Three-times Golden Heart® ̶̶̶̶̶̶̶̶̶̶̶̶̶̶̶̶
learned to pack her suitcase ̶̶̶̶̶̶̶̶̶̶̶̶̶̶̶̶
learned to read. Born to a m̶̶̶̶̶̶̶̶̶̶̶̶̶̶̶̶
lived in the United States, Puerto Rico, Portugal and Brazil. In addition to travelling, Tina loves to cuddle with her pug, Alex, spend time with her family, and hit the trails on her horse. Learn more about Tina from her website, or 'friend' her on Facebook.

Lifelong romance addict **JC Harroway** took a break from her career as a junior doctor to raise a family and found her calling as a Mills & Boon author instead. She now lives in New Zealand and finds that writing feeds her very real obsession with happy endings and the endorphin rush they create. You can follow her at jcharroway.com, and on Facebook, X and Instagram.

Also by Tina Beckett

Las Vegas Night with Her Best Friend

Buenos Aires Docs miniseries

ER Doc's Miracle Triplets

Alaska Emergency Docs miniseries

Reunion with the ER Doctor

Sexy Surgeons in the City miniseries

New York Nights with Mr Right

Also by JC Harroway

Forbidden Fiji Nights with Her Rival
The Midwife's Secret Fling

Buenos Aires Docs miniseries

Secretly Dating the Baby Doc

Sexy Surgeons in the City miniseries

Manhattan Marriage Reunion

Discover more at millsandboon.co.uk.

SECOND CHANCE IN SANTIAGO

TINA BECKETT

ONE NIGHT TO SYDNEY WEDDING

JC HARROWAY

MILLS & BOON

All rights reserved including the right of reproduction in whole or in part in any form. This edition is published by arrangement with Harlequin Enterprises ULC.

This is a work of fiction. Names, characters, places, locations and incidents are purely fictional and bear no relationship to any real life individuals, living or dead, or to any actual places, business establishments, locations, events or incidents. Any resemblance is entirely coincidental.

Without limiting the author's and publisher's exclusive rights, any unauthorized use of this publication to train generative artificial intelligence (AI) technologies is expressly prohibited. HarperCollins also exercise their rights under Article 4(3) of the Digital Single Market Directive 2019/790 and expressly reserve this publication from the text and data mining exception.

® and TM are trademarks owned and used by the trademark owner and/or its licensee. Trademarks marked with ® are registered with the United Kingdom Patent Office and/or the Office for Harmonisation in the Internal Market and in other countries.

First published in Great Britain 2025
by Mills & Boon, an imprint of HarperCollins*Publishers* Ltd,
1 London Bridge Street, London, SE1 9GF

www.harpercollins.co.uk

HarperCollins*Publishers* Macken House, 39/40 Mayor Street Upper, Dublin 1, D01 C9W8, Ireland

Second Chance in Santiago © 2025 Tina Beckett

One Night to Sydney Wedding © 2025 JC Harroway

ISBN: 978-0-263-32508-9

06/25

This book contains FSC™ certified paper and other controlled sources to ensure responsible forest management.

For more information visit www.harpercollins.co.uk/green.

Printed and Bound in the UK using 100% Renewable Electricity at CPI Group (UK) Ltd, Croydon, CR0 4YY

SECOND CHANCE IN SANTIAGO

TINA BECKETT

MILLS & BOON

To my family. I love you!

PROLOGUE

CRISTÓBAL DIAZ ARRIVED just in time to see a vehicle packed with stuff parked at the curb. But that wasn't what caught his attention: it was the person in the back seat—his high school sweetheart. They'd agreed to let last night at the park be their final goodbye, but he hadn't been able to stand the thought that it might be the final time he saw her. And today he'd been compelled by his emotions to come here.

But was this any better?

Vivi's dad frowned at him, letting him know that his presence wasn't exactly welcome, but that was nothing new. He'd never thought Cris was good enough for his only daughter. The problem was that Cris agreed with the man.

She'd been crying, as evidenced by her red eyes and the way she swiped her palm over the moisture on her cheek. And his chest contracted at the thought he might be the cause of that pain. It probably would have been better if he'd never given her that ring with the little red crystals last Christmas, the only thing he could afford on his salary at the local grocery store. She'd tried to give it back to him last night, but he'd placed it back in her palm, curling her fingers over the thin gold band.

He would never get over her. Ever. They would both go on with their lives, because there was no choice, and time didn't stop. Not for him. Not for Vivi. And not for whatever the future might have held for them if her father's change in his diplomatic posting hadn't happened. Vivi said it had been mandatory, and that may have been true, but he was pretty sure her dad wasn't unhappy about being relocated to Santiago. Before they moved there, though, they were going back to the United States for vacation. Vivi's mom was American, but Arturo had been a Chilean exchange student in Kansas, where the couple had met. Vivi was born soon after they were married. He was now a US citizen and had worked his way up the ranks in government work.

And Mrs. Araya, although she'd never disliked him, wouldn't quite meet his eyes right now, so Cris focused his attention on Vivi. And her gaze was fixed on him. His heart twinged again. The urge to rip open the door and ask her to stay with him was strong, but what would they do, even if she agreed? They were both minors and he didn't make enough to support them, and he was pretty sure his parents wouldn't approve of him trying to override Vivi's parents' wishes.

So he forced the impulse back, and instead, placed his palm on the window, fingers splayed. Vivi hesitated, then placed her left hand—where her ring was back in place—on the glass matching his hand, mouthing, *Yo amo ti siempre.*

But would she? He couldn't bring himself to say anything, because despite that ring, nothing had been formalized. Arturo started the car, so Cris lowered his hand to his side and took a step back, even as the man put the car in gear and pulled away from the curb. Cris watched as it turned a corner and disappeared from view, taking what felt like his whole life with it.

The hardest thing was knowing this really was the last time he would ever see her. Especially if her dad had anything to do with it. Cris shut his eyes for the longest time, before glancing at the empty house where they'd spent more than one evening giggling on the porch as he kissed her goodbye. It was now just a shell. A house without a soul.

He nodded at it. "I know the feeling."

Stepping back to his old beat-up car, he put a hand on the hood, letting the residual heat from the engine warm it as he took one last look at the driveway, wondering who would park there next. It didn't matter, because it wouldn't be the Araya family. Then he got in his car and slowly drove away.

CHAPTER ONE

THE ROOM WAS awash with light from almost every angle to avoid having shadows from the team interfere with the surgical field. Viviani Araya should be used to being in an operating room. After all, she'd been a surgical nurse for the last fifteen years.

But not in Valparaiso.

It wasn't the first time she'd dealt with heartache in this place. And now, on the heels of a painful breakup, it had seemed natural to run here. She thought the town she thought of as home would nurture her and help her heal. Instead, she was being inundated with memories of a different time. Memories of sitting in the back seat of a car and crying her heart out.

Estevan had made her cry too. But now she was older and wiser, right? If she could survive the pain of a youthful love that never had a chance to grow, she could survive this. She just needed to give it time.

"Forceps."

She went stock-still, her breath stalled in her lungs. *Dios.* No! There was no way on earth fate could be that cruel. But that low gravelly voice—one that had once washed over her and made her shiver in the dark—she would know it anywhere.

Time seemed to move in slow motion. There were so many hospitals and clinics in her home city—how could she have wound up in the same medical facility as the ghost from her past?

Dark eyes met hers and his frown made her swallow. She wasn't wrong. It was him.

"Forceps." He repeated his request. And while his voice may have still been soft, she dared not mistake that for a softening in his attitude. He was angry at her hesitation in handing over the instrument he needed. She quickly found the right one and placed it in his gloved hand. The second she did, he stiffened and his gaze swung to her face, scouring the part of it that he could see for several long seconds. He said something under his breath and a muscle worked in his jaw.

He *knew*. Knew it was her. Knew she was back where they'd first met almost twenty years ago.

But he said nothing, just turned back to his patient and resumed the surgery—no faltering, no pause—as he moved on to the next step. A knee replacement was undoubtedly a very routine procedure for him. It was probably like driving home at night: it became a series of muscle memory stops and turns that required very little conscious input. It should be the same for her, but it wasn't. Not when Cris was standing just a few feet away. She'd been running late on her first day at the new hospital and had skidded onto the floor and was told where to scrub in and which room she needed to be in.

She hadn't even looked to see if there was a board that listed the patient or the surgeon.

She'd just been desperate to get away from Santiago and hadn't cared where in Valparaiso she landed. She did now, though.

Maybe it was better that she hadn't known that Cris was doing this surgery. She might not have come into the room at all. Might have backed away from her old life and its heartaches.

Not that her present life was any happier.

Cris bit off the name of another instrument and this time she didn't pause or fumble. She deftly placed it in his outstretched hand, doing her best to ignore the electrical current that traveled along her fingers and up her arm as she did so. He was married. Or so she'd heard from a friend who'd since moved away. She hadn't been keeping track of him. At least not anymore. It had been too painful to hear that his parents had died in an automobile crash only a year after she'd left the city. But it was inevitable that friends had shared tidbits of information, although that rarely happened anymore. They had all moved on with their lives. Vivi included.

So why was the presence of a childhood romance now crowding her thoughts with memories that should have died long ago? It wasn't like she'd joined a convent. She'd had a few romances since then, including almost marrying Estevan. But Cris…

He. Was. Married.

So stop it, Vivi!

He must be as horrified as she was that they would meet up again.

Or maybe he didn't care. *She* shouldn't care.

Somehow she got through the next hour with no more missteps, and Cris basically ignored her. So maybe things were going to be okay after all.

Okay. Ha! Somehow she doubted she was going to get off that easily.

"Closing the site." That low voice rumbled over her again as he carefully placed a series of staples along the skin with a precision that sent a flash of heat over her.

She could always go somewhere else.

Really? A swear word slid to her lips, and she had to press them together to prevent it from escaping. How many times was she going to run from things that were uncomfortable? It seemed to have become the norm for her, recently. Actually, it wasn't just recently. She tended to shy away from people when they got too close. And those romances she'd thought of earlier were pretty short-lived, really. Except for Estevan, who had somehow worked his way into her life with a stubborn resolution that had made her laugh. Before she had time to take a few breaths, they were engaged. And that had proved a mistake because he'd evidently worked his way into someone else's heart with the same insistence that he had hers.

It was only after she'd had time to reflect that she realized he was probably more in love with the process of wooing a woman than he was with the woman herself. He'd probably done it more than once. But not with her.

Not again. She'd ignored his texts, finally blocking him from her life altogether.

Which is how she'd wound up back in Valparaiso.

Valley of Paradise. Valpo for short.

It had been once. Paradise. A very long time ago. Something she needed to put from her mind. Because if Estevan had taught her anything, it was that she'd been right about not letting men get too close. She wouldn't make that mistake again.

"Good work, team. Our patient won't play soccer again after his injury, but he'll be able to coach or mentor, which is hopefully what he'll decide to do."

She hadn't realized their patient was an athlete, although she had thought he'd seemed awfully young to need a knee replacement. That was hard: having your whole life change in the blink of an eye and being unable to ever go back. Hadn't that been what had happened to her? First with Cris, then with Estevan? Her parents had urged her to stay in Santiago after her breakup, but she'd been adamant that she needed a change. And so, here she was. With a change she neither expected nor wanted.

Busying herself with organizing her trays while the patient's anesthesia was reversed, all she wanted to do was get out of the room before she had to speak to Cris again. She needed time to gather her thoughts. Thankfully, once he was assured that his patient was awake and starting to communicate, he stepped out of the room. Her muscles went slack and she stood there without moving, pulling down some deep breaths before forcing her mind back to the job at hand.

The time went by fast and soon she had things separated and in order, and the patient had been whisked away. A new team arrived to clean and sanitize the operating room and get it ready for another patient so she stopped to discard her scrub gear in the trash bin, reaching to check that her hair was still secure in its twist. Then she slid through the double doors and glanced to the right at the nurses' station, hoping that was also the way to the staff lounge. She could really use a coffee right now—the stronger the better—since she hadn't had time to unpack her French press. She would have gotten to Valpo a week ago, but a car repair and severe weather had delayed her arrival. She barely made it in last night after nightmare traffic had turned what was normally a two-hour drive into seven.

She started to head toward the main desk, noting the board that listed the surgeries. She needed to find out the other ones she'd need to scrub in for today. Her eyes closed for a second; she hoped those surgeries would not include Cristóbal.

"Vivi, wait."

Santa Maria. Not now. Not when she was still trying to get over the shock of standing next to him. She needed time to process what had happened. Both with Estevan and her discovery that Cris was still in Valparaiso.

She slowly turned and found a man where once had stood a boy. Everything except those intense dark eyes had been covered by surgical gear a few minutes ago, and what she could see now blew her away. His lanky runner's frame had filled out in the best possible way, but the shock of dark hair still curled in every direction and was just as mouthwateringly sexy as it had always been. It would have been so much easier if he had lost most of his hair. But would it? Really?

Besides, fate couldn't be that kind. In fact, fate had been kind of a bitch over the last several weeks.

She tried on a fake smile. "Hi! I didn't know you were at Valpo Memorial. At least not until I saw you in the operating room."

That dark gaze stared her down for a minute or two. "Didn't you?"

His words took her aback and she frowned. "I'm not sure what you mean by that."

"Surely my name was on the list of hospital staff when you came here looking for a job."

He made it sound like she'd been desperate or something.

"Actually, I didn't 'come here looking for a job.' I saw a posting at the hospital where I was *already working* as a scrub nurse and applied. I didn't scour the website looking for familiar names." She threw in another remark. "Besides, I might not have even recognized your name if I'd seen it."

That was a mistake, and he knew it because one side of his mouth curved. "Oh, really? I got a few letters that seemed to indicate otherwise."

Yes, she had written several long pages of prose that reiterated what she'd said the last time she saw him... that she would love him forever. That she would never ever forget him.

Her face heated. "I was a child back then." And she didn't talk about the fact that he hadn't written her back because she didn't want him to know how soul-crushing it had been that he hadn't cared enough to respond.

The way she'd never responded to Estevan's texts? No. That was not the same. She was convinced that he'd never really loved her—or he wouldn't have been able to jump into another relationship so quickly. It seemed she was forever doomed to love men more than they loved her. But not anymore.

"It seems we both were." His face turned serious. "And now we're both adults, so I assume we can both work at the same hospital—the same *quirófano*—without it causing a problem, correct?"

The inflection he'd given to the term "operating room" gave it an intimacy that made her wonder if she really would be able to function working that closely with him. But she had to, or had to pretend he had no effect on her. At least until it became a reality. They really had been kids the last time she'd been here. She neither wanted nor needed to stand around mooning after him. Since he was married, he'd obviously moved on as well. She was glad for him. And honestly, she was glad for herself. He was safely off-limits—even if there had been any temptation. Not that there was.

"*Absolutamente*. It will be no problem." And she meant it.

"That's good to hear. Because I just checked the scheduling and it seems we'll be working quite a few surgeries together, since one of our other scrub nurses retired a few weeks ago."

He'd looked to see if they'd be doing more surgeries together? So maybe *she* wasn't the only one who was going to have problems. Maybe he was too. Except she'd already tried to peer at the schedule board from a distance. She just hadn't been able to read it. And it sounded like he'd looked ahead at the procedures that were on the calendar and not just on the white board. That could always change, though, if she wound up stuck in an emergency surgery with another surgeon when one of Cris's patients was due to be operated on.

But how often was that likely to happen? She could at least hope it ended up being more than the norm, though, couldn't she?

She tilted her chin. "I'm ready for anything."

He gave her a cryptic look, then nodded and turned to go in the opposite direction.

She couldn't help but watch him go, and even though his frame had filled out a bit, he still had that lanky runner's walk that she'd always found so endearingly sexy.

She sighed. This was going to be hard—and honestly that was a good thing, since it meant she would be on guard—but if she had to work with him, maybe it was better that their first meeting had happened the way that it had—in an operating room full of people. Because having it come as a complete shock was better than having fretted over it during the weeks leading up to the move. That would have been worse. So much worse. She probably would have changed her mind about coming to Valpo Memorial.

But at least she would have been prepared. He disappeared around a corner, and she let muscles that she hadn't known were tight relax a bit.

Well, she really was prepared for anything now.

Right?

Cris shook his head as he sat in his office chair and stared at nothing. The shock of seeing her had thrown him into a tailspin, and it shouldn't have. What they'd once had was child's play compared to what life had thrown at him since Vivi's family had moved away. His parents' deaths, his uncle's help getting through medical school, finally finding love again at the age of thirty, the three-year struggle to have a child, then his wife's cancer diagnosis that left him a single dad raising his beautiful daughter alone.

Yes, Vivi had written to him for almost six months after they'd left, but he hadn't had the heart to write back. It had felt kinder to rip off the Band-Aid and let them both heal and to let her form new connections, since her dad had mentioned maybe going back to the States after their assignment in Santiago. And she hadn't come back to Valparaiso after graduating from high school, so it had seemed Cris's decision had been the right one. Besides, he'd been grieving the deaths of his parents a year after they parted ways.

It had taken a while for Cris to move on with his life, but he had, and he'd hoped she had too.

So why had her return affected him the way it had? He'd lost his focus for several minutes while operating on Roni Saraia, which was not like him. At all. The thought had run through his mind that she had come back on purpose after all these years, which was ludicrous. He'd practically accused her of doing so, in fact. He groaned aloud. That hadn't been a proud moment.

It was obvious she hadn't known he was at the hospital before applying for the position, which was a relief. Because they couldn't take up where they'd left off. Not that he thought she wanted to. Nor did he. He had Gabi to think of nowadays. At five years old, she was impressionable and attached easily to people like her teachers and friends, so he had kept his love life simple and uncomplicated. It wasn't ideal. But it worked. And he had no intention of changing the way he did things.

His aunt and uncle were always willing to watch her on the rare occasions he went out on a date with someone, and he had never brought anyone to the house—even when Gabi wasn't there. And Cris wouldn't for a few more years until his daughter was better able to understand that people wouldn't always be permanent fixtures in her life...a lesson he didn't want her to learn for quite a while. His late wife had been estranged from her own parents—who'd been abusive—so there weren't even grandparents in the picture.

He was grateful for his aunt and uncle who'd stepped up to the plate and had been there for both him and his daughter, taking on the role of grandparents, since they had no children of their own. And although he'd been eighteen when his parents had died, they'd brought Cris into their home while he did his undergraduate work, and for most of his time as a medical student. Then he'd rented an apartment they had in the city up until he and Lidia had married. He wasn't sure what he would have done without them. He might not be where he was today without their help and he never let himself forget that.

He sighed and forced himself to look at the paperwork that was waiting to be completed, and then he still had rounds to do, including looking in on Roni to make sure the former soccer star was doing okay. He couldn't afford to spend a half hour every day hashing over things of the past, so he'd better learn how to deal with Vivi's presence in Valparaiso. Soon. Or his work was going to start suffering and that was something he was never going to let happen. Nor would he let it affect his family life.

Finally settling in his chair to catch up on paperwork, he put Vivi from his mind.

"How are you feeling?" Cris caught up with Roni the next day as the young soccer star sat in a wheelchair in physical therapy. The therapist was demonstrating how to do an exercise, but the athlete just sat there and did nothing, acting like he hadn't even seen her. Cris cocked his head at the staff member in an unspoken question and she shook her head to say no. That she hadn't gotten anywhere yet.

"Can you give us a few minutes?" he asked.

"Sure. I'll go see if we have some resistance bands for my next patient." Undoubtedly she already knew the answer to that question, but she was giving them some space like Cris had asked.

Once she was out of earshot, Cris sat in the chair she'd vacated and didn't say anything for a few seconds, just took in the hopelessness he saw in the man's face. A hopelessness he remembered well after his parents passed away.

"Talk to me, Roni." After a catastrophic injury to his knee that had required a complete replacement—an attempted repair at another medical center had failed—it was possible he could still run on the limb, but not at the same level as before. And putting that much stress on a new joint was never a good idea. Especially since it had been dicey getting things to work with what was left of his femur.

"Soccer is—*was*—my life. What will I do now?"

"You're going to take it one day at a time. But you have to try. Otherwise that surgery might as well have never happened."

"Maybe it shouldn't have. Maybe the other surgery would have eventually worked."

This was the hard part. Telling the patient a truth they didn't want to hear. "A portion of the bone had lost blood flow and was dead. If you hadn't had surgery yesterday, things could have been much worse."

"I don't see how."

"You could have faced amputation."

Roni went pale as he stared at him, the pain in his eyes going beyond physical discomfort. "Didn't I already?

The part of my life that I loved the most was taken away from me. Isn't that a form of amputation?"

He was right. It was. Just like when Vivi and his parents had been taken from him. Like when Lidia had died. But those were things no one could change. And Roni's leg wasn't going to be restored to normal, no matter how long he sat in that chair and did nothing.

Had Cris's life ever been restored to normal? No. But he'd learned ways to move forward. Had learned how to wall off portions of himself in an effort to avoid the pain of additional loss. Not that that was something he wanted Roni to do. He was young and deserved to be happy. And he still could. If he could just get past this hurdle—which was a big one.

"You're a legend. Is this the way you want that story to end? With you sitting in this room day after day, refusing to try? Giving up? Is that the message you want to send to kids who idolize you? Who want to be just like you?"

"I'll soon be forgotten."

"And you will be if you just sit here. It's up to you to make sure that doesn't happen. You can still give back to the game. You can help other kids who have little or nothing—like you did—make their dreams come true."

"How? I can't play anymore."

"Maybe not. But you know what it's like to play the game. You know exactly how it *feels* to kick that ball past the goalie and rack up those points. The exhilaration that comes with it. You can share that knowledge with others."

"I don't know…" But Cris thought there might be a

touch less resignation in his look than there had been moments earlier. The orthopedist had never played soccer, but he did know what it felt like to mourn what could never be brought back. And yet he'd somehow made a life for himself—a good one—even though he no longer remembered exactly when or how that decision had been made. He hoped Roni would get to that point as well.

And maybe Cris could help make that happen. "Listen, I can't promise anything, but I can look into camps for boys and girls who want to play and see how you can connect with them. Not just soccer but basketball and other areas. Or maybe we could have some kind of 'meeting of the minds' happen here at the hospital with experts from several sports weighing in. You could be involved with the soccer aspect. But only if you're willing to put in the work on your own recovery."

The man shrugged. "I can't promise anything either. But I'll try."

The PT specialist had come back, resistance bands in hand, and overheard that last phrase. "That's good to hear. So if you're ready, how about we get down to work."

Cris held out a hand and Roni shook it. "Well, I'll let you two get to it. I'll check in on you again before I leave for the day. I'm hoping we can release you tomorrow. You have a way to get back and forth to your PT sessions?"

"I do."

"Good. Think about what I said, and I'll see you later then."

They said their goodbyes and he headed to the glass door, blinking when he saw a familiar face just on the other side. Vivi. Great. Just what he needed. Taking a deep breath, he headed for her.

CHAPTER TWO

"How's he doing?" Vivi had come down to check on Roni, and she wasn't even sure why. She wasn't his doctor. She was just a nurse who'd scrubbed in on his surgery. But she still cared, and at her last job she'd often checked in on patients and no one had seemed to mind. But it might be different at Valpo Memorial. Besides, she had an idea and wanted to run it by Cris. But maybe she should do that in a place where they couldn't be overheard.

"I assume you're talking about Roni?"

She bit her lip. Was he about to chew her out? "I am. Is that a problem?"

"Not as far as I'm concerned. You're a nurse and worked on his case. I think he'll like knowing members of his team care about him. It might even help motivate him into doing his PT."

The last sentence slipped by almost unheard, because of what he'd said just before that. He considered her a member of the team? Something about that phrase made a warmth settle in her chest. She hadn't felt like she'd earned her place on that team yet, but he was evidently not going to hold their past against her. Although why would he? It hadn't been her decision to move away—it was her parents. Except she'd heard her dad say something about her being too young to be in a relationship and that their new assignment would help take care of that. Had her father asked to be moved because of Cris? Whatever his reasons it had worked. Her letters to Cris had gone unanswered. Just thinking about that made her squirm in embarrassment, imagining him telling his wife about the lovesick girl who'd written long missives that promised things that were impossible. She wished she'd been more like him back then, able to let things go that she couldn't change. Well, she might not have been strong enough to do that twenty years ago, but she was now. There was no going back, and she had no desire to.

"He's resisting doing his therapy?"

Cris glanced over at where the physical therapist was standing with a walker. "I think it's part of the grieving process. His career has been a huge part of his identity. Trying to shift gears from the past isn't always easy, but it is necessary."

Her head whipped around to look at him, but the surgeon was still looking over at Roni. There was no way he'd been talking about their childhood romance. Besides, he was married and that would be inappropriate.

"Well, I'll go over there and say hello," she said.

"Let me know if he starts doing some work."

"I will." She gave him a smile that she hoped looked friendly but not too friendly, noticing that he didn't wear a wedding ring. Lots of surgeons didn't, though. They would have to be taken off every time they scrubbed in and then put back on. It got to be a huge pain. If she were married, she doubted she would wear her ring to work either. For some reason that simple little ring he'd given her came to mind. She shoved the thought back into its sealed compartment.

Just because he didn't have one on didn't mean anything. And unless he'd divorced in the intervening years, he was still unavailable. Actually, even if he had divorced, she'd do well to steer clear of any romances here at work or anywhere else. Estevan had showed her all the reasons why that was a terrible idea.

Walking over to Roni, she noted he was still seated. The smile she gave the PT was genuine as was the one she gave the patient. "Hi, Señor Saraia. I know that Dr. Diaz was just here, but I wanted to check on you as well and you weren't in your room. I figured you might be down here."

The nurses dealt with wound-dressing and checking on vitals anyway, so she wasn't out of order in coming. But after what Cris had said, a glimmer of worry had appeared about their patient's state of mind. If she ever couldn't do her job, it would rock her world as well. Maybe not to the same extent, since her whole identity wasn't wrapped up in her job, but it would still be hard.

He looked slightly peeved at having yet another medical person pestering him, so she held her hand out to the therapist. "Hi, I'm new here. Viviani Araya. I'm one of the nurses on the surgical floor."

"Bella Trasseti. Nice to meet you. Roni and I were just

getting ready to do some walking on his new knee, isn't that right? Isn't that what you told Dr. Diaz?"

As if caught red-handed, the man made a sound that sounded like exasperation, but then nodded. "I guess I need to keep my promise to him."

Bella moved the walker a step or two closer, holding it steady as Roni grasped the handles and then hefted himself up on his good leg.

"You're allowed to put weight on your injured leg, and I won't have you do anything that might damage all of Dr. Diaz's hard work, okay?"

Roni nodded, but his jaw was tight, a muscle jerking in his cheek. Vivi wasn't sure if it was due to pain or concentration or a mixture of both. When he glanced around the large open room, which was bustling with other patients and PT staff, she realized what it might be. He was embarrassed to be caught barely able to walk and there were quite a few patients who were glancing their way, probably recognizing their celebrity patient.

She knew a tiny bit about what he was experiencing. Hadn't the looks of pity at her other hospital made her want to melt into the woodwork? Her fiancé had been a surgeon she'd worked with on occasion; it was how they'd struck up a friendship that had turned into more. And the aftermath of finding out he'd been secretly romancing another nurse hadn't been fun. Her friend in Human Resources reminded her that she'd tried to tell her she was headed down a slippery path, but Vivi had been so sure that it wouldn't happen to her. And yet it had. Hopefully she'd learned her lesson.

"Do you mind if I pull a couple of those rolling partitions over here?"

Bella tilted her head and then her eyes widened in understanding. "No, go ahead."

It actually would work perfectly, since Bella's cubicle area was in the far corner of the room. Even blocking the view from the door would probably help. So she pulled two of the devices over and unfolded them so that together they made an eight-foot wall.

Roni sighed. "Thanks. I didn't think having people watch me would bother me—I should be used to it, right? But this..." He motioned down at the dressing on his leg.

The physical therapist gave his shoulder a squeeze. "You need to tell me when you feel uncomfortable, so we can find a way to fix it. I'm glad Viviani thought of it."

"So am I." The look he gave her was one of gratitude with a little something mixed in. Something that made her pause.

No. She was imagining it. This was a man with legions of fans. And probably plenty of women to boot.

He did as Bella directed, slowly making his way to the end of the partition before turning a big half circle and coming back the other way. By the time he got back to his seat his arms were visibly shaking. "*Mierda!* Why do I feel so damn weak? It shouldn't be this hard to just walk."

"Yes, it should," Bella said. "You've just had major surgery. It's not just the injury. It's the aftereffects of anesthesia, which hang on for a while—not to mention the body's attempts at healing use a lot of energy. Give yourself a little bit of grace."

"Grace. Maybe my body should give me a little bit of that and cooperate."

Vivi started to touch his arm before thinking better of it. "Bella is right. It takes time. You'll be surprised at how fast you'll bounce back. Muscle memory will kick in and you'll be on your way."

"On my way to what? Sitting on the sidelines watching the sport I love being played out in front of me?"

She understood that he felt helpless about what was happening to him. Powerless to stop it. But letting himself linger too long in those thoughts was just going to make him sink deeper and deeper. It was like a quicksand. If you ventured too close, you'd have trouble extricating yourself from it. If anyone knew that, she did.

Before she could say anything, though, Bella did what she'd been afraid to do and touched his hand. "You'll do a lot more than sit on the sidelines. For our next session, you're going to help me brainstorm a list of things you can do using your knowledge and experience in the sport."

"It's going to be a mighty short list."

"You might be surprised. Now, that's all the torture I'll put you through, since it's our first session, but don't expect me to be so soft on our next go-around."

He gave the first real smile Vivi had seen. Then he said, "Spoken like a true coach."

"Hmm... I've been called a drill sergeant before, but never a coach. I think I kind of like that." She pulled his wheelchair over. "Why don't you hop into your ride and if Viviani doesn't mind, I'll have her go with you back to your room."

"I don't mind at all." But when she went to help him, Bella stopped her with a slight shake of her head. Ahh, she wanted him to do it on his own. Her nurse mentality was to help her patients whenever she could. A PT's mentality was to let a patient do all he or she could on their own.

So she stood by as Roni awkwardly tried to figure out how to hold onto the chair and turn to get into it. Bella did offer guidance on how to shift himself so that he didn't twist his bad knee. Then he lowered himself into it, slumping forward and blowing out a loud breath.

Bella smiled at him. "It'll come. Don't dwell on the hard stuff. Just tackle each step as it comes and celebrate what you can do, rather than getting stuck in what you still need to accomplish. Getting ahead of yourself won't do you any good and could just cause strain in a different part of your body."

He made a snorting sound that might have been agreement or might have just been an indication that he was withholding judgment.

At any rate, Vivi got behind him and asked if he was ready, to which he nodded. "More than ready. But thank you, Bella."

She was a little surprised to hear him thank the woman who'd caused him to work so hard. But he had. Vivi hoped that was a good sign.

"You're welcome. I'll see you back tomorrow and the

next day and the one after that, until we have you working independently."

"I guess I have no choice in the matter?"

Bella wrinkled her nose and said, "None at all. Take him away, Viviani."

With that, she turned the chair and headed toward the door.

Cris glanced up from a sheaf of messages when a knock sounded at his door. Leaning back in his chair, he tried to figure out if there was an appointment he'd forgotten. "Come in."

Vivi poked her head around the corner. "Are you busy?"

Not someone he was hoping to see. But here she was, and he was fairly certain she wouldn't have come if it wasn't something important, and he had asked her to check in after she'd visited their patient. "Nothing that can't wait. Come in. Is it about Roni?"

She made her way to a chair, and he waited for her to sit down. "Yes and no. Yes, he completed therapy and seemed to have a better mindset by the end of it."

"That's good. And the other part?"

"Well, it's still kind of about Roni, but it's also about the hospital. I assume this department sees their share of athletes walk through the doors, and some of them probably are in the same situation as Roni—not knowing what the future might hold."

"You would be correct."

She seemed to hesitate. "I know I just got here and

haven't earned the right to throw out ideas, but I feel like I have to. What if the hospital had someone like Roni on staff, whether as a volunteer or a paid position, if Valpo Memorial doesn't already do that? He's a recognizable face to most athletes and could talk about career-changing injuries and what helped him make it through."

"Except he's not through it himself."

"Yes, but if he saw that once he was on the track to recovery there was a path opened for him to help others, it might give him something to look forward to. Might give him the incentive to do the work that needs to be done."

He sat back. Her idea kind of went along with his own thoughts, only it took things a step further. In a good way. There was a problem, though. "And if Roni thinks we're just trying to capitalize on his name for the hospital's financial gain?"

"If we aren't blasting his name on social media or using it in advertising campaigns, then I don't think he'll see it that way. He could even give lectures to coaches or professionals in the medical field on how to motivate athletes who become patients. You just admitted there are quite a few of them."

Cris glanced at his watch. "What time do you get off work?"

"I'm actually off right now."

"I have the rest of these messages to get through and I need to make a phone call. But if you're free, can we discuss it a little more over some cafeteria food? I skipped lunch and I'm starting to feel it."

"Oh...um, sure. I don't have plans."

She didn't sound exactly thrilled and he wasn't either, but having her in his office like this with the door closed was beginning to have an effect on him. One he didn't want. And the phone call he needed to make was to his aunt to make sure that she could watch Gabi for a couple more hours. He had no doubt she would be thrilled to. But he was also conscious of the fact that he never wanted to presume. It wouldn't be fair to her or to Gabi.

Why not just make the call with Vivi present? He wasn't sure, and he didn't want to examine the reasons too closely. He was pretty sure she'd heard about his marriage from classmates, although why would she have? He hadn't kept up with where she was or what she was doing.

"If you have plans or would rather discuss it during working hours, I'll completely understand." He hoped she knew that things between them needed to remain on a professional level. So again, why not call his aunt and uncle about Gabi right now?

For that exact same reason. The less they knew about each other's personal lives the better. It was why he'd never answered her letters or kept up communication with her as they went on with their lives. They couldn't be friends without those emotions being dredged up. At least he couldn't. Their romance had needed to stay in the past, and that couldn't have happened if they'd pined away for each other. It still needed to stay in the past. And it was up to him to make sure he followed that rule.

"No, it's not that. No plans. I just don't want to interfere with your home life."

Home life. Did she already know he had a child? Well, if she did, she did.

"No, you won't. So I'll meet you in the cafeteria in, say, fifteen minutes?"

"That's fine, I'll see you down there."

She turned on her heel and exited his office, leaving him to try to get his mind back where it needed to be. He took care of his messages and then locked his office before heading for the elevator and making his call to his aunt.

She answered on the first ring, just as the elevator doors opened on the first floor. The cafeteria was just down the hallway and he saw Vivi waiting in front of it, but she was facing the other way, so he kept his voice low but kept walking. "Aunt Pat, I'm running a little late at work and wondered if you could keep Gabi for another hour or two."

He wasn't sure what he would do if that didn't work for her. He gave an internal shrug. He would just have to cancel and they could discuss whatever idea she had on a different day.

"Oh, are you going into surgery?"

"No, just some unfinished business." He frowned. It was true in the strictest sense, but why had he worded it that way?

"Oh, good," his aunt said. "That's fine. We were headed out to do a little shopping anyway and had to drive by the hospital, so Gabi insisted we come by. We're just coming through the front doors. Are you in your office?"

He'd just reached Vivi and stopped to stand beside her, hurrying to finish the conversation while mouthing "Sorry" to her.

"No, I'm actually down in the..." Things seemed to happen in slow motion as he heard a familiar squeal and automatically turned toward the sound. Just in time to spot a small figure launching herself down the hallway toward him, her aunt calling out to her. He glanced back at Vivi and saw that she had also spotted the pair too and turned to look. Her eyes met his and he could almost see the understanding dawn on her face, although she was still a good hundred feet away.

He broke his gaze and knelt down to greet his daughter, opening his arms. When she crashed against his chest, he closed them again, holding her tight. "Hi, *querida*. Did you miss me?"

"Yes." Small hands patted his face, and a surge of pure love enveloped him. In the midst of his heartache over Lidia's death, Gabi had been the one thing that kept him going. And with her energy and zest for new adventures, his daughter could run circles around him.

Pat caught up with him. "Gabi, you can't just run off like that. Sorry, Cris. She doesn't normally leave my side."

"I know that." He smiled up at his aunt to show her that he wasn't worried about any of that. "She just saw me and wanted to say hi. Where are you guys headed?"

"The *centro comercial* just down the road."

He reached for his wallet. "Let me give you some money for food or a snack."

"Not a chance. I have money. She got an attendance award in school and so we're celebrating."

Cris glanced over to where Vivi had been, knowing he needed to introduce her. But the spot where she was standing was now empty. Had she left? Or just gone inside to give them some privacy?

Turning his attention back to his daughter he smiled, letting her wiggle out of his hug. "Attendance award, huh? That's a pretty big deal."

"Yeah! School is fun! Except for Matias Cabral. He's mean. Maria even says so."

He assumed Matias and Maria were classmates. "Did you try being nice to Matias?"

"No. Because he's *mean*."

Cris couldn't contain his smile. There was no arguing with that kind of logic, and he had no idea if the boy really was mean or if he was just looking for attention, like many other children in that age bracket. "Well, try being nice and see what happens."

"Okay." It was said with a slump of her shoulders, but he had no doubt that Gabi would indeed try to show kindness. If there was a problem with Matias being a bully, he was pretty sure her teacher was already on top of it. She'd been one of his patients a year ago when she needed knee replacement surgery at age sixty. She'd been teaching for a long time and said she loved her job. He believed her when she said she didn't plan on retiring anytime soon.

Gabi went back over and stood beside Pat. "Can we go, Ti-Tia? I'm getting hungry."

Cris's aunt laughed. "You're always hungry. I have no idea where you put all the food you eat."

"In my belly," his daughter said, as if it should be obvious to everyone.

He rose to his feet. "Well, then, you'd better go get something to put in that belly. And I have a meeting to go to. I'll see you in an hour or so?"

"Better give us three," Pat said. "Just in case we find something interesting."

He wasn't sure where he would be if it weren't for his aunt and uncle. Oh, he would have gotten by, but he would have had to hire a nanny or a sitter. And though he knew people did that every day with good results, he was glad Gabi could stay with family. When he'd broached the subject of bringing someone else into the equation as a way to give the couple a little more time to nurture their own relationship, they'd acted hurt and so he hadn't mentioned it again. He had made them promise to tell him if they couldn't watch her for whatever reason. They had, but so far had always seemed thrilled to spend time with her.

So he said goodbye then and promised he'd see them soon. How easily the words slipped from his tongue, even though no one ever knew if they could keep that promise. Shaking those thoughts from his head, he waited for them to disappear from sight before giving a sigh and heading into the cafeteria, hoping there wasn't going to be a need for an in-depth explanation about Gabi or worse, about Lidia or what had happened to her.

He frowned when he went in and saw her sitting at a

table with nothing in front of her. Then he realized that there were no workers in the normally busy place, except for one lone person who was restocking the napkin holders on the tables. When he glanced at his watch, he saw that it was after six. He couldn't remember exactly when they closed, but it must have been recently.

He headed over to her. "I'm sorry. I didn't realize they wouldn't be open."

"It's okay. And it looked like you were busy. If you need to go be with your family, I'll understand." Her voice sounded strained somehow.

"My aunt is going to watch her for a while. They just stopped in to say hi before they headed out on a shopping trip."

"Your aunt?"

He frowned. "Yes." Ahh, he got it. His aunt looked much younger than her sixty-one years, and he could see how Vivi might have mistaken her for Gabi's mom. There was nothing to it but to tell her the truth, because if he let it hang, things might get even more awkward than they already were. And it would feel like he was lying, even though he hadn't been the one giving her that idea "Gabi's mom…my wife…died about a year after our daughter was born."

Her eyes widened. "Oh, Cris, I'm sorry. I didn't realize. I'd heard from Paulette that you were married years ago, but I didn't know she'd passed."

They'd undergone fertility treatments in order to have Gabi, and although the doctors had tried to reassure him that it had probably not played a role in her ovarian cancer, he'd had a hard time believing that and had carried a load of guilt that he still hadn't completely shed.

"It's been a while. Gabi doesn't even remember her." Why had he even added that last part? It was true, but saying the words sent pain through his midsection just like it did whenever his daughter asked to see pictures of her mother. Fortunately, his wife had thought to make a video for Gabi as a way for her daughter to get to know her. She'd taped birthday wishes for her first ten birthdays, all she'd had time for before she became too sick to do any more. They were now through half of the tapings and when they came to the end of the messages, Cris knew it would be hard. It would be like losing her all over again.

"I can't even imagine." She stood and touched his hand before dropping her own by her side.

He frowned. "Sometimes I can't either. It hasn't been easy. But Pat and Guilherme have always been there for me and Gabi."

"I'm glad." She tilted her head and studied his face. "Do you want to meet another time? I'll completely understand, if so."

"No, I'd still like to, if you have the time. We'll just need to do it somewhere other than the cafeteria. Do you have any favorite places to eat?"

"Here in Valparaiso? I haven't been here in so long, that I really don't. I'm fine with anything really. Even just *pastel de choclo*."

The iconic Chilean dish consisted of corn puree, basil, ground beef and a few other ingredients. It was simple and filling and there were few people in the country who didn't eat it on occasion.

"I know a place that makes a lot of comfort-style foods. And it's just around the corner, so we won't need to drive."

"Sounds perfect. Let's go." She slung the strap of her small purse over her head so that it hung diagonally across her chest and waited for him to lead the way.

CHAPTER THREE

HE WASN'T MARRIED. At least not to a living person. Not anymore. But that didn't mean he wasn't married to her memory.

That reality floated through her head over and over again—random thoughts. *Dios!* The safety net she thought she'd had with Cris being married had just been yanked from beneath her. But it shouldn't matter. And it wouldn't. He wasn't divorced, hadn't chosen to leave the relationship like Estevan had—his wife had died. And they'd been very much in love. She thought she'd seen a glimpse of that in his face as he talked about her—even though he hadn't really said much, other than the fact that it had been hard.

And like she'd thought a few moments ago: it shouldn't matter. And it didn't. She wasn't getting involved with another coworker. And definitely wasn't getting involved with someone from her past. Both paths would lead to heartache—she knew that from experience. She'd rather not repeat the same mistakes. She was older and wiser now. And she was going to be a hell of a lot more careful about where she let her heart venture. She was going to keep it close, like a pet dog that might bolt the first time she let it off its leash.

They turned the corner and, *gracias a Dios*, Cris was right. The restaurant was close. Nestled among the vibrantly colored buildings that Valpo was known for was a mint green bistro that had a scattering of white wrought-iron tables and chairs on the cobbled area out front. It didn't take long for a hostess to find them a spot at the outer band of seating. She gratefully sank into a chair, just realizing how tired she was after the long day at the medical center. It was a shame that they couldn't just sit here and enjoy some tapas and knock back a few drinks while watching the sun set over the city. But they wouldn't even be here if it weren't for her "idea." And she was a little hesitant to really go any further in-depth about it. Especially now that they were off hospital grounds.

What if he ended up thinking it was a ridiculous idea?

A waiter came over to the table, and to hell with it, she was ordering wine of some type. Maybe it would give her some courage. Plus they'd walked to the cafe, so it wasn't like she had to drive anywhere right away. And by the time they made it back to the hospital, she'd be back to normal, right?

"I'd like a Melvin, please." The nickname for *melón con vino*—a popular drink in Chile—the Melvin was their version of the Spanish sangria. Only instead of red wine, Chileans used white wine, adding it to honeydew melon. It was absolutely delicious and refreshing. Especially in the heat of the Chilean summer.

"Would you like that for one or to share?" The server looked pointedly from one to the other.

Dios! She hadn't even thought about that. A lot of times *melón con vino* was a communal drink, served in a hollowed-out melon with multiple straws and passed around for everyone to enjoy. "Just for one, please. One straw," she added as if that wasn't already a given.

Her face was so hot it must be flaming red. There was still something about Cris that made her forget where she was. It was still the shock of seeing him again after all these years. She would get over it in a few days.

"Can you bring a pitcher?" Cris said. "I haven't had a Melvin in ages."

Leave it to him to save the day. Like the time that she'd skidded up the driveway, almost late for curfew after they'd spent hours at a stream after school. Her dad had been furious, but Cris had diffused the situation by saying they'd had a school project to do. It wasn't true—they'd been making out—but it had kept her from getting into trouble.

The waiter left to get their drinks and she tried to lighten up what had almost been an embarrassing situation. "I would have taken you for a dark ale kind of guy."

"Me? No. I hate beer, actually, even though I know it's expected at sporting events. I don't drink much, for the most part."

That surprised her, for some reason. But should it have? They'd been so young when they were dating that they hadn't had a chance to learn what either one of them would be like as adults. The fact was, they really didn't know much about each other anymore. They were essentially strangers. And as angry as she'd been at her dad for dragging her away from Valparaiso, looking back, she could see that he really had been looking out for her welfare. If they'd stayed, it was very probable that she and Cris would have married right out of high school. Who knew if either of them would be where they were professionally if that had happened?

But they could certainly enjoy a drink together now without messing up either of their futures. And without the effects of teenage hormones entering the picture.

The waiter brought the spiked fruity beverage in a clear glass pitcher, complete with chunks of melon, and two goblets, each with its own straw. She smiled. At least the server had asked and not assumed, or that could have been a tricky situation.

She kept her order simple, just bread slathered with a healthy amount of mashed avocado. She'd never understood how the pairing could be so delicious but it was, which was why it was so ubiquitous in Chile. Cris ended up being the one who ordered a hamburger. When she raised a brow at him, he smiled, igniting that pesky dimple in the side of his face, one of the first things she'd noticed about him when they'd met all those years ago.

"What?" he asked. "You made me want one."

He'd once made her want a lot of things, none of which she'd gotten when they'd been younger. Cris had wanted to wait. She had not.

It was probably one of her biggest regrets about their time together. Because for years afterwards, she'd fantasized about what it would have been like to sleep with him. But again, it made the transition a little easier because sex had not been tied to her memory of him.

"I guess I was in the mood for green today."

When he looked quizzically at her, she motioned to the pitcher of Melvin and mentioned the food she'd ordered.

"Ahh, I guess you were."

She ignored the fact that he was in a dark green polo shirt. Because that was one thing she wasn't getting. Not in the past and not now.

"Is your aunt keeping your daughter overnight?" Too late, she realized how that might have sounded and hurried to add, "I didn't know if that was something your daughter enjoyed. I remembered liking having sleepovers with friends."

"She does, but it doesn't happen as often as she might like, since I like having her at home at night."

Vivi could understand why. His wife had died and a natural reaction to that might be that he was protective of his daughter and his time with her.

She took a sip of her drink and sighed as the sweet liquid hit her tongue. "I don't think I could ever get tired of this drink. It's the perfect summer cooler."

The waiter came out with their food and set it in front of them before moving on to a different table.

Cris picked up his burger, then glanced at her. "So tell me more about this idea you had."

That's right. This wasn't a normal outing. She'd asked for this. "You mentioned that quite a few athletes come through the ortho department. Do you have any idea what the statistics are?"

He seemed to think for a moment. "Probably about fifty percent. We're known for treating sports injuries."

"And how many of those injuries are career-ending?"

There was a longer pause. "I don't actually know. Some patients follow back up with us and some don't."

"I can see how that might happen." She took a bite of her sandwich. "Roni seemed pretty despondent after getting the news that he'd never play soccer at the same level again. Like I mentioned earlier—what if we had someone like him on staff who could help patients work through the various emotions that go along with that kind of a diagnosis?"

He flipped the lid off his burger and took off the pickles, setting them to the side. Another thing she didn't know about him.

"Like a therapist?"

"Not a licensed one, no, since I'm sure the hospital already has someone like that on staff. I'm talking about someone who's actually faced the hard decisions that those patients will face and has a list of resources available or someone who'll just sit and listen and share what's worked for them."

"Got it." He seemed to mull over what she'd said for a few minutes. "I think that's a good idea. And you mentioned Roni might be a good fit."

"I think so. I don't know if he'll go for it or not. But it sure would have helped if he'd had another athlete to talk to. Instead, he got doctors, nurses and PT specialists who probably don't have the foggiest notion what it's like to have to change careers because of an injury."

"True." He took a bite of his food and there was a pause while he swallowed. "But he hasn't even worked through his emotions yet, much less be expected to help anyone else with theirs."

"I get it. But he will be in a month or two. I expect him to start shifting his focus as he heals. He'll be looking for something to replace soccer with. Maybe it'll be coaching, or even sportscasting. But maybe those options will be too painful right now. Not every injured athlete wants a daily reminder of what they can no longer do."

Cris nodded. "I like it. Can you research whether there are centers who are already doing what you're suggesting? They might have some tips on who to look for and what to bill them as. Meaning outside consultants or actual hospital employees."

"Do I need to run it by the administrator before I do any of that?"

"I don't think so. Not yet. Not until we have something concrete to go to him with." He smiled. "And I'll let you broach the subject to Roni and see if that is even something he'd be interested in. I suspect he'll want to give it some thought, since there's no way it will pay as high as what he's getting now. Or as coaching."

"And I should probably see how he handles PT. But even if it's not Roni, I think the idea could still do some good. Maybe a past patient who's looking for a way to give back."

"I would agree. I'm surprised one of our team hasn't

already thought of it." He looked at her for several seconds. "I wasn't sure how I felt about your showing up at the hospital. But it looks like you might do all of us—including Roni—a lot of good. Thanks for speaking up."

She laughed. "If you hadn't listened, I might have gone over your head."

When his smile died, she was quick to cover his hand with hers. "I was kidding."

He pursed his lips. "Actually I hope you never feel that you can't go to someone else. I'm not always the biggest advocate for change, since I tend to be a creature of habit. It sometimes takes me a while to get to where I need to be."

She couldn't imagine him losing both his parents and his spouse, even though the events happened years apart. Hadn't she thought that he'd probably be protective of his daughter? And he'd admitted that he had a hard time with change, maybe also as a reaction to what he'd been through. She finished her drink, then poured another one. She held up the pitcher in silent question and he shook his head no. "I need to drive home from the hospital. And like I said, I rarely drink."

Yes, he had said that. Hopefully he didn't think she was fond of being tipsy. She wasn't. Using a clean knife, she fished out a couple of pieces of melon from the pitcher and added them to her glass. That would be her dessert.

She finished the last of her avocado toast and dabbed her mouth with the napkin.

When Cris pushed back from the table, she thought

for a second that he was going to leave, but instead, he just laid an ankle on top of his knee. "So where are you staying?"

"Right now? A bed-and-breakfast, since I just got into town. I need to look for a place. I was planning on contacting a realtor this afternoon."

"My aunt Pat is a realtor. I could ask her to check around, if you'd like. Do you have a specific area in mind?"

It surprised her that he would offer. But at least finding a realtor would be one thing off her list. "Something close to the hospital would be great. I'd love to be able to walk to and from work. Do you think she would mind? I know rentals aren't always the most lucrative."

He smiled again, and she stared at his face while trying to appear nonchalant. How was it that the man was a thousand times more good-looking than she'd remembered?

"Actually, she manages quite a few properties and has some rentals of her own. She likes being in the business and helping people. They both helped me a lot after my parents died."

A pang went through her. How lucky she was that her parents were alive and well.

"Thanks, then. I don't really have a preference, other than distance to the hospital. A two-bedroom might be nice in case my parents decide to visit."

At that, Cris's jaw tightened up, although his smile didn't fade this time. "I'll have her get in contact with you. Can I have your number?"

She gave it to him and then said, "She can call me or text. Either is fine."

The waiter came with their check. When she started to ask him if he could divide their orders into separate bills, Cris had already taken it and handed the man his credit card. As if reading her thoughts, he murmured, "I'll put it on my expense account since we were talking business."

So he'd already been expecting to pay. But this was a lot more expensive than the hospital cafeteria would have been. "Let me at least pay for the *melón con vino*. I can't imagine they'll want to shell out for alcoholic drinks."

"I'm pretty sure they do it all the time. And I've put them on my expense reports when going out with other surgeons to brainstorm."

Even though he rarely drank? Well, she wasn't going to argue with him. "Okay, if you're sure. But if there's a problem, please let me know."

"I will. But there won't be. Will you talk to Roni soon?"

"Are you okay with that? You said you wanted me to do some research first."

He nodded. "I do, but even if there's not a precedent for doing like you'd suggested, maybe we'll be the first hospital to adopt something like this. Let me know what he says."

"Do you want to be there to hear it in person?"

He glanced at his watch and then got to his feet and waited for her to follow suit. "No. I trust you."

She looked outside and realized it had gotten dark.

How long had they been here, anyway? She certainly hadn't meant to monopolize his entire evening. It had gone by fast, and that made her uneasy. And now they still had to walk back to the hospital.

But, when they stepped outside, the lights were beautiful and there was a warm breeze blowing. The familiarity of the city she called home washed over her in a wave and she had to stop for a minute. Santiago had been beautiful too, but this was just…home.

"Are you okay?"

She nodded, blinking back sudden moisture. "I'd forgotten, that's all. It's just so damned gorgeous."

He turned toward her, looking into her face. His hand rose as if he was going to touch her before he let his arm drop back to his side. "Yes. It is." A long moment went by and a tingly sensation rose up inside of her. The last time he'd looked at her like this, he'd…

Cris took a step back, ending the intimate moment with a suddenness that made her lightheaded. Or maybe that was the wine. Whichever it was, she stiffened her backbone and forced a smile. "Sorry for the maudlin sentimentality. It's just been a long time since I've been here."

"I get it. I'm not sure I could ever leave the city."

She could understand that for sure. His feelings about the city had to be tangled up with those he'd lost. Staying here would make him feel close to them.

And that look he'd given her? There was no way he'd been about to kiss her. That would be ludicrous. What they'd had had been childish and fleeting. Nothing like marrying someone and then living life with them. Having a child with them. And it made her feel more alone than she'd felt in her whole life. Even more than when her fiancé had walked away from her to be with another woman.

"Shall we go?"

They walked in silence and the beauty of her surroundings had ceased to captivate her. All she wanted right now was to get back to her hotel and hibernate for the night. Hopefully she'd feel better about things tomorrow. Actually she'd felt fine during dinner. She'd enjoyed his company and the conversation. It was only afterwards that her own thoughts had spoiled things.

But things always seemed worse at night. At least that's what people said, right? Tomorrow would be another day.

It took ten minutes to get back to the hospital, and when they got to the doors, he started inside, but she didn't. "I'm headed home."

"Are you driving?"

"Yes, my car is here—why?"

"You were drinking. Let me take you."

She tried to assess her faculties, but she was smart enough to know that she probably wasn't the best judge of that. But she'd only had two drinks.

"Come on, Vivi. It's dark and you're no longer as familiar with the landscape like you once were." And there was something in Cris's eyes that had gone hard, and she had a feeling if she tried to argue her point he was going to lose respect for her. But why? She knew she wasn't drunk. Not by a long shot. But what she'd thought moments earlier was still true.

"Okay. I can take a taxi to work in the morning. Thanks."

The hard look softened. "Good. Which hotel?"

"Esquina da Val. Actually, the name is written in English, Val's Corner, 'cause the owner's name is Valeria and her house is on a corner." She giggled and then put a hand over her mouth, shocked by the sound. Maybe the alcohol had hit her a little harder than she'd expected.

"I see." The side of his mouth flicked up for a quick second.

Dios. The man was more than gorgeous. Getting in a car with him was probably more of a colossal mistake than eating with him had been.

Except it wasn't. He'd thought her idea had merit, so that made it worth it. And her muddled feelings had to be because of the alcohol, even though it didn't normally affect her. She'd been thirsty, though, and had downed the first glass fairly quickly and then had eaten most of the wine-soaked melon chunks after she'd finished the second. She gave an internal groan.

He was right about her not driving.

"I'll bring my car around. Wait here."

Two minutes later, he drove up in a sleek, sporty-looking SUV. She was sober enough to realize that it was an expensive vehicle. He got out and opened her door, and she climbed in.

Within minutes they were on one of the roads leading from the hospital, heading up a hill, past one of the city's funiculars, which were much needed due to the steep terrain. Thankfully she didn't need to use any of them to get to Val's Corner, although the place was on a hill.

"I think I know where the place is, but if you can remember which street it's on, that would be a huge help."

"It's on Gaeta." Somehow she remembered the name, even though she'd only been there once.

A short time later, he pulled up in front of the pink building. It was a good thing, because she'd almost fallen asleep in his car.

"Thank you. And thanks for letting me discuss my thoughts on adding a staff member for our athletes."

"Not a problem. Let me know what you turn up once you look into it. And if Roni seems to be in favor of helping with it."

"I will." She got out and slammed the door behind her and headed for the gate.

Val's Corner had a cobblestone sidewalk leading up to a path of the same material. It ended at the front door, a huge wooden affair that had an intercom. She buzzed the door and let Val know it was her. Her suitcase was still on the bed. She should unpack, butut that might need to wait until tomorrow. She was suddenly exhausted, both physically and mentally, and quite honestly, emotionally as well.

A clunking sound let her know that the door's lock had been released, so she went in and headed up the stairs to her room, one of three on the second floor. And she was as surprised this time as she was the first time she'd set foot in the place. Her room had its own bathroom rather than a shared one on the hallway and was as spacious as her bedroom had been in her childhood home. And that was saying a lot, because her house had been one of the larger ones in the city, since her dad was a diplomat.

She set her suitcases on the ground and then went to the overstuffed chair that sat in one corner and dropped into it with a sigh. Then she pulled out her phone and texted her parents, letting them know that she was settled in and that work had gone well. The one thing she'd left out was a biggie, and that was that she was working with Cris. Although she wondered if her parents would even remember who he was. Her dad might, though. He'd been unhappy with her choice of boyfriends, since Cris's family had definitely not been from the same part of town as her family had, although they hadn't been poor.

None of which mattered now.

She pressed Send and then curled up in the chair and leaned her head back against the cushion. Today seemed so unreal. Who would have ever thought she'd dine with an old high school flame? Certainly not her.

But she was pretty sure she was going to wake up tomorrow and find her situation unchanged.

One thing that would be changed, though, was her attitude. She'd be over the shock of seeing him again. Of hearing his voice. Of having him look at her. And she'd be able to regain control of a situation that had almost spun out of her grasp today. And no more drinking around him.

Or wondering what might have been.

Tomorrow she was going to slip into a part she needed

to learn how to play. A part she should have been playing her whole adult life. That of a colleague who never ventured beyond the boundaries set before her. She'd seen what could happen when she colored outside the lines. And there would be no more of that. Not with Cris or any other work acquaintance. It would be strictly business.

She'd come here to push a work romance into the past, where it would stay. And then she was going to look toward the future and embrace all that it could be.

And Cris wasn't part of that future. Nor would he ever be.

She was going to remember that and stick to it. Even if the going got tough.

CHAPTER FOUR

CRIS SHOVED HIS unruly hair out of his face as he turned a corner and continued his run. The Quinta Vergara park had always been his locale of choice when it came to getting out of the gym and into the real world. Running on a treadmill was one thing, but stepping onto a real road surface with a variety of surfaces was another. And so far, even today, it hadn't disappointed him, even if he was sweating a whole lot more than he would have in the climate-controlled space inside the gym.

The parallel between running and life didn't escape him. The difference between the controlled atmosphere of the hospital, with its sterile environment and mostly predictable events, was at odds with life outside those walls. He'd gotten an up close and personal reminder of that fact two nights ago when he'd gone out to dinner on business and it ended up being a whole lot more personal than he'd planned for. At least on his part.

He turned a corner and stepped off a dirt pathway and onto a concrete sidewalk, feeling the change and how his body automatically adjusted to it. Why hadn't he been able to do that when he and Vivi had stepped outside the restaurant into an evening filled with stars, rustling leaves and hushed voices? Maybe because of the obvious emotion in her voice when she'd looked up and gazed at the sights and sounds of the evening and murmured at how she'd forgotten.

Cris, on the other hand, had forgotten nothing. The instantaneous attraction he'd always felt when she was near. The beautiful tilt of her smile. The painful edge of seeing tears on her lashes.

He'd almost tilted her head up for a kiss. Had almost lost sight of why they'd been in that restaurant. What if Lidia had still been alive? Would he have lost his head then too?

No. He'd loved Lidia deeply. But their relationship had been different. Comfortable. They'd been from the same world, both born and raised their whole lives in Valpo. Being with her had felt so natural. They'd been happy and fulfilled and he was never going to forget that.

He would have remained faithful to her no matter what. But she wasn't here as a talisman to ward off danger. She was gone and no matter how much he might wish otherwise, she wasn't coming back.

And so when he'd stood there with Vivi, the past had come rushing back. The carefree impulsive love of youth. It had arrived out of nowhere and almost overtaken him.

He pushed himself harder, made his muscles work for each step, showing them this wasn't some game. He wasn't a carefree teenager anymore. He was an adult with adult responsibilities. He was a single dad doing the best he could to raise a daughter. To be father and mother to her. The thought of her being hurt because he couldn't control his libido was an unacceptable trade-off. He might have lived through the reality of losing Vivi when he was a teenager. He'd also lived through the wrenching pain of Lidia's death. But that didn't mean he couldn't do his damnedest to protect Gabi from the pain of loss. Loss didn't always come through death. It also came by choice or by circumstances.

So if he could prevent her becoming attached to someone who might or might not stay, he could prevent the pain that came if that person did, in fact, leave. Or worse.

The burning pain in his thighs reminded him that he wasn't out here running as a form of self-flagellation. He slowed his pace to a more tolerable level. But were his thoughts any better? Wasn't he punishing himself for something that hadn't even happened? Cris hadn't kissed her, no matter how tempted he'd been. He'd stopped. Had pulled himself back from the brink. And now that he knew what could happen, he would be on guard.

And really, he didn't know the Vivi of the here and now. He only knew the childhood version of her. If he could remind himself of that and that any feelings he might have were generated out of distorted memories of what they'd once had, he should be able to avoid a repeat.

It hadn't helped that Gabi had asked later about the pretty *señora* she'd seen him standing next to at the hospital. He'd given her a vague answer about her being a new nurse, but the look in his aunt's eyes said she'd recognized Vivi and knew exactly what she'd once meant to her only nephew. Worse, when she'd dropped Gabi off that night, she'd apologized for bringing her to work and said in a low voice meant for his ears only that she hadn't realized Vivi was back in town.

He'd been honest and said he hadn't known it either until they stood across from each other in the operating room.

She asked if he was okay with her being here.

It was a question he hadn't been able to answer then and one he still couldn't answer now. It had certainly been easier before her arrival.

He slowed to a walk, putting his hands behind his head as he went through his cooldown routine. He'd only seen Vivi in passing the last two days, since he did most of his surgeries on Wednesdays and Thursdays, unless it was an emergency surgery like Roni's had been. And she hadn't contacted him about whether or not she'd done the research he'd asked or whether she'd spoken to Roni, who had been released from the hospital and was coming to PT on an outpatient basis. He was due to see the athlete in his office again on Friday of the current week. Hopefully his patient was in a better frame of mind.

And hopefully by that time, Cris would also be in a better frame of mind and sticking to his plan of not socializing with Vivi outside of office hours. Next time the cafeteria was closed, there would be no going off campus to discuss anything. And there definitely would be no alcohol involved. Because when he'd thought she was going to drive, a surge of anger had come over him. Alcohol and driving did not mix. No one knew that better than he did. And he took great care to make sure he put no one at risk. Including his daughter.

Gabi was number one in his life and that's the way things needed to stay. At least until she was old enough to understand that bad things sometimes happened. And at five years of age, he hoped she was a few years away from needing to know that.

He got back to his car and took a towel out of his gym bag, dragging it across his face and arms and then tossing it back. Glancing at his watch, he grimaced. He'd taken longer with his run than he'd meant to, so he didn't have time to go home. Thankfully he had a change of clothes back at the hospital and would shower there in the bathroom that adjoined his office.

And then he would start his day.

Vivi was in at the nurses' station when *he* got off the elevator. Looking like a bronzed Adonis in gym shorts and a T-shirt that clung to his form in a way that should be illegal, he'd obviously been working out.

And he's off-limits, Viv. At least to you.

But that didn't mean she couldn't admire the hair that hung almost to his chin in decadent curls. That was one thing that hadn't changed about him. He'd always worn his hair a little longer than was conventional and let it be a little wilder.

It had driven her wild as a teenager, just like it had all the girls. She'd always been in awe that he'd chosen her out of countless others who would have loved to be with him.

But that was then and this was now.

His dark eyes met hers for a second longer than necessary before veering away in the direction of his office. Where he obviously was headed to shower. And her mental reminder leaped off a cliff and vanished.

Her eyes closed in an attempt to block the images that were now pounding at her lids demanding admittance.

Please, no.

"He's a hunk, isn't he?"

Her eyes jerked back open, horrified at being caught. Then she realized the comment wasn't aimed at her. It was between the two other nurses at the desk. She blew out a breath in relief and pretended to be doing some paperwork that was so engrossing that she couldn't possibly have heard what they were talking about.

"What do you think, Viviani?"

She glanced over, blinking. "Oh. About what?"

The other nurse chortled. "Never mind. If you'd seen it, you would know."

Oh, she'd seen it all right.

Vivi gave a half shrug as if she were totally confused. But it served as a wake-up call. What if word got back to one or both of them that she and Cris had a history? How would that possibly happen? She was pretty sure he wasn't going to say anything, and Vivi definitely wasn't going to. So she just had to make sure no one saw her making eyes at him or seeking him out. Or going out to eat with him again. Which she had no intention of doing.

Except she did need to talk to him about what she'd found out about other hospitals employing athletes or having programs similar to the one she was talking about. There were none in the area. Theirs would be the first. She wasn't sure if that was going to be a plus or a minus as far as that went.

She just needed to find a way and a time to go talk to him. And that time definitely wasn't now. But what she could do was text him. Or send an email to his hospital mailbox. Once she talked to Roni, which she still hadn't done. But she had gone down to PT and talked to Bella, since she was still handling his case. She said that Roni was still going through the stages of grieving and hadn't completely given up hope on returning to the field as a player.

He was going to eventually have to come to terms with it or risk wrecking all the work that Cris had done on that knee. She'd smiled and asked if she could come down during his next session. The physical therapist was thrilled. "He seemed to really connect with you, so I think it would do him good to see you."

And that session was today at three this afternoon, so she had a while. A few minutes later, Cris came out dressed in fresh clothes, an iPad in his hand. He looked straight at her. "Can I see you about our athletic patient?"

She played dumb, even though both of the nurses from earlier had gone to treat patients. "Athletic patient?"

He threw her a look which made her cringe. She wasn't very good at acting clueless. So she'd better get up and moving before anyone came back and saw her talking to him. "I'll be over in just a minute."

"Okay." He headed back to his office.

Dios! She at least needed to tell someone where she'd be. If it looked like she'd disappeared from the desk, someone might want to know where she was, especially since she was so new to the hospital. So she headed to the patients' rooms and found Dora on the first try.

"I need to go consult with one of the doctors about a patient. Are you good?"

"Yep, go."

She assumed that happened quite often here, just like it had at her previous hospital. There were all kinds of reasons. Medication changes, scheduling changes and so on. It was normally just taken at face value, and Dora didn't ask which doctor needed her, which was a relief. "Just page me if you need me, but I shouldn't be long."

"It's not Dandalia, is it?"

She had no idea who that even was. "No. Why—is he or she long-winded?"

"He. And the longest. Okay, see you."

With that, Vivi headed back down the hallway, dread filling her as her steps took her ever closer to the man's office. When she was there, she hesitated before knocking.

"Come in."

She did as directed, almost falling over herself to get to one of the two chairs that were parked in front of his desk. "You wanted to see me?"

"Yes, any information on what we talked about?"

He made it sound almost clandestine. And that was the last thing she wanted: to feel like they had some kind of secret between them. Well, they did, kind of. But this wasn't from twenty years ago.

His hair was still damp from his shower and the room

was filled with the warm scent of some kind of wood. Cedar, maybe?

She tried to ignore it. "I did call all the area hospitals that might have some kind of program but struck out. As far as I can tell, they have mental health specialists on staff but nothing other than that." She went on before he could ask. "I was going to text you. I did go talk to the PT here at the hospital about how Roni is doing and it sounds like he's still in denial. But he has a session today at three. I plan on going down then."

"He has an appointment with me on Friday as well. If today doesn't pan out, maybe you can come to the appointment."

"Which is at what time?"

Cris checked his electronic device. "Eleven. Are you scheduled for surgery on Wednesday or Thursday?"

"Both days."

He didn't say anything to that, and since they were both procedures that he was involved with, she tried to read his body language, but if he cared one way or the other, he wasn't showing it. "Will you let me know what Roni says today?"

"Do you want me to actually ask if he would be interested in helping with a program like the one I mentioned?"

"Yes. Don't make him any promises but ask if it's something he could see himself doing—helping other athletes who find themselves in his position."

"Got it. But I have to tell you…if I get there and feel like it will hurt his session or his chances of recovery,

I'll hold off. I'd rather say nothing than do more harm than good."

"We're in agreement there." He looked at her, then said, "About the other night."

Heavens. What on earth could he want to say about that? That he was disappointed in her for letting the booze go to her head?

"What about it?"

"I'm sorry if I made you uncomfortable. We should have probably sat somewhere at the hospital and talked."

He hadn't made her uncomfortable. In fact, she was pretty sure he was the one who felt uncomfortable about what had happened. "It was fine. But you're probably right. We should stick to the hospital grounds for work-related subjects."

He looked at her a little closer. "And those are the only subjects we should be talking about."

Ahh, so he was warning her off. Well, there was no need for it. She'd done plenty of warning herself off when it came to that. Especially after the comments made by Dora and Elena. "I agree. We can just act like we didn't know each other before I came to work at the hospital."

"I didn't mean that. Eventually someone is going to know and say something about our past. It'll make it worse if people think we lied about it. Because they'd start wondering why."

"I'm pretty sure no one is going to be interested in my past."

But they might be interested in his. Actually, she was pretty sure they would be. But it would be easier if they just thought of him in terms of a man who had lost his beloved wife.

"Have you never worked in a hospital before? People want to know everything about everything. Even if it's none of their business."

She laughed. "True."

He paused. "I've always liked your laugh."

"And this is related to hospital business how?" But she didn't stop smiling. Because she couldn't. And he'd just showed her that the task of keeping to impersonal subjects might be harder for him than he made it sound. Because no matter what else had transpired in her life, she would always have a soft spot when it came to him. That whole first love thing. How could she not allow those good memories to sometimes overshadow the present? And she hoped that he might still have at least a memory or two that he cherished about her.

He'd been married, and she'd been almost married, and yet they did have history. Nothing would take that away no matter how much they didn't want the past to bleed over to the present.

"It's not related to business. But it is the truth."

"Well, as long as we're talking about truth—I still like your hair. I'm glad you never completely cut it off." When they were together, his hair had been almost down to his shoulders.

"I've thought about it. Many times. But Lidia…" He shook his head. "Sorry. None of that matters."

His wife had liked his hair too. Somehow, the thought of him finding someone else—rather than being painful—brought comfort. And she was sad that he'd lost what they'd had. Vivi had thought she'd found love as well. Only to find that the universe evidently didn't have that in store for her. At least not with Estevan. And not with Cris, either.

"I'm sorry she's not here for you now." She wasn't sure why she'd said that, but it was true.

"Thanks. Me too. I'm sad she won't be here to see Gabi grow up."

"I think maybe somehow she can. At least I'd like to think so."

He smiled. "I'd like to think so too." He stood. "Anyway, I won't keep you. But thanks for checking into the other area hospital thing and for trying to feel Roni out about the program."

"He might respond better if it came from you, since you're his surgeon."

Cris seemed to think about that for a minute. "I don't think he believed me completely when I told him he'd never play soccer on the same level again. That his repaired knee would not be able to handle the stress of pro soccer."

"Well, I'll try. But don't expect him to jump up and down over the prospect."

"No. And he won't make nearly as much from a hospital job as he would from advertising endorsements. People will recognize him for a long time to come. He could still make a lot of money."

She didn't think that's the route he would go, though, and she couldn't put her finger on why she thought that.

"I don't think he's about the money, honestly. I know a lot of these athletes are, but I think Roni truly loves the game. He never once mentioned money to me. Not about losing his income or anything else like that."

"No, me either. Which is why he may opt to coach. It would keep him in the game. And if that's what he wants to do, then more power to him. But I would still like to see what we can do for the future Ronis that come through our doors."

"Me too. Okay, I better go. How hush-hush do you want all of this?"

"For right now? Until we've talked to the hospital administrator about it, I'd like it to stay pretty much between us. I don't want him to think we're going behind his back with anything. And as soon as you talk to Roni today, I'd like us to go together to talk to the powers that be about it."

She could understand that. "Do you think the administrator will go for it?"

"Marcos is a pretty big soccer fan himself. I can see him finding an angle that helps the hospital raise funds. He's good at the money side of things, which might make it tricky, since I don't want Roni to think this is just a fundraising tactic. But I also think he'll be interested in doing the right thing for the athletes themselves."

Vivi hadn't met the man yet, but since there was a staff meeting next week for all new hospital employees, she would meet him then, if not before. "I'm fine if you want to present it to him on your own."

"It was your idea. I want you there. You'll be the one who can present it to him with passion."

She wasn't really sure about that, but she did understand Cris not wanting to try to talk about it on his own. And she did have some thoughts on how to kick-start this thing and get the word out there. And it would have the side benefit of attracting some of the top players, who would come to them for treatment if they knew that Roni endorsed the hospital.

"Okay, as soon as I see Roni today, I'll try to feel him out. And I'll let you know."

"Sounds good. And like I said, regardless of how this plays out with him, I'd still like to present the program to Marcos. Are you okay if I set up a time with him?"

"Sure. That's fine."

"Okay. Talk soon."

With that she left the office, wondering how good of an idea it was for them to "talk soon." Because they'd been talking a whole lot more than she envisioned when she saw him on the other side of that hospital bed and realized he was the top orthopedic surgeon in the hospital and quite probably the city. She'd been determined to avoid him if at all humanly possible. And now all of a sudden they were brainstorming an idea that she'd come up with. So instead of avoiding him, she'd just committed herself to seeing a whole lot more of him.

And she wasn't sure what she thought of that.

But one thing that she was pretty sure was going to haunt her long into the night was the fact that he still liked her laugh.

She kept replaying those words in her head. It was just an offhanded comment and meant nothing more than the words themselves. So why did she keep hearing so much more behind them?

She didn't know. But she'd better find a way to minimize that comment and anything else he might say in the future. Or she was setting herself up for a whole lot of heartache. Maybe even worse than what Estevan had handed her. Because it would mean she was turning her sights toward a man she couldn't have back when she was a teenager and for a man she still couldn't have today. Whether it was the whole rebound thing or not, it wasn't healthy. And she, for one, was not about to let herself go there.

Roni's face turned red and Vivi flinched, waiting for him to flambé her for even thinking that the great Ronaldo Saraia would deign to be assigned to giving pep talks.

"You want me to head up a program at the hospital for injured athletes?"

"Well, we need to run it by the hospital administrator, first. But basically, yes."

He looked at her as if she were crazy. "Why do you think they would listen to me?"

"Are you kidding? You're every kid's fantasy for the future. You pulled yourself up from nothing and played your heart out each and every game. They'll listen."

His brows went up. "Okay. I'll think about it. I have some folks I'd need to talk it over with to make sure it wouldn't affect my brand. Because even if I'm never able to play again, I still love the game and want to support it in any way that I can."

Wow, his attitude had done some shifting over the past several days and she was glad to see it. Before, he'd been afraid his "brand" was going to disappear off the face of the earth if he couldn't play. And now he seemed to be moving past that kind of thinking.

"I get that completely. And we don't want to do anything that will hurt your ability to do that either. I just know you could do a lot of good for the individual athletes who make up soccer. They're just as important as the game itself, don't you think? Without them—without *you*—there wouldn't even be a game. It's made up of individuals just like you."

"Wow, that's a lot of weight on my shoulders." Unexpectedly, Roni worked his way over to her, using his walker, and enveloped her in a big hug. "But thank you for everything."

"Hey, it's you I need to thank for even considering it."

When she looked up, her eyes going over his shoulder, she saw that Cris was in the doorway staring at them, and for some reason he didn't seem very happy. What was he doing here?

She pulled free and waved him over. "Here's Cris… er… Dr. Diaz now."

When he made it over to them, Roni reached out to shake his hand. "Vivi was telling me about the idea of starting an athletic support group."

Cris's eyes were on her, though, rather than on the

other man. "And what do you think about the idea? It's hers, you know."

"I figured that out almost immediately. And I think it's a great one. I told her I need to iron out some things before I can agree to help, but I think the folks in my camp will be happy that I'm still able to do something for soccer."

"We'd appreciate anything you can do. But now I have to steal Vivi away. We have an emergency coming in and I need her."

"An athlete?" Roni asked.

"No, not this time. I'll see you on Friday at our appointment?"

Roni nodded his head. "I'll be there." He shifted his glance to her. "And thank you. I mean that. I guess that means we'll be working together on this, if it all gets approved?"

"I don't know about that. It depends on what the administration wants the program to look like. But you're welcome." She wanted to be careful where he was concerned. Patients could easily become attached to their doctors or caregivers. And even if the whole patient/staff relationships thing wasn't forbidden, she wasn't interested in him that way and she didn't want him to get any ideas.

It had nothing to do with the strange look Cris had given her when he'd walked through that door. And speaking of Cris, he was already headed toward the door, and it was clear that he expected her to follow him. So she did, hoping that whatever emergency it was, it would have a good outcome. Because she could use some good news. Her phone pinged and she looked down at it, not recognizing the number. Then she went stiff. She didn't recognize the number but she recognized the first couple of words of the text, because she'd seen several of them before she'd left Santiago. It was from Estevan. And he wanted to talk.

Not happening. She pressed some buttons and blocked the new number, almost running into Cris as she did. She pulled herself back to allow some space to come between them and sighed. What could she and Estevan possibly have to talk about. When she had some time, she would sit down and compose a text that made it clear that they were done. That chapter of her life was closed. Just like the chapter between her and Cris was.

Closed. Forever.

Yes. She could definitely use something that had at least the possibility of a good outcome right about now. Crossing her fingers behind her back, she got onto the elevator with Cris.

CHAPTER FIVE

THEY SCRUBBED IN side by side without saying a word to each other. She still didn't understand what she assumed was a glare that he'd given her down in PT or the cold shoulder she'd gotten on the way back up to orthopedics. He'd told her that their patient—a fifteen-year-old female—had been injured in a car accident. She'd been going to celebrate her Fiesta de Quince when a drunk driver hit the side of her car. Her mom was killed instantly, and her dad had been severely injured as well. Clara had been left with a shattered femur that would need to be rebuilt.

It was a terrible tragedy. But when she'd said as much, Cris had shot her a look and said that the tragedy was that people still got behind the wheel of a car after having too much to drink.

Was it a commentary on how he'd had to drive her home after dinner the other night?

He was right to be angry about the accident. She was too. He'd just been so vehement about it.

He finished scrubbing in first and there was a nurse waiting to snap his gloves on. She did the same for Vivi.

When she arrived in the operating room, she went

up to take her place at the instrument table and checked them over before glancing at the patient, who'd already been intubated and was ready to go. She had on heavy makeup, but there was blood spatter on her face—from her own injuries? From one of her parents? The fifteenth birthday ritual was such a big part of Latin American countries that the thought of something like this happening was heartbreaking. Clara would wake up in a different world from the one she'd just come from where she'd probably laughed as her hair and makeup were done, surrounded by friends and family.

Her mom was gone and her world shattered, just like her leg.

She pulled her thoughts back to the surgery at hand. None of those things could be changed. But they could help Clara regain the use of her leg.

She glanced up at Cris and it was déjà vu. All she could see were his eyes. He was looking at her as well, and she couldn't tell if he was still angry or not. Although realistically if he was angry at her for some reason, they were going to have it out after the surgery, because she was not at fault here.

"Are you ready?" His voice wasn't hard anymore, though.

"Yes."

When they unwrapped the dressings that the EMTs had put in place, she could see that the actual injury was a mess. The part of the femur that was in one piece had perforated the skin and had been exposed to the air and all kinds of contaminants. Even as she looked, she spotted a dime-sized piece of bone stuck just inside the wound.

"Cris." She brought his attention to it, only realizing afterwards that she'd said his first name. But that probably wasn't an issue because a lot of doctors didn't stand on formality.

He nodded and retrieved the piece, dropping it into a jar of saline, the way they would do with any other pieces that were floating loose in the wound. They would piece together what they could and hope the bone would fill in what they couldn't. The piece he'd just dropped in the jar probably wouldn't be able to be reattached, but it was crucial that they clean out any fragments that could cause complications later on. Miraculously, there were no large severed vessels, but there was still a lot of blood.

"Scalpel." This time, she handed it over without the hesitation of that first surgery. He opened the wound further and began carefully flushing the wound to remove any debris, using forceps to pick out more bone fragments as they came to the surface.

He gave a running commentary both for the benefit of those in the room as well as for the recorder, which was in use for every surgery. "Displaced open fracture of the femur with multiple small fragments. Three main sections of bone that I can see."

He glanced around. "We're going to be here a while. Can someone check and see if we have the staff to scrub in as needed to relieve us in shifts?"

Someone left to do that, while the rest of the surgical team continued doing their jobs.

He finished flushing until he was satisfied that no foreign material was left in the wound and then set out to reconstruct what was left of her bone.

Three hours went by as Cris began forming a type of scaffolding that would hold the three main sections of bone in place while it hopefully healed, and then added in two other pieces that were large enough to screw into.

"Length looks to be good."

So there was still enough bone that the overall length would be close to what it was pre-accident. Which meant if all went well one of her legs wouldn't be noticeably shorter than the other. Where there had been one fragment in the glass jar when they started there were now seven. Fewer than Vivi thought there would be. And so far, she hadn't fumbled at all during this surgery. It gave her hope that she'd be able to maintain a professional demeanor even when things like that puzzling look he'd given her down in PT happened. She'd been trained for this and it was important that she be able make it through. If she ever felt patient care was going to suffer because of her personal life, then she needed to put in for a transfer or relocate, just like she'd done after discovering her fiancé had fallen in love with someone else.

Dios. She did not want to have to write Estevan back, but it looked like at this point that she had no choice. But it would be the last time. And if he contacted her again, she would change her own number.

Five hours after they had started, Cris finally seemed happy with the way the leg had been reconstructed. "I'm going to close up, starting with the inner sutures."

Even though he had to be mentally and physically exhausted after standing over the patient for so long—it had taken a couple of tries to get things fitted the way he wanted them to be—he continued on as if he still had plenty of energy. The tables and floor gave another story, though. They were littered with gauze and metal pieces— symbols of the hope of a leg that might heal.

Then he was done. "Let's wake her up."

The anesthesiologist gave a reversal agent and once he deemed she was ready, they extubated her and waited for her to stir. Cris went to the head of the table and talked in low soothing tones. "Clara, can you hear me?"

Her eyelids fluttered and then she looked up, obviously still in that confused fog that surrounded the anesthesia medication. The girl nodded and tried to say something but Cris put his hand on her forehead. "Don't try to talk yet. We're going to put you in a room and let you wake up a little bit more, then I'll come in and see you."

The girl nodded again, before letting her eyes slide shut.

"Wheel her down to recovery. I want to check her hemoglobin and make sure she won't need supplemental plasma. I'm going to check on her family."

Oh, God, that was right. Her mom was gone. And her dad? Were there any siblings?

Cris turned to the team, "Good job, everyone. That went as smoothly as it could have, and that's thanks to all of you." His eyes landed on her and then away before he headed out the door, leaving them to complete their tasks. This went much quicker than the surgery and everyone filed out, leaving the room to be thoroughly cleaned and disinfected for the next surgery.

She headed down to the cafeteria to get a coffee, even though she only had a half hour left of her shift. A surgery like that drained her, even though she wasn't the one who was performing the operation. She was pretty sure everyone on the team felt the same way.

She got her coffee and headed back out, her gaze tracking to the left for a second and spotting a familiar head of hair. It was just the back of him, but the slump of his shoulders and the way he was kind of hunched over as if in pain made her stop and head toward him. Rounding the table, she saw that the rest of him didn't look any better. He was pinching the bridge of his nose as if his head hurt and his eyes were closed.

"Cris, is everything okay?"

He opened his eyes, the brown irises so dark that they seemed almost black. "It's fine."

Before she could stop herself, she pulled out a chair and sat down. "No, it's not. Is it the patient?"

"No. She's fine. At least until she wakes up and realizes what happened."

"I know." Maybe that's all this was about, but she couldn't shake the feeling that there was more to it.

"It's just so senseless. Why would someone get behind the wheel of a car if they weren't fit to drive? Why wouldn't his friends stop him? Or whoever served him those drinks."

"Maybe he was drinking at home. With no one around to intervene."

"I know. And ultimately it boils down to being his responsibility and his alone. But, dammit, no one should have to go through what I…" He shook his head.

Her throat dried up. "Is that how your wife died?"

He blinked as if remembering she was there. "No. It was my parents. They were killed as they went to celebrate their twentieth wedding anniversary."

"By a drunk driver."

"Yes."

"I'm so sorry. I knew your parents had passed in an accident, but I didn't know the circumstances. Your comment about not drinking much. Is that why?"

"Yes."

If she remembered right, he didn't even finish his glass of Melvin. And there she'd been with no idea why he'd seemed so irritated with her for even considering driving. Her heart ached for all of the loss he'd experienced.

"You don't have any more surgeries today, do you?"

"None scheduled. But who knows what will come in next."

She put her hand over his. "Cris, you can't change the world or prevent people from doing things that hurt others no matter how much you may want that to happen."

Her fiancé had hurt her deeply by tossing her aside for someone else. She'd had no control of that or of what Estevan was doing now in repeatedly contacting her. Even her dad had hurt her deeply by tearing her away from all her friends and from Cris when he'd moved the family to Santiago. And even though she could see why now, it had changed the way she'd viewed her father for a long time afterwards. She'd thrown some terrible words at him, and even though she'd later apologized for them, they'd both done some things that they regretted.

"I know. But I wish to God I could change what that girl is going to go through as the realization hits her."

"What happened to the driver of the other vehicle?"

"He wasn't hurt at all."

She frowned. "But he was arrested, wasn't he?"

"Yes. From what I heard he was driving without a license. It seems he was a repeat offender so it had already been taken away. He'd been to jail, rehab—and still couldn't get his life turned around."

"Addiction is a terrible thing. I'm not excusing him. He should not have been behind a wheel and I truly hope he won't have access to alcohol for a long time to come."

"Me too." He gave a wan smile. "Roni is right. You are a pretty persuasive person."

"Come on. My shift is over, and my coworkers have already told me to go home. The last thing you need to do, though, is go home and dwell on what happened." Then a thought hit her. "Your daughter. Is she waiting for you?"

"No, she's with my aunt. I wasn't sure how long the surgery would take so she offered to keep her for the night."

So he really would be alone at home. After his announcement, Estevan had moved out of their apartment the next day while she'd been at the hospital. So she went home to a very different place. It had been a terrible feeling and one of her reasons for leaving Santiago and starting over.

But fate had a funny way of showing her that she'd never be truly free of her past. Things she'd thought were left behind came back to haunt her at the oddest times. And now here she was with Cris again after twenty years away. That wasn't to say that she hadn't thought of him over those years. She had. More than once.

He probably felt the same way about his parents' deaths and the death of his wife. They would never completely leave him. And that's how it should be.

"I know we said we'd keep this professional, but surely we can break that rule just this once. I promise not to pounce on you or anything."

One side of his mouth went up in that delicious smile of his. "As I remember it, no one pounced on anyone."

"All right—so there shouldn't be a problem, right?"

"Persuasive. Yes, you are." He sighed and slapped his hands on his knees. "But I really don't want to go home. What do you want to see?"

Ha! That was a loaded question and one she'd better not dig into too deeply. Because it might break the rule they'd just made. "One of my favorite places as a kid was the Cerro Alegre overlooking the bay. We would go up the funicular and find a restaurant that had a good view and enjoy it. But we don't have to eat. If I remember right, there's a sightseeing spot just as you get off the lift."

The funiculars of Valparaiso looked like odd train cars that traversed terrain too steep for a car or other forms of transportation. The ones that were still in operation were considered national treasures and were a top tourist destination. And the views at the top of those hills couldn't be beat.

"I took Gabi there once and she liked it. But I think the funicular was her favorite part of the whole excursion."

"I bet it was." The little girl was the spitting image of her father with her dark curls that fell over her eyes despite the little bands that had been used to try to hold those locks at bay.

"Okay, let's go. Do you need to change?"

Cris was already back in street clothes, but she still had her scrubs on. She took a sip of her coffee, which was now lukewarm, and made a face. "Yes. I have some clothes in my locker. I can meet you back here in say fifteen minutes."

"That sounds like a plan. I'll let my aunt know where we are. Oh, and I talked to her about your need for housing and she said she'd look into it and try to get a list together of available places in the next couple of days."

"Oh! Thank you. And please say thank you for me. See you in a bit."

As she was changing in the staff locker room area, she started having doubts about what she was about to do. But since it was her idea and she didn't want to have to explain what she was worried about, she'd just have to grit her teeth and bear it. The problem was that she was looking forward to the outing a little too much. And that gave her pause.

But surely she could get through this without any problems. She was an adult. She'd met plenty of men she found attractive and hadn't gone to bed with them. And even if she were willing, Cris promised to be on his best behavior. Well, not in those exact words but close enough.

She glanced in the mirror to see the worry on her face, though, and gave herself a mental lecture.

You are helping him get over a terrible memory. Nothing more, nothing less. Got it?

With that, she headed back down the elevator to meet him.

Cris leaned back in his chair, glad for the diversion. He hadn't been lying when he said he didn't want to go home. Although he wasn't living in the same apartment where he and Lidia had lived—he'd moved closer to his aunt and uncle so that it would be more convenient to take Gabi back and forth—there were still memories everywhere he looked. Every picture of them together or of his parents was a reminder of his loss. Of all that his daughter would miss out on. He was used to it and most days it didn't bother him, but tonight?

Oh, yeah, tonight it would. Especially if he didn't have his daughter's presence to help distract him.

Vivi reappeared and she was now dressed in a white gauzy skirt and navy blouse. A silver bangle enclosed one slim wrist. She looked very bohemian and matched the city's vibe perfectly. And yet it was who she was. It was what he remembered of Vivi from their teenage years.

In reality, she was more beautiful with tiny lines fanning from her eyes that spoke of laughter and a happy life than she'd been back then. And he was glad for her. Glad that she'd been able to find joy in living. Cris's joy came mainly in the form of his daughter and his work. And he frowned, realizing he didn't have much of a life outside of those two things anymore. So this trek up Cerro Alegre would be good for his…what did they call it? His soul? Although he wasn't so sure anymore that he had one of those. His ability to forgive seemed to come less and less easily nowadays.

He stood. "Ready?"

"As ready as I'll ever be."

The way she said that gave him pause. "You don't have to go, you know. I'm not going to go out and do anything crazy."

"Neither am I, so we're both good." But the nervous laugh that accompanied the words didn't make him any more confident in going along with her suggestion. But other than calling her a liar, he was going to have to take her at her word.

"So we're going to be sane and rational, then?"

Her laugh when it came this time was real and happy-sounding and made him smile.

"Since when have we ever been sane and rational when we were together?"

His smile widened, thinking of all the crazy stunts

they'd pulled back then. "I don't regret any of it, though. Do you?"

"No, I don't. Not a minute of it." She held his gaze for a second before looking out the window at the gathering dusk. "But if we're going to do this, we'd better go now."

"Are you okay taking my car to the funicular?"

"Yes, since you probably know the way better than I do. It's going to take me a while before I relearn the city."

Before they relearned each other.

The thought came and went so quickly that he almost missed it. But as long as that relearning involved friendship, there was no harm in shared memories. Right?

Right.

They got in his car and despite the traffic of those heading out to various clubs and nighttime activities, the main rush hour was already finished. Various buildings had spotlights on them, highlighting the street art that Valparaiso was known for. He thought again that Vivi looked like she could have been born and raised in Chile despite spending her earliest years in the States. Maybe because her heart was Chilean, that blood handed down from her father. He almost snorted. A father who, although he bore the last name that announced his heritage, seemed almost embarrassed by that fact. Or maybe it had just been Cris, who hadn't grown up in the best part of town. But his parents had been hardworking individuals who loved him.

He shook himself free of his thoughts. And glanced over at her to find her staring out the window.

"I'd almost forgotten how much I love this city. I

think it was home for me more than any other place I've ever lived."

"Santiago is nice too. It's a bigger city with more choices of things to do."

One of her shoulders flicked up in a half shrug. "It is, for sure. But I never really considered Santiago home. Although if my engagement had worked out, I probably would have stayed there."

She'd been engaged? He hadn't known that.

"I'm sorry for whatever happened."

"Me too. It wasn't the most pleasant breakup, but, like most things, it was for the best."

It made sense now. "That's why you came back to Valparaiso."

"Yes."

Hell, and he'd allowed himself to think that it might be because of him. That seemed so egotistical now. "It had to have been hard to leave your parents and all that you cared about."

Including her fiancé? He was pretty sure Vivi had never lacked for male attention. He'd even seen it in Roni and hated to admit that he'd felt a hint of jealousy over it. A jealousy he had no right to feel.

Vivi sighed. "I'm glad for the chance to start over, honestly."

Start over? He swallowed. Did she realize that those words could be taken more than one way? And the way that had flitted through his skull had better be discarded immediately. There was no starting over for them.

"Well, now you're back."

She nodded. "Now I am."

He turned left at the next stoplight. "We're almost there." The streetlights would start popping on soon. Tourists were always warned not to go out after dark, and maybe it was wise advice. But the best advice of all was to look like you belonged here and to not present any temptation.

Vivi definitely looked like she belonged. But temptation? She was that. But he was not about to admit that to anyone, not even himself.

He found a place to park in a public lot and paid the attendant. Then they walked the short distance to the funicular station.

"The *ascensor* is just ahead."

Unlike the ubiquitous street art that adorned many surfaces of the city, the funicular cars and stations had been painted in a linear pattern by professionals. At least the ones that were still in good repair. Cris paid for the tickets, shaking his head when Vivi started to pull out her wallet. "Next time."

Since there probably wouldn't be a next time, it was an easy way to be able to do something nice for her. Just like her offer to keep him company. He'd appreciated it more than she would ever know. He had a few friends, but most he kept at arm's length and he wasn't sure why. Maybe the niggling fear of loss that never quite went away? Maybe because he just didn't do much outside of parenting Gabi and work. Most friends did want you to at least spend some time with them. He used to go to sporting events, but that was before Lidia died.

Maybe he should start doing some of those things again. His aunt and uncle had offered time and again to watch Gabi, and Guilherme had invited him to go to various soccer events, but Cris had always found some excuse not to go. Instead, he'd stayed at home watching the game on TV.

They went through the turnstile and got their seats in the small car and waited for it to start up the hill. There were those who were dressed for dinner out, since Cerro Alegre had a lot of nice boutique-style hotels and restaurants. It was also a big hit with tourists, since it boasted a scenic overlook of the bay.

Then the funicular started moving. A slight sound next to him made him look at her. "Are you okay?"

"Yes, I'd just forgotten how steep a climb this is. I probably shouldn't look back."

He smiled. "That's why a few of these things are still in use. They don't take up the real estate that a road would need to navigate the hill. They can climb almost straight up. And it's not quite as scary as a ski lift would be, right?"

"I wouldn't know. I've never been up one of those and have no intention of doing it anytime soon."

"Your dad never took you to the Portillo ski resort?"

"No. He never did. He's never been a big fan of the cold, even though I would love to see snow."

An interesting fact that he'd never known about Vivi's dad. But that made sense. She'd grown up in south Florida, which boasted warm weather most of the year. "Santiago doesn't get very cold either, so almost no chance of seeing snow there. Or here, for that matter."

"Nope. Maybe someday, though. As long as it doesn't involve a ski lift."

The *ascensor* made it to the top and stopped with a loud squeak to let its passengers off. Fortunately, the way the funicular had been built kept the actual car level the whole ride up, so it didn't feel like a steep incline, even though it was.

They got off and went to the lookout. By now the lights had come on and although it wasn't pitch black yet, the view of the Valparaiso Bay was spectacular. There were some tall buildings, but they didn't obscure the view of the boats and the lights shining off the water. In the remaining daylight, the bay looked midnight blue, the deep color drawing you in.

"*Dios*. I'd forgotten. How I'd forgotten…"

Her words drifted away, but they carried a thousand sentiments that he recognized: familiarity, love…loss. Hadn't he thought that about his parents and wife? He could remember the second that he could no longer summon his mom's voice in his head. He'd tried for months, picturing her face and the movements of her mouth, but not the sound of her laughter, or the way she told him she loved him. It had been an awful time when he'd still been grieving Vivi's absence, and his parents were killed barely a year later.

"I know."

She turned to look at him. "You do, don't you."

"Yes." His eyes sought out hers. "And for what it's worth. I really am sorry about your engagement."

"He left me."

"Hell. I'm sorry, Viv." He knew all too well that loss was not always associated with death. In his mind, he'd always hoped that Vivi was as happy as he'd been during his marriage to Lidia. But it seemed maybe that wasn't the way things had gone for her.

He wasn't sure what else to say, so he stood there with her for several long moments looking out over the water. Then he felt the tentative touch of a hand over his, even though she never said a word. He turned his own palm up and curled his fingers around hers, never looking at her, but the familiarity was there all the same. He forced himself to just enjoy her presence and companionship in a way that he hadn't felt since…

Well, in way too long. And he didn't want to go there. He just wanted to stand here with her and not think about anything else. Maybe she felt the same way. Maybe she needed a few minutes not to think of the heartache of having a fiancé walk out on her.

Someone bumped against him as a person tried to squeeze in to take in the sights. It forced Cris to press shoulders with Vivi. He thought about moving away, but he didn't want to. He would have to go home sometime tonight and he wanted it to be with a good memory rather than the tragedy that had happened to Clara today. Even Roni had been weighing heavily on his mind. Both of their lives had changed in a split second.

And so had his. And evidently, so had Vivi's. Enough

so that she'd left Santiago to come back to Valparaiso. And he couldn't help the feeling that came over him: he was glad she'd returned. Whatever the reasons.

On impulse, he let go of her hand and draped his arm around her shoulder. The only reaction was her burrowing closer. He closed his eyes and breathed in deep, the warm air filling his lungs with the scents of the water below and Vivi's own personal fragrance that was reminiscent of vanilla and citrus. Yes. He remembered. But only after capturing the scent for the first time in twenty years. Wisps of her hair blew in the breeze every once in a while, sliding across his cheek. That he remembered too. How those long strands felt against his face, against his arm, and sliding through his fingers as he kissed her long and hard.

He would have married her had she stayed. He knew that deep within his being. But if that had happened, he wouldn't have Gabi or have had Lidia and it was an exchange he was not willing to make, even if he'd known ahead of time the heartache that would await him later.

When another strand of her hair blew across his mouth, he lifted a hand to brush it away and ended up holding the silky soft section for a few brief seconds before setting it back in place. What kind of man would leave her? She hadn't said it outright, but he got the feeling that she'd been blindsided by the breakup.

He wasn't sure if it was an attempt to comfort her or for some other reason, but he slid his fingers in the hair by her nape and let it slide back through like a waterfall, something he'd habitually done when they'd been a couple. It had become muscle memory after thousands of times doing it. And he blamed that now.

But when he did it a second time, she turned toward him with a warm smile. There was something secretive behind her eyes, and he realized this was what he really wanted. For her to look at him like she had in the past. Just once. With a mixture of want and need that had almost driven him to do things that he knew their parents wouldn't approve of. But he didn't. And how he'd regretted that in the days after she'd left. He'd wished they had done it. Wished her wanting to have a baby with him. Anything that would have kept her there.

But then again. Where would they be if that had happened? Would Vivi have gone after her degree? Would he have gone to medical school knowing the grueling hours that it would bring?

And that meant Lidia and Gabi never would have been in his life.

No. He'd done the right thing.

But he was older now. Old enough to know that one thing did not necessarily lead to another. And that he didn't need or want anything that would bind her to him anymore. When her fingers reached up to touch his face, though, he knew he was lost. He wasn't sure if her thoughts were moving in the same direction as his were, but he wanted to experience what he had not back then. It didn't have to mean anything for either of them. And maybe it would even bring a closure that they'd never gotten. And maybe it would help whatever heartache

Vivi was still experiencing from her breakup. He caught her hand so that she would look at him.

"Do you want to stay here and sightsee some more?"

She shook her head. "I want to go."

Taking a deep breath, he leaned down. "Where? Home? If no, then…?"

She went up on tiptoe, her lips touching his jaw and moving along it until she reached his ear. "Can you guess?"

He could guess a whole lot of things. But this was one thing he needed to be sure of.

"I think I need a little more to go on."

Her teeth nipped her ear. "That might get us kicked out of here."

Sensation traveled straight down the midline of his abdomen making a beeline for a place where, if noticed, might also get them kicked out of there. "I know a place."

"I don't care where."

The images those words drew up were insane. Of them naked in the bay below them, with him drawing her onto his hips. Of Vivi on the grass in some park, reaching up to pull him down to her. Of showers and beds and countertops, of bare tile floors. He would have rejected none of them.

Taking her hand, he towed her behind him as he left the lookout area and headed toward a hotel that he knew. One that he'd used a time or two in the past. But once he got there, he bypassed it for the one two doors down. One he'd never been to. With anyone. And he wasn't sure why it mattered. But it did. He wanted none of those other memories tainting the ones he was about to share with her.

They went in the door to the hotel, and he let go of her hand to go up to the reception desk.

CHAPTER SIX

VIVI HALF EXPECTED that she'd misunderstood him. That despite the intimate little touches, the talk about sightseeing and going home and wanting to know where else she wanted to go might have meant just that.

And yet here they were in the lobby of one of the fancy little hotels in the Cerro Alegre district and he was registering them as Mr. and Mrs. Diaz. Not even a phony name. Just a phony relationship. Because they weren't married and this wasn't about relationships or promises—it was about the here and now and needing something that only he could give. On the heels of hearing from Estevan again, she found that she needed it. Needed to know that she was still attractive. Still desirable.

He came back with a key card. "Third floor."

This was really happening. On the third floor. Somehow the thinking part of her brain filed that away in her memory banks to be retrieved later on.

"Elevator or stairs?"

His brows went up. "Is that a challenge?"

She blinked and then tilted her head up to look at him. "I think we might be arrested. I'm pretty sure they have cameras in both of those places."

He bent down and kissed her mouth, and that first touch of his lips against hers made her shudder as a thousand memories came over her. His arms went around her waist and drew her to him, as his head turned to deepen the kiss. She buried her fingers in his hair and pressed herself against him, taking in the sensation of his body against hers. And although they were both fully clothed, Vivi swore she'd never felt the intimacy that she did at this moment. With this man. And she had no idea why that was.

He finally lifted his head, dark eyes staring down at her. "The last thing I want is to be arrested. At least not yet."

She shivered when his meaning came across and leaned into him. *Dios!* This wasn't a dream. He really did mean to take her up to a room and share a bed with her. "Elevator, then. It's faster."

There was no wait and no one in the car when the doors opened. But when they boarded and the doors closed, she nodded at the corner where there was indeed a camera in plain sight. "See?"

"There won't be one in the room. There'll just be me… and you." He swept in to kiss her again, and suddenly she wasn't worried about cameras or the police as his tongue slid deep into her mouth. His hand at the back of her head, he held her there as he made his intentions very clear, turning her whole body red-hot. He could have taken her right then and there and she would have let him, consequences be damned.

But the elevator arrived at the third floor with a loud

ding, which sent them—like fighters in a ring—back to their respective corners. Then he held his hand out and she took it, weaving her fingers through his as they disembarked with him glancing at the key card and then making his way down the hallway and a short string of doors. "Here. Three-oh-nine."

She squeezed his hand until he looked down at her. "Are you sure you're okay with this? I won't expect anything more from you than one night."

She'd said the words, but could she stick to them? One night and then it was over? If not, then it was going to be over before it even started, and she couldn't bear that thought.

"I won't expect anything more either, I promise. I just always wondered."

"Me too. You were always the one who wanted to wait."

He chuckled and handed her the card. "I know. I was a fool."

Vivi had no trouble swiping the card across the reader, hearing a satisfying click as the mechanism unlocked. She pushed the door open and went in, sensing him behind her.

The room was more spacious than she expected with white linens and pale beige walls. There were touches of color in blues and greens, probably meant to echo the water in the bay. She walked around, touching things, nervous all of a sudden. She could say it was because it had been a while since she'd been with anyone, but that would be a lie. She'd been with Estevan a little over a month ago. But this was different. The hum of anticipation was stronger than anything she'd felt with her ex.

Cris was right. It was because they'd both wondered what it would have been like for them to have been together. And that anticipation was...

"What are you thinking?" His low voice came from behind her and she turned toward him.

"I'm thinking how much I want this."

His arm went around her waist and he reeled her in. "Good. Because I was thinking the exact same thing."

Her palms splayed on his chest, relishing the feel of him against her for the first time in all those years. "I can't believe we never did this. I wanted to, you know."

He smiled in a way that made her pulse quicken. "I know. I wanted it too. I just didn't want to..."

"Didn't want to what?"

"Rush anything. I wanted us to be sure. And then time ran out."

"Yes, it did."

His hands cupped her face. "Until now."

Bending toward her he kissed her. Really kissed her, as if they had all the time in the world. And for tonight, they probably did. And it was old...and new...all at the same time. They melded together to form something that was unique to both of them. Her arms wrapped around his neck trying to hold on to him in case he might try to back away. But he didn't. If anything, he moved closer, crowding her and cocooning her all at the same time. It was decadent that she could be standing here with the man she'd once loved and be about to make love with him for the first time ever.

She wanted to rush and have him take her in an instant, and she also wanted it to go so slow that time stood still and became an eternity.

When his head finally came up, he looked into her eyes for a long time, and as if satisfied with what he saw there, he scooped her up in his arms and carried her to the bed in the middle of the room. "Do you have to be home tonight?"

"No." The word came out breathlessly, because it meant he wanted to take his time, too. The thought of having sex in various places in the room filled her with need and want and so many other things.

They'd done some heavy petting in their day. So heavy that, looking back, she'd been amazed at his control. And that control intrigued her now. How long could he hold out before going over the edge? How long could she hold on? Probably not as long as he could.

Dios.

He was still holding her, as if not quite sure what to do with her. Hopefully he wasn't having second thoughts. "Cris?"

His smile was slow and decadent. "Just going through my options."

"We have options?"

"Mmm...we do. Shower? Bed? Against the plate glass windows in the dark? In front of the bathroom mirror with me pleasuring you until you cry out—all the while watching yourself as you come apart?"

Her mouth went dry. Her list sounded so much tamer than his did. And she wanted his.

He turned from the bed and headed to the bathroom and suddenly she knew which one he was going to choose. For a second she thought she was going to explode right then, but somehow she kept it together long enough to get inside the room.

Cris didn't bother kicking the door shut, because there was no one there to see. No one there to hear anything. No one except for them.

He set her down in front of a huge mirror that spanned the space between two sinks and along a huge vanity. His arms went around her waist and he crowded her against the hard surface of the vanity. She could feel him in the small of her back, already hard, already ready.

He nuzzled her hair aside and kissed her neck, slowly working his way up until he was at her jawline. He pressed his cheek against hers and stopped there, meeting her eyes in the mirror. She sucked down a quick breath, when his hands slid up her belly and cupped her breasts, squeezing gently.

"So soft. So full. I can't wait to taste them." He found her nipples and rubbed his thumbs over them, sending a wave of heat straight down. "Do you *want* me to taste them?"

She tried to make her voice work, but whatever came out sounded strangled, so she had to nod instead.

His hands bunched her shirt, pulling it up so that his hands could tunnel under it. But he didn't stop there. He also slid under the band of her bra and then his skin was against hers. And still he held her gaze in the mirror. She could see herself bite down on her lip as the sensations grew more intense, then she shut her eyes only to have him sharpen the pressure until they flew open. "I want to see your eyes. Want to watch your pupils expand as you grow more and more aroused." As if to highlight his point, one of his hands moved and dipped under the elastic waist of her cotton skirt. When they edged beneath the band of her lace undies, she shuddered, knowing what was coming. He was going to do exactly what he said he was going to do. Watch her while she watched herself have an orgasm under his touch.

"Cris..." She wasn't sure if it was a plea for mercy or for him to continue, and he didn't ask. And she didn't say no. Because he wasn't the only one who wanted this. She did too. Estevan had never done anything remotely like this. Had never rumbled words against her skin and then moved to carry them out.

His fingers moved further down, over her bare belly, over her mons until he reached the juncture between her thighs. At his first touch, her hips jerked forward.

"Yes, Vivi. I like that." His touch moved further, dipping over her. "You're so warm. So wet. I can't wait to feel you squeeze me to completion, can't wait to push so deep that I can't tell where you end and I begin."

He set up a slow rhythm of sliding across her, and she couldn't stop herself from joining him, moving her hips back and forth in time. She rocked back and forth and then suddenly he stopped his own movements.

She blinked, looking into his face.

"Shh... Move, Viv. I want you to do it. I'm right here. Sharing in it. But I want you to use me for your own pleasure." He nudged her with his hips and she felt herself slide over the finger that was pressed against her most sensitive spot. "Just like that, *querida*."

His hips backed off and she couldn't take it anymore. She wanted it all, wanted to experience this through his eyes. So she did as he asked and moved against him and it was luscious. And when his finger curved and entered her, the world turned into vibrant colors that she didn't even recognize. She pumped her hips against him, feeling him slide into her and over her at the same time.

His other hand pulled her blouse and bra up over her breast, baring it, and then he gripped her nipple between his thumb and forefinger and squeezed it every time her hips moved forward. It was exquisite and moving and she couldn't help but feel her whole existence was about to undergo a huge shift.

Her movements increased as the need within her grew, and the whole time Cris was there, pressed close, the cradle of his arms supporting her, holding her, whispering to her, and she could tell he was as enraptured by what was happening as she was. She wanted to give them both what they wanted. *Dios*, and she wanted it now.

Now!

The tide rose within her, its current fast and strong, carrying her in its rush to reach its destination. Her hips jerked over and over and her head fell back against his shoulder as raw sensation erupted within her, blotting everything else out.

She was vaguely aware of him moving quickly behind her, catching her as her legs gave out. Then he picked her up and carried her to the bed and, peeling the coverlet back, set her gently down on the cool soft sheets.

Blinking up at him, she felt him climb in beside her and hold her, his arms nestling her against his side. She'd expected him to rush and enter her and seek out his own pleasure, but instead, he murmured to her and stroked her hair.

She looked at him. "But you…"

His smile said it all. But as if to make sure she understood, he whispered. "Don't worry. The night is still young. And I have several more ideas to try out."

And as if a few moments ago had never happened, she felt her body reacting to his words, slowly waking up again. He'd said that, but she'd had her doubts that they would go more than one round. Maybe that's why he'd done what he had. Maybe he'd gotten a different kind of pleasure from watching her break apart in front of him.

Although she couldn't imagine anything more fulfilling than what had just happened.

But it seemed that Cris was pretty sure he knew otherwise. And she was happy to let him try to prove it. All night long.

Cris's cell phone pinged once, then twice. In the distance he heard a second phone go off as well.

Still in a kind of exhausted, trancelike state, he fumbled to reach the nightstand. But it wasn't his room and the body pressed to his back wasn't his…wife.

He fell back onto his pillow. The night came back to him in a rush. Every single guilt-ridden moment. He was in a nameless hotel with Vivi. A ghost from his distant past. The one he said he was going to avoid. The one he said he was going to be able to work with without getting involved. The one he said Gabi was never going to get a chance to get attached to.

And he could still keep the last of those promises, even if he'd shot the first two to hell last night. Because he'd gotten involved the first time he'd touched her. And now he was going to have to figure out how to extricate himself without hurting her.

But would she be hurt? She hadn't asked for anything from him other than what had happened last night.

His phone pinged again. And so did hers. This time she stirred against his back and moved to get her mobile device.

Then she turned in his direction. "Cris, wake up. There's an emergency with Clara."

"Clara?" He reached for his own phone and quickly scanned the text. "*Maldicion!* She's spiking a fever and her wound is seeping. I've got to go."

"I got the same text. I think they're reassembling a team knowing we're going to have to go back in."

He sat up and threw the covers back. "I was so sure I got all of the fragments out."

"It was an open fracture. Who knows what contaminants were in there or how deeply they were pushed into the tissues. It's not your fault."

Clara might not be his fault. But this thing with Vivi?

That was his fault, only he didn't have the luxury of trying to figure out how to get back out of it right now. Right now, they needed to get to the hospital. "I'll go."

"I'm coming with you. Besides, you drove us to the funicular station, remember?"

That's right—he had. So there was nothing left to do but get dressed and put this all behind him.

He turned toward her to tell her, only to have her shake her head. "No need. It's okay. We both went into this knowing what it was. And now we can move forward." She smiled. "No more wondering. Now we know. And it was pretty damned good."

She sounded like she was going to have no trouble moving forward. Just categorize the night and file it away, never to be bothered by it again.

He wasn't so sure he could do it quite as easily. Especially not after waking up and expecting to find life just the way he'd left it four years ago. And that carried its own guilt. Even though he hadn't consciously tried to swap her out for Lidia. And yet his subconscious? Was that what it had tried to do?

He could sort through all of those things at a later time. Right now they both had somewhere they had to be.

They pulled on their clothes in silence, with Vivi dressing in the bathroom while he put his clothes on in the main room. They'd both showered last night, but they didn't have a clean change of clothes, so they'd just have to make do with what they had. When she came back out, fully dressed, he asked, "Do you need me to take you home so you can change?"

"I'll do that at the hospital. I always keep a couple of sets of scrubs in my locker in case I need to change after a surgery."

Not that she'd done that many at Valpo Memorial. But she probably had done that at her old hospital and just carried the habit over to the new one.

They hurried to check out. It was only five in the morning and so the desk clerk looked a little worse for wear, probably being at the end of his shift, but he did his job with a smile. Then they were on their way, catching the funicular and riding it to the bottom of the hill.

The drive back to the hospital seemed to take forever and Vivi was quiet. A little too quiet. "Is there anything I can do to help make this go back to the way it was?"

"Do you want it to? I say we each just process things in the way that's best for us and then go on with our lives. Nothing's changed. Not really. We had sex. Damned good sex. But that was yesterday and now we've moved to a different day. We can leave it in the past, just like we did twenty years ago."

And, yes, she did make it sound easy. A little too easy. He looked at her a little closer trying to see some chink in her armor and finding none. It was like she was immune to regret or guilt or any of the things he'd woken up to this morning. Or maybe it was because she was still hurting from the breakup of her engagement to worry about anything else right now.

Yet another reason for him to regret what had happened. She'd obviously been deeply hurt, and yet there he was, ready to jump into bed without giving the slightest thought to how she might feel.

Mierda!

They got to the hospital and went their separate ways to change and check in. Cris promised to let her know what the plan was as soon as he'd been to see Clara and had read her charts. But at the very least, they were going to need to go in to flush the wounds again, because if bacteria got lodged in the hardware he'd installed they were going to have a devil of a time eliminating all of it. Worst-case scenario was that they'd have to redo some, or all, of the surgery and replace all the screws and plates. Best-case scenario was that they flush everything with an antibiotic solution and then put her on strong intravenous meds that would hopefully get rid of anything they might miss.

He went to his office and changed his clothes yet again and then headed to Clara's room. He found her flushed and murmuring things that didn't make sense. Not good.

The chart showed she'd been given the antibiotics he prescribed and all had seemed well up until an hour ago when her temperature had suddenly risen to a hundred-and-three degrees. Peeling her dressings back, he could see that there was indeed some seeping, and a red angry line marked an area next to the sutures. He agreed with the doctor who'd taken a look at her. They were going to have to go back in and pray that she hadn't developed a staph infection. Those kinds of infections could steal limbs or even lives if not stopped in their earliest stages.

He knew Vivi was right and it wasn't that his surgery was faulty, but more likely a pathogen from the environment had entered the wound at the scene of the accident. A pathogen that the first round of antimicrobial flushing hadn't reached. But he was determined this next round would get anything and everything that was in there. They could still stop this in its tracks, but they did need to work fast. He went from her room to the nurses' station and placed orders for a surgical suite and team. He was gratified to see that the hospital had been on top of this right from the first sign of trouble. Vivi wasn't the only one who'd been called in. Several other members of the original team were here, including the anesthesiologist.

When he asked if Clara had been told about her mother, they'd replied that her family had told her and that she'd seemed to go downhill from there. While he knew she would need to know about her mom, he also knew that the shock could cause her immune system to tank and allow anything that was in there to go wild. Which could be part of what had happened. And evidently the dad was still in pretty bad condition.

"What time are we scheduled for?"

"We're just waiting for Viviani and Dalton."

He frowned. "Vivi is here, but I don't know about Dalton. Were you able to reach him?"

"He's on his way." The nurse glanced at her chart. "You say Viviani is here? I don't show her answering her text yet. I have an alternate who is already here."

Mierda. She hadn't, because it hadn't crossed either of their minds to act independently. As if they'd heard individually rather than being together when those texts had arrived. "I know she's here because I saw her down in the lobby. We spoke for a moment. Maybe she typed out a reply and didn't hit send."

And there was the first batch of lies, signed, sealed and delivered. And if Vivi gave a different response, then he was toast. And yet there was no time for him to find her and get their stories straight.

This nurse doesn't care, Cris. She's just putting pieces into place, not sitting there trying to work out why Vivi didn't respond to her text.

"Okay, then, that takes care of that problem. Dalton is just a few minutes out and they're prepping Surgical Suite One even as we speak. Clara is already in pre-op, and there are a couple members of her family who are coming in. Permission has been granted to do whatever we deem necessary."

"Good. I'll go scrub in then. Here's what I'd like to see in there." He handed the head nurse the list of medications he'd need for the wound-flushing and there were orders for the antibiotics he wanted to use after surgery was done. "I'll also want to take a sample to be grown to see exactly what we're dealing with."

And he hoped to hell that it wasn't MRSA, a staph infection that was resistant to many antibiotics. But if it was, they needed to know which ones could be used to fight it. Thankfully they had quicker ways of "typing" the infection nowadays and the ability to figure out the best way to attack it.

Vivi came up on the floor just before he headed out

and he heard the nurse say, "I guess he was right about seeing you in the lobby. I wasn't sure you'd gotten my text."

Her eyes darted to his for a second before agreeing with what had been said. "Sorry. I meant to reply, but was in such a hurry to get here that I must have forgotten. Anything I need to know before I go scrub in?"

The nurse said, "We're still waiting on one team member so we're about fifteen minutes out from the patient being brought in. Can you hold off on scrubbing in until we get everything in place?"

"Sure. Just shoot me a text. I promise to reply this time. Sorry again. Is the cafeteria open? I think I need a sip of coffee."

"If not, there's a coffee pot in the lobby that's refreshed every hour."

"Great. Anyone want anything?" Her glance encompassed both him and the charge nurse, who shook her head.

He replied that he didn't need anything either. Caffeine tended to wind him up a little too much. He preferred to be slow and methodical in the operating room.

Unlike last night at the hotel?

Better not to even think about that right now or it was going to shoot his concentration to hell. And Clara deserved to have a surgeon who was fully attuned to accomplishing what needed to be done. Every time he turned around, something seemed to be telling him that last night was a mistake.

Something else that he wasn't going to think about

right now. Not if he wanted to be at his best. Thank God he had actually gotten a couple of hours of sleep last night. Not that he hadn't wanted to go another round or two with Vivi.

And there it was again. He watched the woman in question get on the elevator, their eyes meeting for a split second before the doors closed.

How was he going to get her out of his system? That was what last night was supposed to have been about. And yet, it seemed like she was now embedded in there somewhere, just like Clara's infection, and it was up to him to figure out how to get it cleared out so that it didn't recur.

And that was the truth. Last night was not going to recur. Not if he had any say in the matter. Because if it did, he was going to have even bigger problems on his hands than spending a sex-filled night with a former flame. It would mean that his whole plan to keep Gabi and his love life in two different hemispheres might be in danger. And that was not something he was willing to let happen. So he would figure this out one way or the other. And he was going to do it soon.

CHAPTER SEVEN

She hadn't seen Cris since Clara's surgery yesterday morning. She'd gone home for a couple of hours' sleep and then come back for her afternoon shift, checking on the girl almost as soon as she'd arrived—while she was in a good deal of pain, the procedure and meds afterwards seemed to be doing their job. She hadn't seen Cris once.

And today seemed to be headed in the same direction. At least so far. She didn't know if he was even at work today or if he was just holed up in his office.

Avoiding her? Maybe.

They hadn't spoken about what happened in that hotel room, either, and that was troubling. She at least wanted to hear that they could continue working together. That's what they had said, right? That it wouldn't affect anything. And after they woke up to their phones pinging, she'd said as much.

We both went into this knowing what it was. And now we can move forward.

Except she wasn't doing the greatest job with that. She wasn't moving forward. She was doing nothing but thinking about the night they'd spent together. She'd been able to do her job in the operating room, but his voice had made her senses come alive as he'd asked her to hand him one surgical instrument after another. She hadn't fumbled or hesitated, but she'd had a hard time not picturing him moving over her as they'd continued making love. On the bed, this time. And it had been even better than the first time, even though she didn't know how that was possible.

She got back to the nurses' station after checking on the patients that were on their floor and Elena was there waving at her. "Dr. Diaz asked if you could go down to the hospital administrator's office for some reason."

Dios. He wouldn't have found a reason to get rid of her, would he? Her heart contracted in her chest. She would never have taken him for the kind of person who would do something like that, but how well did she actually know him now?

You know him. You saw the real Cris when he was hunched in that chair broken up about Clara's mom being killed. You saw the real Cris when he saw to your pleasure first and then still saw to it that the next time was just as good for you. You saw the real Cris when his daughter ran up to him and he made it clear that there was no one more special to him than she was.

A few of her muscles relaxed. There's no way he would have tried to have her fired. So this was about something else. "Okay, I'll head down there now. Is he there?"

"I'm not sure where he was calling from. I do know he

had a visit yesterday afternoon from that soccer player he did the surgery on."

Roni had gone to see him? Did that mean he was agreeing to help with the program she'd talked about? If so, why hadn't Cris contacted her and let her know that they had a meeting today?

She went down to the first floor, trying to remember where that office even was. It was unreal that she'd been here just under a week and so many things had happened since then. She found the office and knocked.

"Come in."

She peered inside the door and saw not only Cris and Marcos, the administrator, but also Roni. She swallowed, feeling a little left out. They'd planned this meeting and she hadn't even been invited. Until just now.

Marcos stood and came around to shake her hand. "Have a seat. From what I hear, you're the brains behind this idea."

So again, why was she just hearing about this now? Roni grabbed her hand as she moved to a chair next to him and gave it a quick squeeze. She smiled and greeted him softly. But when she glanced at Cris, he was looking straight ahead, not even acknowledging her.

"Roni called my office yesterday afternoon and asked to come and speak to me about an idea you had had." He smiled. "I was going to try to schedule a meeting with all of you next week, but a spot opened up on my calendar and Roni is anxious to get this project underway. He's a pretty persuasive person."

She swallowed. That's what both he and Cris had said

about her. So why was the surgeon giving her the cold shoulder now?

Marcos nodded at Roni. "Do you want to tell them?"

"Sure." He looked at her. "When Vivi came to me with the idea, I felt like it was just a pep talk. A way to get me to start doing my physical therapy. That lady down in PT should be a soccer coach, by the way—she doesn't let me get away without trying my best. But when Vivi came and talked to me about it again, I could see that she really meant it. That she was excited that the hospital might be able to use me to help hurt athletes. But I needed to check with my team."

He slid a folder off Marcos's desk and handed it to her. "I didn't want to talk to you about it until I knew for sure. This is what they came up with and I think it's a solid plan."

Cris still hadn't said a word. She had to know. "Have you already seen this?"

"I saw it yesterday afternoon. You were with patients at the time, so I was going to talk to you this morning, but—" he did manage a quick smile that made her heart quicken "—I think you'll like it."

She opened the folder and started reading, her eyes widening as what it said hit her. Her head jerked to look at Roni. "I never meant that you should put up the money for the program."

"I wanted to. Listen, I came up from nothing. And the idea that I can help not only injured athletes, but other kids who are like me is something bigger than just me. If I can use my money for that, then it will be all worth it."

Roni was donating two million dollars to start an athletic support center in the hospital that included group sessions on how to cope after a life-altering injury... or any injury, really. A career planner that had a list of resources to help athletes plan for the future once their career on the field was over. And it included something that Vivi had never even thought of. A coach who would run two sports camps a year for at-risk kids. One for soccer and one for basketball, which was also popular in Chile. Kids whose parents couldn't afford to send their kids to any kind of camp. It meant buying a small parcel of land somewhere in the city where a soccer field could be set up. The salaries for the part-time coaches and group leaders would be paid out of a portion of the money that would be put into a fund. Roni would head up the soccer camp and they would need to find a coach for the other team.

She glanced at him. "This is amazing. Thank you for being willing to do all of this."

"Don't thank me yet. My team had one caveat, because they are all about the brand and keeping it going. They want it to be called The Ronaldo Saraia Sport and Support Center." His lips twisted as if unsure how they would take the news.

She smiled. "I think it's perfect."

"Good."

Marcos held up a hand. "I have one caveat of my own. Roni has agreed to it, but I need you and Cris to sign off on it as well. You had the initial idea and I'd like you to still be a sounding board for any changes to the program and Cris will need to be involved on the medical side of the program, okaying any kind of training techniques to make sure they're good for kids' growing bones and muscles. So saying that, I'd like there to be a picture of the three of you together that will go out in a press release announcing the new program. Vivi, I believe you said this will be the first one of its kind in the city."

She nodded, seeing now why Cris had been so quiet. He didn't want there to be a picture linking the two of them that would be out there for the world to see. Well, it wasn't like they were announcing their one-night liaison to the world. It was a sports program, for heaven's sake. "As far as I could tell it is."

Roni broke in. "My team also checked on that aspect, and we couldn't find anything other than the normal support groups that weren't exclusive to athletes, so hopefully the concept will catch on. Athletes expend a huge amount of calories and their diets reflect this. But if they can't play, that will need to be altered, so having nutritional advice as well as career advice is going to be important."

Vivi felt like she was stuck in some surreal world where people were talking but she was unable to completely understand what they were saying. She glanced at Marcos again. "So you're agreeing to let this go forward?"

"Just like Roni has a team, the hospital does as well and I'll need to get board approval. But since the money and support have basically just been handed to us on a silver platter, we would be fools to turn this down. And

I think Roni is right. This could help a lot of kids. And a lot of adults for that matter. And putting my administrator's cap on, it would be great publicity for the hospital itself."

Marcos glanced at Cris. "Once we get approval, can you figure out a time to get the three of you together for a photo op? Roni and his people are going to look at land and then the hospital will also need to approve the location and make sure the taxes and so forth are manageable. It's just a lot of red tape and working between teams. But I can definitely see it happening. So it may take a couple of weeks, or maybe even a month."

"I can do that."

"Good. Then if there's nothing else?" He stood. "Roni, thank you again for helping Valpo Memorial. I think this is going to be a great addition to our current services."

"I'm glad to be a part of something that will hopefully outlive me. Let me know when you're ready to move forward or if your team has any concerns."

Marcos came around and shook the man's hand. "I'll be in touch. Thank you again."

They all filed out of the office and Roni, now sporting a cane rather than a walker, waved it in the air. "I've been working, see?"

"Did your physical therapist okay that?" The words may have been stern, but Cris's smile was anything but. He liked the soccer player. It was there on his face and in the way he clapped the other man on the back.

Roni gave him a rueful grin. "Yes and no. But I'm being careful, I promise. I have some coaching to do.

I'm in talks to maybe even coach a professional team. But don't worry—the sports camp will be a high priority and will need to be included on any contract I sign. Well, I'm off to my torture session. Catch you later."

With that he slowly made his way to the hallway that led to the physical therapy wing of the hospital.

This time, Cris actually looked at her. "Well, that went faster than I thought it would."

"Me too. Did you just hear about the meeting this morning?"

"I did or I would have tried to warn you ahead of time."

She had to ask. "Are we okay, then?"

There was silence for almost a minute. "Why do you ask?"

Okay, he'd just gone from smiling to tense in the space of a few heartbeats. "I think it's obvious."

"I'd rather not talk about this at the hospital."

It wasn't like there were a whole line of people going back and forth down the hallway. So what was he afraid of? "I'm not going to tell anyone, if that's what you're worried about."

"I am worried. The nurse couldn't figure out how I knew you were here this morning or why you hadn't responded to her text. I can picture there being a thousand more little things like that that will be hard to explain away."

She snorted. "Well, unless someone actually saw us check in or leave that…place, no one will be any the wiser."

"Maybe I am overreacting." He sighed. "By the way,

my aunt told me that she did some research on apartments and has a little list of possibilities made, if you're still open to going to look at some."

"Wow!" Her eyes widened. "I know you mentioned it earlier, but didn't want to get my hopes up. I do, for sure. Living in a hotel room is getting a little old, even though it's more like a bed-and-breakfast with really nice owners. But it would be nice to have a place of my own. I appreciate her doing this."

"And that's part of it. My daughter may be with her when you all go to look, since it would have to happen during business hours, and I'll more than likely be here at the hospital. If you could not give her any encouragement, I would appreciate it."

"Encouragement? Do you mean your aunt or your daughter?"

"Either. Both. Aunt Pat remembers you from…before. I already told her not to think along those lines, that it wasn't happening, but she can be willful. And Gabi has been through a lot in her life. I'd rather her not get…attached."

"To anyone? I mean what about her teachers? Her peers?"

"I think she understands that those people are not permanent—that they're a year or two at the most."

Now she understood what he was saying. He didn't want his daughter getting attached to her, specifically. Because he sure as hell wasn't going to. She didn't know why that was a kick in the gut, but it was. Yes, they'd all but said there was no future to them, but to have him act like they couldn't even be friends. Or rather, maybe they could, but she just wasn't allowed to be a friend who came around the house and hung out with him and his daughter.

"Don't worry, I don't plan on stalking you to get to her. Or vice versa. Your secret rendezvous is safe with me. And your aunt is a grown woman. I'll let her choose her friends." She knew her words had come out in acid shades, but she couldn't help it. When someone hurt her, she tended to give back in kind. Not to strangers, but to those she cared about. And as much as she hated to admit it, she still cared about him and had hoped they could find a path to friendship. But it seemed that wasn't the case.

He moved a step closer. "Vivi, I didn't mean it like that. I don't want Gabi hurt. It's why I've never brought any dates home."

"And why we had to use a hotel room, even when your daughter was spending the night elsewhere. I get it."

Tilting up her chin, he looked her in the eye. "That's not fair, and you know it." He lowered his voice. "The hotel was the closest place, and I didn't feel like either of us wanted to wait to get to one of our residences."

She took a deep breath. He was right. That had been the reason. But she got the feeling he probably wouldn't have brought her into his home even if they'd been making out right in front of it. "You're right. I'm sorry. You just reminded me of my dad for a minute and how you accused him of saying you weren't good enough for me. I'm evidently not good enough for your daughter."

He sighed. "No, that's not it either. I just don't want her to assume we'll end up together. Relationships are too uncertain. You just broke it off with your fiancé, didn't you?"

"Yes." It was funny how he turned that around to make it sound like she'd done the leaving and not Estevan, even when she'd told him it was her fiancé who'd made the choice. "So now that you've laid out the ground rules, I'll be sure to follow them. Although it might be better if I found another realtor. One who doesn't pose a danger to your comfort level."

He held up his hands. "I'm waving a white flag here. I don't want to fight. And I want you to use Pat. She wants to help. I just wanted all of us to tread carefully. And to keep Gabi off the playing field."

She smiled, knowing she'd overreacted, just like he'd mentioned doing moments earlier, and tried to move back to neutral ground. "I'll be on my best behavior, I promise, and try to make sure she stays on the bench. And I'm sorry if you thought I would do otherwise. I don't want to hurt Gabi any more than you want her hurt. So I won't encourage her. And if your aunt starts down that path, I'll head her off and assure her that neither of us wants a relationship. At least not with each other."

His sudden frown puzzled her. And she wasn't even sure he realized what his face was doing. Did he really think his aunt would try to play matchmaker? If so, she was in for a rude awakening, even if it didn't come from Vivi. Her nephew had no intention of going back in time and renewing what they'd once had.

She was doing her best to hold true to that promise too. But when she'd thought her universe might be imploding in that hotel room, she was right. She just wasn't sure what the damage was and until she could mentally remove the rubble that had rained down on top of her, she would have no idea what was left unscathed. But there was this crouching fear that whatever remained was entirely different than what she'd hoped it would be.

He thought about that encounter long after she'd walked away, hips swishing as she made her way to her next destination. Cris knew that he had messed up royally in how he'd handled things today. But all during the meeting, he'd been hyperaware of the moment Vivi had entered the room. How she'd sat next to Roni. And how Roni had addressed almost all his remarks to her. She hadn't flirted with the man; in fact, he was pretty sure that she'd been unaware of his attention, but he could feel it in his bones. The man was attracted to her. He'd noticed it before, but today it seemed as clear as day.

It shouldn't matter. But somehow it did. He'd been irritated by it, like a clam with a grain of sand lodged in a sensitive spot. But when she'd stood in front of him a minute ago and said if they did wind up in relationships, it wouldn't be with each other, it had made him wonder if Roni wasn't the only one harboring a secret crush. If so, Vivi was a hell of a lot better at hiding that attraction than Roni was.

Imagining her coming apart for someone else the way she'd come apart for him was...unsettling.

And hell, it was a lot more than that. It was jealousy plain and simple, but it was also misplaced and unfair. He should want her to be happy. And he did.

So what was it, then? Did he just not want to know about it, the way his daughter would never know about their past relationship?

He wasn't sure. But then they'd come out of that room and he'd almost immediately thrown out that he didn't want her to try to be friends with Pat or with his daughter. How pompous and self-serving that had sounded. And she was right. He'd sounded just like her father, dictating who she could and couldn't fall in love with and who would go so far as to remove her from the vicinity if she dared trespass on forbidden ground.

And if Gabi started to like Vivi a little too much, would he do the same thing, swoop in and carry her away? He hoped he wouldn't. But at this point he couldn't promise. Because he might be in danger of liking Vivi a little too much himself. And he was doing his damnedest to backpedal and pretend that the night in the hotel hadn't happened at all. But it had and there was no going back. They'd slept together and that was going to hang between them for as long as they knew each other. He just hadn't thought through how to handle it yet.

But he'd better figure out a way that was a little more helpful and less like a warning gong.

Surely this didn't need to be as complicated as they made it out to be. Colleagues slept together from time to time and went on with their lives. What the hell was he so afraid of?

You're afraid you'll fall in love with her all over again, and that there's nothing you can do to stop that from happening.

Oh, yes, there was. He could be friendly and nothing more. Surely he could do that. And if he spent as little time as possible with her outside of the operating room where things were basically scripted and rehearsed until they ran like clockwork, that would be a first step. No more sightseeing tours. No more letting her comfort him, which she'd done after he'd operated on Clara.

And if she spent time with Pat and Gabi, what was the harm, really, as long as he didn't give them any reason to think that she might be a permanent fixture in their lives? There was none. At least that was his fervent hope.

Vivi was off on Wednesday, even though it was a surgical day. Actually she had asked for it off, citing that she still hadn't found a place to live. And that was true. She was planning on meeting Pat and going to look at a few places. But she'd also needed to decompress from everything that had happened over the last couple of days. She'd slept with him and then had almost immediately been whisked away to perform emergency surgery and then the next day she'd had the surprise meeting with Roni and the hospital administrator and then the confrontation with Cris afterward.

She needed time. In a place where she wasn't afraid of running into him or having to face him over an operating table. And she was looking forward to being outside the hospital and finding a more permanent place to stay.

She met Pat in front of the first of four apartments she would be looking at. When she arrived at the address, the realtor was already there. The woman exited the car and then went to the back seat to do something there. She realized quickly that it was to release Gabi from her car seat. Even though Cris had warned her that his daughter might be along for the ride, she felt a kind of nervous energy rise up inside her. She didn't want to say or do anything that might upset Gabi or Pat. But the second that the child's feet were on the ground, she ran over and embraced Vivi.

"Hi!" she said. "I remember you. You were with Daddy!"

Vivi couldn't stop the smile, despite the way the child had worded it. This was her second time seeing Gabi, but she was again struck by her uncanny resemblance to Cris. She even had a dimple on the exact same cheek as he did. Her heart lurched as a wave of affection crashed over her for the child. It was wholly unexpected and entirely…well, terrifying. She could see why Cris was worried. Gabi was absolutely adorable and anyone would be hard put not to love her at first sight. Like Vivi had done with the girl's father twenty years ago?

"Hi, Gabi. Your dad told me you might be coming along."

Mistake number one: she'd linked herself with Gabi's dad instead of just pretending to be a random client. She needed to be more careful. And she would be.

Pat came over and gave her a kiss on the cheek in true Chilean form. "It's so good to see you again."

"I know—it's been a long time." She embraced the woman.

Mistake number two: she'd assumed Pat was talking about the twenty years that had passed when she could have simply meant since their last meeting at the hospital.

She quickly added, "Thank you so much for helping me find an apartment. When Cris mentioned you were a realtor and probably wouldn't mind helping me with my search, I didn't expect you to drop everything. I hope I'm not putting you out."

"You're not—don't worry. This is what I do for a living. And I truly enjoy it. And the fact that it's for my only nephew makes it all the more special."

At first Vivi thought she meant that she was finding the apartment for her nephew, but then understood that she meant that she was doing him a favor. "Well, you have no idea how overwhelmed I was at the thought of finding something. My dad helped me find my place in Santiago, so I've never had to go out and scout properties before."

Pat motioned toward the apartment complex, and she had a key card that gave her access through the front gate. "Well, let's go look at the first one. It's a one-bedroom one-bath and on the second floor, but it's supercute and the landlord is a dream. I know her personally." She gave a smile that was full of mischief, or at least that's what it looked like to Vivi.

"I can't wait to see it."

They went up the stairs. "The only downfall is that it's not on the ground floor."

"I kind of like going up stairs. It's like a built-in gym membership."

"Speaking of which, it's not far from where Cris goes to work out."

She swallowed, hoping that wasn't a hint. Especially since Vivi had seen the results of his workouts firsthand. And they were pretty incredible. She closed her eyes for a second to block out the images of the muscles in his arms rippling as he balanced his weight above her on the bed.

She didn't say anything, because she didn't think she could without her voice coming out as a squeak and giving her away.

There was a keypad on the front door. Once Pat punched in a number, a mechanism unlatched and the door swung open into a front foyer. There was a table with a beautiful silver bowl on it, obviously made to catch keys and small items as you came into the apartment. "Is it furnished?"

"It is. Although if you have your own furniture, the landlord can put this into storage."

"Really? They would do that? But no, I didn't save any of my furniture from Santiago, other than a rocking chair from my great-grandmother. My parents will have that sent once I find a place. So furnished is a plus."

She had the rest of her boxes in the room at the bed-

and-breakfast. A couple of them had keepsakes that she hadn't had time to go through yet.

"The landlord has pretty good taste, if I do say so myself." There was again that smile, which was contagious.

"I agree. It's beautiful."

They went through an arched doorway and found a great room, a long table in the dining room acting to separate the kitchen from the living room. On one wall there were sliding glass doors that Pat went over to and opened to show a small balcony that was just big enough to hold a couple of chairs and a café table. It looked out over a pool area, which was empty at the moment.

It was quiet and peaceful, a few palm trees dotting the landscaping. "It's really a lovely complex. There's the pool, of course, and there's a communal party room where you can hold celebrations and so forth. It's equipped with a stove, fridge and a large serving bar. We've actually used it for a few of our own celebrations."

Wow, she must know the landlord really well for them to have allowed that.

The rooms were white stucco with beige furniture and green throw pillows. The same green fabric was on the seats of the dining room chairs. The contrast was beautiful as were the beams in the ceiling and the hardwood floors that Pat said went throughout the space.

Vivi loved it. It was exactly her taste. "Does it come with pots and pans and dishes?"

"Everything in here is included."

Unbelievable. The dining room table was made up with white china that was rimmed in gold, the simplicity of the place settings making it all the more elegant. There were olive green cloth napkins fanned onto each plate and a large wooden bowl in the middle looked like it was ready to receive whatever delicious food you chose to serve. She could see herself putting a large salad in there or meats that were cooked to perfection on the small grill she'd seen on the balcony.

"And we have the bedroom through here." Pat walked through the door, while Gabi stayed in the dining room and played with a couple of toys that the realtor had pulled out of her bag. The girl must be extraordinarily well-behaved to be left alone in there. But Pat evidently knew what she was doing.

The bedroom was just as gorgeous, the bed with a white damask coverlet that was turned down to expose white sheets that looked soft and welcoming. There was a green throw tossed across the lower third of the bed and an aged steamer trunk against the footboard.

There was also a long dresser that looked like it would hold every piece of clothing she owned.

"*Dios*. I never imagined... This is perfect."

Pat smiled. "You haven't seen the bathroom yet."

They went through the bedroom to the ensuite bath. Inside was a freestanding soaking tub with a beautiful chrome faucet set that had been placed at the side of the tub. It wouldn't interfere with the bather reclining their head on the sloped porcelain back. A live-edge board was placed so that it spanned the width of the tub, allowing the user to place a book or beverage and a candle on it to further enhance the experience.

The shower was small but certainly adequate, and chrome bars were mounted on the wall just outside the shower. They looked like they were heated. The place took her breath away.

"I'm afraid to ask how much this is."

Pat named a monthly amount, and Vivi's eyes widened. "Are you sure that's right? It must be worth twice that much."

"It's been sitting here empty for a while, just used to house family that fly into Valpo. The landlord is ready to lease it out, but will be very picky about who she leases to. It was hers before she was married and it was leased to other family members for years. It holds sentimental value. The whole complex was remodeled just a few years ago, which is why it's so nice."

"Will she even lease to a single woman?"

"She would lease it to you." Pat's voice was soft. "I can guarantee that."

"How do you know?" Vivi looked at her as understanding dawned. "You're the landlord, aren't you?"

"I am. Cris rented this place for years after he graduated from medical school before he and Lidia got married. Then they moved to a different place and got pregnant with Gabi."

That gave her pause. "What would he think about me living here?" To have an ex-girlfriend living in the apartment might not go over too well.

"It's mine to rent to whomever I please."

"I know, but…"

She touched Vivi's arm. "He won't care. He hasn't asked about this place since Lidia died."

"What happened to her?"

It was *so* none of her business, but the words came out before she could stop them. She knew how his parents died, but not how his wife had.

"She died of ovarian cancer. It was diagnosed almost as soon as Gabi was born. She died a year later. We were all devastated."

That was why she could leave Gabi playing in the other room while they checked out the rest of the apartment. "I think you should ask him before you agree to rent it to me."

"I promise, he won't care. He's happy where he is."

"Is this the furniture that was in here when he lived here?" She didn't think she could live there if it was. It seemed too personal, somehow. Especially if he and Lidia had made love in that bed after they started dating.

"No. I furnished it with new stuff after Cris moved out. I would just ask that we be allowed to use the party room for Gabi's birthday parties if Cris wants to hold them here."

"Of course. But your rent is way too low."

"No. It's the perfect price for the perfect person."

She tried again. "I can give you references."

Pat smiled, even as Gabi came into the room carrying the small doll her aunt had given her and leaned against Vivi's leg.

"I don't need them," she said. "My mind is made up, if yours is. But don't take it just because it's mine."

"I wouldn't. But I love it. Truly. And it's a great distance from the hospital. I could jog in or ride a bike if I chose to. Would you mind my bringing my rocking chair in? I think it would look wonderful in the corner of the bedroom. And it would make it feel like home. My home. That chair goes everywhere I go. Do you want a year's lease?"

"How about we just go month by month. No deposit needed, and you can move in whenever you're ready."

She laughed. "How about this Saturday? I'm off duty and all I'd be bringing over would be my suitcases and some boxes of books and memorabilia. My parents could bring the rest when they come."

"Speaking of parents. The sofa pulls out into a bed and the curtains that are at the balcony are extralong and actually pull along a track you'll see on the ceiling and provide privacy for anyone sleeping on that couch. No need for them to find a hotel."

"I don't know how to thank you. I really don't."

Pat gave her a tight hug. "No thanks needed. It's so good to have you back in Valpo."

Vivi smiled. She'd been questioning her decision to come back ever since she found herself across the operating table from Cris. Their time at the hotel had only added to her confusion and made her second-guess everything. But she couldn't go back to Santiago. It was a huge city, but not big enough for both her and Estevan. Even the thought of moving back there and possibly running into him made her queasy. The same feeling she'd gotten when she saw his text. She'd replied and asked him not to contact her again. So far he hadn't.

"Thanks. I'm hoping I made the right decision to come back."

Pat put her arm around her and leaned her head against Vivi's shoulder. "I think you are just what this city needed."

What a strange thing to say. Then she remembered Cris's warning not to encourage his aunt. Was this what he meant? Surely she wasn't talking about her nephew. Their relationship ended twenty years ago.

And that time in the Cerro Alegre hotel room?

That wasn't a relationship. It was a ticking time bomb. One that could very well blow up in her face. As could her decision to rent this apartment from Cris's aunt. But that's what she was going to do. Both because she loved the apartment and because it was the right price and in the right place. Just because it didn't come with Mr. Right didn't mean anything.

Dios. Cris was not Mr. Right. At least not hers. Her throat contracted when Gabi caught her hand and held on tight. But this wasn't her family. It was Lidia's and she was pretty sure Cris was not anywhere near moving on after her death or he would have done so by now. And he'd talked about protecting his daughter from being hurt. Who could argue with him about that? Certainly not her.

So did she shake her hand free of the child's grasp? No. Because that would be cruel and Vivi wasn't about to be that person. So she smiled down at the girl and hoped to hell she was doing the right thing.

And because he was bound to find out about her renting this place, she decided to take the bull by the horns and tell him the next time she saw him at work. Where she would assure him that she'd done nothing to encourage his daughter to like her. No matter how much she'd been tempted to do exactly that.

As they went back down the walk, Gabi was talking about a picnic with her dad that was set to take place today at a local park. "You can come, Vivi. I'm sure Daddy would like it. You smell nice."

Her face flamed and she tried to discreetly take her hand back from the child's grasp, but Gabi's grip tightened.

"Oh, yes, you must. Guilherme and I will be there as well. I'm sure Cris won't mind. I'll call and ask him myself right now."

"Oh… I don't think that's a good…"

But Pat was already dialing. "Cris, hi! I'm not interrupting, am I?"

He was going to go through the roof. Vivi tried to wave and shake her head no, but Pat tilted her head like she didn't understand. "Oh, yes, she found the perfect place. At least she said it was." The woman sent her a smile that was so genuine that all Vivi could do was hunch there in misery.

"Yep, Gabi's right here with us. She asked Vivi to come with us on the picnic and I assured her it would be all right with you. It will be, won't it?"

She waited for Pat's face to change when faced with whatever Cris was saying at the other end of the line. But it didn't. She just smiled and then gave Vivi a thumbs-up sign. He'd said yes? That was almost unbelievable. And it only made her stomach shrivel up even further than it already had.

"Okay, we'll see you in a couple of hours, then. Love you."

Then she disconnected the call and acted like all was right with the world. Little did she know that she'd just helped Vivi to commit mistake number three. And that was to accept an invitation to lunch issued by his daughter. She honestly believed Pat was trying to be friendly and that there'd been nothing nefarious about the invitation. But it still didn't make her feel any better. She just hoped that Cris knew that she'd had nothing to do with being wrangled into a family gathering. If not, then she hoped she could convince him of her innocence.

CHAPTER EIGHT

CRIS DROVE TO the park amused, rather than irritated. His aunt and his daughter were both strong-willed when they wanted something. And it was partially his fault that Gabi had been with Pat this morning when she'd taken Vivi apartment hunting. Evidently, they'd found "the perfect one." Which was great. Because now he could show up at the park and pretty much be assured that it would be the last time that his daughter would have an outing with the scrub nurse.

So if he could make it past today, it should be smooth sailing from here.

He parked in the lot and got out of the car and stretched. Soon Gabi came sprinting from a nearby picnic area and grabbed his hand. "Bivi is here too!"

His nose wrinkled. "You mean Vivi."

"That's what I said. Bivi."

The woman in question was over at the table helping his aunt set up the food and his mouth went dry. She was wearing the same gauze skirt and blouse that she'd been wearing the night they made love. There was no way she'd done it on purpose, since she hadn't even known about the picnic until this morning.

And she wasn't meeting his gaze. Probably because she was horrified at being roped into this monthly picnic thing. It normally happened on Saturdays, but Pat had something with a group of friends this week, she'd said.

Gabi pulled him toward the group. His uncle was already at the grill, and the smell of steaks filled the air, reminding him that he hadn't eaten since breakfast. He'd had back-to-back surgeries this morning and then a meeting that he'd just come out of.

"Cris! I was wondering if you were going to make it. We were getting worried."

He glanced at Vivi, but she still wouldn't meet his eyes. After the lecture he'd given her on not letting Gabi get too close, who knew what she was thinking. The best thing they could do was get through this in one piece. But first he had to reassure her that it was okay.

He decided to make the first move. "Glad you could make it, Vivi."

Her head swiveled toward him and a look of utter shock came over her. This was evidently not the reaction she'd expected out of him. And he could see why. Maybe it was time for him to lighten up. For all Gabi knew, Vivi was simply a friend and a genuinely nice person. Why would she think otherwise? It wasn't like Vivi was stepping into any kind of substitute mother role. And he believed her when she'd said she wouldn't purposely lead Gabi on. It was what had helped him keep his cool when his aunt had sprung the news on him.

He'd had time to think things through after he'd gotten off the phone with her.

"Thanks. I couldn't turn down the invitation."

She gave him a pointed look that said, *Really, I couldn't turn it down. They wouldn't let me.*

"I know." The words were accompanied by a nod that he hoped conveyed his understanding.

She blew out an audible breath that made him laugh and pull her aside. "That bad, huh?"

"I expected the phone to explode in her hand when she called you."

"It's okay. We'll just go with the flow and in a couple of hours it'll be all over."

Pat interrupted them. "I think we're ready, if you're hungry."

"Famished," Cris said. And he realized it was true. He was hungrier than he could remember being. And he actually was glad that Vivi was here.

Because that meant she wasn't out with Roni?

Not fair, Cris. Just get over it.

But as they ate and he watched Vivi laugh at the terrible jokes that his uncle told and let Gabi talk her into letting her sit on her lap, Cris got a warm feeling in his chest that he recognized from four years ago. He and Lidia used to attend these family picnics and it felt very much like this. But instead of the loss and crushing grief that he'd felt at these events since her death, today he was able to look back at those times with an affection that had become almost foreign.

He quickly shook the feelings away. But what he couldn't shake away was the fact that he was able to enjoy watching Gabi hang out with a woman who wasn't his aunt. Not that anyone had ever attended these picnics with them before.

It wasn't the disaster he'd envisioned it being. And when it was time for Vivi to go, citing that she needed to do some things before heading back to her hotel, Gabi didn't pitch a fit or cry or do any of the things that he'd been afraid she would do.

Maybe it was going to be okay. Gabi had made a friend, and it had happened seamlessly and without trauma.

As they waved goodbye to her, he hugged his daughter tight, both proud and afraid of how much she'd grown over the past year. One day she would be an adult and on her own. And then he would be free to pursue his own dreams. Except Cris wasn't sure he had any of those anymore. And if he did, his heart sure wasn't sharing those dreams with his mind. And maybe it was better that way.

Come dressed for a picture.

She hadn't checked her hospital email in a day or two and when she opened it up this morning, she saw this caption on a message from Marcos. *Dios!* She checked the date. It was for today!

She'd just finished moving into the apartment over the weekend and still hadn't told Cris about renting it. She just hadn't found the right time, since it had been crazy at work. And at the picnic, he'd been in such a good mood that she'd been afraid of somehow destroying that.

And that picnic had been so much fun. Almost too

fun. She kept waiting for the other shoe to drop, but it never had. Unless there was some kind of delayed reaction.

She'd had two surgeries on Wednesday and Thursday with Cris. But they'd barely spoken other than him asking for surgical instruments. She wasn't sure if that was on purpose or if he was simply stretched for time. He didn't come into the room until just before the surgery started and didn't stick around after it ended.

And she hadn't heard any more from Roni about the new project either. Until now. And it seemed like she was going to have to pose for publicity pictures with both Roni and Cris. And she immediately felt sick. All she could hope was that the pictures were individual ones and not ones where they would have to pose together. She wasn't even sure why she was so fearful of having them done. The picnic had been good and fun.

If anything, maybe it had gone too well. Maybe Cris's quietness in the operating room was a delayed regret about letting her spend time with his daughter. Although she hoped not.

The other thing that made her queasy was that she had opened a small box of keepsakes, expecting to give it a quick perusal and tuck everything back away. But out had tumbled a small ring with familiar red crystals.

The ring Cris had given her twenty years ago. She didn't even remember keeping it. She'd stared at the thing for close to fifteen minutes, trying to will herself to toss it back into the box and tape it shut. But she couldn't make herself and she didn't know why. So she'd set it on the dining room table until she could figure out what to do with it.

And now she had to pose for pictures with him. She wasn't sure she could do it.

She'd been instructed to wear clothing in light colors. She didn't have much that fit that description except for that gauze skirt she'd worn for both the trip to Cerro Alegre and to the picnic. But if she paired it with a pale pink top, Cris wouldn't recognize it as such, would he?

Dios, she hoped not.

She took care in getting ready, brushing her hair until it shone and then pulling it up in a high ponytail. It was a look she deemed cool and professional. No sexiness to it. And that's what she wanted. The last thing she wanted was for Cris to think she was dressing for him in hopes of getting another night with him.

Not that she would turn him down. Once she'd gotten used to the fact that she hadn't committed professional suicide by sleeping with a coworker, she'd started to relax a little. Especially after his laid-back attitude at the picnic. It had been a week since their night together and the world had kept on turning. She'd spent a few more hours in the company of both his aunt and his daughter as they signed forms required by the condo association and switched the electricity and gas from Pat and her husband's names into hers. And although Gabi had taken to hugging her tight, she hadn't started to call Vivi mama—which she was pretty sure was one of Cris's biggest fears. Instead she called her Bivi, which warmed her heart in a way that made her uneasy.

She could admit that she was smitten with his daughter. She was charming and smart and well-adjusted. She talked nonstop about her preschool and all the friends she had there. Vivi loved listening to every word the girl uttered. But Cris was never going to know about any of that, because she was not going to tell him. And she was pretty sure that Pat wouldn't either. His aunt seemed oblivious to it. Or maybe she just wasn't worried. But if she'd seen Cris's face when he'd warned her not to encourage his daughter, she might be.

Looking at her reflection and blowing out a breath, she deemed herself as ready as she'd ever be. She glanced at the ring on the table with a growing sense of foreboding before locking the front door. On a hanger she carried a set of scrubs with her to the car so that she could change into them as soon as the pictures were done. Hopefully it wouldn't take long. And then afterwards she could tell him that she'd moved into the apartment he used to occupy.

She would much rather the news come from her than from Pat. And she would just act surprised if he said he'd once lived there. She hadn't died from anything that had happened so far. So this would just be one more hurdle to get over before the road cleared and they could go on as if nothing had happened.

At least she hoped that was possible and that he wasn't avoiding her for some unknown reason.

Clara had been released, her infection almost totally cleared, although her father was still in a coma and it had been touch and go for the past week. There was no word on how the girl was dealing with her loss. All Vivi knew was that she was staying with close relatives until her father got better. Vivi prayed for that to happen with all that was in her, even lighting a candle for the man at the church she had attended with her family.

The drive to the hospital took less than fifteen minutes, despite the traffic this time of morning. She could almost run it in the same amount of time, but since she didn't want to arrive at the hospital hot and sweaty or try running in her wedged heels, she opted to drive.

Parking in the employee lot, she picked up her purse and the hanger containing her scrubs and walked through the front doors to the hospital, then stopped dead. The foyer had been transformed into a soccer field, complete with two goals and what looked like artificial turf where the information desk had once stood. And there was photography equipment set up along one wall. On the other side was a set of barricades that formed a narrow corridor where hospital visitors could come and go without interfering with the setup.

But it looked like people were standing along the barricades, hoping to catch sight of Roni, whose picture covered almost one entire wall where a vaulted ceiling allowed it to stretch upward to around twenty feet.

She'd hoped these pictures would be done in the conference room or something, which was where pictures for staff lanyards were taken. It looked like the press release, though, was going to be a public event.

Had the email said anything about this? She couldn't remember. And right now she was stuck in that corridor with all the other gawkers and feeling more and more self-conscious by the second. Especially dressed as she was. Hopefully no one would guess who—

"Vivi, there you are. Come on through." Marcos stood holding a gate open so that she could step onto the Astroturf. There was a crunchy feel as she walked over the surface and she could almost feel the whispers of the onlookers as they tried to figure out who she might be.

Well, she could tell them. She was just a nobody and wasn't sure exactly why they needed her picture. Or why they needed her on their brochure at all.

Marcos ushered her into a room on the other side of the foyer. They'd actually needed to cut the door out of the huge picture of Roni. And inside the room was the man himself, along with Cris and about ten people she didn't know. Maybe they were part of Roni's entourage or photographers or something. But all of a sudden this thing seemed blown so far out of proportion that she wondered if it had been such a good idea at all. She hadn't wanted the sports program to become a farce that was about any one person and she hoped Roni didn't want that either.

As if guessing her discomfort, Cris came over to her and whispered, "It's not as bad as it looks."

"Really? Because it looks pretty horrible from where I'm standing."

Roni came over to join them, still using his cane, enveloping her in a big hug before stepping back to give her a rueful grin. "Sorry for my big *rostro* messing up your hospital. But I've been assured that it will bring in even more money for the program. It won't be all about me. I promise."

She believed that's what he wanted and what he thought. But right now it was going to be a hard sell as far as she was concerned.

He made his way back to where a big stack of books sat and then Marcos headed their way. "The photo op is going to be in about thirty minutes and will be open to the public by invitation only and with a donation. And Roni will autograph his biography and all of those proceeds will also go for the program."

"Why do you need us here at all? I'd rather this be about the program rather than about me or anyone else."

"It will be. But it has to get off the ground if it's going to work. Think about how new departments in the hospital get started. There's usually a group picture of the staff, along with a short bio of each member highlighting his or her contributions to the program."

She couldn't argue with him there. She'd seen the one that had been made up for the orthopedics team. She wasn't on it yet, but most of the other staff members were, as well as all of the physicians and surgeons. And she agreed. That's what drew people in.

Okay. She was willing to give them the benefit of the doubt. And for sure Roni was a huge draw, and she'd sensed during their initial talk that his heart was in the right place, so maybe she should trust what the experts said and just roll with things. Everything would probably pan out in the end.

Thirty minutes later, they were ushered out onto the

fake field, where Roni held a soccer ball. She and Cris were placed a few feet back on either side of him. The rest of the PT staff were lined up behind all of them. So the effect was that of a large team of staff and at the center of it all was the biggest star of them all, Ronaldo Saraia. They took several pictures of the whole group, then the PT team were dismissed to go back to their department.

The hardest picture was the one they took of her and Cris together. They were asked to stand with their arms crossed over their chest and angled in to kind of face each other, although they were still looking forward at the camera. It was supposed to give them a look of authority while still working together as a team.

But all she could see was Cris as a person and not as a surgeon. And when they edged them closer together until their shoulders were touching, it felt very intimate and very public. Kind of like that voyeur scenario that he'd hinted at in the hotel about making love in front of the plateglass window. That one had never happened, and she wasn't sure she could have gone through with it if he'd wanted to unless she was sure they couldn't be seen.

But in this instance, she didn't have a choice. They were basically being asked to make love to the camera with an actual audience standing there watching. It was surreal and she felt very, very vulnerable about the whole thing.

When they were told their part was done, Cris squeezed her hand for a brief second as if realizing exactly how she was feeling, and she appreciated it more than he could imagine. She was glad it was over. And if they were asked to repeat any of the shots, she wasn't entirely sure she would agree. But Roni was now seated at a table in front of his picture on the fake field autographing books and a few soccer balls and other items that would be raffled at the end of the gathering.

Right now it all felt as fake as that field. She could only hope it ended up being worth the effort. Big promises came with even bigger expectations. Could she, Cris, Roni and the hospital deliver on them? She wasn't sure at this point. Maybe once they found the land for the field and were able to bring in some specialized staff for the counseling programs they'd talked about, it would seem more real—more feasible.

Marcos came over and shook their hands. "I just saw the digital proofs. They look good. We'll make sure you each get some copies of them."

The idea of having a picture of her and Cris together made her heart ache. She knew it was just about their professional union, but her heart said that it went beyond that. And the picture would just be a reminder of what had happened between them. Both twenty years ago as well as a week ago.

You don't have to keep it or display it in your home, Viv.

She knew that, but she was so afraid of what she might see reflected on her face in those pictures.

Because somewhere between the flash of lights and the clicking of camera shutters she realized something. Something that she'd foreseen happening as they'd made love that night. Her world had indeed imploded. And she'd done the unthinkable. She'd fallen in love with Cris all over again.

And it was both a thrill and a tragedy. Because he'd made it more than clear that he did not want a relationship. Not with her. Not with anyone. Because of his daughter. And very probably because of his late wife. He'd found love again after their childhood romance. And from what it sounded like, nothing was ever going to match up to what they'd had. She was glad he'd found that kind of love. But there was a little part of her that was jealous that he'd gotten the happy ending and she had not.

Happy ending? His wife had died. How was that happy?

It was happy in that Cris would probably do it all over again, even knowing what was going to happen. Maybe it would have been the same if she and Estevan had married. But she wasn't so sure. Their relationship must have had holes in the fabric that she hadn't seen. And when the wrong person had come along, it had all unraveled until there was nothing left.

Was that what that night with Cris had been about? Proving that she was still attractive as a woman? A rebound romance? If so, that plan had backfired terribly. But the biggest question of all was a crucial one: would she undo that night with Cris if she could? If it meant not realizing she loved him?

No. She wouldn't. Because she'd experienced something she thought was long beyond her reach. Something she never would have guessed possible. And she would cherish that memory for the rest of her life.

Cris gave her a quick wave and then left the area, probably headed to his own office. He hadn't sounded any more overjoyed than she had been at the offer of a free set of pictures of the two of them along with the shots with Roni and the other PT staff. For her own part, she would gladly display the one of the whole team. But the one of just the two of them? She didn't think so. Someday her children would probably find it tucked into a book along with that promise ring and ask who that man was.

She would simply say it was someone she'd once cared about very much.

Really, though? Did she think she'd have children? She was thirty-seven years old and her fiancé had basically run off with another woman. She didn't see herself starting over anytime soon. And since she was an only child, there would be no nieces or nephews. And her parents would have no grandchildren. Unless she decided to go it on her own. But then she'd probably need to move back to Santiago to have a support system.

It was no use, though, rushing into life-altering decisions. And, right now, railing against a loss she'd never experienced would solve nothing. So all she could do now was live her life and do good to others.

And that should be enough for her. And if it wasn't, then she somehow needed to make it enough. Because it was all that she had.

* * *

Gabi burst through the door to his office and leaped into his arms, making him laugh. He'd half expected Vivi to march in complaining about the pictures that had just hit his inbox. There were a couple that were real doozies. Because one of the group ones must have been taken before she realized what was happening and she was looking at him with this soft expression that made his heart lurch.

He forced his attention to move back to his daughter. "Have you never heard of knocking, Gabs?" He must have sounded more severe than he realized because her lower lip stuck out.

Pat came in, apologetic. "Sorry, Cris, she had some exciting news and wanted to tell you about it."

Now he felt doubly bad. He was letting his thoughts take over when he should be focused on the here and now. The things he *could* change and not the things he wished he could change.

"Sorry, *querida*. What's your news?"

"Ti-Tia is getting a new puppy and is going to let me choose a name for her. She's so cute! I picked her out and she loves me already."

His aunt and uncle had lost a dog a little over six months ago and had been talking about adopting one from an animal welfare agency.

"Well, Gabi," her aunt corrected. "She's not a puppy. Not really. But she does need a name."

Cris hugged his daughter. "That is exciting news. Is there a picture of this pup?" Because of their schedules, he and Lidia had never gotten a pet, so his aunt and uncle's dog had become kind of a communal pet, and he was grateful to them for letting her take a big part in its life.

Gabi jumped out of his arms and went over to Pat. "Can you show him?"

"Of course, honey." His aunt pulled out her phone and opened the camera. "She's going to be spayed and get her shots today and we should be able to bring her home tomorrow." She pulled up a couple of pictures of what looked to be a smallish dog that was definitely a mixture of breeds and that mix hadn't been the kindest, from the looks of her: pug nose, wiry hair and legs that looked far too long for her short body.

He looked up at Pat. "You didn't let her pressure you into this one, did you?"

His aunt chuckled. "She might not look like much, but she took a definite interest in Gabi and sat with her quietly as if sensing she needed to be gentle. And when we had to leave the enclosure, she gave the most pitiful howl and…well, I couldn't resist. I think she's going to make a great companion. Guilherme agrees with me. He was as taken with her as Gabi was."

"So do you have a name picked out?" he asked his daughter.

"Mollete. But I'm going to call her Molly for short."

He wasn't exactly sure the dog looked like a muffin, but kids saw things differently than adults did, he'd found. "I like it."

"She already knows her name. She's supersmart." His

daughter was so sure of this that she'd popped her palms up, elbows tucked into her sides as if she had discovered a surprising fact.

"I'm sure you'll teach her lots of things. Like manners." He smiled.

Pat laughed. "To change the subject...did Vivi tell you that she's renting our old apartment?"

"What apartment?"

"The one that your uncle and I've had for ages. Don't tell me you don't remember it."

He frowned and then tilted his head. "The one I lived in during medical school?"

"Yep."

When he could speak, the words came out slowly as if he'd had to drag them out kicking and screaming. "I didn't realize you were going to show her that one."

"She's the perfect tenant. You know I wouldn't trust that apartment to just anyone. We did quite a few updates to it."

"Yes, I know." He'd once thought that he and Lidia would share that apartment. But she'd wanted something that was theirs and theirs alone and so he'd moved out and they'd found the place where he currently lived.

He hadn't been to that apartment in ages, except to have a couple of Gabi's birthday parties in the communal room in the complex. "When does she move in?"

Why had he asked that, unless he was actually toying with the idea of talking her out of it?

"She already did. Over the weekend."

"That was fast. Was there a reason for it?"

Pat shrugged. "It was my suggestion. She doesn't have any furniture to speak of and so it was only a matter of moving her suitcases and a couple of boxes over there." This time it was Pat who frowned. "Is there a problem?"

He realized he was making a bigger deal than necessary over a piece of property that didn't even belong to him. But it just seemed weird to think of Vivi as living in a space he'd once inhabited. But if he knew Pat, she'd downplayed all of that and maybe even strong-armed Vivi into taking the place. And she was right. Vivi would be the perfect tenant if her work in the operating room were anything to go by. She was meticulously careful and ultra-organized. It was as if she'd mentally catalogued all the instruments and their position on the trays in front of her. Except for that first surgery, she hadn't made a misstep yet. And even that one time it had only been a slight hesitation. He could understand why now. Because he'd been just as shocked once he realized his new scrub nurse was none other than his high school flame.

"No, it's not a problem. Just with our past, I'm surprised she would want to—"

"The only thing she was worried about was how you might handle her living there. I'm guessing she was right?"

It looked like she was. He was being a first-class *culo*.

"Let's just say your nephew is being a jerk. Of course it's okay that she lives there. It's a great space and I know she'll love it."

"She loved it the moment she set eyes on it. So please

don't be a—how did you put it?—a jerk if the subject ever comes up."

"I won't. And thanks for telling me. It just caught me by surprise. I'm sure she appreciated the help in finding a place."

Pat came over and leaned down and hugged him. "It'll be okay, Cris. I just have a feeling deep down in my bones."

All his senses went on high alert again. "You would not be trying to do anything sneaky, would you?"

She stood up and glared at him. "I would not play around with your future. So no. If you're worried about me matchmaking, that never even entered my mind. Because if it had, I would be a lot better at it than that."

Which was exactly what he was afraid of. But he no longer thought she had any ulterior motives in leasing the apartment to Vivi. And maybe he needed to make sure that Vivi knew he really didn't mind.

Even if it wasn't entirely the truth.

The buzzer rang at her front door just as she'd finished making her dinner of *chile relleno* soup, one of her favorite easy dishes. Pat had said she might stop by one of these days to check in on her, so thinking that must be who it was, she unlatched the door and opened it, eyes widening when she saw who it was.

It wasn't Pat. It was Cris, and he was standing there in all of his brooding male glory, hands stuffed in the pockets of his chinos, the sleeves of his blue dress shirt pushed up his forearms. The breeze outside lifted his hair off his forehead and sifted through the curls.

"Cris. What are you doing here? How did you even know I *was* here?"

"Pat said you were renting the place and mentioned you were worried about how I might react. I wanted to make sure you knew I was okay with it."

She realized he was standing there in the wind and quickly stepped aside. "Come on in. I don't know what it looked like when you lived here, but Pat said they remodeled the whole complex not too long ago."

He stepped into the foyer and glanced around. "I had furniture in here, but not much. It was kind of a bachelor pad. But since I was in medical school there was none of the partying that goes along with that."

Vivi smiled. "Medical school doesn't leave a whole lot of time for that. Come on in and sit down. I was just making soup. There's plenty if you want some."

Following her into the kitchen area he glanced at the pot that was on the stove. "So that's what that wonderful smell is. I'd love a bowl, if you're sure there's enough."

"Believe me, there is. Have a seat at the bar. I have wine, if you want some, or water or some cola."

"Water will be fine."

She hesitated. "Will it bother you if I have wine with mine?"

"Not at all."

Vivi took down a wineglass and a tumbler from one of Pat and Guilherme's well-stocked cabinets and set them in front of the bar stools and poured the drinks. Cris was sitting there looking far too "right" in the space and she reminded herself that she'd better not get used to it. He wasn't interested in permanence and there was no way she wanted him to realize how much she cared for him.

He dragged a hand through his hair to get it off his forehead as she got down two bowls and some spoons and set them in front of their spots. "I have some extra cheese if you want yours topped with it."

"However you're having it will be fine."

Well aware that he was watching her every move she got the cheese she'd grated earlier and put it into a bowl and poured some cream into a little pitcher she found in another cabinet. Then she cut slices from a rustic bread she'd purchased at the store and set the pot on top of a trivet. Ladling some of the soup into the two bowls, she came around to sit on the other stool. Right next to him. Somehow this was different from sitting across the table from someone. Sitting next to him felt much more intimate, somehow, as if they'd done this a thousand other times. And back when they'd been an item they would have sat next to each other in the booth of a local diner they liked to go to.

She took a sip of her wine, letting it swirl on her tongue for a moment before swallowing it. "There's bread. And help yourself to the cheese or *nata*. I like to pour a little more into my bowl."

She added some cream to her own soup and then sprinkled some of the cheese on top. He did the same. Then he took a spoonful.

"Wow, delicious. It's been ages since I've had this."

"Thanks. I'm hoping to grow my own poblanos out on the balcony. I use a lot of them when I cook."

She then took a swallow and had to admit it was good. And it had felt good to cook something for herself rather than going out to eat, like she'd grown accustomed to. Estevan liked to eat out. And as weird as it sounded, he seemed to prefer prepackaged food to eating something that was homemade. He'd said it was because his family had rarely eaten out and it felt like a luxury to be able to go out whenever he wanted. They never actually fought about it, because Vivi had tried to keep the peace, something she tended to do to her own detriment. Her dad used to tell her to speak up if she wanted something. But when she'd spoken up about wanting to stay in Valpo, he hadn't listened and insisted that the move had been necessary. And being her normal easygoing self, she hadn't pushed the issue after that. But she'd cried herself to sleep for months after the move.

"I'm a pretty big fan of poblanos myself. My mom used to dry the red ones and grind them into powder to add to dishes. It's one of the things I remember most about her. Her love of cooking."

How he must miss them. "Your parents were always nice to me."

He smiled. "They were nice people. Their deaths were a huge blow."

"I'm sure. I'm so glad your aunt and uncle lived nearby."

He took another spoonful of soup as if contemplating his answer. "Yes. My aunt grieved losing her sister, but they took me in and made sure I knew that I still had family. That I was not alone."

"You're not. You've got a wonderful family who loves you and a sweetheart of a daughter. She looks just like you, you know."

"Really? I don't see it."

Her brows shot up. "Um…curly hair that goes every which way. Check. Long dark lashes. Check. Deep brown eyes. Check. A dimple in her left cheek. Check."

"I'm a bit offended by that comment about my hair going every which way." Even as he said it, he pushed it off his forehead again only to have it drop right back to where it was before.

"I rest my case."

That made him laugh and the sound filled her apartment like nothing she'd ever heard. He was… In. Her. Apartment. She didn't know why, but that seemed so monumental. They didn't have to stay outside and talk. Or find a park. Or sit in a car in order to be alone.

And they could do anything. Without having to hide it.

"So you rest your case about my hair?"

"Yep. I used to wish I had hair just like yours. But it wouldn't have looked nearly as good on me as it does on you."

He spooned the last of the soup into his mouth and watched her for a minute. "So you think I have crazy hair, but that it looks good."

"Exactly." She laughed, because when he put it like that it did sound kind of ludicrous. "See? It makes perfect sense."

She got back to the reason he'd come by in the first place. "So you really don't mind me renting this place?"

"No. And my aunt says you are the perfect person for the place. She knew it from the moment that she heard you were looking for an apartment. She was going to save it to show you last, but she just couldn't. She was afraid you'd settle for something else and never get to see it."

"I didn't know that. Well, I'm glad she showed it to me first, because it really is perfect for me. Right down to the location and everything." She used her bread to mop up the last bit of soup and ate it, then motioned at the pot. "There's plenty more of everything."

"I think I'm okay for now. It really was good." He put his napkin on the bar next to his bowl. "I don't want to hold you up, though. I'm sure you're ready to put your feet up and be done for the night."

Suddenly she didn't want him to leave, and she wasn't sure why. Maybe because she would likely never have him here again. Never again have him share a meal that she'd made. And it felt like those were things that should have happened a long time ago, but that they never got the chance to experience together.

And despite everything, she grieved that loss more than she grieved the rest of it.

"I could make us some coffee and we could drink it on the veranda, if you have time." She realized she was forgetting something. "You probably have to get home to Gabi, though."

"My aunt and uncle took her to Santiago for the day shopping, so she's spending the night with them."

"Got it." She stood up. "So…coffee?"

"Yes, that sounds good. It's been a while since I've just taken my time eating or had a coffee after dinner. Life is so busy. Too busy."

"I know what you mean." She got up and ground some beans she'd bought just the other day and loaded her French press with those and poured boiling water over them. As she waited for the coffee to brew, she got out mugs, cream and sugar.

Chileans traditionally drank more tea than coffee, but Vivi's mom had always made coffee thanks to her American roots and her dad had followed along and started drinking the beverage as well. So it was kind of surprising that when she met Cris all those years ago, he liked coffee as well, even way back then before the coffee industry started growing.

Pushing the plunger of her coffee maker down to trap the spent ground at the bottom of the carafe, she divided the brew between the two mugs, offering him cream and sugar and finding that he still liked his black rather than sweet like she did. "Are you okay with going outside? I know it's warm, but there's normally a nice breeze blowing up here."

"I know. I used to live here, remember?" He smiled. "And yes, I'm great with that."

They took their mugs and went outside, sitting at the café table that sat just outside the sliding patio door. It was already dark out and there were lights on at the pool and a few people were in it, enjoying the night. But even with that, it was still quiet and there was a peacefulness to the complex that she found surprising. But maybe that was one of its best-selling features.

They sat in the dark and drank their coffee in silence for several minutes, before he said, "I used to love sitting out here after a hard day of school. I would just keep the light off and drink tea. Or coffee. Or whatever I had available and just decompress after the day. I won't tell you the number of times that I fell asleep with my head on this very café table."

"Oh, so this was here when you lived here?"

"It was one of the few things that they kept. It brings back memories."

Her chest ached for what he must have gone through back then. "I hope not all the memories are bad."

"No, not all of them." He glanced at her for a long time. "Definitely not all of them."

She held her breath. Was he talking about twenty years ago? Because when she looked back at all of the upheaval they had both gone through it was hard to find the good among the rubble of the bad.

"Which ones?" She was genuinely curious.

"The ones of us together in the park come to mind. It was where I think I felt the closest to you. Where we could be ourselves completely because there were none of our family or classmates around. I had you all to myself."

That surprised her. But in a good way. "I felt the same.

It was kind of 'our' place. Where we went to talk, to laugh, to…"

Her voice died away because she'd been about to say where they'd gone to kiss. It had been. That had been a big part of their time there. And when someone looked at them askance, they simply moved to a different spot in the park and started up all over again.

"Yes. I remember it all. And more."

Her fingers slid across the table and clasped his. "It was good back then, wasn't it? Carefree and simple."

"It was." He suddenly leaned across the table and pressed his lips to hers. And there was no hesitation on her part. She kissed him back with all that she had in her, reveling in the way his fingers slid into the strands of hair at the back of her head, at the way his tongue almost immediately sought entrance.

And she could deny him nothing. And would instead give him anything he wanted. For as long as he wanted.

CHAPTER NINE

CRIS WASN'T SURE exactly what had triggered it. This deep-seated need to kiss her. He didn't know if it was the food or the peace and quiet of the veranda or if it was just the memories of their time together. But something sparked it. He'd halfway expected to kiss her for a second or two and then back off, but Vivi was evidently having none of it. She was immediately kissing him back as if she'd been waiting for this very thing.

Maybe she had been. And maybe he had as well.

And when he stood from the table and held out his hand, she immediately put hers into it. And this time it was Vivi who led the way into the space and moved to the bedroom with a certainty that said he didn't have to ask her if this was what she wanted. Because it obviously was.

And there'd been no planning. No matchmaking. No half-thought-out plans. He hadn't come here with the intent of making love to her. Had simply come here to put her mind at ease. But he wasn't sad that it was morphing into something else. He'd had a hard time putting their last session out of his mind and had ended up not only thinking about it but dreaming about it. Long lazy dreams that had them tracing patterns over each other's bodies.

They got to the room and where there was urgency and rushing the last time, it was obvious that this was going to be about taking it easy and getting it right. Not that they hadn't done that last time, but so much of it seemed like a blur. It had moved with a speed that was hard to savor when looked back on.

If it was going to become a memory, he wanted it to be a long sliding of bodies together. Of kissing deep into the night. And this was the first time that he'd been okay with it happening in someone's home rather than in the impersonal space of a hotel. And it was something he didn't need to examine. Not right now.

Vivi undressed him with slow movements that were intoxicating and sensual. What skin she uncovered, she kissed. His shoulders. His pecs….his nipples. And his body went rigid at the intimate touch.

His shirt fell to the floor and she started on his belt buckle, moving to undo the button and fly on his slacks. And then she was pushing them down his hips until he could kick his legs free of them as well as his shoes.

"My turn."

She smiled a slow sexy smile that made his mouth go dry. "No. It was your turn last time. I want equal billing." Her fingers slid into his briefs and found him with ease.

And then she proceeded to show him in ways he hadn't dared to imagine that she was going to get as much as she could from him before she finally set him free.

* * *

Vivi woke up first and felt the pressure of his arm around her waist. She'd fallen asleep just like this with her back pressed against his warm chest, their legs tangled together in the bedclothes. It felt so right that it made her want to weep. If they could have stayed together here in some kind of limbo while the rest of the world stood still, she would have gladly done it.

She retrieved her watch from the side table and looked at it. It was just now eight o'clock. She wasn't due at the hospital for another two hours, although she wasn't sure what time Cris's day started. Maybe he had today off for some reason.

Trying not to wake him, she slid free of his embrace and got into the shower, soaping her hair and body before leaning her head back and rinsing the shampoo from it. A cool breeze from somewhere made her blink and she realized that the door to the shower stall was open and Cris was standing there in the opening. And what he wanted was very evident in the rigid flesh that stood ready.

The man was evidently insatiable.

She thought they'd done as much as they possibly could last night. But it looked like he was out to prove her wrong.

She held her hand out to him and then froze when the buzzer to her front door went off. Oh, God. It couldn't be. Not now.

She jumped out of the shower and threw him a towel. "Hide in the bedroom."

"Hide? Are you kidding me? Are we back in high school? Just tell whoever it is to get lost and then you come back in here. Or better yet, we can just ignore it."

"My car is down there. They'll know."

This time he looked at her in a way that made her cringe. "Are you expecting a specific person?"

"No. But if it's who I think it might be, you're not going to want to be caught *in flagrante*."

"*Maldicion*. Are you saying it could be my aunt?"

"I don't know." The buzzer rang again. "Hurry."

This time he grabbed the towel and wrapped it around himself and then stalked into the bedroom. "Do not tell her I'm here."

"I won't. Of course I won't."

She was sick that he would even think that.

She pulled on her long terry robe and cinched the belt tight, wrapping her wet hair in a towel. Then she padded to the door and peered through the peephole. It was indeed Cris's aunt and she wasn't alone. Her sense of nausea grew. He was not going to be happy. In fact, he was probably going to regret ever coming over here. But there was nothing she could do about that now. Pat had to know she was home.

She opened the door and forced a smile. "Hi, you guys. Sorry for not getting to the door earlier. I was showering."

"No, we're the ones who should be sorry. But Gabi wanted to bring you something we bought in Santiago before she has to go to school."

The child was practically dancing at Pat's side. "Show her!"

"I'm trying to, Gabs. Give me a chance." She pulled a bag out of her purse and gave it to Gabi. "You show her. Then we have to go or you're going to be late."

Gabi opened the bag and brought out a kitchen towel. When she turned it over, Vivi's eyes watered for no good reason. Displayed in bold print were the words My Favorite Nurse Lives Here.

"Oh, Gabi, I love it. Thank you so much." She leaned down to hug the child. "I'll hang it in my kitchen."

"Can I see where?"

Before anyone could stop her, Gabi had walked through the living room and into the kitchen. Pat mouthed, "Sorry."

"It's okay." But inside she was panicking that Gabi might go and open the bedroom door. Taking the little towel, she opened it up and threaded it through the first door handle she could find for one of the cabinet doors. "Right here. This is where I'll keep it. Where I can see it right as I walk into the kitchen."

"You really like it?"

"Yes, Gabi. I love it. Very much. Thank you."

Pat took hold of the girl's hand. "Now it's time for us to go." She drew Gabi to the door and went out, looking into the parking lot and then stopping still. Her head slowly swiveled back toward her. "Oh, Vivi. I'm so sorry. I had no idea. If I had we never would have come."

There was no denying it. The woman had obviously

spotted Cris's car parked next to hers. "Please don't let her see it."

"See what?" Gabi asked.

"Nothing important. I'll tell you later." She turned to go, towing the child behind her as they made their way to the stairwell. Then they were gone. And she hoped and prayed the little girl did not see her father's car parked in her lot. Or realized that he'd just spent the night in her bed. Because Gabi's "favorite nurse" might have to let her down hard when she found out that Daddy and Vivi were probably not going to wind up together. Especially not after what had just happened.

But there was nothing to do but go and face the music.

When she got to the bedroom, she found Cris there fully dressed. Even though she already knew they weren't going to take up where they left off, the resigned look on his face made her want to weep.

"Did you know they were coming?"

"I swear I didn't. I mean I know Pat was planning on coming sometime, but there was no specific time or day."

"They know, don't they?"

"Pat saw your car and guessed. I asked her to make sure Gabi didn't see it."

"Mierda!" He came into the kitchen and spotted the towel, his eyes closing. "I asked you not to let her get attached."

The words were so soft and so even that they made her swallow hard. And when he came back into the dining room he touched something on the table, picking it up and turning it over before his head came up and he fixed her with a look before setting it back down. She moved closer and realized it was her ring. The one he'd given her when they were seventeen.

God, he must think she'd planned all of this. The ring. The night spent in her bed. His aunt catching them this morning.

"I didn't! Do you think I would purposely set out to ingratiate myself with an innocent child? I've only seen her a handful of times and you were there for two of those times. First at the hospital and then at the picnic."

"You're right. I know you wouldn't." He shook his head. "I can't do this. I'm truly sorry, Vivi, but I can't. Gabi is everything to me and I won't see her hurt. I won't let her experience any more loss than what she's already experienced."

A thread of anger came over her. "You say that like you think I'm going to try to trap you in something you have no desire to be a part of. I think I already assured you that I wasn't going to do that. The ring fell out of a box of mementos, that's it. But because you're worried about it, I think it's better if we make sure we're not alone again. If you don't want it, then don't put yourself in situations where things might just flame out of control."

She went on. "We'll see each other at work and that's it. You can tell your aunt whatever you want to. She knows you're here, and she's not stupid. She knows exactly what we were up to. If you want to tell her I changed my mind, feel free. If you want to tell her it meant nothing, that's fine too. Because really it's the truth. We had sex. So what? You once gave me that little ring, if you remember, and it also turned out to mean nothing in the end."

"Vivi—"

"No. Just go." She sighed, suddenly more tired than she'd been in ages. "I can't do this again. I can't think that things are going to work out only to discover that there was nothing there. I came to Valpo to get away from a relationship that had gone wrong. I'm not about to step into another one that I already *know* is wrong."

When he acted like he might say something else she just shook her head. "Please, Cris. Just go."

And so he did. And rather than watch as yet another man walked out on her without a backward glance, she shut the door so she wouldn't have to look.

Cris had done two more surgeries with Vivi over the week that followed. But he hadn't seen her in the last two days. Not a word passed between them that didn't have to do with the procedures at hand. Pat had handed over Gabi without a word the day of her encounter with Vivi. She never said anything about seeing his car or that she knew he'd been there. She simply gave him a hug and then kissed Gabi goodbye. But as she'd left she said, "Don't hurt your daughter just because you're afraid." And then she was gone.

He'd pondered her words for the next week, even though he already knew exactly what she was talking about. But Pat wasn't the one who had to live with the fear of losing someone else. With the fear of his daughter being devastated when someone she cared about left, either by dying or by just moving out of their sphere.

So no, he wasn't going to risk it. Not again.

But he did owe Vivi the courtesy of telling her why he couldn't take things any further. But when he went to the nurses' station, he was told that she'd left early and had said she was headed to Santiago for a while.

She was going back there?

Evidently. And it was because if him. It had to be. And if he hadn't already felt bad enough about the way things had ended, he now felt even worse. He'd had no business letting things go as far as they had. But he hadn't been able to resist her or the lure of the might-have-been.

Well, now he knew what could have been and he wished he'd never ventured into those waters. Because his feet did not want to pull free of those last few inches of liquid. Did not want that last droplet to dry into nothingness.

But why? Why did it matter so very much?

The truth hit him so hard that he had to sit down. Had to cradle his head in his hands to deal with the throbbing pain that pierced through his skull.

He loved her. Hell, he'd probably fallen back in love with her that first day he looked across the operating table and realized that Vivi was back in Valpo.

But what did he do with all of the other "stuff"? He'd lost both his parents and his wife to tragedies that had been none of their doing. What if it happened again? What if he couldn't stop that fear from bubbling up every time he looked at her? Every time he took her in his arms and wondered if this was the last time?

Well, it was either somehow find a way of dealing with it and trust that Gabi would be okay no matter what happened. Or he needed to shut Vivi out of his life once and for all.

Hell, he did not know what to do. Or which way to turn.

But weren't there more ways to experience loss? And if you did the wrong thing, could you actually *cause* the loss that you hoped to avoid?

He blinked as that realization washed over him like a flood. If he pushed Vivi away, he was effectively doing the very thing that would cause Gabi pain. She loved Vivi already. It was as if she was able to read who Vivi was and knew that she was the "right" person to complete their family. And if he didn't see that and recognize it for what it was, he would be the reason she experienced a loss that would undoubtedly affect her. And what would be gained in doing that?

Nothing. Absolutely nothing.

He couldn't see anything right now, but his own stupidity. But what if he wasn't seeing past his own lust? Past his own desire to be part of a relationship again? He was too close to the situation. But he knew someone who wasn't. And so he drew out his phone and dialed the number of the people who had helped him weather some pretty awful crises. Maybe they could help prevent him from creating another one. This one of his own making.

"Uncle Guilherme? Do you and Aunt Pat have time

for me to come over while Gabi is in school? I need to talk to you about something. And if you say what I think you're going to say, I want to talk to my daughter and ask what she thinks about it all."

"Of course, Cris. Come over now. We're home. We'll always be home."

Vivi lounged by the pool of her parents' rental house and tried to make sense out of what had happened. She'd moved to Valpo to get away from Estevan only to run smack dab into another situation that was just as bad, if not worse.

Because Cris was the real deal, where Estevan had only been a shadow that had looked real until you peered under the surface and saw that it was all just pretend. Playacting. Their relationship had never been made of the stuff that lasted. If she and Cris had made a go of it, she knew it would have worked.

But they would never get the chance, because Cris wasn't willing to risk failure or whatever the hell else he was afraid of. Yes, he'd suffered some terrible losses. But so did thousands of other people in this country. And most of them didn't give up on…life. And that's what he'd done. Just as surely as Roni had after he'd had his knee replacement and realized he'd never play soccer again. But Roni had regained his footing and was finding a way to deal with his loss rather than just saying no to everything good that came his way.

And she and Cris would be good together. She knew they would be. If only he had been willing to take a risk.

She flipped over onto her back, trying to force herself not to think about him anymore. Because in the end it did nothing but make the ache in her chest come back.

Putting her arm over her eyes, she tried to focus on the warmth of the sun as it played across her skin.

When she'd shown up on her mom and dad's doorstep, they hadn't asked what was wrong; they just pulled her into their arms and let her cry it out. In the end, it was her dad who'd asked her if she was sure she wanted to give up on Cris. She simply replied she didn't know. But she hoped she'd come to a decision by the time she left Santiago.

She lay there for what seemed like ages, knowing she should probably go in and help her mom prepare lunch, but the sun felt so good. So healing. And right now, it was what she needed.

A chill came over her, and she blinked to see if clouds were gathering. Then her breathing stopped when she realized it wasn't clouds that were blocking the sun. It was the very man she'd come here to forget. Or at least figure out what to do about.

"Cris? Is Gabi okay?"

He sat on the lower part of the lounge chair and faced her. "Not really."

She sat up in a rush and found herself inches from his mouth. "What's wrong with her?"

He touched her hair, his warm fingers sifting through it. "The same thing that's wrong with me. We miss you, Vivi."

"But you…" Confusion rolled over her like a wave,

and she couldn't figure out what he was even trying to say. "You said you didn't want me near her. That you couldn't do this."

He closed his eyes for a brief moment before reopening them. "I know I did. And I was wrong. I see that now. I even went and talked with my aunt and uncle and they assured me that coming here was not the wrong thing to do. It was the only right thing I *could* do under the circumstances.

"Circumstances?"

"I love you, Vivi. I know that now. And I'm hoping I'm not too late…that maybe you feel the same way about me. That maybe you can forgive me for pushing away something good. Something healing. Because I realize now that I *have* been healing. And it took you leaving to make me realize it."

She tilted her head, not moving out of his proximity. "I didn't leave. Not really. I just came here to do some thinking."

"And if that thinking had you wondering if maybe you should leave for good? I don't think I could endure that a second time. I lost you once, Vivi. I don't want to lose you again. Please say you'll come back to Valpo."

Her fingers went up to touch his cheeks, still not positive that he was really here, but hoping beyond hope that this wasn't a dream. The warmth of his skin, though, told her that she was very much awake and that Cris was no phantom. He was here. Telling her that he loved her and that he wanted her to come back to Valparaiso.

"Why? Why do you want me to come back?"

"Because I want my aunt to lose the tenant that she just signed. I want you to move out and move in with me and Gabi. I want to spend my life with you. The place doesn't matter. What does matter is that you and me and Gabi are together."

"Does she know you're here?"

"Yes. I told her in words she could understand, and she's even more excited about you coming to live with us than she is about Mollete."

"Moll…who?"

"Never mind. Just know that she's all in favor of it."

She licked her lips, afraid this was all going to fall apart somehow. "Are you sure? You're not going to change your mind in a month's time?"

"I'm not going to change my mind. That much I can tell you. I don't know exactly what it'll look like…this life that we'll share. But what I do know is that I don't want to do life without you. As long as you say yes."

She smiled and kissed his mouth. It was a long time before either one of them came up for air, but when they did, he pulled her to him in a hug that threatened to crush all her bones. And she loved it.

"I don't have a ring yet, but when I do…"

"That's where you're wrong." She didn't give him a chance to say anything—she just walked into the house, very aware of his eyes on her bikini-clad form. She went to her room and picked up the thing he'd seen on her dining room table. The thing she'd brought back to Santiago to help her make a decision about her future.

She sat down next to him and opened her palm, revealing the thin gold band with its tiny crystals. "I couldn't leave it behind on the table. It just seemed…wrong."

He took it from her and examined it. "I can't believe you kept this all these years."

She nodded. "Not because I ever thought this would happen, but because I couldn't let go of that little piece of my childhood. I wanted to remember. Because as hard as it was, those memories were good. Some of the best times of my life happened in Valpo."

"Are you sure, Vivi?"

"Very sure."

He slid the ring on her finger and looked at it for a long moment before lifting her hand and kissing it. "It still fits."

"I know."

"In that case, will you marry me?"

"I will. And I don't need any band other than this one. It's the only one I want."

He wrapped his arm around her shoulders and pulled her against his chest, resting his chin on her head. "Your dad isn't going to make you move again, is he?"

She laughed. "No. And if he even tried, I'd tell him to forget it. He actually apologized yesterday for any part he may have played in our rift. I assured him that if things were meant to be they'd work out. And it looks like maybe they are." She twisted her head to kiss his shoulder. "He's happy for us, this time."

"He did seem a little more pleased to see me than he was the last time we saw each other." He leaned over and pressed his cheek to hers. "I want to spend my life with you. Um…is it too soon to talk babies?"

That made her laugh. "Yes, it is. But I'm not saying it's off the table. But let's give us a chance to get to know each other again. This time knowing it's for keeps."

"For keeps. I like that."

"For keeps," she agreed. "Shall we seal the deal?"

"Out here on the deck? I don't think your dad would approve."

She took his hand and helped him to his feet. "No. Not on the deck." She nodded at the water. "That was more what I had in mind."

Still holding his hand, she walked to the edge and jumped into the pool, her grip on his hand hauling him into the water with her. When they bobbed to the surface she turned and kissed his mouth, treading water. "I love you, Cris. And I always will."

"I'm going to hold you to that. For the rest of our lives."

EPILOGUE

THE PORTILLO SKI resort was as beautiful as she'd imagined it would be, and she couldn't have asked for a better place to honeymoon. Vivi had even ventured onto one of the ski lifts yesterday, although she'd gripped Cris's hand so hard that she'd probably bruised it.

And the snow... *Dios,* the snow. It was white and soft and it sparkled under the stars tonight. Just like the little crystals in her ring. It was a magical place, and she never wanted to leave.

But they would have to soon. Gabi was staying part-time with Cris's aunt and uncle and part of the time with her folks, who were camped out in the apartment she and Cris had just bought. They'd wanted a new start for their new life. They'd waited six months to get married, just to give Gabi and themselves time to adjust to being a family. But there'd never been any doubt that it would work this time. Because they were willing to put in the hard work. They were worth it. Their love was worth it.

And there were talks of adding a baby to the mix, both agreeing to start trying as soon as they got home.

Roni had made it through physical therapy and the new program at the hospital was up and running and was going even better than she could have imagined. And none of her fears had materialized. It was a team effort and Roni had welcomed any and all advice, and instead of coaching a big professional team, he had opted to coach school kids who were just learning about the game. He said it fulfilled him in a way that his career never had.

She was glad for him. And glad for the kids whose lives would be enriched by the time and effort he put into them.

And Clara's dad had unexpectedly come out of his coma a month after the accident and surpassed all of the predictions, seeming to have made a full recovery. Her big strong husband had actually shed a few tears as he told her the news. And she loved him all the more for that display of emotion.

Although their separation twenty years ago had been difficult, she had to believe that things had worked out the way they should have. She insisted on having a large picture of Lidia displayed on a wall in their living room and she intended to scatter photos of her with a baby Gabi throughout the house.

It was twenty years after the fact, but Vivi knew they were meant to be together. It was the timing that had been the question. They had both grown into the people they needed to be to make a strong healthy marriage and it made them appreciate being together even more.

She gathered some snow in her hand and pressed it into a ball. "Do you think we can take one of these back with us?"

"Hmm…probably. But it might not be in the same form by the time we get home."

"True. Maybe I'll just leave it here, where it belongs."

He wrapped his arms around her and cupped his hands around the snow. "I'm glad you're where you belong."

"Me too. I wouldn't want to do life without you."

He kissed the top of her head. "You don't have to. I love you, *querida*."

She twisted until she was facing him, the snowball falling to the ground. "How much?"

"Too much. Too damned much."

"Really? Maybe you can show me exactly how much 'too damned much' is." She sent him a smile and hoped he caught the inference.

He did, judging from the way he grabbed her hand and started towing her to the nearest entrance. "Oh, it's a lot. A whole damned lot."

Vivi laughed, the sound carrying across the grounds of the resort and into the night. "That's exactly what I'm counting on."

* * * * *

*If you enjoyed this story,
check out these other great reads from
Tina Beckett*

New York Nights with Mr. Right
Las Vegas Night with Her Best Friend
Reunion with the ER Doctor
ER Doc's Miracle Triplets

All available now!

ONE NIGHT TO SYDNEY WEDDING

JC HARROWAY

MILLS & BOON

To the team at Mills and Boon Australia,
who always make me welcome every time I visit.

PROLOGUE

WEARING THE HOTEL'S fluffy robe, Londoner Gigi Lane emerged from the bathroom to find the sexy Australian guy she'd spent the afternoon and evening with pulling his T-shirt over his yummy ripped torso. She breathed a happy sigh, glad that she'd both embraced a foreign adventure in Sydney and trusted her instincts with this guy. Their perfect anonymous night had certainly helped banish Gigi's lying ex from her mind for good.

'I'll be off then,' he said with that killer smile he'd worn all evening, his blue eyes sweeping over her with impressive hunger given they'd not long finished having the best sex of Gigi's life.

'Okay.' Gigi nodded, watching him tie his shoelaces.

Newly arrived from London, she'd connected with *D,* as he'd introduced himself, on a dating app. They'd met at the iconic Sydney Opera House, chatted and laughed and flirted as he'd given her a tour of the city's waterfront before coming back to the bar in Gigi's hotel for drinks. Their chemistry had been off the charts and she'd wanted to mark the beginning of a new chapter in her life. One where she was so much more than a woman who'd been lied to, betrayed and humiliated.

He stood, slid his phone into the back pocket of his jeans and then, with another smouldering look hot enough to negate the sheet-clawing orgasm she'd experienced not ten minutes ago, he snaked one arm around her waist, pulling her body flush to his hard, muscular chest and thighs.

'It was great to meet you, *G*.' He pressed his lips to hers and hummed a sexy little sound at the back of his throat as if he couldn't bring himself to leave.

'You too, *D*,' she said when he released her from the lazy kiss that sent heat flooding throughout her satiated body. 'Thanks for showing me around this corner of Sydney.'

Despite sharing plenty of laughter and banter and stories of their respective cities, they'd deliberately avoided personal details. For his own reasons that they hadn't discussed, D had been fully on board with a casual hookup.

'You're welcome.' He grinned, pushing her hair over her shoulder. 'Have fun being a tourist. I hope Australia is everything you thought it would be. But watch out for those snakes, yeah...'

They moved to the door. Gigi pulled it open, but before he could step over the threshold, she rested her hand on his chest. 'I had a really good time. Thanks.' He'd helped her exorcise some memories of Will at least, although four years was a long time to love someone who would go on to betray her in the worst way.

D reached for her hand and slid it up to his mouth, peering at her while he pressed her fingers to his lips. 'I did too.'

Heart thudding with renewed excitement, Gigi dropped her hand, fighting the urge to ask him if he wanted to do this again in a month when she returned to Sydney to work as a locum emergency doctor at one of the city's hospitals. But that would spoil the fantasy and break the unspoken hookup rules. And their one night had been perfect as it was.

A second night might require the sharing of her most humiliating and painful secret, something she'd come there to put behind her.

'Safe travels,' he said with a wink, stepping out into the hotel corridor.

As he headed for the lift, she knew she should go inside and shut the door. But he had a great backside in his jeans, and she couldn't resist one final drool. After all, she'd never see him again.

Before he turned the corner out of sight, he looked back as if he'd known she was watching. Their eyes met the way they had when he'd moved inside her, and he smiled a knowing smile she returned with a delicious shudder.

She waved and ducked into her hotel room, resting back against the closed door with a long, satisfied sigh. Now that she was here, so far from home, she had a really good feeling about this trip. Three months in Australia, one as a tourist and two working as a locum, would be good for her emotional healing. She could rediscover herself and return home to London with her confidence renewed and a new job identified, one that avoided any accidental bumping into her ex or her best friend, the woman he'd cheated with, whose betrayal still felt somehow worse to Gigi.

But that sorry episode of her life was far behind her now.

CHAPTER ONE

A month later...

ON HER FIRST shift at Sydney Harbour Hospital, Dr Gigi Lane scoured the abdominal X-ray of her latest patient, a ten-year-old boy with suspected appendicitis, looking for signs of intestinal perforation. She'd arrived back in the city late the night before after her month-long tour which had included the Gold Coast, Cairns and the Great Barrier Reef, Darwin, Uluru and the wineries of the Yarra Valley. Exhausted from travelling, she'd used the key code to enter the apartment she was renting from some Australian friend of her cousin, had the world's fastest shower and collapsed into bed. Fortunately, the self-contained accommodation she was renting was clean, affordable and close to the hospital, where she was excited to start her two-month locum position as an A & E doctor.

Relieved to see that her patient's X-ray appeared normal, she labelled the blood vials she'd taken for testing and dropped them into the basket marked for the lab, before speaking to the boy's worried parents once more.

'The X-ray looks normal,' she told them. 'So that's good news. We'll wait for the blood test results to confirm or exclude the diagnosis of appendicitis, but I'll be back with an update soon.'

As it was early and the emergency department seemed quiet

for now, Gigi had time for a quick coffee before seeing her next patient. The emergency department at SSH, as the hospital was abbreviated, had a designated staff room, but there was also a small kitchenette beside the nurses' station. Gigi flicked on the kettle there and reached for a mug from the wall cupboard. Laughter from the nearby nurses' station caught her attention. Clearly the nurses were quiet too…

'Then why did you agree to let her the apartment in the first place,' one of the nurses asked, 'if you're so worried she'll cramp your style?'

Having added a spoonful of instant coffee to her mug, Gigi paused and listened more intently, her sixth sense tingling that they might be talking about her.

'What can I say. I'm a nice guy,' a deep male voice drawled, full of flirtation and laughter and vaguely familiar, although all Australians sounded the same to Gigi's English ear.

'And I owed her cousin a favour,' the man went on. 'I stayed with him in London ten years ago.'

The hairs on the back of Gigi's neck stood on end, her heart banging with embarrassment and indignation. They were talking about her. The *nice guy* currently gossiping about her to impress the nurses must be her landlord, the man she'd yet to meet, Dante Scott. He was a surgeon at SHH who'd done her cousin, and Gigi, a *favour* by renting out the apartment in his Surrey Hills home.

Gigi shook her head in disgust, adding hot water to her coffee and stirring vigorously. With the exception of that one guy, her anonymous one-night stand a month ago, she'd yet to meet another man who'd changed her belief that she'd done well to avoid marriage and that all men seemed to be jerks. She'd even been warned about the one currently talking about her by Katie, the department's senior nurse, when she'd arrived that morning. Apparently, Dante Scott had an appalling reputation as the hospital's worst playboy. No wonder she no longer believed in naive happy ever afters.

'Maybe you won't see much of her,' the female nurse went on as Gigi silently fumed while still eavesdropping. 'If she's working here, she'll be busy.'

'I hope so,' Dante replied, sighing dramatically. 'I don't have time to babysit an English tourist, what with my professional surgical exams coming up.'

Her cousin had told her that her landlord was a surgical registrar. He must be about to sit his final fellowship exams before becoming a consultant.

'And training for the fun run,' someone else said. 'Although you're clearly in tip-top shape already.' The woman giggled girlishly.

Gigi rolled her eyes. She'd yet to meet her landlord, but she was certain that his ego required no massaging, and obviously he was used to charming the nurses.

'Not to mention your dating life,' someone sounding like Katie added. 'Which reminds me—you just leave our locum alone. I've already warned her about you.'

Gigi smiled, as she splashed too much milk into her coffee, glad to have the senior nurse on her side. They'd hit it off instantly that morning.

'She seems far too good for you,' Katie went on. 'One day, you'll meet someone who'll turn your world upside down and then you'll have to change your ways.'

Honestly...the arrogance of this guy. She hadn't once asked him to show her around Sydney. She'd spent the past month being a tourist. In fact, she'd barely asked her landlord for a thing beyond his bank details for her automated rent payments. The last thing she needed was the company of some arrogant, womanising man she'd also have to see at work.

'So what's she like?' someone asked as Gigi sipped her

rapidly cooling coffee, her face hot with humiliation that she was the topic of conversation in her new workplace. She was still bruised from her previous humiliations. There was nothing more embarrassing than having to cancel a wedding and tell all her family and friends the reason why.

'No idea,' he said, dismissively. 'I think I met her parents when I was in London—she would have been a teenager at the time. Like most Brits, her family seemed a bit stuck-up from memory.'

Gigi gripped her mug tighter, outraged but glad she'd never met this guy ten years ago. Her seventeen-year-old self might have thought the mysterious foreign friend of her cousin dreamy and exotic and total crush material. But she didn't want to hear another word. Her hateful landlord had entertained her new work colleagues with enough of his unfounded stereotypical opinions.

Coffee in hand, Gigi appeared from her hiding place, her humiliation boiling over. 'Dr Scott,' she said to the back of his offensive head. 'Can I ask what part of me legally renting your room for a thousand dollars a week, paying you one month's rent in advance plus a deposit, is you doing me, or my cousin for that matter, 'a favour'?'

The man had the good grace to freeze, guiltily. The nurses he'd entertained with his gossip glanced away, some of them slinking off in search of a task.

'And what on earth,' she continued, warming to her subject—taking him down a peg or two, 'during our two or three brief, impersonal emails gave you the impression that I would need your assistance for anything while I'm here?'

Finally, the surgeon turned slowly, giving Gigi the shock of her life. It was *D*, the guy from that incredible perfect night a month ago, the man she'd thought she'd never see again.

For a second, his shock matched hers as they faced each

other and Gigi's words deserted her. Then his expression turned sheepish for all of two seconds before he grinned a cocky smile, straight white teeth gleaming.

'So you're Dr Lane, right?'

'Yep.' Gigi's fingers tightened around the handle of the mug, shock still rolling over her in waves. *D* was Dante Scott, her landlord, work colleague and friend of her cousin. *D*, the man she'd had swoony daydreams about for the past month, recalling his gorgeous smile and sexual skills, was the jerk bad-mouthing her at work to impress other women.

'And you're my landlord.' Gigi's insides trembled with mortification and rage, her emotions heightened, because her memories of his outrageously handsome looks had done Dante Scott a disservice. He was hotter than she remembered. Tall, dark hair, blue eyes made brighter by the green surgical scrubs he wore with all the confidence and swagger she'd expect from a surgeon and with that damned smile that had probably parted many a woman from her underwear, her included.

Gigi closed her eyes, seeking strength. If there was any justice in the world, his outsides would be as unappealing as his deceitful, arrogant show-off insides. Boils, body odour and rotten teeth. When she looked up, raising her chin proudly, the remaining nurses he'd entertained with his tales had drifted off, leaving her and Dante alone at the nurses' station.

'I wasn't expecting to see you here,' he said carefully, clearly as annoyed by her appearance as she was by his. He even had the audacity to glance around to see who might be listening.

Gigi snorted. 'It's a little late for discretion, D,' she huffed.

'You said you were a tourist,' he accused, his stare narrowed.

'I *was* a tourist for a month,' she said through gritted teeth, cursing her stupidity that she'd fallen for his charms. 'As of today I work here.' She paused, sensing his discomfort, then added, 'I know…awkward. But then you most likely bump into women you've slept with all the time. Maybe if you'd told me your first name when we met before, we might have avoided this embarrassment.'

She should have known that men were likely all the same and couldn't be trusted, no matter what continent you were on…

He smiled and shook his head, incredulous. 'I could say the same, *G*,' he said, crossing his muscular forearms over his broad chest as if he regretted nothing. 'You were the one who said no personal details, if I recall.'

'You can't blame me for this. I was new in town,' she challenged, lowering her voice to a furious hiss. 'And we both agreed it was just going to be one night.' She was too horrified and confused to go easy on him. And he still hadn't apologised for the gossip she'd overheard.

'Oh, I remember,' he said, watching her with amusement, the merest hint of heat in his eyes, as if he was indeed thinking about that night she now regretted.

But Gigi's body responded to that look as it had the night he'd rocked her world. Only now the memory of her perfect night with a sexy stranger was tainted forever by the reality of the jerk standing in front of her. Just another man selfish enough to humiliate her, another man who couldn't be trusted.

'Oh, really?' she snapped, stepping closer and looking up because he was so much taller than her, something she'd once found wildly attractive but now resented. 'I'm surprised you remember me at all given your reputation around here. And gossiping with the nurses? Really?'

What a pig. How could she have such appalling taste in men, even the casual ones?

With talk of his reputation, she seemed to have touched a

nerve. His bright blue eyes hardened, sweeping over her face. 'What reputation is that?'

Gigi ignored the warning in his stare, uncaring that she had to not only live with the guy but work with him, too. 'Don't be coy, Dr Scott. You of all people know how much the staff around here love to gossip. When my new colleagues found out I was single this morning, you were the first doctor they warned me about. The nurses call you *The Flinger*—did you know that?'

'Oh, that...' He shrugged, unapologetic, as if he'd heard the name before and embraced it, his attitude only adding fuel to the fire burning in Gigi's veins.

'Yes, you're legendary,' she said. 'Apparently, your relationships rarely last more than two months and are never serious. You should probably come stamped with your own expiration date so everyone you meet is clear.'

To her amazement, he gave a carefree shrug. 'At least I'm honest. Anyone dating me knows exactly what they've signed up for, you included. Is that such a bad thing?'

Gigi gaped, wondering if he'd already heard from Katie about her cheating ex and aborted nuptials. But when Katie had asked why Gigi had come to Australia, she'd admitted it was to get over a bad break-up. Of course Gigi hadn't told Katie in confidence, and she would be the first to admit she was sensitive to gossip, having been the reluctant topic of her very own soap opera thanks to her ex.

'Look, about just now,' he went on, changing the subject, 'and whatever you overheard—it was just banter. Obviously I didn't know you were listening.' He smiled a smile he probably considered charming, not in the least embarrassed to be caught out.

'I overheard plenty,' she said. 'But let me get this straight. You're saying it's *my* fault you were talking about me? My fault you were making fun of me, because I shouldn't have been within earshot? Well, at least I was good for something: your pathetic attempt to impress the twenty-something contingent of female emergency nurses. No doubt you're lining them up to be your next conquest, if you haven't slept with them already, that is.'

She was being rude and judgemental, but she couldn't stop herself given her understandably damaged trust and her shattered fantasies of her one perfect night.

Finally, he appeared contrite. 'Look, perhaps we got off to a bad start—'

'I agree,' she snapped, cynically. '*You* did.'

He shrugged, as if his easy charm was excuse enough. 'Well, it's not quite the introduction I imagined, but welcome to SHH, I guess.'

Inflamed that he could act so…normal after sleeping with her and then humiliating her, Gigi pasted on an insincere smile.

'Thanks,' she said. 'Don't worry, I definitely won't be cramping your style. In fact, why don't we make a pact: you stay away from me and I'll be more than happy to steer clear of you.'

'If that's what you want,' he said looking a little remorseful.

But having seen his true colours, it was too late to repair the damage. She'd never met someone she disliked so strongly and instantly as Dante Scott, who seemed so different from D, the gorgeous, fun and entertaining guy she'd met a month ago. What a mistake that had been…

'Great,' she said, holding her head high. 'I'm glad we got that sorted. Excuse me.' Wondering if she could switch hospitals and find a new rental so she never had to see him again, she turned her back on the obnoxious Australian and went back to work.

CHAPTER TWO

DANTE WAS JUST about to chase after the infuriating English woman, who also happened to be the seriously sexy blonde he'd slept with a month ago, and finish apologising when Katie reappeared and blocked his path.

'I'd leave her alone if I were you, D,' Katie said shrewdly. 'Besides, there's a suspected appendicitis case in bay four for you. The blood tests should be back by now.'

'Thanks,' Dante muttered, marvelling at how quickly Gigi Lane had got under his skin when he rarely allowed anything to upset his awesome life, least of all a woman.

He'd made the choice, many years ago, to keep his life simple and his relationships short and sweet. If that earned him the reputation she'd pointed out, the reputation he normally laughed off, so be it. He was always honest with the women he dated the way he'd been honest with Gigi, and it wasn't a crime to doubt the existence of love, commitment and successful marriage that worked for both parties. The trouble was that this particular woman had stayed in his head way longer than he'd anticipated after that night. And now she'd been re-thrust upon him, both at work and at home. What were the chances…?

Shoving away his frustrating reunion with Gigi, Dante made his way to his next patient, Leo. Having examined the ten-year-old boy's chest, he looped his stethoscope around his neck and gently palpated his abdomen, noting the rebound tenderness and guarding in the right lower quadrant, over the appendix.

'Your blood tests show that you might have appendicitis, Leo,' he said to the boy, seeing that Leo was also Gigi's patient. 'That's what's making your tummy sore.' Dante turned to address the concerned parents. 'Leo's presenting symptoms—abdominal pain, vomiting and fever—are classic for an inflamed appendix. But we'll need to perform an ultrasound scan today. If the diagnosis is confirmed, I'm afraid we'll need to remove the appendix surgically.'

The couple nodded, looking worried, but smiling reassuringly for the benefit of their son.

'I see the emergency doctor, Dr Lane, has already prescribed some antibiotics and something for the pain,' Dante went on, the flash of humiliation in Gigi's lovely green eyes haunting him. 'I'd like to admit Leo to the surgical ward and review him when we have the results of the scan, okay?'

'Thanks, Doctor,' Leo's dad said, and Dante made his exit.

He'd just finished typing up his observations in Leo's file, his mind stubbornly returning to the infuriating emergency doctor and his sexy tenant, when the emergency department's alarm sounded. Rushing to the resuscitation bay, he found Gigi with a male patient who appeared to be in his sixties.

So much for steering clear of each other...

'This is Mr Anderson,' she said, shooting Dante a panicked look as the blood pressure monitor sounded another shrill alarm. 'He presented with acute back and abdominal pain and a fainting spell. I think he has a pulsatile mass in the abdomen,' Gigi added, pointedly meeting Dante's stare so he knew they were on the same page with their working diagnosis: a leaking or ruptured abdominal aortic aneurysm, a life-threatening condition that was often fatal unless quickly repaired.

There was no time to be annoyed with each other, apologise or explain away any misunderstandings.

While Gigi placed a second cannula in the patient's arm and attached an intravenous saline drip, Dante quickly assessed the man, who was sweating profusely, appeared short of breath and showed signs of hypovolaemic shock.

'Have you cross-matched for transfusion?' Dante asked her, quickly performing his own examination, then saying, 'I agree with your findings, by the way.'

'Yes,' she said, reaching for the portable ultrasound machine and passing Dante the probe.

'We might need to operate on you urgently, Mr Anderson,' Dante explained, quickly applying gel to the abdomen so he could pass the ultrasound probe over the palpable mass and seeing confirmation of his and Gigi's diagnosis. 'You have an aneurysm here and we suspect it's leaking. I'm going to transfer you around to theatre.'

The blood pressure alarm sounded once more and Gigi's stare flew to Dante's, almost pleading, any trace of her earlier annoyance gone. Putting their patients' needs first had a way of reprioritising what was important, and when it came to their work, they seemed to be a team.

'Can you speak to his next of kin?' Dante asked Gigi as he unlocked the wheels of the stretcher bearing their shocked patient and headed for the exit doors. 'And get the blood sent round to theatre,' he called over his shoulder, pulling out his phone to dial the anaesthetist as he marched towards the operating suite.

'Of course,' she said, holding the door open so he and the nurse could wheel Mr Anderson from the resuscitation bay and run towards the surgical department.

There was no time to spare. Certainly no time to apologise to Gigi for their disastrous reunion this morning. But whatever their other issues, she seemed to be a good doctor and would certainly understand that in cases like this, every second counted. Their personal lives, the reinstatement of Dante's immovable boundaries, even his strategy to forget the woman he'd wondered about every day for the past month, would need to wait. His job was his life, the one thing, along with his casual relationships, he could control. He'd worked long and hard to ensure he was good at it.

A week later, determined to fall into bed too exhausted to give Dante Scott another thought, Gigi returned from an evening run of his suburb having pushed herself hard. As she'd hoped, she'd managed to avoid her obnoxious landlord since that disastrous first day they'd met again. Unfortunately that hadn't stopped her thinking about him daily, or banished the dread-like roll of her stomach whenever she'd seen a surgical patient at work and wondered if he would answer the call to A & E.

Pausing in the driveway of his house, Gigi braced her arms on her thighs and caught her breath. What a mess she found herself in. But after what her ex had put Gigi through, was it any wonder her judgement of character was still massively skewed? She should never have slept with a stranger, because what should have been one perfect night was tainted, turned into a hellish nightmare, just like the kind she'd come to Australia to forget.

Looking up at the view, the evening sun sparkling off the turquoise waters of Sydney Harbour, she sought her equilibrium. Despite accidentally sleeping with the guy she had to not only live with but also work with, she still couldn't bring herself to regret that she'd come all this way. Sydney was vibrant and bustling with heaps of trendy bars, glamorous restaurants with sea views and a hip café on every corner. And the people were so friendly, probably something to do with all the sunshine and the laid-back, hedonistic vibe of the city.

Or maybe it was simply that, even having run into her anonymous one-night stand again, London was the last place Gigi wanted to be right now. There were too many reminders of her failed engagement, the cancelled venues for the aborted wedding of her dreams. Not to mention the chance that she'd run into Will or worse, her ex-best friend, Fiona.

Swallowing down her humiliation, both for the past betrayals that had sent her running overseas and for her current embarrassing predicament with...*him*, she rounded the side of the house with her head ducked, intent on the entrance to the self-contained flat she was renting.

Her feet skidded to a stop, her heart rate spiking anew. Up on the deck off the main part of the residence was a shirtless Dante, dressed in nothing but a skimpy pair of workout shorts that showed off his deliciously tight backside and manly thighs. Sweat glistened over his back, which was to Gigi, his defined muscles bunching and bulging as he performed a series of chin-ups on a bar installed under the veranda.

Gigi's mouth, dry from her own exertions, watered involuntarily. His toned body was as yummy as his looks—lean and ripped and bronzed by the Aussie sun. She closed her eyes, momentarily recalling how she'd clung to those broad shoulders as he'd pushed her towards ecstasy. Too bad his true personality was so odious. Between Dante and her lying, cheating womanising ex, Gigi was so done with men.

Snapping open her eyes and disgusted by her weakness for Dante's physique, Gigi debated her next move. If she unlocked her door now, he might hear her and turn around in time to witness her scurrying inside as if she was ashamed, when she'd done nothing wrong. But not only did she want to avoid another heated exchange with him, she'd already seen enough of Dante Scott naked. She didn't need fresh images of his chest dusted with manly dark hair in her head. Nor was she remotely interested in the very generous contents of his gym shorts. But if she just stood there in the garden dithering, he was certain to reach his chin-ups limit and turn around anyway, catching her watching with her mouth hanging open.

Before she could decide on the best course of action, he dropped from the bar with a final grunt. Gigi froze, wondering if she should turn around and go for another run, just to avoid him. But then he picked up a towel from the nearby patio seat and spun around so they were face-to-face.

A slow grin lifted his gorgeous mouth, zapping Gigi's nervous system to exquisite awareness.

'Enjoying the show?' he called, rubbing the towel over his sweat-darkened hair and face, completely at ease with his near nakedness. But with a body like that, not to mention his skills in the bedroom, why wouldn't he be comfortable? The man was…delicious.

'No,' she lied, lifting her chin. 'I just got here, actually. I was trying to sneak past so I didn't have to talk to *you*, so feel free to just pretend you haven't seen me.'

Self-conscious about her own appearance, she crossed her arms over her chest. Her face was probably puce from running, her hair likely stuck to her skull by perspiration. She could only pray that her damp T-shirt wasn't semi-transparent so he'd see her perked-up nipples.

'Too late,' he said with that same easy smile, and hopped down the steps from the deck. He came to a stop in front of her, the grin smug and the towel now looped casually around his neck.

For a glorious second, Gigi imagined strangling him with it. Why couldn't he just have ignored her as promised? Why, out of all the men in Sydney, did she have to end up living and working with *him*?

Because she didn't want him to think she was bothered by his presence, she held her ground. 'I see you can't follow even the simplest suggestion,' she said, her irritation blooming where he merely shrugged.

'Been out for a run?' he asked, his stare sweeping over her Lycra-clad body.

She broke out in a fresh sweat, rolling her eyes that he'd stated the obvious. To change the subject she blurted the first thing she could think of that had nothing to do with either of them being naked. 'What happened to Mr Anderson? That aneurysm patient I referred you on my first day.'

Dante immediately dropped the confident smile, his eyes clouding over with regret. 'I'm afraid he didn't make it. The aneurysm had ruptured and by the time he made it to theatre, he'd lost too much blood. He had a cardiac arrest in theatre and I...couldn't save him.'

Gigi swallowed, briefly closing her eyes on a wave of sadness. She should have expected it. Ruptured abdominal aortic aneurysms had an eighty percent mortality rate. But it never got any easier to lose a patient.

'Hey... I know,' he said, his voice soothing and his hand resting on her arm. 'I'm sorry. It wasn't your fault. Your speedy diagnosis bought him some time.'

She shook her head and stepped back from his touch, too confused to take comfort from him of all people.

'I'm sorry, too. That must have been hard on you,' she mumbled begrudgingly. 'But I'm sure you did everything you could.' Despite the mess they'd made of their personal life, instinct told her he was probably a good surgeon. She'd heard as much from Katie, who Gigi suspected had a massive soft spot for Dante, or D as she called him.

'I know that.' He shrugged, his expression watchful in a way that left her feeling hot all over. 'But none of us likes the statistics. In better news—' he brightened, shoving his fingers through his hair, pushing back the damp strands from his forehead '—the acute appendicitis case you referred on your first day is making a good post-op recovery.'

'That's good.' Gigi nodded, still uncomfortable with his reassurance. It worked better for her if she could put him a neatly labelled box—*men she couldn't trust*. Of course it would also help if she could switch off her attraction to him and forget about that incredible night.

'So…' he went on, 'how are you settling in at SHH?'

'Good, thank you,' she replied primly, pulling herself together. 'Well, I'll um…leave you to your workout.' She inched towards the apartment, towards escape from the memories of that night and how he'd made her feel desirable again, replacing the sense of betrayal and shame she'd brought to Australia with something more hopeful. But that was before she'd seen his true colours.

'Wait,' he called after her. 'I'm glad I caught you, actually. I thought we should talk.'

Gigi frowned. Talking to him while he stood there half-naked looking like a pin-up for a fitness magazine…? While she could still feel the silkiness of that hair between her fingers and scrape of his hands over every inch of her body? No way.

'Didn't we say everything we needed to at the hospital last week?' she asked, pointedly glancing at her watch. She'd already experienced enough of Dante Scott's brooding sex appeal for a lifetime. 'It's bad enough that I have to run into you at work and here when I thought I'd never see you again.'

He smirked, as if onto her. 'Well, *you* said plenty the other day—'

'And so did you,' she interrupted, her irritation simmering just beneath the surface. 'How did you describe me?' She tapped her chin with her index finger, pretending to think. 'The annoying English tourist out to cramp your style.' She huffed indignantly.

Pressing his lips together in a tight smile, he scrubbed a hand through his messed-up hair. 'Look, I'm just used to living alone, having my own space, that's all.' He tilted his head towards the house. 'And I didn't know anything about you when your cousin asked me to let you the apartment. I love my life, and I guess I was worried that having a lodger would create issues.' He shrugged, the move raising his well-defined shoulders and accentuating his pecs, drawing her traitorous stare there where a happy trail of dark chest hair bisected his ridged abdomen and disappeared into the low waistband of his shorts.

A hysterical bubble of nervous laughter built in her chest as she pictured him naked. 'Of course, you'd never have rented the apartment to me if you'd known your tenant was your one-night stand…' she said, trying and failing to think of anything but that night. 'Well, you needn't worry. I won't be keeping tabs on the company you keep. Fling as much as you like.'

He shrugged again, smiling. 'Nor would you have taken the lease if you'd known. But thanks for the permission.'

His calm logic inflamed her further. 'Yes well, like I said, I'll stay out of your way and you stay out of mine.' She made to pass him but he held out a hand, stalling her.

'Hang on a sec,' he said. 'I think we've proved that avoiding each other is impractical under the circumstances. And don't you think you owe me some sort of apology?'

Gigi gaped at the audacity of the man. 'Me owe *you* an apology?'

He nodded, his stare full of amusement.

'What for?' she asked, outraged, rushing on. 'You called me stuck-up in front of my new work colleagues.'

'You hurled your fair share of insults my way,' he said with an easy smile. 'I never lied to you the night we met or tricked you into sleeping with me. We were both on the same page. No personal details and just one night, you said.'

'Yes, and it was supposed to be one perfect and anonymous night.' Gigi winced, hating that he was right, that her own words and her reckless impulse had come back to haunt her. 'Not this…mess.'

Dante shrugged. 'I think you had a good time,' he reasoned, his stare dipping briefly to her chest. Clearly the mutual physical attraction was still pretty intense, not that Gigi had any intention of acting on it this time.

'So did you,' she snapped, oblivious to the ridiculousness of their argument.

'Just because I date casually,' he said in the same easy-going and playful tone, 'and don't believe in commitment, there's no reason to resort to name-calling.'

Gigi stepped closer in case he was hard of hearing. '*I* didn't invent your nickname,' she fired back, fisting her hands on her hips and leaning closer. 'Your reputation is your responsibility. If you don't like it, do something about it.'

'Right…' He nodded slowly as if coming to a decision. 'I get it. You're clearly the kind of woman who feels threatened because a guy is honest about wanting to avoid commitment and marriage.'

'I am not.'

'Would you rather I lied?' he asked, ignoring her assertion.

Her body flooded with the heat of humiliation at how close he was to the mark. She'd once believed that marriage to Will would make her life complete. She'd excitedly pored over wedding dress designs and glamorous venues with Fiona, who'd later admitted she'd been sleeping with Will for months. Gigi's naive dreams for the perfect wedding had been utterly crushed when she'd seen a sexy message from Fiona on Will's phone and caught them out.

'See, you're right,' she said to the man who personified the opposite of everything she'd once wanted. 'You *don't* know anything about me. But I don't think you need to worry about avoiding commitment. What woman in her right mind would want to marry *you*?'

Smiling, he held up his hands in surrender. 'Wow…don't pull any punches, will you.' Then he added, 'So that's all you have to say?'

'What…?' she asked, everything about this man confirming her belief that for men, monogamy was improbable. 'Having insulted and humiliated me, now you expect us to be friends? Is that it?' Her breathing sped up as her temper spiked.

'I don't need any more friends.' His gaze swept over her from head to toe, making her flush with a different kind of heat. 'I just assumed we could be civil, seeing as we're living together and working together.'

'This is me being civil,' she snapped.

He shook his head with disbelief. 'Well, remind me to never get on your bad side.'

A red mist descended before her eyes. 'Oh, it's a little late for that, I'm afraid.'

He stepped closer, his startlingly blue eyes flashing. 'I think you're being a bit uptight, if I'm honest. You're giving a very different impression to the fun and flirty woman I met that night. The one who knew what she wanted and was honest about it.'

'And I think, aside perhaps from your skills as a surgeon, that you're a jerk. I have no idea what I ever saw in you…or how I was so stupid to be fooled by this.' She waved her finger at his handsome face, still wreathed in that now infuriating smile and his semi-naked body. 'But I am so done with men, especially you.'

He was so close now, she felt the heat from his body, remembered his weight on top of her, the scent of his skin and the sexy groans he'd made into the side of her neck. How could she still find someone she disliked so strongly attractive? Clearly she'd been a terrible person in a former life and was now paying the price.

'What is your problem, lady?' he said, his easy-going charm finally cracking.

Gigi blew wisps of hair out of her eyes. 'I don't have a problem. I was quite happily minding my own business when you came along and bad-mouthed me at work, just to impress the nurses. Haven't you already dated all of them anyway?'

'What if I have?' he asked with a curl of his lip. 'Are you jealous?'

Gigi scoffed. 'Don't be ridiculous.'

'I don't lie to any of them, just like I didn't lie to you,' he went on. 'You've heard of my reputation, so you know I'm completely uninterested in anything serious or long-term and everyone knows that.'

Gigi covered her mouth with her hand in mock horror as if she was about to burst into tears. Then she dropped her hand and slapped on a straight face. 'Well, there's a surprise,' she deadpanned. 'You know, I feel glad for the female population of Australia. At least your commitment phobia means some poor woman won't end up stuck with you for the rest of her life.'

She was so furious now, she couldn't decide if her feelings were directed at him or her ex. But maybe they were two peas in a pod.

'Just because I refuse to feel…trapped. It's not a crime,' he went on as if she hadn't interrupted. 'Maybe you're the liar. Maybe you're a commitment and marriage type, after all, despite what you said that night. Despite how much you deny it now.' His stare raked hers with suspicion, as if she'd duped him that night and then deliberately hunted him down, rented his apartment and scored a job at his hospital simply to trick him into a relationship.

'Wrong,' she said triumphantly. 'Not any more. Not thanks to men like you.'

He frowned, looking momentarily confused, but Gigi had revealed enough.

'I have never met a bigger ego than yours,' she muttered, stepping back. 'You probably think I deliberately tracked you down because I'm so lovestruck after having sex with you once. Believe me, it wasn't that great.'

The lie tasted bitter, but she couldn't let him win the upper hand. She headed for the apartment entrance, feeling his eyes on her with every step.

'So that's it?' he called out as she keyed in the code to unlock the door. 'You're not going apologise or accept my apology?'

'When I hear it,' she said, casting him a final look over her shoulder, 'I'll let you know.'

With her heart pounding and her terrible impressions of Dante Scott cast in stone, she entered the apartment and closed the door, praying that tonight, for the first time since she'd met him, that out of sight would also be out of mind.

CHAPTER THREE

DANTE HAD BEEN all set to apologise to Gigi last week when he'd spied her returning from a run, but two things had happened to derail him: one, her sensational body, her every perfect curve encased in skintight Lycra running gear, had wiped his mind clean of all coherent thought. And two, she'd checked him out just as enthusiastically in return, her lips parted and her stare tracing his naked torso as if she was thinking about that night they'd slept together. It seemed that despite his own casual rules and the fact that she could no longer stand his guts, their chemistry wouldn't be silenced. Of course she'd ruined all that when she'd needled him, as good as throwing his attempt at an apology back in his face.

Heading for the emergency department where he would no doubt see her again, Dante tried to recall why she was exactly the type of complication he avoided at all costs—a love and marriage kind of woman. Despite their anonymous night together, instinct told him that Gigi believed in all that romance and love rubbish. Except her *not any more* comment had spun through his mind ever since, even though his curiosity was pointless. So what if she'd been hurt in the past or maybe lost someone she'd loved? As far as he was concerned, it changed nothing.

His life was just the way he wanted it. Having seen a bad

marriage in action with his parents, he had no intention of falling into the same trap or ever being caged.

Entering the department, he looked around for her, seeing no sign. As he'd pointed out, they couldn't avoid each other, no matter what they'd agreed or how eager he was to maintain his easy life, at least until she went back to London in six weeks.

Katie spied him from across the room and pointed towards one of the curtained-off bays. 'Bay sixteen,' she called, rushing off while tying a disposable apron around her waist.

Dante poked his head into the bay, finding the patient with Gigi. Just his luck...

She looked up as he entered, her smile sliding from her lovely face. 'Oh... Dr Scott.' She flushed and cleared her throat then glared at him. 'This is Mr Neale. He's presented with a large painful swelling on his back.'

Dante introduced himself to the patient and pulled on some gloves, trying to ignore how Gigi's mauve top brought out the green of her eyes and how her light floral scent made it that much harder to forget how passionate she'd been that night.

'Mind if I take a look, Mr Neale?' he asked the patient, who nodded. Dante slid in next to Gigi at the bedside. She stiffened, stepping as far away from him as the cramped space would allow. Interesting. She might detest him, but they were definitely still attracted to each other. Unfortunately...

'So, what's your diagnosis, Doctor?' he asked her while he gently palpated the red, angry swelling, which was approximately ten centimetres across on the man's upper back.

'My differential diagnosis includes an abscess or a ruptured, inflamed epidermoid cyst,' she said, casting him a challenging stare that told him she wasn't remotely intimidated by his seniority or the fact that they'd been intimate with each other.

'Good, I agree,' he said, flicking her a smile as he removed his gloves. 'See how easy that was,' he muttered, grateful they could set aside their issues and be civil when it came to work.

She narrowed her eyes at him behind the patient's back, but Dante ignored it.

'How long have you had a lump there, Mr Neale?' Dante asked the patient.

'A long time… Maybe a couple of years,' the man replied, sheepishly. 'But it's recently got bigger.'

Dante nodded. 'We think it might be what we call an epidermoid cyst. It's completely benign, but it seems to have ruptured and is causing the pain and inflammation, probably a bit of infection too.'

'Okay,' Mr Neale said, glancing between him and Gigi, perhaps picking up on the weird tension.

'Unless we remove the ruptured cyst,' Dante went on, 'it will keep on growing and may become inflamed again in the future. For now, Dr Lane or myself will drain the cyst and give you some antibiotics for the infection. When the inflammation and swelling has settled down, you can see your family doctor who should be able to remove the cyst under local anaesthetic. Sound like a plan?'

Mr Neale nodded gratefully, and Gigi told the patient, 'I'll be back in a moment.'

Dante followed her to the treatment room, where she reached for a kidney dish, a syringe and some local anaesthetic, her movements brisk as if she wanted him gone from her sight. And she was right. He should make himself scarce. This patient didn't require admission. But maybe because he hadn't been able to get her off his mind since he left her hotel room that first night, he lingered.

'Do you want me to supervise?' he asked, wishing they hadn't left things so hostile last time they spoke. Part of his role as a specialist was to support the emergency doctors with surgical cases, even if the patients weren't being admitted.

'No, thank you,' she said, keeping her stare averted. 'I don't need you.'

He nodded, finding the rigid rod of her spine amusing. And because she wanted him to leave, he dug in his heels. 'Obviously if it's not an epidermoid cyst,' he went on, 'but an abscess—you should know as soon as you stick a scalpel in— then I don't need to remind you to take a swab for culture and cytology in case it's something else.'

'No. You don't,' she replied, shutting down the conversation with the minimum number of words.

Dante sighed, reluctant to leave things so tense. 'Should we talk about last week sometime?' he pushed. He'd never actually had the chance to utter the words *I'm sorry*. And no matter what she thought of him, he wasn't a jerk. Like her, he'd just never imagined their paths would cross again after that awesome night.

Her head whipped around, her glare caustic. 'No need. There's nothing more to say.'

'I doubt that.' Dante tilted his head in a way that called her out. 'I told you it was impractical for us to avoid each other and after you left last week, I realised that I never actually had the chance to apologise. That had been my intention when I saw you, but we kind of got sidetracked by all the name-calling and the ogling.'

'I wasn't ogling you.' She glanced up, the merest hint of a blush across her cheeks.

'Okay, well, I'm sorry I was talking about you on your first day. You're right—it was unjustified. I've since discovered that you're an exemplary tenant.'

She shot him a suspicious look. 'Okay, consider your apology accepted.'

'Great…' Dante scrubbed a hand through his hair. 'Because we obviously need to find some way of working together until you go back to London.' Until his life could return to normal. Because Gigi Lane was a distraction he just didn't need. Ever.

What he needed was to find a way to ignore how sexy she was, how they clearly had heaps in common beyond unforgettable chemistry. How her remaining six weeks in Sydney had the potential to feel endless.

Just then Katie bustled into the treatment room.

'This is the guy to ask about running routes,' Katie told Gigi as she tossed her disposable apron in the bin and began to wash her hands. 'He's doing the hospital fun run, aren't you, D?'

'Yeah,' Dante said, observing the stiffening of Gigi's shoulders at Katie's mention of his shortened name. 'Are you in training,' he asked Gigi, trying to be friendly even though it seemed like a dead end, 'or do you just run for cardio?'

For what felt like the millionth time, he wondered what it was about this woman he couldn't seem to move past. Was it simply that she was the sexiest woman he'd ever met? Or was it his regret for having talked about her behind her back, topped with a dollop of protectiveness because he knew her cousin and knew what it was like to work in a foreign place?

'Just for exercise,' she said, glancing nervously between him and Katie.

'You should sign up for the fun run,' Katie urged, clearly oblivious to the tension in the room. 'It's a great laugh. A bunch of people dress up, and it's a good fundraiser for the hospital. I'm manning the first aid tent this year. You two could train together, seeing as you live together.' Katie raised her eyebrows at Dante with all the subtlety of a sledgehammer, clearly urging him to agree with her suggestion.

Gigi laughed nervously, almost hysterically. 'I'm only here for another six weeks.' The tone of her voice became higher, tinged with panic. 'And I think Dr Scott and I see quite enough of each other as it is.'

When she realised what she'd said and how they'd seen each other naked that night, she flushed and busied herself with the local anaesthetic.

But they hadn't just seen each other naked, they'd also clicked so perfectly together, it had momentarily taken him aback until she'd said she was leaving Sydney for a tour of the northern states.

'Maybe Dr Lane likes to run alone,' Dante pointed out to Katie, smiling when Gigi shot him another challenging glare. She really didn't want to be alone with him again. Did she despise him that much for his clumsy comments on her first day, or was she just as aware of their still pretty intense attraction as him? What had she called their one-night stand? One perfect, anonymous night?

No matter how determined he was to keep his life free and easy, he couldn't forget that night—her moans, the way her breath had caught when he'd touched her, how she'd smiled with an addictive kind of dreamy satisfaction before he'd gone to the bathroom to dispose of the condom.

'It's safer to run with a buddy,' Katie said, pointedly glancing Dante's way as if he should be friendlier, but he couldn't force the woman to run with him.

'I'd be happy to show you the best routes through the parks in my neighbourhood,' he said because he didn't need to worry that Gigi would want more from him than he was willing to give. She clearly could no longer stand him.

'I'll even keep you company if you want,' he added, thinking he could run half a kilometre behind her so they wouldn't need to talk, aka argue. But then he'd be tortured by a great view of her backside…

'Maybe,' she said with an overly bright, bordering on maniacal, smile. 'Well, excuse me. I have a cyst to drain.' She sounded as if that or any similar task would be preferable to spending another moment in Dante's company.

He and Katie watched her hurry away.

'I don't think she likes me enough to run with me,' he told Katie. 'She'd probably prefer to take her chances with the creeps and murderers.'

Katie smacked his arm and tutted. 'You could be a little more welcoming. She doesn't know anyone here, and she's not long ago been through a really bad break-up. Plus you owe her after talking about her that way on her first day. I've warned you before to not flirt with my nurses.'

'She told you that? About the break-up?' he asked, ignoring the parts of Katie's reprimand he deemed irrelevant, his curiosity for the intriguing Gigi flaring. Whereas most women he met found him charming or hot or at the very least found the doctor thing swoon-worthy, Gigi had taken an instant dislike to him when they'd re-met. Clearly she was off men in general. She'd told him as much last week. Some guy had obviously hurt her, which would explain why she'd come all the way to Australia alone, why his casual attitude to dating bothered her so much and what she'd meant by her comments *'not any more'* and *'no thanks to men like you'*.

'Yes,' Katie said. 'I'm a good listener. You should try it sometime.'

Dante smiled blandly, used to the regular ribbing he received from the emergency nurses. 'You had another patient for me to review?' he said, shoving Gigi and her accusatory green eyes from his mind.

'Bay twelve,' Katie said, and they both went back to work.

CHAPTER FOUR

FORGETTING DANTE SCOTT didn't seem to be working. For several nights in a row after her conversation with him in the emergency department and despite her long evening runs, she'd dreamt of him kissing her, touching her, pushing her to the brink of climax until she jerked awake in a cold sweat. Hopefully, tonight's even longer run would exhaust her into a solid eight hours of dreamless unconsciousness so she could get some reprieve from the infuriating man.

With her music playing through her ear buds, she left the park, her ultimate destination the closest beach. She'd just crossed the road and turned a corner, when her foot hit a patch of gravel and skidded from under her. She fell to one side, her knee, elbow and forearm scraping the ground with enough force to bring tears to her eyes.

Wincing in pain, she muttered a few swear words under her breath, removed the ear buds and assessed the damage, relieved that nothing felt sprained or broken. But there was a hole in the knee of her running leggings and a nasty graze beneath, as well as along the edge of her forearm, which was bleeding badly enough to look terrible.

'Are you okay?'

From her position sprawled on the pavement, Gigi looked up, squinting into the evening sun to see Dante bent over her. Dressed only in another pair of gym shorts, he filled her vision, his yummy bare chest glistening with sweat. She pressed her lips together in annoyance. Did he only wear a shirt at work? Was he incapable of covering up his sublime body? Or maybe for him, running was just another opportunity to pick up women.

'I'm fine,' she mumbled, cursing fate that he of all people had been the one to see her fall. 'I just skidded on the gravel. Don't let me interrupt your run.' She waved him on and tried to clamber to her feet, wincing again as the Lycra rubbed at the graze on her stiff and throbbing knee.

Dante's hand encircled her uninjured elbow as he helped her up. 'You're bleeding, and there's dirt and gravel embedded in those cuts.'

'I'm fine,' she said, feeling stupid as she pulled her arm from his warm grip. 'Just a bruised ego and a couple of grazes. Nothing fatal.' But now that he'd touched her, he seemed to invade every one of her attuned senses.

The scent of the sunscreen he'd applied, the heat from his big manly body, the vision of his muscular and hairy chest close up triggered memories she'd rather she could forget. Why couldn't she stop thinking about him?

'If you stick to the parks,' he explained patiently, 'you can largely avoid the roads. I normally run a loop from home with short cuts from one park to another. That's what I was doing when I saw you head this way. I can show you the route if you like. It might be safer.'

'Thanks, maybe,' she muttered, wishing it had been anyone but him to see her on her backside in the dirt. 'So... I'll see you.'

She stared to limp back the way she'd come, planning to clean up at home and nurse her bruised ego in peace away from his easy smile and the way he seemed to possess a hide tougher than a rhinoceros.

'Let me walk back with you,' he said, pulling his T-shirt from the back pocket of his shorts and slipping it on. 'I have a first aid kit at my place, and you really should get those grazes cleaned up. You might want to grab a tetanus shot at work tomorrow if you're not up to date.'

'I know that,' she snapped. 'No need to state the obvious.' Why couldn't he just be the jerk she knew him to be and leave her to hobble back home alone?

'No need to bite my head off.' He held his hands up in surrender but kept walking at her side with that easy smile of his. 'But I understand why you'd be embarrassed. I would be too if it had been me on my arse in the road.' He winked cheekily.

She stared up at him, searching her mind for another caustic comeback to put him in his place. But maybe as a result of her dwindling adrenaline or the fact that even sweaty from a run he was still ridiculously attractive and oozing self-confidence, she laughed at herself instead. He was right. She was just embarrassed. It wasn't his fault she'd fallen.

'Wow, you can still smile,' he teased, spoiling the moment. 'I'd forgotten what that looked like.'

'Are you always a jerk?' she asked, rolling her eyes. 'How on earth do you manage to find so many women willing to sleep with you to have earned yourself that nickname?'

'Don't be so hard on yourself,' he quipped, his lips twisted in a sexy half-smile, his eyebrows waggling suggestively. 'You know I have other talents beyond surgical skills.'

Gigi shook her head in disbelief at his sheer arrogance, but her lips twitched in an involuntary smile. It was hard to constantly dislike someone so confident, especially when he spoke the truth—he was the best sex she'd ever had.

'Or women are simply stupid,' she said in defiance, 'willing to overlook a man's obvious and numerous shortcomings.' Herself included.

His comment about being trapped from their conversation at his place swirled in her mind, forcing her to take another look at him. Maybe his commitment avoidance wasn't just a lifestyle choice. Maybe he'd had a bad experience too, putting him off long-term relationships. There must be something redeemable and likeable about him to have earned him Katie's respect.

'Ah... I see you're a fellow cynic.' He smiled playfully and then sobered, shooting her a cautious look that left her more exposed than when she'd been naked with him. 'Katie said some guy had let you down. If it's any consolation, I'm really sorry that happened to you.'

'Thanks.' Gigi looked away, relieved to see he'd dropped the light-hearted banter and appeared genuine, throwing her even further off balance. 'Katie has that nurse thing going on,' she continued, embarrassed that she'd opened up to the other woman, not that she'd spoken in confidence. 'Either she's trying to fix everyone's problems or you find yourself opening up without knowing it or wanting to because she's such a good listener.'

Dante nodded. 'Do you want to talk about it, now?'

'Nope.'

'I figured as much.' He shrugged as if not insulted in the slightest. 'I'm no expert on commitment, as you've heard, and I'm not belittling what you've been through, but most relationships could benefit from a healthy dose of honesty.'

She observed him, recalling the things he'd said to her the night they'd met. He hadn't actually lied or manipulated her in any way. *She'd* been the one to insist on no personal stuff, because she'd wanted to get away from the Gigi who'd been betrayed and had her heart broken. *She'd* latched onto the way he'd introduced himself as D, playfully withholding her name. *She'd* told him she was travelling to the Gold Coast the next day but not that she'd taken a locum position in his city, because she hadn't wanted to be vulnerable with anyone else so soon after Will. What if she'd told Dante she was returning to Sydney and he hadn't wanted to see her again? She hadn't been ready for the possibility of rejection then.

'So about this honesty thing,' she said, 'I'm curious—what do you tell these women you date?' Whatever his methods, they seemed to work for him.

'I tell them the truth,' he said with another shrug. 'That I'm not sure love is real, and I don't believe in marriage. That as far as I'm concerned, it's an outdated institution often used to control or dominate or entrap. That's what I would have told you the night we'd met if you'd asked, by the way. Instead you made it very clear you wanted one night, which obviously suited me just fine.'

'Have you ever been married?' she asked, reluctant to absolve the man she'd dismissed as untrustworthy, just like her ex. He was in his thirties, old enough to have been divorced. Although the one personal thing they *had* shared that night, was that neither of them had any children.

Dante looked mildly uncomfortable. 'No, but it works both ways. Marriage can be just as detrimental for the guy, too.'

She watched him, fascinated. 'So have you always felt that way?'

'There's no heartbreak to report, if that's what you're fishing for,' he said, looking straight ahead. 'But my parents are divorced, so I grew up witnessing a bad marriage in action. My dad is the sweetest guy. He could have left my mother years before he did, but he wanted to keep the family together for me. I don't know, seeing how unhappy he was, seeing how even after they split my mother used me to manipulate him to get her own way or get revenge... I reached the point where I couldn't see any plus side to that kind of commitment.'

'I see…' Gigi said, left strangely flat by his admission. 'Well, I don't wholly disagree with you actually, although my opposition to marriage is relatively new.'

'The guy?' he asked, peering at her in that intense way of his that made her shiver. 'The bad break-up?'

'Yeah,' she admitted warily, reluctant to share too much with him in case it came back to bite her. But carrying around her betrayal like a sack of bricks was exhausting. Yes, she'd been humiliated, but the shame belonged to Will and Fiona, not her. 'He cheated,' she added. 'With my best friend, no less.'

'I'm sorry,' Dante said with a scowl, now completely serious. 'That really sucks.'

Gigi nodded, his outrage on her behalf flattering. 'At least I found out what he was like *before* I married him.' She laughed but the sound was hollow. Maybe it was still too soon to joke about. And she'd lost more than a man not worth having. She'd also lost a friend she'd assumed she'd have forever.

'You were engaged to him?' Dante asked, clearly appalled.

'Yeah.' Gigi nodded, confused that she'd confided so much and to him of all people.

Perhaps sensing she wanted to change the subject, he paused and indicated a path between the trees. 'If you cut through here, you emerge opposite my place.'

Gigi nodded and moved ahead of him along the track, her heart rate picking up. How many times could this man surprise her? And how would she keep her still fierce attraction to him at bay if forced to admit that the longer she knew him, the more she saw that he was every bit as much D, the sexy and interesting guy who'd shown her a great time the day they'd met, as he was Dante Scott?

Dante dipped the gauze in the antiseptic solution and gently wiped it over the nasty graze on Gigi's elbow, watching her for her reaction. 'Sorry. I know it probably stings like anything, but there are bits of gravel embedded in here.'

She tensed, pressing her lips together against the pain, and urged him to continue with a nod. 'It probably would have washed out in the shower,' she muttered.

'But why struggle on alone when you have a damn fine doctor on hand?' He smiled, a strange protective urge coming over him that she'd not only been hurt physically tonight, but also emotionally in the past by some unscrupulous loser. There was no excuse for cheating and with Gigi's friend of all people. No wonder she'd wanted to get away from London. No wonder she was defensive and distrustful and done with men.

Without thinking, he reached for her hand and turned it over so he could follow the graze along her forearm, cleaning up as he went. Her warm fingers flexed against his, a soft, barely audible gasp gusting over her lips.

'Am I hurting you?' he asked, all too aware of the subtle scent of her shampoo, the impossible length of her eyelashes that he'd marvelled at as they'd traipsed around Sydney that night they'd met, the soft pout of her lush lips that had distracted him from what she'd been saying that day, even though he'd found her interesting and funny and smart.

She shook her head and withdrew her hand from his as if she too could recall every detail of that night. It seemed this attraction was going nowhere, even in the face of their misunderstandings and the fact that they worked together.

'Want me to have look at your leg, too?' he asked, his heart banging as he stuck a sterile dressing over the cleaned wound on her arm.

'In your dreams.' She snorted, shoving him playfully in the shoulder. 'I'm not dropping my trousers for you, Dr Scott.' She stood, looking a little flustered.

'Shame,' he said, grinning and standing too. At least she

could laugh at herself and him. 'Why don't you take the first aid kit with you, so you can clean it up yourself.' His stare was drawn to her lips, his pulse pounding at her closeness. She was so sexy and the sex between them had been seriously unforgettable. He should know, because he'd tried and failed.

She looked up at him. He stood stock-still, scared to move in case he did something stupid like kiss her again. An hour ago, they'd practically hated each other. But now that he'd seen past her prickly outer shell, his attraction to her was…deafening. She was gorgeous and only in Australia for another few weeks, and she already knew his standpoint on relationships so she wouldn't expect hearts and flowers and romance from him.

'Tell me,' she said, her breathing speeding up as she looked up at him, her stare shifting over his face, 'does it always work for you? The honesty about commitment? The marriage line?'

Dante frowned. 'It's not a line, Gigi.' His voice croaked with lust. 'It's how I genuinely feel.' He never wanted to be in the same position as his father, trapped in a bad marriage, bullied and belittled on a daily basis, manipulated because he'd been a good father and hadn't wanted to break his family apart for Dante's sake. But at least his dad had eventually left the toxic relationship. Of course then Dante had been thrust into the piggy in the middle role, mainly by his mother, who'd played every game in the book to punish John Scott for leaving her.

She nodded, her intelligent eyes seeming to see him more clearly. 'But I bet women think they can change you, right? That they'll be the one to make your head turn. Am I wrong?'

He smiled, his head shaking at her cynicism. 'This might surprise you to know, but I'm not always the one who ends it. Sometimes they leave first.'

She rolled her eyes. 'Because you've already cleverly primed them to know the relationship won't last,' she pointed out triumphantly.

'Do you want to change me?' he asked.

'No,' she scoffed. But she was still standing close, still looking up at him, still breathing too fast.

'Like I said—' he shrugged '—I'm honest.' Now he wished he'd simply kissed her when the impulse first washed over him. 'Surely you can appreciate that? I've never once cheated, *ever*, and I never would. That's hateful and cowardly and selfish.'

Her pupils dilated. 'Can *I* be honest?' she whispered, her breasts rising and falling with her breaths in a highly distracting way.

'Of course,' he said, keeping his stare locked on hers and not an inch lower, no matter how tempted he was to stare at her sublime body. 'But I think I know what you're going to say. The night we met I was your rebound sex, right?'

She gasped then shook her head. 'You were actually, but that wasn't what I was going to say. What I wanted to say was that I don't like you much.'

'Yeah, I'd figured that out.' He smiled, his pulse accelerating because he liked that she was a straight talker and she could use him for as much casual sex as she liked. 'But there are no hard feelings on my part,' he added. 'I *was* a jerk that first day at the hospital.'

She nodded in agreement but then went on as if he hadn't spoken. 'That being said, I stupidly find myself still really wanting to kiss you,' she surprised him by saying.

Dante froze, his breathing stalled as need pummelled him. 'Even in spite of my terrible reputation? My feelings on commitment? The fact that I don't believe that love is the answer.'

'Maybe *because* of those things,' she said, her voice breaking slightly with nerves or maybe vulnerability. 'I meant what I said too. I have no interest in a serious relationship, least of all with you, and I'll be going back to London soon.' She looked down then and stepped back. 'I know, it's a stupid urge. Forget it... Maybe I bumped my head when I fell.'

Dante reached for her hand, gripping her fingers to stop her moving away. 'What if I don't want to forget it?'

She looked up, their stares locking before his dipped to her mouth. 'What if I want to kiss you again too,' he said, 'despite the fact you don't like me? I'd say that's also a pretty stupid urge, wouldn't you?'

Her teeth scraped her bottom lip, her mouth forming a slow smile as she nodded. 'Really stupid.'

The hand holding hers reached forward and curled around her waist. He pulled her close, his other hand cupping her face, tilting up her chin. 'We could be stupid together,' he whispered over her lips which parted invitingly.

'This doesn't mean I like you.' She smiled wider and wrapped her hands around his upper arms, drawing him closer.

'Noted,' he said, pressing her body to his, her heat scalding him. 'Don't worry, I won't be all clingy.'

With a moan of surrender or maybe frustration, she surged up to meet his mouth with hers, her kiss the same passionate glide of lips and tongues and breathy pants that had made him almost lose his mind that night they'd met.

Her breasts pressed against his chest, his arm easily encircling her waist as he hauled her closer still, his growing erection crushed between their bodies. She moaned again, her fingers tunnelling through his hair. Energy flooded his body, hot and potent. He scanned his mind for the location of the nearest condom as he cupped her breast and rubbed at the nipple through her clothes.

'That night,' he said, when he pulled back a fraction. 'I haven't stopped thinking about it.'

'It was a great night,' she agreed, then yanked on his neck and kissed him again, her sexy body writhing against his. This could be the perfect fling. They wanted the same thing and they already knew how hot they were together.

He crushed her body flush to his, stepped forward so his thigh settled between her legs. She moaned again, rocking her hips, and he slipped his hand under her T-shirt, his fingertips grazing the skin of her waist, higher and higher until he found her hard nipple peaking through her sports bra.

'Do you want to come inside?' he asked, his lips grazing her earlobe and down the side of her neck so she dropped her head back to give him better access.

'I'm not sure that's a good idea…' she muttered, her hands on his backside as she shunted his hips closer.

'What?' he asked. 'Don't tell me you've forgotten how good we are together?' He pulled back and she stared up at him with dazed eyes, blinking and panting.

Her eyes glittered with desire and a hint of challenge. 'I've had better,' she said with a shrug, licking her bottom lip as if to torture him.

'That's probably because I'm not really trying,' he said, tilting up her chin and brushing his lips over hers, confident that she was as into it as him. Her heart was thudding against his chest, her breath panting past those lovely lips and she was still rubbing herself on his thigh.

With a soft snort of laughter, she gripped his biceps and shoved him playfully away. 'Yeah, I bet you don't often have to work for it at all, right?'

'I wouldn't go that far.' He scrubbed his hand through his hair and took some deep breaths, willing his body to calm down. 'But maybe you're right. I don't want to take advantage of you given that you suffered that head injury, earlier.'

Shaking her head as she smiled at his joke, she scooped up the first aid kit. 'There's no rush this time… Why don't we start running together and see how we get on. See just how stupid we actually feel like being, shall we?'

Dante smiled, catching the slight tremble in her voice that hadn't been there before she kissed him. But she was right. There was no sense rushing into this, not when they lived together and would see each other at work tomorrow.

'Goodnight, Dr Scott,' she said as she headed for the steps. 'Thanks for the rescue.'

'Dr Lane,' he called after her. 'Sleep well.' He watched her walk away and then went inside for a very cold shower, hoping that she would need to do the same.

CHAPTER FIVE

A WEEK LATER, after a run of night shifts where she failed to see Dante at the hospital, Gigi was still obsessed with that dangerous kiss that had almost gone all the way. She hadn't planned to kiss him again that night, but nor did she regret it. Running together daily meant they were getting to know each other better, although they kept their chats light-hearted. Focussing on the delicious flirtation with Dante was also helping Gigi to forget that if her ex had been a decent human being, she'd be about to walk down the aisle any day soon, helping her to rationalise that maybe in cancelling her wedding she'd actually had a lucky escape.

Shutting down the fresh wave of humiliation that she'd been taken in by her ex in the first place or missed the signs that he was cheating, Gigi rushed to see her next patient, who'd just arrived in resus.

'Thirty-one-year-old male with blunt force abdominal trauma,' the paramedic said, thrusting an ambulance assessment form her way. 'Surgeon is on his way down.'

'Thanks.' Gigi got to work, quickly taking as much of a medical history as the patient was able to give and filling in the gaps with the information the paramedics had gleaned from the witnesses who'd seen the man fall after a drunken brawl in the city.

She'd just reviewed the patient's urgent X-rays when Dante

marched into the resuscitation room, his excited eyes briefly meeting hers, before he quickly slid on his game face.

'What do we have?' he asked, peering at the screen, which showed a chest X-ray with two fractured ribs, over her shoulder.

'Thirty-one-year-old male with blunt force abdominal trauma,' she said, relieved that he was surgeon on call tonight.

'He has bruising of the left abdominal wall and fractured eleventh and twelfth ribs,' she told Dante, trying to get the restless, groaning man to keep on his oxygen mask. 'As you can see, he's heavily intoxicated and history from the friend who accompanied him states he got into a physical altercation and fell, landing across the kerb.'

'Good work,' Dante said, quickly examining the man's abdomen, which was tender and showed clinical signs of peritonitis. 'Let's do a quick ultrasound,' he said, reaching for the portable machine kept in A & E.

While he performed the bedside test to look for damage to the spleen or internal bleeding, Gigi tried to take blood from the thrashing patient.

With his examination complete, Dante met her stare, his eyes full of concern. 'The spleen is ruptured,' he said quietly. 'And there's a sizeable haematoma. He's going straight to surgery.'

Gigi nodded, still wrestling with the man. 'Okay. Can you help me hold him still so we can get venous access. He pulled out the cannula the paramedics inserted.'

'Of course,' Dante said, touching her elbow and stepping up beside her to help.

While Dante and the emergency nurse did their best to immobilise the patient's arm, Gigi selected the largest cannula available and quickly inserted it. The emergency nurse attached a bag of saline and Gigi hurriedly labelled the blood tubes for the lab, as the patient was likely to require a blood transfusion.

'Let's get a second line in, just in case,' Dante said, reaching for another cannula. The last thing they needed was for him to go into shock. 'Can you call the anaesthetist and ask him to come down?' he asked another nurse, who nodded and hurried off to make the call.

Gigi straightened the patient's other arm and Dante inserted the cannula, the two of them working quickly, side by side, anticipating the other's needs.

'Thanks,' she said, casting him a grateful look. They'd just splinted both elbows to stop the confused man undoing all their efforts, when the patient's blood pressure fell slightly, the alarm sounding.

'Get another bag of fluids up, please,' Gigi told the nurse who hurriedly obeyed.

'I'm taking him to theatre,' Dante said, unlocking the wheels of the trolley before shooting Gigi a calm and reassuring look.

She nodded, hoping that this time the patient would make it through the emergency surgery. 'I'll call the lab, get the crossmatched blood sent around to the operating room.'

Dante and the nurse manoeuvred the stretcher towards the door, which Gigi held open. 'Good luck,' she said, briefly touching Dante's arm as he passed by. This was becoming a habit—her referring him patients he then whisked off to theatre for urgent surgery. As teamwork went, it was exhilarating.

'Thanks,' he said, his stare silently communicating with hers for a second, as if he was just as aware that they made a pretty good team. Then, as quickly as he'd arrived, he was gone.

The next morning, after a night spent operating on various surgical emergencies that had been admitted, Dante loitered outside the emergency department, idly scrolling his phone while he waited for Gigi to appear. It was Saturday, another stunning sunny Sydney weekend forecast. He should go home and crash for a few hours, wake up and do some exam study before heading to the beach for an evening surf. But as he'd been leaving, his feet had automatically slowed outside A & E, his thoughts turning to Gigi and what kind of night shift she might have had.

Trying not to overthink his impulse, he acknowledged he was entering new territory with this woman. He'd never lived with anyone before, not that they were properly living together or in any sort of relationship. But the circumstances of them not only sharing a residence and a workplace but also a whole heap of pretty addictive chemistry meant she was always on his mind.

His patience was rewarded when she appeared, looking tired after her night shift but offering him a knowing smile.

'No need to work this hard for it,' she teased, bringing up their flirty conversation the night they'd kissed. 'I'm heading home to shower and fall into bed, *alone*. I have another night shift tonight.'

'I guessed as much,' Dante said, slipping his phone into the pocket of his scrubs as his pulse leapt with the excitement of seeing her. 'And I'm heading home to crash too. But we have to eat. I thought we could be stupid together over breakfast.' He winked, letting her know there were no hard feelings for what she'd said before she'd kissed him like she wanted a replay of their first time.

She smiled but narrowed her eyes. 'Oh, yes…what did you have in mind?'

Enjoying the return of her fun and flirty side, Dante tilted his head. 'There's a great café across the street. Then I can give you a lift home after.'

'Okay, thanks.' She shouldered her bag and together they left the rear of the hospital grounds and crossed the street to Morning Brew, the closest café that also specialised in their delicious breakfast menu. Having ordered, they sat in the window and Dante poured them glasses of water.

'How was the rest of your night?' he asked, stretching out his tired legs under the table. He'd spent most of the night standing in theatre operating on one patient after another.

'Hectic,' she said. 'I saw three heart attacks, a stroke and two diabetic ketoacidosis patients.' She took a sip of water. 'How about yours?'

'Busy, too,' he said distracted when she licked her lips. 'I spent three hours saving that guy's spleen and then a post-op patient from the ward started bleeding and had to return to theatre.'

'Poor you,' Gigi teased. 'But I'm sure the spleen guy will be grateful, when he sobers up. Well done.'

'I'll let you know.' He raised his eyebrows playfully, his fatigue disappearing in her exhilarating company.

'You love your job, don't you?' she asked, looking at him in that curious way he'd grown accustomed to.

'Yeah, I do. Don't you?'

She half shrugged, half nodded. 'I used to. Before my life imploded. Then I was just desperate for a change.'

'Were you already working in A & E?' he asked, sensing she was talking about her ex.

She nodded and Dante waited, curious for more details and aware that her trust was a delicate thread he couldn't tug too hard.

'Yeah, but I worked at the same hospital as my ex and my friend,' she added with a sigh, dropping her gaze to the table. 'So it kind of became claustrophobic after what happened.'

'I bet. So that's why you came to Sydney?'

'I needed to get away. From my life, my friends, even my family.'

She looked up and he urged her to continue with another nod.

'Don't get me wrong,' she went on, 'everyone means well. But when you have to cancel a wedding after you've sent out all the invitations, everyone you know discovers exactly why there'll be no happy occasion. There's no hiding that kind of humiliation, no matter how much you wish you could.'

Dante reached for her hand across the table and snagged her fingers in his. 'I'm sorry. I didn't realise you'd actually planned the wedding. I can see why all that would feel claustrophobic.' No wonder she'd needed to get away, why she'd wanted one anonymous night when they met, why she was definitely off relationships for now. He actually hated her ex and he'd never even met the guy.

'Yeah.' She shrugged but her stare was haunted. 'I thought I'd be over it by now, but with the cancelled wedding date looming, I'd started to feel worse all over again. My friends, even my family had started to walk on eggshells around me when all I wanted was to feel normal again. But London has too many reminders.' She smiled brightly. 'So here I am, running away from my problems instead. I have an aunt who lives here, in Bondi. I've always wanted to visit Australia, and I thought why not?'

'I don't think you're running away,' he said quietly, aware that she hadn't pulled her hand from his and how much he liked that. 'Maybe you just needed space to heal. I think you did a very brave thing actually. Many people might go ahead with the wedding, feeling that they had no choice but to forgive and forget.'

'Would they? Maybe.' She shrugged. 'But you're right— aside from the emotional devastation and all the lost deposits we'd paid, there was also the communal disappointment to manage. Anyway, what about you?' she asked, changing the subject. 'Did you grow up here?'

He nodded. 'Yeah, in Manly, a beach suburb in northern Sydney.'

'So your family lives here? Your parents?'

'I'm an only child,' Dante said, eager to avoid talking about his childhood. 'I'm closer to my dad, who lives in Rose Bay. Do you surf?' he asked, his overactive imagination picturing Gigi in a teeny tiny bikini. Better that than thinking about his strained relationship with his mother, who even to this day with him a grown man still played emotional games, urging him to visit and then bringing up his father, fishing for details.

'Never tried,' she admitted, tugging her hand from his and smiling up at the handsome barista who placed their coffees on the table.

'I can teach you if you want,' Dante offered, swallowing down the irrational surge of jealousy. What was wrong with him? He never got possessive over a woman. Maybe it was just because he was her landlord and work colleague and knew her cousin... Or maybe it was their chemistry still bubbling away in the background, fanned by that kiss and the memories of that one night.

'I thought you were too busy to *babysit a tourist*.' She smirked his way over the rim of her cup, sipping at the foamy layer of her drink.

'A guy needs a break from the textbooks every now and then,' he argued with a wink. 'And said tourist has kind of grown on me.' He flashed her his most charming smile, heartened when she laughed.

'Okay, I might take you up on that offer sometime,' she said, resting her elbow on the table and her chin on her palm.

'But first tell me this: What's the longest relationship you've ever had?'

'Ooh, this isn't really the best location for pillow talk,' he teased, leaning forward too, 'but okay, I'll take the bait. Eleven weeks.'

She raised her eyebrows as if pleasantly surprised.

'How long were you with the guy who clearly didn't know what a good thing he had?' he asked, those possessive and protective urges building.

'Four years,' she said, looking down at her cup. 'Engaged for two.'

'You deserve so much better, you know,' he said with a wince, feeling defensive on her behalf. 'Only cowards and narcissists cheat.'

When she nodded and met his stare he asked, 'Do you mind me asking how you found out?'

She shrugged, but he understood her well enough now to know his question had pushed her to the edge of her comfort zone. 'I got home from a night shift where I'd lost two elderly patients in a row. Will was in the shower, but he'd left his phone on the bed. The phone lit up, catching my attention. I saw a suggestive text on the screen, from my best friend, Fiona.' She met his stare boldly. 'So I'm sure you can understand why I didn't want to talk about anything personal the night we met. That's one big can of worms to open when all you're trying to do is forget.'

'Of course I understand,' he said, wishing he still had a hold of her hand. 'So you confronted them both?'

She nodded, shifting in her seat as if uncomfortable. 'Yeah. Of course, he tried to deny it at first, said Fiona's text was just a joke, tried to gaslight me, which made it even worse. But even though I'd been awake for over twenty-four hours and had worked a crappy and emotional shift at the hospital, I instantly knew he was lying.'

'I'm so sorry. That's horrible.'

She shrugged, watching him closely. 'Losing Fiona was somehow even worse. We'd been friends since medical school, and there's supposed to be a code of sisterhood. She was supposed to be my chief bridesmaid. Needless to say being here, away from all that mess was a big part of my motivation to travel.'

Dante nodded, reaching for her hand once more, his respect for her soaring. 'I think I'd do the same.'

She smiled sadly, tilting her head. 'But you wouldn't have got yourself into that situation in the first place,' she pointed out. 'You don't believe in marriage. I'm not sure I do any more, either.'

'Good point.' Dante nodded in acknowledgement. 'Want to talk about something else?'

She nodded, looking relieved. 'Yes please.'

'So…about that kiss,' he started, grinning when she laughed and tossed a packet of sugar at him across the table.

'I plead a moment of weakness brought on by that head injury when I fell,' she said, glancing over at the kitchen behind the counter, presumably hoping to be rescued by the timely delivery of their breakfasts.

'But you didn't bang your head,' he said, refusing to let her off the hook this time. 'I think what you need is a holiday fling. Something stupid and casual, to help you forget, same as before.'

She was right; there was no rush, but their chemistry was clearly going nowhere.

She laughed and he smiled, glad he could return her good spirits. 'Let me guess,' she said, her eyes dancing with humour and the excitement he recognised, 'you're bravely volunteering for the role?'

'Why not?' Dante shrugged. 'You already know we're amazing together—'

'Do I?' she challenged teasingly.

'And neither of us is interested in anything long-term,' he said.

'I'm leaving in just over a month,' she added so he nodded encouragingly.

'See,' he said. 'One perfect night could become a perfect holiday fling.'

With her amused stare locked on his, she dragged in a deep breath and released a shuddering sigh as their breakfasts arrived.

'You just can't help yourself, can you?' she said, sprinkling pepper over her eggs Benedict.

'I just know when I'm onto a good thing.' He winked, picking up his cutlery and tucking into his smashed avocado with bacon and poached egg. 'Anyway, you know where I live if you like the idea.'

'Eat your breakfast, Dr Scott,' she said, with the kind of smile that let Dante know she was beyond tempted.

CHAPTER SIX

THE FOLLOWING WEEK, on what should have been her wedding day, Gigi found herself smack bang in the middle of a shift from hell.

'ETA on that stabbing case, two minutes,' Katie said, glancing at her with sympathy because, so far, Gigi's day had been hectic and emotional. She'd lost a cardiac patient first thing, had two more patients brought in dead whom she'd had to certify deceased in the back of the ambulances, and she'd just admitted a critically ill one-year-old with whooping cough to paediatric intensive care. Clearly it was going to be one of those days.

Making her way to resus, Gigi intercepted the paramedic and patient and got straight to work, Katie at her side.

Taking one look at the man's injuries, she said to Katie, 'Can you call Dante, please.'

While Katie made the call, Gigi took blood from the man, ordered some urgent X-rays and performed a more detailed examination. Having only seen Dante this past week for their evening runs which followed a predictable format—sweating, flirting, a goodnight kiss that lasted for just a second too long to be anything other than restrained—Gigi nearly sagged with relief when Dante marched into resus moments later, his eyes landing on hers, the smile there shoved aside by the professional questions he had.

'This is Mr Green,' Gigi told him as he quickly assessed the urgent situation. 'A twenty-eight-year-old male with right sided stabbing injuries to the chest and abdomen. He has a small pneumothorax on the right. Blood pressure is stable but he's tachycardic. My main concern, beside the pneumothorax, is that the knife has penetrated the liver.'

While Dante quickly introduced himself to the groggy patient before removing the gauze covering the abdominal wounds and carefully palpating the man's abdomen, Gigi brought up the X-rays.

'He needs an urgent CT scan and a laparotomy,' Dante said, joining her at the computer terminal and scouring the X-rays over her shoulder. 'But let's insert a chest drain first. I don't want that pneumothorax tensioning on the way to surgery.'

Gigi nodded towards the nearby tray. 'I have a drain kit already set up for you.'

'Then let's do this,' he said, with a nod that told her he had complete confidence in her, which today, probably because she was emotional, gave her self-esteem an enormous boost.

'Mr Green,' Dante addressed the patient once more. 'You have a punctured lung. We need to place a tube in your chest to remove the air. We need you to hold nice and still, okay?'

Together, he and Gigi washed their hands in preparation for the procedure and pulled on sterile gloves. While Dante readied the chest tube, Gigi injected the patient's chest wall with local anaesthetic then made a small incision between the ribs. She'd just correctly positioned the tube and sutured it in place when the patient became agitated and began to thrash, tugging off his oxygen mask and throwing out his arm, catching Gigi on the chin and chest.

'Calm down, Mr Green,' Dante said, and together with Katie and another emergency nurse held onto the man's flailing arm to stop him hurting either himself or others.

'Are you okay?' Dante asked Gigi, wearing a frown of concern.

Gigi nodded, a little winded. 'I'm okay. His saturations have dropped, so he's probably hypoxic.'

With the oxygen mask repositioned over the patient's mouth and nose, Gigi quickly unclamped the chest tube, relieved to see bubbles of air escaping, which meant it was correctly positioned and draining the escaped air from around the lung, which would now be able to reinflate.

'Hopefully that will help with his agitation,' she said to Dante, glancing at the monitor to see a slight improvement in the patient's oxygen saturations. 'I'll order a chest X-ray to check the position of the tube.'

With the man stabilized, Gigi peeled off her gloves and re-washed her hands, which trembled slightly from the adrenaline of both performing the procedure and being accidentally hit in the face. But it was an occupational hazard and another tally to add to her bad day.

As the radiographer arrived to take the repeat chest X-ray, Dante stood at her side at the computer station. 'That was quite a blow,' he said, his hand touching her elbow.

She offered him a small smile, her breath shuddering at his thoughtfulness. 'I'll live.'

He peered at her closely, his concern touching. 'You sure you're okay?'

'I'm fine,' she said. 'But thanks for checking.'

'Gotta look out for my favourite emergency doctor,' Dante said with his signature cheeky smile, although his concern lingered in his eyes.

'Just having one of those days,' she added, knowing he would understand what she meant.

'Why don't you come over after your shift and you can tell me all about it.'

Gigi nodded, dangerously close to tears that he was being so supportive. 'Okay, thanks.'

'Right,' he said, resting his hand on her shoulder, 'you book the urgent CT and I'll book him in for surgery.'

'Sounds like a plan,' she said with a grateful smile, her spirits rising slightly, as they set about their separate tasks. Sometimes laughter was the best medicine. But who would have known that when they'd started working together and after that disastrous first day, they'd become such a well co-ordinated and supportive duo? She couldn't imagine getting through today of all days, without him. How had that happened? Fortunately, duty called and she had no time to think about an answer.

Later that evening, after three hours of study after work, Dante pulled open the door to find a more relaxed-looking Gigi on his doorstep.

'Fancy a beer?' she asked with a smile, holding up two bottles sweating with condensation.

'Absolutely, thanks,' he said, trying not to stare at her gorgeous bare legs in her short denim shorts. Since he'd seen her at work she'd changed into casual clothes, her hair damp at the ends as if she'd recently taken a shower.

'What are we celebrating?' he asked, guiding her to the comfy outdoor sofa he kept on the deck, which had distant views of the ocean.

Instead of the only single chair, she settled into the sofa next to him with a small sigh. 'To the end of a crappy day,' she suggested, clinking his bottle with hers.

They each took a sip and he added, 'And to three hours of study when it was the last thing I wanted to do after work.'

Another clink and another sip, another of her lovely smiles that never failed to brighten his day.

'And to a beautiful Sydney sunset,' she added, staring at the view while he stared at her profile, the urge to kiss her beating at him like powerful waves.

Before he could stop himself, Dante brushed her hair back from her cheek and rested his arm on the sofa behind her. 'Want to tell me about your bad day?' he asked.

'Yeah,' she said, 'in a second. But tell me—how was our punchy patient after surgery?'

'Punctured liver and diaphragm and two perforated loops of small bowel,' he said, the floral scent of her shampoo teasing his senses. 'Don't think he'll be punching anyone for a while.'

He took a sip of beer, his stare drawn to the smattering of freckles across her nose. 'It's always a shock when patients become aggressive. No one expects to be assaulted at work, even if it is unintentional as in this case.'

'I'm okay,' she said, her eyes amused but haunted by that sadness she'd carried since earlier. 'I'm tough. But who knew you were so thoughtful.'

Dante winked playfully, flirting with Gigi a great way to end a busy day. 'I know I have a terrible reputation, but I'm not just a jerk.'

She nodded, watching him keenly as she teased. 'I'm starting to see there are deeper layers to you. On the surface, you have a lot going for you, I guess. Good job, nice house, great body, not to mention the chat.'

'I bet you say that to all the boys,' he replied, bumping her arm with his and joining her when she laughed at him. 'So, are you looking forward to the fun run?' he asked, wanting to keep the conversation light until she was ready to open up. Any distraction to help him take his mind off how badly he wanted to kiss her and not stop this time. His mind had unhelpfully inflated the memories of how great their one night was to mythical proportions.

Gigi nodded. 'Katie's lent me a tiara and a Union Jack so I can represent my country.' Her smile warmed him but she still seemed off and fell quiet.

'You don't have to tell me,' he said after a moment, his fingers stroking the back of her neck where his arm was stretched along the back of the sofa, 'but if you want to talk about it, I'm here and I've been told by Katie I should practice my listening skills.'

She smiled thoughtfully, looking as if she might brush him off again. Then she dragged in a deep breath and spat it out. 'Today was supposed to be my wedding day.'

Dante froze, shock stalling his breath. That was the last thing he'd expected her to say and wasn't sure how to react.

'I guess it was fitting,' she added, glancing away, 'that my work day was so…challenging.'

Dante winced, feeling out of his depth when it came to relationship advice but desperate to be there for her the way they had each other's backs at work.

'I'm sorry. That *is* particularly cruel of the universe,' he said. Their work was intense and demanding, sometimes devastating. It tended to push personal problems to the back of your mind.

'Do you have any regrets?' he asked quietly, hoping for her sake that she didn't. But maybe she was sad because she still had feelings for her ex.

She shot him a sharp look, placing her unfinished beer on the coffee table. 'No way. Apart from the fact that I wasted so many years with a man who managed to deceive me and lie to me.'

'It's not your fault,' Dante said, reaching out to sweep her hair behind her ear, his thumb lingering on her cheek bone. 'The responsibility is totally his.'

'I know.' She nodded, tilting her face towards his palm,

leaning into his touch as if she needed comfort. 'I guess I just feel stupid for not seeing through him sooner, for allowing him to lead a double life and keep me in the dark. Plus it's changed me as a person. It will be a long time before I can trust someone again, and I resent him for that.'

'That's understandable,' he said, wishing he could say something, anything, to make her feel better. 'I struggle to trust when it comes to relationships and I have nowhere near as good a reason as you.'

'Why is that?' she whispered, watching him intently, a small frown pinching her eyebrows.

Dante shrugged, clueless as to how he'd survive what she'd been through—falling in love, committing to someone then picking up the scattered pieces after being betrayed.

'I don't want to ever be that vulnerable with someone,' he said. 'For years I watched my parents argue. My mother would make what seemed like unreasonable demands, and my father would get beaten down by her manipulations and tantrums to keep the peace for my sake. Even after their divorce, she still had a hold over us both. Until I was eighteen and I left home, she would use me to guilt-trip Dad into getting her own way. It used to make me so mad but as a minor, I couldn't leave.'

'That's awful,' she whispered. 'I'm sorry.'

Lost to how powerless he'd felt growing up, Dante went on, confessing more than he'd meant to. 'Nothing I did was ever good enough for her either. It was…suffocating. And until I became an adult, I was literally trapped because my parents had shared custody of me.' He paused, feeling raw and exposed from the sympathetic look of understanding on her face. 'I don't know…' he went on. 'I never felt I could be my own person in my mother's house, or in that relationship. Even to this day, we're not close.'

She rested her hand on his bare knee, her touch just the

distraction he needed. 'I'm sorry that was your experience,' she said. 'It must have been hard being caught in the middle. No one wants to feel that there's no way out of a situation.'

He shrugged, placing his hand over hers on his thigh. 'I escaped eventually. But when my first girlfriend started pressuring me to see things her way and then dumped me because I was 'too emotionally distant', I realised that the safest bet was to keep things casual. This way I won't disappoint anyone. I can just be myself. I'm free of expectations.'

'And it's worked for you ever since,' she said, her lips pressed together in a sad frown. 'Maybe you've got something there…' She tried to smile and make light of it.

'My approach to relationships doesn't suit everyone,' he said. 'I guess I'm only telling you all this to show you that many of us struggle to give another person the power to hurt us. And in your case, you have a very good reason to be cautious going forward. For what it's worth, I think you're incredibly strong. I admire you. And now that we know each other better, I can totally understand why you took an instant dislike to me when you heard me talking about you that first day. I did behave like a jerk.'

'I'm also pretty cynical these days,' she said, her vulnerable stare on his. 'Always second-guessing people's motives and my own judgement of character. There's an outside possibility that I might have overreacted.'

Dante shook his head in understanding. 'Not all men cheat and lie. I know it's easy for me to say, but you should trust your instincts. They're good. You saw through me, didn't you?'

He smiled and brushed her cheek with his thumb. But she didn't join him smiling this time. The atmosphere shifted as she stared. She was suddenly looking at him as if he was reciting love sonnets, the way she'd looked at him the first night they'd met, her stare dipping to his mouth and her breathing fast. It was there between them again, the unavoidable attraction a constant buzz of static it was growing increasingly hard for him to ignore. He surely deserved some sort of endurance medal for ignoring it this past month.

'I think I'm ready to be stupid again,' she whispered, peering up at him with desire and a hint of uncertainty. 'How about you?'

Dante placed his beer on the table next to hers, encircled her waist and tugged her astride his lap, the desire he felt whenever she was around heavy in his belly. 'I'm always ready to be stupid with you. I want you, Gigi.'

She smiled a satisfied smile that made his chest tight then leaned forward to brush her lips over his.

'I've wanted you every day since you came back to Sydney,' he said, holding her waist in both hands, his fingers flexing, ready to curl into the fabric of her T-shirt and crush her close. 'But you're in an understandably emotional state today. I don't want to take advantage of you or pressure you into something you'll regret. I'm not that much of a jerk.' He tried to smile, but his need for her was so intense his face felt rubbery, his restraint stretched to snapping point.

'What if *I* want to pressure *you*?' she asked, trailing her lips seductively along the side of his jaw and down his neck so he groaned aloud, his good intentions crumbling. 'And I'm no more hung up on my past today than the first time we met.'

He closed his eyes because she was rocking on his lap, the heat between her legs and the way her lips traced his skin making him hard.

'But I didn't know that then,' he said, his throat tight with want as he clung to every second of this exhilarating seduction in case she agreed with his logic, came to her senses and moved off his lap.

'When I said you had to work for it,' she whispered against

his earlobe, driving him wild, 'I didn't mean this hard. I want you too. Just a no-strings holiday fling like you said. I'll be gone in a month.' She sucked his earlobe between her lips and he gripped her hips harder as lust boiled in his blood, shoving aside every last trace of logic and reason.

With one arm around her waist, he scooped her forward so their hips were flush, his erection bathed in the heat between her legs. She gasped in delight, her lips returning to his, sliding and parting, her tongue a flirty little tease in his mouth, making him forget everything—his caution, her vulnerability, even the reasons she'd just reiterated why a holiday fling could work out perfectly for them both. He groaned, crushing her to his chest as their kiss deepened and quickly escalated out of control.

'I haven't been able to stop thinking about you,' she said when she let him up for air. 'About that night and believe me, I've tried. Don't make me beg.'

'No need for that,' he said, turning serious as he slid his hands inside her T-shirt, trailing his lips down the side of her neck, sucking in the heady scent of her skin. 'Man, you're sexy. I've been going out of my mind, thinking about you.' He cupped her breasts, his excitement spiking. He had a month of memories to refresh. She had a great body and this bra felt lacy. He couldn't wait to see it, then get her out of it.

'So are we done talking about it yet?' she asked, twisting his hair between her fingers then pulling back to look at him, all dewy-eyed with desire.

'Absolutely,' he said chasing her lips. 'I'm not an idiot. One holiday fling, coming up.'

She laughed, stood and pulled on his hand to urge him to his feet. 'Let's go inside.'

In his bedroom, Gigi pushed him down on the edge of the bed and re-straddled his lap, kissing him again with renewed passion that left him seeing stars. He cupped her backside in her denim shorts, then slid his hands up her ribs, taking the T-shirt she wore up and off, exposing her gorgeous breasts in their sexy black bra. He kissed her, popping the bra clasp with one hand, yanking it down so her breasts spilled free. Then he swooped down and took one nipple in his mouth because he recalled how it had made her moan the last time.

'Yes,' she said, her head falling back and her hips rocking, torturing them both with the friction. 'Why did we wait so long?'

'I have no idea.' He shifted her aside, laid her down on the bed and started to remove her shorts. 'But I'm happy to make up for lost time.'

She smiled up at him, then yanked him down on top of her. 'You don't have to keep working for it. I've already decided to sleep with you again,' she said, parting her lips enticingly so he couldn't help but kiss her.

'I'm not sure I can have sex with someone who doesn't even like me and thinks I'm a jerk,' he teased, cupping her breast and rubbing the nipple erect so she moaned through her smile.

'You've grown on me a bit, too,' she said on a gasp.

Then they both turned serious. While their tongues duelled, Dante slipped his hand inside her underwear, finding her wet for him, probing her slickness, stroking her clit so she parted her thighs and tugged frenziedly at his shirt. He helped, tossing it to the floor, shoving off his shorts and boxers, then scooping off her underwear so they were finally naked.

'You are so sexy,' he said, taking a moment to stare at her body. His heart pounded hard with excitement, made stronger by the wait and the knowledge that he and Gigi just clicked in bed like a match to a box of fireworks. Her ex was an idiot. Gigi was smart and caring and passionate and so gorgeous, he was struggling to breathe. But that guy's loss was Dante's gain. He'd make sure that no matter how she'd begun this day that should have been her wedding day, she'd fall asleep with a smile on her face.

Tugging him down on top of her once more, so they were chest to chest, skin to skin, their hearts banging together, she speared her fingers into his hair and kissed him, wrapping her legs around his hips.

He burned everywhere their skin touched, need pounding through him, hot and insistent.

'I've thought about this every day since that night in the hotel,' he said, trailing kisses down her neck, sucking first one and then the other nipple.

'That was a pretty spectacular night,' she said, dragging her fingernails down his back, reaching between them to stroke his erection.

'Then let's make tonight better,' he said, shifting to slide his lips down her abdomen, finishing between her legs, smiling when she moaned his name and shoved frantic fingers through his hair. Having waited this long, Dante had no intention of rushing this.

'Yes,' she moaned, as he pleasured her with his mouth, looking up to see her watching, her expression slack with desire.

His heart soared in his chest. That he could put that dreamy, lust-drunk look on her face, today of all days, after what she'd been through, made it worth every second of the wait. He wanted to rock her world, banish the thought of any other guy from her mind, obliterate the bad memories with pleasure.

Keeping the strokes of his tongue rhythmic, he pushed a finger inside her, working her closer and closer until she cried out his name, her orgasm rippling through her core in wave after wave until she was spent.

'Oh, wow…' she said, panting, pulling him back down on top of her.

He grabbed a condom from the nightstand and quickly covered himself, leaning in to kiss her because suddenly, he couldn't seem to be close enough.

'He's an idiot,' he said, his voice strangled as he rested on his elbows and held her eye contact. 'I hope you know that you deserve so much better.'

Then before she could remember the other man who'd betrayed her and made her doubt herself, he covered her mouth with his, parted her thighs with his knees and pushed inside her, gritting his teeth to stem the wave of pleasure.

She moaned into their kiss, crossing her ankles in the small of his back. Dante flexed his hips, pushed deeper, his possession primal, as if he wanted to be the only man she thought about from now on. But that was just great sex talking. Their connection was superhot. Even hotter than the first night, because now they knew each other, had formed an easy friendship, a supportive working relationship all topped off with intensifying chemistry.

Dante reared back to look down at her, sliding his fingers between hers and pressing her hands into the mattress as he rocked into her, taking his time to drive them closer and closer to the edge.

'You're beautiful,' he said, watching as pleasure streaked across her face, her lips parting, her breaths snatching once more.

'Dante,' she moaned. 'Kiss me.'

Releasing her hands, he scooped his arms around her waist and crushed her close, raising one of her thighs over his hip, kissing her again as desire for her overwhelmed him and he acted purely on instinct, wanting this moment to last forever.

'Stay with me,' he panted, cupping her breast and teasing the nipple, dragging a series of breathy moans from her that he swallowed up with his deep kisses. He slipped his hand between her legs and stroked her clit, encouraged by her grip on his shoulders and the way her mouth clung to his with increasing desperation as if she was close again.

'Dante,' she gasped and he picked up the pace, braced on his forearm, his lips brushing hers in increasingly erratic kisses.

With a final groan from him and a broken cry from her, they climaxed together, his body racked with spasms as he bucked and crushed her close, chasing every last second of the high, the moment so perfect, he feared he might grow addicted to sex with Gigi. After all, if the first time had been unforgettable, how would he get over this time?

'Oh, wow,' she said, still holding on to him for dear life. 'You are seriously good at that.'

Her chuckle brought a lump to his throat as he came down from the high. He'd done it, he'd taken her awful day and put a beautiful smile back on her face. Only where he should feel elated, a niggle of doubt pinched his ribs. It was a good thing she'd be leaving Sydney in a month and there'd be no time to become addicted. He didn't do long-term and the last thing he wanted was to hurt her after what she'd been through.

Groggily, he raised his face from the crook of her neck and pressed a soft kiss to her lips. 'It's all your fault. You're too sexy.' He smiled and she laughed, touching his face, pressing her lips to his.

'Want to do it again?' she said, her panting breaths drawing his attention to her lovely lips and her pert breasts, making him almost forget his own name and that he'd vowed, only seconds ago, not to get hooked.

'Absolutely,' he said rolling onto his back and taking her with him so she was sprawled on top. 'This time you drive.'

He crossed his hands behind his head and grinned up at her, their playfulness settling any residual doubts he might have that this would creep towards something serious. Gigi wasn't stupid. She'd never fall for a man like him.

'No way,' she said, straddling his hips and leaning down to kiss him around her smile. 'You still have to work for it.'

'Okay. If you insist,' he said, wrapping his arms around her and tugging her back down to his side. 'Give me five minutes.'

Her throaty laughter and the way she wrapped her arms around his neck and tangled her legs with his made his heart kick at his ribs.

CHAPTER SEVEN

THE NEXT DAY at work, Gigi couldn't seem to wipe the dreamy smile off her face. Every time she tried, some memory—laughing at nothing with Dante, kissing Dante until her lips were chapped, moaning Dante's name as he thrust her towards another orgasm—would plaster it back there.

That was how Katie found her staring into space moments later.

'Incarcerated inguinal hernia in bay two for you.' Katie handed Gigi the GP referral of her next patient, a curious but knowing smile on her lips as if she could read the contents of Gigi's mind.

'Thanks,' Gigi said, trying to keep her face straight and not wreathed in a satiated smile. Why had she waited so long? Dante was the perfect candidate for a holiday fling and Gigi had to return to London in four weeks, so there was no chance he'd be freaked out that she'd want more.

'What's up with you?' Katie asked as Gigi quickly scanned the referral letter. 'You're acting weird. You haven't won the lottery, have you?'

'Nothing and no,' Gigi said. 'I just had a good run this morning before work. I'm still a little high from the endorphins.'

Of course she was also still high from spending the night in Dante's bed. She'd thoroughly banished any lingering memories of her hateful ex and what should have been her wedding day with the kind of sheet-clawing all-night sex-a-thon that would almost certainly ruin her for any future relationship. Then, energised in spite of only three hours' sleep, they'd gone for an early run together before work and grabbed takeaway coffee and croissants on the way home.

'Dante is the surgeon on call today,' Katie said, shooting her a disbelieving look. 'In case you need him.'

Katie drifted off, leaving Gigi to find her patient, an elderly man in his seventies.

'Mr Taylor, I'm Dr Lane, one of the emergency doctors. I need to ask you some questions.'

The man nodded and Gigi took a quick clinical history, learning that he'd had a lump in his groin for many years, but during the past couple of days it had become tender and swollen.

'Any vomiting?' she asked, noting his pulse, blood pressure, respiratory rate and that he had a fever of thirty-nine degrees.

'Yes,' Mr Taylor said. 'A couple of times.'

'I need to examine you if that's okay?' Gigi asked, already suspecting that the hernia might have strangled a segment of bowel, which starved of its blood supply might be necrotic and would need to be removed.

With her examination complete, she took some blood and ducked out to call Dante. Katie was at the nurses' station where Gigi paused to label the blood vials for the lab. 'Is he already here?' she asked about Dante.

Katie nodded. 'He's just with another admission,' she said, 'And Mr Taylor's daughter is on her way in.'

'Thanks,' Gigi said, looking up as Dante appeared. Suddenly the emergency department seemed short of air and Gigi felt naked, as if every one of her colleagues would know what they'd done last night.

'Hi,' she said in an embarrassingly breathy voice. 'I was just about to call you.'

He nodded, a hint of a heated smile in his eyes. 'What have you got for me?'

Gigi swallowed, pulling herself together. 'A seventy-seven-year-old man with an incarcerated strangulated inguinal hernia and peritonitis,' Gigi said, focussing on her case and not how pleased she was to see Dante after everything they'd shared yesterday.

'Any medical conditions?' he asked, taking a look at the patient's notes over her shoulder.

'Yes,' Gigi said, her concerns for Mr Taylor building. 'He has type two diabetes and ischaemic heart disease.'

Dante sucked air through his teeth, presumably because the man's comorbidities presented an added risk for surgery. 'Let's get the anaesthetist down to assess his fitness for surgery,' Dante said to Katie, who nodded and went into the office to make the call.

'Shall we see Mr Taylor together?' he asked Gigi and they headed for their patient side by side.

With Dante's examination complete, he glanced her way with concern. 'I agree with your diagnosis,' he said. 'Have you prescribed antibiotics?'

'Yes, Katie is organising those now,' she said, sharing his concerns for the patient. A strangulated hernia was a surgical emergency that required an operation, but this patient was frail and with his additional medical conditions, not a great candidate for surgery under normal circumstances.

'We think you need an operation to sort out this hernia, Mr Taylor,' Dante explained. 'Have you had a general anaesthetic before?'

The patient nodded and told Dante the same thing he'd told Gigi, that he'd had his wisdom teeth extracted in his twenties.

'I'm going to organise an ultrasound scan,' Dante went on, 'and an X-ray of your abdomen, then I'll be back to talk to you and your daughter, who I believe is on her way.'

Outside the bay, Dante drew Gigi aside and lowered his voice. 'He doesn't look very fit and active,' he said with a small frown. 'We'll see what the anaesthetist says, but I probably don't need to tell you that he's a high-risk candidate for a general anaesthetic.'

'I know,' Gigi said, nodding. 'But what choice do we have?'

Dante scrubbed a hand through his hair, already looking a little fatigued. 'I'll admit him to the surgical ward and review him with the test results. I'll let you know how it goes.'

'Okay, thanks. I'd really appreciate that.' Gigi winced, feeling a little guilty that he might not have slept as soundly as usual with her in his bed. 'I hope your on-call isn't too horrible.'

'I'll cope.' He smiled. 'I'm looking forward to a surf this weekend. Can I tempt you to join me?'

'You can.' At this point he could tempt her to anything, although she couldn't get carried away by great sex and the kind of once in a lifetime holiday fling she'd most likely remember on her deathbed.

Then with a confident and playful flash of his killer smile, he left her to intercept the on-call anaesthetist who'd just arrived, no doubt catching him up to speed on their high-risk patient.

That Saturday, Gigi placed her surfboard on the sand next to Dante's, her arms and legs trembling with the fatigue of hauling her body onto the board time and time again while being buffeted by the sea's currents and waves. And maybe still a little jelly-filled from the early-morning sex.

'That was so hard,' she said, laughing and shoving wet ropes of hair from her face, which despite the cold was wreathed in smiles. 'How dare you make it look so easy.'

She wrapped her arms around his neck and gave him a salty kiss that made her belly flutter. They'd driven to Bondi, the iconic white sand beach popular with surfers, early that morning and planned to call on Gigi's aunt Naomi before heading home.

Dante scooped his arm around her waist, bringing her lips back to his in a swoon-worthy kiss that made her instantly warm all over. Even wearing a full body wetsuit, he was ridiculously handsome. And good at *everything*.

'I have been doing it since I was fourteen,' he said with a smile that gave her warm gooey happiness in the pit of her stomach. 'I have an unfair advantage.'

Still attached to her surfboard by the ankle leash, she leaned into him, slipping her arms around his waist, awash with good vibe emotions.

'Had enough for one day?' he asked her, tugging her down to sit on the sand between their boards to undo their ankle straps. 'Wanna grab coffee from the Beach Shack?' He jerked his head towards the road. 'Don't worry, it's not what the name implies. It actually serves really good coffee and all the café usuals including the best chocolate brownies you'll ever taste.'

Gigi smiled. 'I'm definitely up for coffee and a brownie,' she said. 'Although I could watch you surf all day, I'm not sure my legs can even carry me back to the car.'

'I'll carry you,' he said, slinging his arm around her shoulders and pressing a kiss to her temple while they watched the world go by for a few contented minutes.

Gigi leaned her head on his shoulder and released an endorphin-fuelled happy sigh. Bondi was everything she'd imagined—a perfect crescent of golden beach, sparkling blue ocean and people enjoying another gloriously sunny Sydney day, walking, jogging and swimming, and families playing in the sand.

'Thanks for bringing me here,' she said. 'I know your time is precious at the moment what with your exams coming up, but I really appreciate having such a great surf instructor.' That she could enjoy this moment with Dante, who also happened to be the lover of all her wildest dreams, left her more content than she'd been in months. Last night, after he'd crashed for a few hours' sleep following his on-call, he'd knocked at her door. They'd had frantic sex on the sofa of her apartment, desperate for each other as if they'd been apart for months, not the twenty-four hours of reality.

Gigi hid another sigh at how addictive this fling had turned. 'I'm starving,' she said, looking up at him.

'Me too,' Dante said, sliding his palm against hers, their fingers intertwined as they clambered to their feet. 'Breakfast feels like a long time ago.' He tilted up her chin and gave her a heated stare before he pressed his lips to hers. Of course they'd only managed a slice of toast before heading back to bed for deliciously slow morning sex.

When he pulled back with a knowing smile, Gigi shuddered. This was the perfect distraction she'd dreamed of when she'd left London. Her past, the uncertain future of where to work when she returned to best avoid her ex and her ex-friend who were also both doctors in the city, having to make new friends because she would never forgive Fiona and they'd shared a social crowd.

'Let's go,' Dante said, leaning down to kiss her again as if he couldn't get enough, and then laughed.

Grinning at each other, they'd just gathered up their surfboards when Dante glanced down to the other end of the beach and froze. Gigi looked up to see one of the surf lifesavers tear down the beach from their watchtower and run towards the swimming flags clutching her bright yellow Rescue Tube.

'Someone's in trouble,' Dante said, squeezing her hand tighter as the lifesaver waded into the shallows then dived into the surf and swam towards a group out in deeper water who appeared to be making their way ashore. 'There are rips here,' he added. 'You should always swim between the flags on the beach.'

'Let's go see if they need help.' Dante dropped his board and took off running with Gigi not far behind. By the time they'd made it to the other end of the beach, the casualty, a man who appeared in his forties, had been dragged from the water and was lying unresponsive on the sand.

'We're doctors,' Dante said, sliding to his knees beside the pale and unconscious swimmer. Gigi knelt opposite as they both checked for a pulse and signs of breathing.

'He's in cardiac arrest,' Gigi said, tilting the man's head back and delivering five rescue breaths via mouth-to-mouth.

While the second surf lifesaver arrived out of breath but with a resuscitation mask, Dante positioned his hands over the man's sternum for cardiac compressions, counting aloud to thirty as he compressed the chest. When he'd finished, Gigi gave another two breaths, this time through the mask.

'Has someone called the ambulance?' Gigi asked in the pause while Dante counted out another thirty chest compressions. The surf livesavers had also brought blankets and windbreakers to screen off the emergency from the other beachgoers.

'On their way,' one of them said, glancing up the beach to the nearest road.

She and Dante continued CPR, pausing regularly to quickly check for a pulse or signs of spontaneous breathing to no avail. By the time the paramedics arrived with oxygen and a defibrillator, she, Dante and the surf lifesavers were exhausted from taking turns with CPR and almost resigned to the fact that the poor man wasn't going to make it.

The paramedics relieved Gigi and Dante from CPR and then shocked the patient's heart with the defibrillator. She and Dante watched, feeling helpless when the patient remained in cardiac arrest, despite everyone's best efforts. Dante wrapped his arm around Gigi's shoulders, his breathing hard after all the exertion, his grip comforting but tight, as if he needed her by his side as much as she needed him to hold her.

'Try again,' he urged the paramedics, a deep frown of concern slashing his brows.

'They're doing everything right,' she said quietly, watching the paramedics follow the CPR protocol. But she understood Dante's desperation, the growing sense of futility making her shiver uncontrollably as if she was back in icy cold water.

'It's been forty minutes,' she said eventually, the atmosphere from the gathered rescuers turning even more sombre.

Glancing around as if he'd just become aware of the people on the beach staring, Dante snapped out of his concentration. 'Let's transport him to the ambulance. We're attracting a crowd of onlookers.'

Together, the six of them lifted the man onto a stretcher, continuing the CPR as best they could as they moved him to the ambulance. The last thing they needed was the curious bystanders filming events on their phones.

Inside the back of the ambulance, the paramedic continued with CPR, while the second jumped into the driving seat and turned on the flashing lights, while she and Dante held each other, feeling helpless.

It was only when the vehicle pulled away, sirens wailing that Gigi finally turned into Dante's arms for comfort, burying her face against his neck and holding him just as tightly as he held her, their lovely morning at the beach turning to what they both clearly expected to be a far too common tragedy.

CHAPTER EIGHT

BACK AT HOME, Dante stepped under the shower with Gigi, pulling her into his arms once more. 'It's okay. We did everything we could,' he said, pushing her hair back from her face and pressing his lips to hers. 'Sometimes, it's just not enough.'

He hated that her first taste of surfing had ended in a senseless tragedy. Gigi had been understandably quiet on the drive home. They'd called the hospital as soon as they'd arrived back from the beach and learned that the drowning victim hadn't made it.

'I know...' She gripped his waist tighter, her head resting on his chest as another wave of protectiveness swamped him. 'I just keep wondering about his family. If he has children. Imagine your loved one goes for a swim on a beautiful sunny day and never returns.'

'I know,' Dante said, his mouth against her forehead. He'd never witnessed a drowning before and it killed him that he and Gigi hadn't been able to revive the man. 'I keep thinking what else we could have done, even though I know I'm just beating myself up.'

She looked up at him, pressed her lips to his and sighed. 'Don't do that,' she said. 'You're right. We tried everything.'

He nodded, realising that they were both likely in shock, even though their work meant they'd sadly experienced losing patients many times before. But this was different.

They'd been off duty and enjoying the beach so it had been totally unexpected.

'I'm so glad you were there,' he said, his emotions surprisingly close to the surface. 'I would have hated to go through that alone.'

'I'm glad you were there too.' She tilted her face up to his and he brushed his lips over hers, unable to stop touching her and kissing her.

'Turn around,' he said, reaching for the shampoo. 'Let me wash your hair.' He lathered up her hair and then his own, washing out the sand and salt before filling her hands with shower gel, soaping her back and shoulders and them himself before ducking under the spray to rinse off.

'Take your time,' he said, passing her the body wash. 'I'm going to make you a cup of tea.'

He stepped out of the shower cubicle and towel dried his hair before wrapping another towel around his waist and leaving the bathroom. Gigi had such a big heart, was such a dedicated and talented doctor. She deserved so much more than the betrayal and deception she'd experienced. She deserved a man who would worship her, celebrate life's highs and commiserate the lows with her. But his thoughts only left him strangely restless, maybe because for now, all she had for comfort was him.

She emerged five minutes later wearing one of his T-shirts, her hair blown dry, her big eyes watchful and haunted. Dante swallowed, aching to have her back in his arms, where somehow, the sadness of what had happened at the beach lessened.

'Will you stay tonight?' he asked, taking her hand. 'I think you should. For the shock. I don't want you to be alone.'

And he had a sneaking suspicion that without her by his side, he might also toss and turn the night away.

'Okay.' She followed him into the bedroom where he sat her tea on the bedside table, pulled on a pair of boxer shorts and climbed under the covers next to her, drawing her into his side with his arm around her shoulders.

Gigi snuggled into his side, her head resting on his chest as he stroked her arm. 'Thanks,' she whispered. 'For the surfing lesson and for the tea.'

'You're welcome.' He pressed a kiss to the top of her head and clutched her closer, needing her every bit as much as she seemed to need him. 'Not quite the day I had planned...'

Left reeling by how quickly tragedy could strike, he felt closer to Gigi than ever. Yes, this was only temporary, a holiday fling and nothing serious, but what should have been a fun day surfing had turned heartbreaking in the blink of an eye. It made you think and most likely explained his strange emotional turmoil.

'I had a really good time until...you know,' she said, and he nodded in agreement.

'Thanks for staying the night,' he added. 'I probably wouldn't be able to sleep if you weren't here.'

'You're welcome,' she said, snuggling closer.

As they drifted asleep wrapped in each other's arms, Dante's final thought was how quickly they'd grown closer than he could ever have imagined. He hadn't changed his mind about relationships, but Gigi Lane was certainly the whole package—smart, sexy, fun and caring. Until she left for London in a month, he would need to be careful to keep their expectations aligned. After all, she'd been hurt enough. Dante didn't want to be the one to cause her any more pain.

The hospital fundraising fun run the following weekend began at the harbourside Pirrama Park in the inner-city suburb of Pyrmont. From the start line, the six-kilometre route followed the waterfront south to The Rocks, the historic district settled by early European convicts, and then on to the Opera House, finally finishing in Hyde Park, Australia's oldest park.

On the final stretch, as they ran side by side, Dante threw his arm around Gigi's shoulders so they could finish the race together. She smiled up at him and they held out their flag capes in celebration, hers the Union Jack and his, the Aussie flag.

'We did it.' Gigi grinned up at him as they crossed the finish line to cheers and clapping from the crowd.

Abuzz with endorphins and after their emotional week following the drowning at Bondi, Dante pulled her close and pressed a triumphant kiss to her lips. 'Congratulations. You're practically Australian now that you've run your first city race.'

She laughed and took a bottle of water from one of the volunteers, passing him another as they joined the crowds cheering for the competitors that were finishing behind them, which included a man dressed in a kangaroo suit who must have been sweltering and two runners in nursing uniforms pushing a full-sized hospital bed complete with a fake patient.

'I'm going to sit down,' Gigi said, walking a short distance away to sit in the shade of a tree from where she could still watch the race.

Dante flopped down beside her, chugging a drink to rehydrate. That they'd done this together delivered ten times the satisfaction than if he'd run alone. Despite his caution, they'd spent every night together this past week. Dante would get home from work, shower and hit the books for a few hours. Then either she'd come up to his place or he'd go to hers, where they'd spend the night together, rise early for a run and head into work. Gigi had kept her side of the bargain, embracing their holiday fling, throwing herself into enjoying her time in Sydney, while also giving him space to study.

Was it any wonder he was addicted to such good sex, good

laughs and good company? Every time he started to feel doubts, he reminded himself that she'd be leaving in another three weeks. Unless he decided to once more visit London, they likely wouldn't see each other ever again.

Ignoring the momentary flicker of disappointment in the pit of his stomach, Dante watched Gigi untie the flag from around her neck and fan her face.

'Are you okay?' he asked, noting that she'd gone a little pale.

'I just feel a bit light-headed,' she said, putting a hand to her forehead. 'I didn't eat breakfast because I didn't want to get a stitch.'

Dante frowned and sat up. Temperatures were going to reach a high of thirty-five degrees today, hence the early start time for the fun run.

'Maybe you're not used to the heat,' he said. 'Have another drink.' Concerned, he glanced around for the first aid tent that was usually present at these events, spying it a short distance away behind the finish line.

Gigi took a hesitant swallow, her hand trembling. 'Oh... I feel faint.'

Before he could help, she lay back on the grass and propped her feet up against the trunk of the tree, her colour turning ghostly grey.

'Gigi. Talk to me,' Dante said, trying not to panic. He felt for her pulse, which was reassuringly strong but fast. 'Are you okay?'

'Just dizzy,' she said, her fingers squeezing his. 'I'll be okay. Need some sugar.'

Reluctant to leave her, Dante called over a volunteer. 'Do you have any sports drinks or bananas? My friend is feeling light-headed.' Why hadn't he thought to bring something?

The woman nodded and rushed off, returning moments later with a carton of coconut water and a banana.

'Can I help you to the first aid tent?' the woman asked as Gigi raised her head and took a few sips of the drink through the straw.

'No... I'll be fine,' she said to the woman, trying to sit up. 'I feel better already.'

'Don't get up too soon,' Dante said, his protective urges and concern flaring. After their aborted surf date last weekend, he'd been determined that she enjoy today's fun run.

The volunteer watched Gigi peel the banana then traipsed away. But Dante wanted to be sure. 'When you've finished eating that, we're going to the first aid tent,' he said, in a voice he hoped would cut off any argument. 'You're very pale, so no arguments. Besides, I'm pretty sure Katie is on duty there and she'll kill me if she finds out this happened and I didn't bring you in to be checked.'

'All right.' Gigi sighed reluctantly, and took another bite of banana.

After another five minutes and with her colour improving, Dante helped Gigi to her feet. 'Okay?' he asked. 'Just take it slowly.'

She nodded, taking his hand. Inside the first aid tent, the volunteer first aiders were twiddling their thumbs. With the exception of one man who'd obviously slipped and grazed his knee, the tent was empty of casualties.

'What happened?' Katie asked when she saw them, helping Gigi onto a stretcher and urging her to lie down.

'She just got light-headed after the race,' Dante explained, never more relieved to see the competent, no-nonsense nurse he respected.

'I'm fine,' Gigi said as Katie applied a blood pressure cuff to her arm and pressed the button to inflate it.

'Let me be the judge of that,' Katie said, shooting Dante a

suspicious and accusing look as she placed a pulse oximeter on Gigi's finger.

Dante held his ground. Katie could shoot as many accusing looks his way as she liked as long as she made Gigi better.

'What can I do?' he said, shuffling his feet and feeling like a spare part, a role that didn't sit well with the surgeon in him.

'Nothing,' Katie said. 'Other than maybe call a taxi. I don't think she should walk home in this heat.'

'We drove to the start line,' Dante said. 'I'll go and get the car, bring it closer to the park.'

'I'm fine now,' Gigi said to deaf ears as both he and Katie ignored her pleas.

At least they were of one mind when it came to checking Gigi over thoroughly.

Katie nodded to Dante as if Gigi hadn't spoken. 'If you come down College Street, someone can raise the barrier for you so you can bring the car right up to the tent.'

Dante hesitated, his hand still holding Gigi's, reluctant to leave her alone when she wasn't feeling well. 'What's her blood pressure doing?' he asked Katie because he couldn't switch off the doctor mode, his eyes on his running partner.

'One-ten over seventy,' Katie reported.

'That's normal for me,' Gigi interjected, looking tired but with more colour in her cheeks. She even looked mildly annoyed that they were treating her like a patient, which was a good sign that she was feeling better.

'Go,' Katie told him. 'She's in good hands here and the St John's ambulance is just outside.'

Gigi nodded and squeezed his fingers. 'I'll be fine. Come back soon, but don't speed, obviously.'

'I won't.' He hesitated again, glancing Katie's way, uncertain if Gigi would want anyone at work to know they were sleeping together. Then he made up his mind and pressed a swift kiss to her lips before rushing off at a run to retrace the route back to where they'd left the car.

CHAPTER NINE

'How are you feeling now?' Katie asked as another volunteer handed Gigi a takeaway tea and a chocolate biscuit.

'Fine. Just a bit embarrassed. I don't know what came over me.' Gigi dutifully ate the biscuit and sipped the tea under Katie's shrewd observation. 'Sorry for all the fuss.'

'No need to apologise,' Katie said, taking a seat next to Gigi. 'This is exactly why the first aid tent is here.'

'I didn't have breakfast,' Gigi admitted. 'Rookie mistake.'

Katie eyed her thoughtfully. 'I have to ask you—any medical conditions that might have caused the dizzy spell?'

Gigi shook her head. 'I'm as fit as a flea. Although I normally run in the evenings when the heat has gone out of the day. Maybe I was just a bit dehydrated.'

Katie looked uncomfortable, glancing at the door of the tent through which Dante had disappeared five minutes before and then meeting Gigi's stare once more. 'Any chance you could be…pregnant?'

Gigi scoffed, doing a quick calculation of the date of her last period, which had been before she'd left London. 'No… I've never been regular but… No,' she said more forcefully, trying not to panic. She'd gone off the pill after dumping Will, but she and Dante had used condoms. Lots of condoms.

'It might be worth doing a test, just in case,' Katie said quietly in her compassionate nurse voice, leaving Gigi more uncertain than ever. 'I only raise it as a possibility because—'

'Because he kissed me,' Gigi interrupted, ducking her head. The other woman had warned Gigi about falling for Dante's charms on her first day at SHH. Of course Katie hadn't known then that Gigi had already slept with him a month before.

Fear squeezed her chest. What if she was pregnant? What would she do? Dante would freak out, and his life was here, hers back in London. She had three weeks left on her locum contract and then her temporary work visa would expire.

'Well, that,' Katie said, her voice and stare sympathetic, 'but also, I'm pregnant, too. Twelve weeks. And I had a dizzy spell the other day.'

'Congratulations.' She tried to smile, pleased for her friend. 'I'm so happy for you, but... *I'm* not pregnant.' Her denial carried less conviction, her doubts growing by the second, so she broke out in a cold sweat.

Katie nodded and gave Gigi a sad smile. 'Okay.'

Now that it had been raised as a possibility, it was all she could think about. Panicked, Gigi sat up and reached for Katie's arm. 'What if I am pregnant?' They'd become friends and Katie was wise and practical and caring.

'No need to panic,' Katie soothed so Gigi realised that's exactly what she'd been doing. 'But you should take a test as soon as possible so you'll at least know one way or the other.'

Gigi shook her head, desperate to rewind time and make this conversation disappear. If she was pregnant it was almost laughably poor timing. 'You don't understand,' she said. 'It's just a holiday fling with Dante. We're not in a relationship.' He didn't even believe in those because that kind of commitment made him feel caged. She couldn't have a baby with a man like that. There was no commitment bigger than a child. He was going to freak out big time and she was pretty close, too.

'My life is in London,' she went on in an almost pleading voice, as if Katie could make it all right. 'My work visa expires in three weeks so I have to go back. And Dante doesn't even believe in commitment...' She dropped her head into her hand. 'This can't be happening. It can't be happening...'

'It's going to be fine,' Katie said, urging Gigi to take another sip of her tea. 'I know we tease him for being a ladies' man, but he's a decent man too. You'll figure the logistics out between you if it comes to that, but don't go jumping the gun. Just take a test.'

Gigi nodded, clinging to the unlikely possibility of her being pregnant by her fingernails. 'I'll stop at the pharmacy on the way home and buy a test, take it as soon as I get back.'

'Finish your tea,' Katie said. 'I'll go see if we have a test in the supplies here.' She bustled off, leaving Gigi to sit and stew and play out every likely scenario in her head so she could prepare for whatever happened.

She just hoped she was worrying for nothing.

Later that afternoon, Dante paced his living room, waiting for Gigi to appear from the bathroom. The minute he'd returned to the first aid tent to take her home, he'd known from the look on her face that something was off. To her credit, she'd told him Katie's suspicions and the reason why she was acting weird the minute they were alone. Trying to stay calm, Dante had agreed that she should take the test as soon as they got home, certain they were worrying over nothing. After all, they'd used protection.

'It says to wait one to three minutes,' Gigi said, as she emerged from the bathroom. She placed the test flat on the coffee table, her wary stare meeting his so he witnessed her panic. 'What if it's positive?'

Dante breathed through the fear rising in his chest and

pasted on his doctor's face. 'Let's take one thing at a time,' he said, taking her hand—although he wasn't sure if it was for her comfort or his—and pulling her down onto the sofa.

'I feel sick,' Gigi said, her stare flitting to the plastic stick every few seconds as if she could will it to disappear or sound out a negative alert at any moment.

'Can I get you anything while we wait?' he asked, his mind whirring at a hundred miles an hour and none of it making any sense. 'Tea, a snack?'

But his surgical training kicked in. Most dilemmas had a solution as long as you stayed calm and in control.

'No... It's just nerves, I think.' She dropped her head into her hands. 'I can't believe this is happening.'

'Hey, it's okay.' Dante stroked her back. 'Everything will be okay.' He had no idea how but if the test came back positive, they'd have to make it okay. After all, they were both adults with good jobs. They wouldn't be the first people on the planet to conceive a baby after a one-night stand, assuming that was when it had happened because Gigi had gone over her dates in the car journey home. But he'd never imagined he'd find himself in this situation.

'I can't wait any longer,' she said, abandoning her phone which still had ninety seconds to run on the timer. She stood and picked up the test stick, her back to him. Then her hand covered her mouth as she gasped.

'It's positive,' he said instinctively, shock numbing him and snatching all other thoughts from his mind. They were going to have a baby...

She turned, nodded, tears building on her lashes. 'I'm pregnant... I can't believe it...'

'Wow...' His heart thundered away with adrenaline as he stood at her side and peered at the test, which was unequivocally positive, for confirmation. But deep down in the pit of his stomach, the first flutters of cautious excitement bloomed. He'd never really thought about parenthood, determinedly focussing on his career up to now, but the very knowledge that he and Gigi had created a life changed everything and made him instantly protective of her and the tiny human she carried.

Then, as if his mind was eager to present both sides of the dilemma, the doubts rushed in. On the whole, babies were something that couples did. What if Gigi expected something of him that he wasn't able to give? His chest started to tighten, his temples pounding, that suffocation feeling he detested so much gripping him.

'Don't freak out,' Gigi said, breaking through the mist.

'I'm not, I'm just…shocked I guess.'

'That makes two of us,' she said, swallowing hard.

'Let's sit down,' he suggested, taking her hand in his as he tried to rationalise his fears. Just because they were having a baby didn't mean they had to have a romantic relationship. They could be parents but he could still keep his autonomy, his independence. And Gigi wouldn't want to rush into anything either, not after what she'd been through.

'Are you okay?' he asked, realising he was being a bit selfish thinking only how this might affect him.

Gigi opened and closed her mouth, clearly equally dumbfounded. She nodded but said, 'Why aren't you freaking out?'

'You just told me not to.' Dante shrugged, scared to vocalise all his feelings and doubts. He might not know the first thing about being a father, but he knew there was a right and a wrong way to handle this conversation and he didn't want to say anything he would later regret. And he knew one thing—if she wanted to have this baby, *his* child would grow up loved and supported by both parents. No manipulative games. No piggy in the middle. No emotional oppression or enforced loyalty.

'Also, me freaking out won't change anything,' he admitted, looking down at their hands.

'But...' She stared at him in confusion, and he cupped her face, brushing aside the lone tear from her cheek.

'It's okay,' he soothed. 'We'll figure it out. Maybe it's too soon to even talk about it today. Maybe we should take some time to come to terms with it before we get into the nitty-gritty.'

Gigi nodded, looking relieved but bewildered. Then she covered her mouth again. 'I'm going to have a baby.'

Dante smiled and nodded, his throat tight. Now that his baby existed, he absolutely wanted to be a father. To be a great father, just like his own. '*We're* having a baby,' he said softly, pressing his lips to hers. 'Congratulations.'

'You too,' she whispered, awed, her wide eyes turning into a frown. 'But how will this even work? You're Australian and I'm due back in London in three weeks. I have another locum job lined up back home, and I only came to Australia on a temporary short stay specialist work visa.'

As if he'd completely forgotten that fact, it struck him like a blow to the chest. She couldn't leave now. Not when there was so much for them to figure out. Because if Gigi left Sydney, then obviously his baby would be leaving too. How would he stay in control of everything then?

'I don't know...' he said again, feeling like a broken record as his doubts roared back to life. 'I don't have all the answers yet...'

Timing wise, this couldn't have been any worse. He had his final professional surgical exams in three weeks. He couldn't up and leave his job and relocate to London. Even if he wanted to move to London, something he'd never really considered, he'd need to pass his exams, register with the General Medical Council of the UK, take the British medical competence tests and secure a consultant surgeon job in addition to satisfying the immigration requirements. But nor did he want to be estranged from his child or thrust into some complex and depressing custody and visitation agreement with their baby being shuttled back and forth like a pawn on a chessboard.

'You're right,' she said, drawing him back to the present. 'We do need to think this all through and come up with a plan.'

Dante nodded, focussing on Gigi's immediate needs to stop the logistical implications from overwhelming him. 'Do you want me to take you to my family doctor? You can register with them temporarily. You'll need antenatal hormones, screening blood tests and a blood pressure check.'

'Yes please.' She smiled gratefully. 'I didn't even think of that.' She bit her lip, her expression hesitant. 'It must have happened that first night we met.'

'I guess.' Dante shrugged, feeling guilty although they'd been safe. 'Sorry for accidentally impregnating you.' He smiled, hoping she'd see the funny side, because he sure needed to. 'You probably got more than you bargained for from your trip to Australia.'

She smiled, swallowing hard as if putting on a brave face. 'It's not your fault, although you must have super sperm. But we're both adults and we did it together.'

He smiled too, the twist in his gut easing that they could be so mature and supportive rather than playing the blame game.

Then she turned serious. 'But I want you to know—I didn't plan this. That's not what's happening here.'

'Of course not,' he said, squeezing her hand. 'I didn't even think that for one second.' Although his self-preservation instincts had kicked in and helpfully reminded him what it felt like to be backed into a corner.

'I just...' Her eyes swam with emotion. 'I don't want you to feel trapped or ambushed. We're not in a relationship. I don't expect anything from you.'

Dante nodded, wishing her words carried the reassurance he imagined they would. 'I know. But let's talk again tomorrow.'

Gigi nodded and stood. 'I'm going to go. I need to have a shower and I need some time alone. Today has been...intense.'

'Of course,' he said, standing too. 'But please don't worry. We'll figure everything out, okay?'

'We will.' She nodded and released his hands, moving towards the door where she hesitated and glanced over her shoulder. 'Please don't freak out. We agreed it was just a holiday fling. Like you said, nothing's changed.'

Dante's pulse pounded, the full implications piling up in his mind. She was right—this situation certainly had the potential to make him feel like there was no escape, but only if he let it.

'I'll walk you down,' he said, following her to the apartment, kissing her goodnight and watching her go inside.

It was only when he was alone that he allowed the freak-out she'd predicted free. It was time to face the consequences of his actions and come up with a plan. And fast. He loved surgery because it allowed him to stay in control and be a man of action. Maybe he could apply that problem solving here. If he stayed in control as if he was in theatre, he could solve this problem, come up with a solution for his and Gigi's situation and figure out a plan for them to be parents, because no matter what, everything was about to change. And he couldn't be reactive or let those changes overwhelm him.

CHAPTER TEN

THE NEXT DAY, Gigi hung up the phone and emerged from the office in the emergency department, her feet dragging with despondency.

'Are you okay?' Katie asked, having taken one look at Gigi's expression.

Gigi nodded, still a little numb with the shock of discovering she was pregnant with Dante's baby. 'I just got off the phone with personnel,' she said. 'I was hoping to extend my locum position for a few more weeks, but they've already filled the role with someone permanent so they don't need me. And without a job I won't be eligible for an extension on my work visa.'

'I'm sorry about that.' Taking her arm, Katie ushered Gigi back inside the office and closed the door. 'But why do you want to stay longer? I thought you had another locum position lined up in London.'

'I do. Did.' Gigi nodded, the mess of her unexpected situation almost overwhelming the excitement she felt that she was going to have a baby. 'But you were right.' She sighed then smiled hesitantly. 'I am pregnant.'

Wordlessly, Katie hugged her, her smile when she pulled back full of understanding and sympathy. 'How do you feel about that?' she asked carefully.

Gigi collapsed into a chair. 'Shocked. Embarrassed. Overwhelmed,' she admitted with a wince. Then she swallowed and reached for Katie's hand, a flutter in her belly. 'And a tiny bit excited.'

Katie nodded and smiled. 'That's all understandable.' She hesitated, then asked, 'Have you told the father?'

Gigi smiled, aware that Katie was astute enough to know the truth but grateful she was also being discreet.

'Dante knows,' she said, rubbing at her temple. 'We took the test yesterday when we got back from the fun run.' Part of her wished she'd done the pregnancy test in secret, had time to come to terms with the result before telling Dante he was going to be a dad. But despite the fainting spell and Katie's intuitive premonition, Gigi had been convinced the test would be negative, which was why she'd mentioned Katie's wild theory to him.

She sighed again, exhausted from considering all the implications over and over without finding a solution. She'd come to Australia for a fresh start, to get over a failed relationship. And now she'd landed herself in an even bigger mess, pregnant by a man who had no interest in a real relationship. Carrying a baby that was half Australian. Soon to be both jobless and deported, unless she upped and went back to London as planned. She was running out of time.

'So you two are…?' Katie asked.

Gigi shook her head. 'No, we're not a couple. We both agreed it was just a holiday fling.' She met Katie's stare. 'You know what he's like. You even warned me about him. And I'm not in a relationship place either after what happened with my ex. It's a mess.' She dropped her stare to her lap.

'I'm sorry,' Katie said. 'But at least you know how you feel about the baby. That part isn't a mess. You're going to be a mother and a great one too.'

At Gigi's snort of choked laughter, Katie added, 'So what do you want to do about the rest of it?'

Gigi swallowed, confused and close to tears. 'I don't know. It's so complicated. I keep going around in circles. I guess part of me assumed Dante would freak out or be angry and would want nothing to do with the baby.'

'But he surprised you?' Katie said with a knowing look.

Gigi nodded. 'He's been really supportive. Said we should take time to come to terms with it and then discuss a plan. But in some ways, it would be easier to do this on my own. At least then I could go home without feeling guilty as if I'm kidnapping his child or denying him his role.'

'I see,' Katie said, a small frown tugging at her mouth. 'That is complicated.'

Gigi looked up, deflated. 'Looks like the decision will be taken out of my hands anyway. Without a job, I'll have no choice but to leave in three weeks. We'll have to figure everything out via email and video calls.'

'Well, at least you'll be communicating, which is the important thing, right?' Katie said, ever the optimist.

Gigi nodded and squeezed Katie's hand. 'Yeah, I guess. Thanks for listening and thanks for urging me to take a test. You're good at this nursing thing, you know.' She stood, sniffing away the sting in her eyes as she tightened her ponytail and prepared to be a competent doctor once more. 'I'd better see some patients.'

'Want me to make you a cup of tea?' Katie asked. 'I'm making myself one so it's no problem.'

'That would be amazing.' Gigi put one hand on the door handle and paused. 'But don't be too nice to me or I'm likely to cry all over you.'

'Got it,' Katie said knowingly. 'But you know where I am if you need a listening ear.'

Gigi nodded, grateful that she'd made a good friend in Sydney, but in desperate need of more than a listening ear. She needed a solution to all her problems. Instead, she opened the door, stepped out of the office and threw herself into work.

That evening, after suggesting a dinner date after work so they could talk, Dante watched Gigi take in the sight of the lit-up Harbour Bridge and Opera House by night from Ascot's, a harbourside restaurant known to have the best views in the city.

'This place is stunning,' she said, turning his way once more, a moment's excitement in her stare before the worried frown returned. 'And the food looks delicious.'

She scanned the menu, not looking up as if she was nervous. And he understood. He had no idea which way this conversation would go, but they needed to talk.

'I went to school with the chef, so I hope you're hungry,' Dante said, topping up their water glasses. 'And I thought we should talk somewhere neutral, away from work and home.'

'Of course,' she said. 'Good idea.'

'Don't look so nervous.' He reached for her hand across the table in spite of his own nerves. 'What are you going to have?'

They studied the menu and made their choices when their waiter returned. When they were alone again, Dante dived into the tricky conversation they needed to have.

'Do you want to go first,' he asked, brushing the back of her hand with his thumb, 'or shall I?'

This wasn't a situation he'd ever imagined he'd find himself in, but now that the shock had passed, now that he'd had a chance to think it all through, he was growing used to the idea of fatherhood. He'd even called his dad, John, and broken the good news.

'First, I just want to say this,' she began with a small

sigh. 'I really don't want you to feel trapped or pressured by this…situation.'

'I know. You said that before,' he pointed out, his heart rate spiking with anxiety.

She nodded and went on. 'We were both clear from the start that this wasn't a relationship, so as far as I'm concerned there are no expectations on you.'

Dante frowned, grateful they were still on the same page when it came to their feelings for each other. 'Right, it's just a fling,' he confirmed.

'You can be as involved as you like with the baby,' she continued. 'And conversely, I'll also be fine doing this alone if you feel it's…not for you.' She paused, looking less uncomfortable, as if she'd got a weight off her chest.

Dante's frown deepened as understanding struck. She expected him to walk away. To take himself out of the equation just because he'd confided in her why he avoided relationships all these years. His insides started to tremble and nausea rolled through his gut. He hadn't changed his mind about relationships, but nor did he want his kid growing up in London without him.

'This isn't a bold wallpaper choice or pumpkin-flavoured coffee, Gigi,' he said, keeping his voice impressively calm. 'This is my child.'

'I know that, but—'

'Maybe I should point out,' he interrupted, losing his grip on his logic, 'that I'd be happy raising our baby alone too, if you decide that it's *not for you*.' This was the last way he'd expected this conversation to go.

'Don't be ridiculous,' she said tugging her hand free of his. 'I didn't mean to imply that you would walk away. I just wanted to remind you that we're not in a traditionally committed relationship.'

'Thanks for the reassurance,' he said, reaching once more for her hand because it helped him to stay calm. 'But regardless of how I feel about relationships, and that hasn't changed by the way, this is an entirely different situation. I'm going to be a dad to our baby, Gigi, every bit as much as you'll be a mum.'

She blinked, nodded, glancing down. 'Of course. I'm sorry. I'm a mess. I just meant...' She sighed and met his stare once more. 'I just meant that obviously because we're not a couple and because we come from the opposite sides of the world, it's going to be complicated. I wanted you to know that it's okay not to have all the answers, because I don't either.'

Dante squeezed her fingers, a calm settling over him the way it did when he reached for a scalpel. 'I understand.'

She sighed and looked up. 'It's a bit of a mess. But as long as we're mature about it, I think we'll be okay. Anyway, so far I've done all the talking. You go.'

'I agree, it's complicated,' he said. 'And obviously the biggest issue is the geography. Also I have my final fellowship exams looming, which means while I'm not averse to relocating to be closer to you and the baby in the future, I'm not really in a position to move overseas at the moment.'

Gigi nodded. 'I totally understand,' she said, looking relieved. 'And obviously I'll call you from London, keep you up to date on the baby's progress throughout the pregnancy... We can talk as often as you want and we can visit back and forth a few times a year as annual leave allows.'

'Hold on,' Dante said, losing his grip again, 'I don't think you should rush back to London, either. There's a lot to discuss and figure out. We have to be practical. I want to be there for you both.'

Gigi gave a small frown. 'I agree but I actually called personnel this morning,' she said. 'I was hoping that I could extend my locum position for another month so we had more time before I'd have to leave. But they've already filled the position.'

'I see...' Dante said, his mind racing and his stomach in his boots. 'That does complicate things.'

Panic sliced through him like a blade. If Gigi left Sydney, the baby would leave with her. And he'd be trapped here.

'It won't be forever,' she soothed, seeing his disappointment. 'You can come to London as soon as you've passed your exams.'

He winced, pressed his thumb and forefinger to his throbbing temples, that cornered feeling roaring to life. 'But I'll miss out. On scans and the first kick and bonding with the baby.'

It wasn't fair. He deserved the chance to be a good father.

'I know...' she said, her frown deepening. 'But like it or not, I'll have to leave in three weeks. I came on a three-month visa, which expires soon. Without a job they won't extend it.'

'I understand that.' Dante's mind spun faster, in full-blown problem-solving mode. In theatre, you needed to think decisively and act fast. 'Maybe...maybe you could stay and not work,' he suggested. 'You can live at the apartment rent-free. I can support you until we figure everything out.'

Gigi shook her head. 'I can't be an illegal overstayer. I'm a doctor. I can't have any sort of record, Dante.'

'No, of course not.' He rubbed at his jaw in frustration. 'But we need more time to come up with a plan for the future that works for us both. Once my exams are out of the way, I'll be in a better position to investigate consultant jobs, whether it's here or in London. We haven't even explored the option of you staying in Sydney.' The panic grew, fluttering in his chest because he'd been over this in his head many times in the past day and wanted more than anything to be a part of this pregnancy and his child's life. He could finally imagine how his father must have felt, wanting out of a bad relationship but patching over and tolerating things so he could stay in Dante's life.

'No, but even if I wanted to stay in Australia, I can't stay indefinitely or illegally,' she said warily, looking frustrated because they were clearly going around in circles.

Dante paused, his heart beating like a jackhammer. There was one solution. A last resort. For him it went against every instinct he had and made him feel sick. But he was trapped either way. If he let Gigi walk away, he'd be denied a chance to be involved in this pregnancy.

'Of course not,' he said taking a deep breath, certain that the solution brewing in his mind was now the only way to stay in control of this situation. 'There is another way... What if we...got married,' he blurted.

Stunned, Gigi laughed, sitting back in her seat. 'Ha-ha... very funny.' She took a sip of water and returned her glass to the table. When her stare returned to his, she froze. 'You can't be serious?'

'I know,' he said with a wince, because this had the potential to be his worst nightmare come true. 'Coming from me it's laughable. But think about it... It would be purely logistical. It will buy us some time. You can stay here in Australia as long as you like. And I can focus on passing my professional exams without missing out on the pregnancy.'

Gigi shook her head dismissively. 'It's the craziest idea I've ever heard. You don't even believe in marriage. You think it's an *"outdated institution used to control or dominate or entrap"*. This is ridiculous.'

'And I stand by my thoughts on marriage in the traditional sense,' Dante said, his panic intensifying because he was losing what little control he had. 'But we're not in love. We're not even in a committed relationship. We each have our own very valid reasons for avoiding those. But unlike when we first started living together and working together, we can at least stand to be in the same room as each other now. Which is why this could be a perfect practical, short-term solution.'

Yes, the idea of a real marriage filled him with dread. But this wouldn't be a real marriage.

When she simply stared, her mouth hanging open, he went on. 'Look, nothing has to change this way. We keep emotions out of it. Carry on the way we are until after my exams. But this buys us some time to figure out a long-term plan like where we're going to live and how we're going to share custody. By the time the baby arrives, we'll have everything figured out. Then we can get a quickie divorce. Problem solved.'

Warming to the idea, he added, 'If you detach emotions from the act of marriage the way people have done for centuries to unite families or sweeten deals, it makes so much sense.'

'Does it?' she asked, incredulous. 'Because from where I'm sitting it sounds ludicrous.'

'It makes the most sense to me.' Dante sighed, his breathing tight at the thought of her taking their baby to London before they'd come to some sort of agreement. If that happened, he'd be just like his father had been, cornered emotionally by a situation out of his control.

'You can stay in the apartment,' he urged, desperate now for her to see the benefits of this unorthodox suggestion, 'As my spouse, you can access my private health insurance for antenatal care, even the delivery if you're still in Australia by then. And perhaps the most important reason is you won't be deported in three weeks, which is by the way when I have the most important exams of my career. I've worked long and hard to get where I am, as I'm sure you have too. I can't afford to be…distracted.'

She stared for a moment, as if debating what to say. 'And what about the sex?' she asked finally, her lips pursing.

'That's irrelevant,' he said, the panicked lurch of his heart easing for the first time. 'A totally separate issue.'

'So as your *wife,*' she made finger quotes, 'I won't be expected to sleep in your bed?'

'Of course not, unless you want to,' he said. 'I'm not suggesting we have a real marriage, but nor am I taking sex off the table. I don't think our chemistry is going anywhere, at least not for me. If you want to think about our arrangement differently, think of it as an extended holiday fling. A marriage in name only.'

'An extended holiday fling until we figure out a plan and then get divorced?' she asked, clearly still sceptical if her tone of voice was any indication.

'Exactly.' He gave a hesitant smile, hopeful that with maturity and mutual respect they could make this work in the short term. 'I know people would say it's not the best reason to get married, but it's probably the only reason that would ever appeal to me. It's not like we planned or expected any of this. Unusual circumstances call for unusual measures.'

'It's still ludicrous,' she said, shaking her head.

Dante dragged in a deep breath, his stomach sinking once more. 'I can see why you'd think that given how we met and what I've shared with you about my parents, but I don't have any other answers, Gigi.'

'Neither do I,' she said in a defeated whisper.

'This is the last resort, the only way for me to be there for you and for my baby until we have the definitive practicalities of custody and visitations, of childcare and child support worked out.' He swallowed, his throat suddenly bone-dry. 'The alternative is that you leave in three weeks and go back to London alone where I can't help you or support you or be a part of this pregnancy in any way. And that just feels wrong and, quite frankly, unfair.'

'I never thought of it that way...' she said, still looking conflicted.

Dante squeezed her hand, because they were in this together. 'I'm all ears if you have any better suggestions...'

She frowned deeper but stayed silent.

'Why don't we both think about it some more. We don't have to decide right now.'

She nodded.

'All I ask is that you give me a chance to be a dad,' he said, his chest burning because he felt completely at her mercy. 'Promise me you'll think about my suggestion.'

Gigi nodded, her hand tightening in his. 'Okay. I will.'

The waiter chose that moment to return with their starters. Gigi pressed her lips together and stared at him across the table. When they were alone again, Dante reached for her hand once more.

'Thanks. Now, let's enjoy our dinner.' He tried to smile, hoping that she'd quickly come around to his way of thinking. Because short of magically rewinding time and having never met and hooked up in the first place, they were running out of viable options.

CHAPTER ELEVEN

'THANKS FOR A lovely meal,' Gigi said as Dante pulled into the driveway and parked the car. 'It was delicious, as promised.'

They'd each kept their word and changed the subject for the rest of the night. Dante had even stuck to water with dinner to keep her company. He'd spent the evening being his funny, charming, considerate self, and despite having a good time and enjoying a delicious dinner, Gigi wanted to sob or scream. How could he drop the bombshell that they should marry and then act so…normal when she couldn't seem to move past how ridiculous it was? Maybe if they were in a real relationship it would be different, or maybe that would make his solution seem worse… She was so confused.

'You're welcome,' Dante said. 'I'm glad you could meet Glen. He's a talented chef and a good guy.' He left the car and opened her door, talking her hand as they walked to the apartment.

Gigi tugged on his hand and drew them to a stop in the beam of the apartment's security light. 'Dante, I know we're done talking about it for tonight, but I just want to say this— I would never stop you from seeing our baby.'

That had been playing on her mind ever since he'd as good as begged her to give him a chance to be a dad. She understood where his fear came from. He'd experienced his parents divorcing, the mind games, being stuck in the middle, but she would never toy with his or their child's emotions.

He ducked his head and looked at the ground. 'I...know.'

'Do you?' she whispered, stepping closer. 'Because I know you've experienced being trapped in the middle as a kid, but that's never going to happen with us.' She took his other hand. 'This baby is as much yours as it is mine. I would never use our child to hold you to ransom.'

He looked up, his eyes meeting hers, doubt and gratitude shining there. 'Okay. Thank you.'

'You're really serious about this temporary marriage thing, aren't you?' she asked, because since she'd had some time to reflect, she could understand how Dante's logic worked. He'd long ago dismissed the idea of a regular marriage based on love and lifelong commitment. What he was suggesting was something else entirely, something clinical and convenient and easily reversed. Zero emotions, zero expectations.

'As serious as I'm ever likely to be,' he said, his stare haunted, as if he genuinely believed there was no other way. And maybe he was right. His solution would solve all their problems in the short term.

'Then I promise I'll think about it just as seriously, okay?' she said, solemnly.

'Thank you.' He cupped her cheek and leaned close, resting his forehead against hers. 'That's all I ask.'

Gigi paused, her heart thudding at his closeness and vulnerability. She'd come to know Dante so well these past few weeks, to learn that while he was protecting himself by avoiding real serious relationships, he had so much more to give. He was funny and kind and a great surgeon. And despite the shock news of her pregnancy and his preposterous-sounding solution, she still wanted him physically. All the time...

'Are you up for a run in the morning before work?' he

asked, pulling back. 'We can take it slow. Don't want you feeling dizzy again.' He smiled, took her hands and glanced down at her stomach.

'Sure,' she said, still confused that she could be thinking about sex when they had bigger issues to digest including the fact that she was having a baby and his outlandish proposal.

'See you then.' He tugged her hand to bring her close, his free arm snaking around her waist. Slowly, he pressed his lips to hers in a chaste goodnight kiss that left her achy for more, even though she had no idea where they stood any longer. Should she even want him at all given the circumstances?

But her body didn't care that it was a complicated mess. Despite all the reasons to be cautious, Gigi prolonged the kiss, her body molten with lust. Dante groaned and gripped her tighter, his lips moving against hers, parting so their tongues slid together and need pooled low in her belly.

No matter what else had happened, this still made sense, their chemistry unwavering. She still wanted him as much as before. Maybe more so, her hormones raging. If she set aside the fact that she'd fallen accidentally pregnant to an Australian commitment-phobe, she was having the time of her life here in Sydney with Dante.

Just as their kiss became more heated, he pulled back, rested his forehead against hers, breathing hard. 'Goodnight, Gigi.' He kept a hold of her hands but straightened determinedly.

'You don't want to…come in?' she asked, looking up at him disappointed and confused by both her own conflicted feelings and his impressive willpower. But if they spent the night together, they'd end up discussing their options again, end up going around and around in circles.

'Of course I want to come in,' he said, his gaze dipping to her mouth as he brushed her lips with his thumb. 'But I figured you might appreciate some breathing space. It's been a pretty intense few days. I've given you a lot to think about tonight and I don't want you to feel pressured that things between us have to continue just because we're going to be parents. Like I said earlier, our physical relationship is a separate issue.'

'Okay.' Gigi nodded, grateful that he at least had the wherewithal to demarcate some boundaries even as her stomach sank. Clearly her hormones were running amok.

'I'm trying to do the right thing for us all,' he said, his expression uncertain. 'But I'm also making this up as I go. It's not a situation I've been in before.'

'Me neither,' Gigi said, squeezing his hands, letting him know that she appreciated his efforts to find a solution they could both live with. 'We'll figure it out together.'

He nodded and stepped back, releasing her hands. 'Go inside before I change my mind.' He gave her small smile and she realised that he still felt their connection too, that no matter what else was going on, it hadn't diminished in the slightest.

'Okay,' she said again, desperate all of a sudden to hurl herself into his arms and sob. Instead, she keyed in the lock code. 'Goodnight then.'

'Sleep well,' he said, waiting until she'd gone inside and closed the door before he headed to his part of the house.

Gigi watched him leave through a chink in the blinds, her heart hammering with uncertainty and fear. Could she really do what he'd proposed, marry him just to buy them some time? Detach all emotions from the act that normally represented the epitome of commitment when she'd come so close to marrying for real not so long ago?

But then look how that had turned out. She'd once thought she had her life all figured out: a career she loved, a fiancé, the perfect wedding planned. But since cancelling that wedding, she'd harboured doubts that marriage was the be-all and end-all anyway. She certainly wasn't ready to trust someone with her heart again. Marrying Dante was a practical way to solve a lot of their immediate problems. And would it really matter that she'd end up divorced as long as she and Dante were still committed to each other as parents?

As she readied for bed, her thoughts returned to the dawning realisation that her life and Dante's were about to change in every way imaginable. She might still want him and he her, but as tonight had proved, sleeping together was more complicated now. Gigi's final thought as she fell asleep was that she might not be ready to give up on their chemistry, but would she be able to have sex with her fake husband while they figured out how they would parent their child together but separately and also keep her emotions firmly in check?

The next day, she and Dante attended Gigi's antenatal appointment and first scan. He looked nervous and her heart went out to him, because until she saw the reassuring tiny flutter of their little one's heartbeat, she too had some apprehension. But after Dante had made his impassioned plea the night before, she was hyperaware of his every emotion.

He held her hand in the waiting room. 'Thanks for letting me attend,' he said.

The lump that lodged in her throat at dinner last night swelled. 'Of course. I'm glad you're here,' she whispered. 'I can't believe we're about to see our baby.' She wouldn't dream of denying him one second of this journey they were on together.

'I wouldn't have missed it for the world,' he said.

They were called into the sonogram room, where Gigi hopped up onto the bed and exposed her abdomen.

Dante squeezed her hand as the sonographer applied gel to Gigi's stomach and adjusted the setting on the machine. She smiled hesitantly over at him, nerves getting the better of her when she saw the worry in his eyes.

'Everything will be fine,' he reassured her in spite of the way he must be feeling, pressing a kiss to the back of her hand.

With her heart thudding with a mix of trepidation and excitement, Gigi nodded and then held her breath as the woman slid the probe over her lower abdomen and clicked a few buttons to adjust the resolution on the screen. Then she turned the screen to face them.

'Here's your baby,' she said, adjusting the angle of the probe.

Gigi froze, aware that Dante had done the same, his hand tightening on hers. She peered in awe at the image of the tiny human she and Dante had created.

'There's the heart beating away,' the sonographer added to her rapt audience.

Gigi swallowed as tears stung her eyes, and gripped Dante's hand tighter.

'I'll just take some measurements to confirm your dates and then I'll send you the images,' the woman said.

Gigi nodded, finally dragging her eyes away from the screen to look at Dante, who'd gone quiet. 'It's our baby,' she whispered, caught off guard by the sight of this big, buff Australian choked and lost for words.

'It's really happening,' he said, his stare wide with emotion. 'We're having a baby.'

Gigi laughed through her tears and nodded vigorously. 'A baby with a reassuring heartbeat.'

With her examination complete, the sonographer handed Gigi a box of tissues to clean up the gel from her abdomen. 'I printed one picture for you. The rest will be emailed through. I'll leave you to clean up. You can leave when you're ready.'

With a final smile, the woman left them alone.

Gigi handed the picture to Dante while she cleaned up and

straightened her clothes, something momentous happening inside her as she watched Dante stare in wonder at the scan picture.

'I can't quite believe it,' he said. 'I know that sounds stupid because I'm holding the evidence in my hand, but I can't believe how perfect he or she looks.'

He tore his eyes away from the picture and looked up at her.

'I know.' Gigi nodded, standing at side so they could look at the image together. 'Tiny hands and feet and a little face.'

She too was in shock, relief making her heart pound and her hormones rage.

'Thank you,' he said suddenly, gripping her shoulders. 'You're amazing,' he choked out. Then he kissed her, snatching her breath.

'I haven't done anything yet,' she said when he pulled back, laughing as the joy of the moment, and his reaction, burst inside her.

'Yes, you have.' He drew her into his arms and pressed a kiss to her forehead. 'You're going to be such an amazing mother.'

Blinking furiously, she buried her face in his shirt, clinging to him for comfort as his words from the night before haunted her.

All I ask is that you give me a chance to be a dad.

She hadn't been able to get those words out of her mind since he'd spoken them. She couldn't forget the anguished look on his face when he'd pleaded with her. And now, his obvious joy to meet their baby and his gratitude that she'd allowed him to be a part of this pregnancy left her suddenly certain that his plan to marry in order to buy them some time was the only fair way to go.

Dante was willing to relocate to London to be a part of his child's life. She couldn't deny him a chance to experience every stage of the journey they were on. And he was right. A temporary marriage ending in an amicable divorce was no big deal compared to the bigger picture: their relationship as parents, not when she'd almost married a man she didn't even know.

'Are you okay?' he asked, pressing his lips to her head.

She looked up at him, keeping her arm around his waist. 'I've been thinking,' she said, nibbling at her lip, 'about what you said last night. About your...solution.'

'Okay,' he said warily.

'You're going to be a brilliant dad,' she said, 'and I don't want to deprive you of anything, so I think we should do it.' Her pulse tingled in her fingertips with nervous excitement, but she didn't regret the sudden impulse to accept his temporary solution to their problems.

He frowned and gripped her shoulders. 'Are you serious?'

'Yes.' She nodded, her doubts from last night silenced. As long as they set some ground rules, what could go wrong? 'I think we should get married.'

His frown deepened even as hope lit his stare. 'Are you sure, because you don't have to rush any decisions.'

Gigi slipped both her arms around his waist. 'I'm sure. I've thought about it and I agree. It's the only way in the short term. And I was watching you watch the sonogram and it hit me, exactly what it meant for me to leave the country without you. I don't want to hurt you by leaving. And you're right. If we're practical about it, it makes so much sense.'

He cupped her face and pressed his lips to hers in a fierce and breathless kiss. 'Thank you.'

She laughed, never imagining that the man she'd first met would be thanking her because she'd agreed to marry him. But he was only relieved because it wouldn't be a real marriage.

'Let's go,' she said. 'We can talk about the rules on the way home.'

They left the radiology department together, Dante still clutching the scan picture as if it were a winning lottery ticket. Grinning goofily at each other, they made their way back to the car.

CHAPTER TWELVE

FACED WITH THE violent highs and lows of the last thirty minutes, when he'd been nervous that their baby was okay, putting on a brave face for Gigi, while also fearful that Gigi would leave Sydney alone and take their baby back to London, Dante tried to assimilate everything that had just happened.

'Are you really sure about this?' Glancing over at Gigi in the passenger seat, he smiled, so grateful that she'd seen things his way now that he'd seen their baby for real, its tiny heart fluttering away.

'I am.' She nodded vigorously. 'I realised that after what happened with my ex, after meeting you and getting pregnant, that marriage doesn't mean as much to me as it did before. I've had my fingers burned. And this reason—' she rested her hand over her stomach to indicate the baby '—it just feels like a better reason all of a sudden. Like you said, it's only for a few months Then we can divorce just as civilly and move on, putting the baby first.'

Before he could speak again, she leaned close and kissed him. Dante was swamped by wave after wave of emotion. Desire for Gigi, excitement that his plan to stay in control of this situation might work, a tiny flash of fear and doubt because he'd never imagined himself married, for any reason. But he couldn't seem to move past the feeling that if he let Gigi and their baby walk away, his life might unravel. And now that he'd seen the scan, that feeling only intensified.

Pulling back from their kiss, he tried to think past the slug of lust fogging his mind. 'So let's talk about these rules before we get carried away.'

'Okay.' Gigi nodded, her hands resting on his shoulders. 'Rule one,' she said, still breathless from their kiss. 'We can keep having sex but feelings are strictly forbidden.'

'Well, I'm not going to argue with that.' He smiled, holding her off when she swooped in to kiss him again. 'Rule two— we keep the living arrangements as they are. I need my space to study and you'll have your own bed, so you don't have to feel pressured to sleep with me unless you want to.'

'I do want to. Now,' she said, kissing the side of his neck and driving him wild because it had taken all of his willpower to walk away from her the night before.

When he peeled her away, she sighed playfully. 'Rule three,' she went on. 'It's a practical arrangement so I don't get deported. I'll print a prenup off the internet that we can both sign stating that we agree to leave the marriage with exactly what we brought to it if things don't work out, which obviously they won't because it's not a real marriage and we plan to divorce.'

Dante nodded. 'Okay. But we don't have much time. I'll apply for a special licence to marry because you're pregnant, and book the registry office.'

She nodded. 'Sounds good, but I have one last rule.' She nibbled her lip, looking hesitant.

'Okay,' he said, waiting.

'No more dates,' she said, 'unless it's for sex. I don't want us to blur the boundaries. I don't want either of us to be hurt. After all, we're doing this for the baby, because we both want to put him or her first so we can't afford to make any mistakes and mess this up. Agreed?'

'Okay.' Dante nodded, thinking she couldn't be any more perfect than in that moment.

Turning serious, she took his hands. 'Neither of us wants to play games. We've both experienced those in different ways.'

'I agree.' Because she was wonderful and he couldn't stop himself, he kissed her again. 'So we're really doing this?' he asked, swallowing down those old habitual feelings that had served him well up to now. But this was a completely different scenario. This was a practical solution to benefit them all—him, Gigi and their baby.

She smiled and nodded. 'We are.'

He kissed her again, his heart thudding wildly.

'Want to go home and celebrate our engagement?' she asked, snagging her bottom lip with her teeth as she peered at him seductively.

'Absolutely,' he said. 'Put your seat belt on.'

Hurriedly and with a squeal of excited laughter, she obeyed as he started the engine and put the car into gear.

The Pyrmont Registry office overlooked Pyrmont Bay, which was a part of Sydney Harbour and located along the route of the SHH fun run. A fitting location for her and Dante's small wedding a week later. They'd asked Katie and John, Dante's father, to be their witnesses. Gigi wore a cream sundress, her hair styled in soft waves and adorned with white orchids that matched those in her simple bouquet.

As they faced each other before their celebrant, she clung to Dante's hand, her stomach full of butterflies. His confident smile soothed her nerves and banished the worst of her doubts that she was making a terrible mistake. But when she recalled how close she'd come to marrying a man who would cheat and lie and betray her, she'd realised that Dante's practical solution carried less weight than she'd initially thought.

He was right, it not only solved their immediate problems, it was also less important than their commitment to each other as parents, which wouldn't end with the signing of the divorce papers in the future. Not that she'd imagined this would be how her wedding day would unfold, of course.

Dante's fingers tightened on hers as he began to recite the vows he'd written. 'Gigi, we exchange these rings today to symbolise our connection to one another. This ring,' he said, placing the gold band on her ring finger, 'represents my trust in our relationship, my commitment to support and protect you, and our partnership in this marriage. I join myself to you, respecting you as an equal, promising to be there for you in good times and bad.'

Gigi smiled encouragingly, her eyes stinging with emotion because regardless of their reasons for marrying, she not only respected him, she was also a hormonal mess. 'Dante,' she began in return, 'I stand by your side as your partner in this journey of marriage. This ring—' she pushed the band onto his ring finger '—represents what we've found together. A union of different cultures and a shared career, of mutual respect and support, of greater strength together than apart. I join myself to you knowing that together, we'll find a way to face whatever the future holds.'

The celebrant smiled and said, 'By sharing vows and rings and making a commitment to each other today in front of your witnesses, you have declared that you choose to live your lives as husband and wife. It is now my great pleasure to pronounce you such and wish you many congratulations.'

Gigi smiled over at her new, fake husband, who looked seriously hot in his wedding suit, and dragged in a shuddering breath, hope blooming in her chest for the first time since her world had collapsed back in London.

She was confident that she and Dante could work side by

side as parents the way they worked as doctors. Unlike her ex and regardless of Dante's reputation and fear of commitment, this man smiling back at her had never once let her down. He'd stepped up and supported her and their child these past couple of weeks. No, they weren't in love, nor was this the most romantic wedding the world had ever seen, but she trusted in him and in them to find a way to raise their baby together. In that moment, that meant more than a million words of love.

With his stare locked to hers, Dante tugged Gigi's hands, drawing her close and pressing a soft kiss to her lips while Katie and John applauded beside them.

They broke apart, Gigi laughing with relief as they shared hugs and congratulations with their overjoyed witnesses.

'Welcome to the family,' John told Gigi warmly, his hand gripping Dante's shoulder and his eyes bright with paternal pride.

His words shoved a lump into her throat, guilt hot in her veins that she was deceiving Dante's lovely father, but she swallowed it down, convinced that the end justified the means in the long run. And irrespective of their marital status, she and Dante would always be a part of each other's lives and families through their bond as parents.

'I knew it would take a special woman to make an honest man of you,' Katie told Dante good-naturedly, pressing a kiss to his cheek before hugging Gigi tight and whispering congratulations. Gigi held Katie back for a few seconds too long, her confession on the tip of her tongue. Katie had become a true friend and supporter. She just hoped that when the truth came out, the other woman would forgive her and understand her and Dante's reasons.

In the whirl of activity that followed—signing the register, posing for photos in the sunshine and making their way to a nearby restaurant for lunch—Gigi had no time to deeply analyse what they'd just done or how she didn't want to let go of Dante's hand. Seen through the lens of her pregnancy, she couldn't tell which of her feelings or emotions were real anyway and which would pass. If she kept a hold of their rules as tightly as she held his hand, surely everything would work out for the best?

Inside the sun-filled restaurant overlooking sea views, Dante ducked his head and said, 'You look beautiful, by the way. I should have told you sooner.'

She blinked up at him, shocked by the heat in the stare he swooped over her. 'Thanks. You look pretty good yourself.' She straightened his buttonhole in the lapel of his jacket, trying to think of anything else apart from how long it had been since they were last intimate. What with work and his study schedule for his looming exams and the fatigue she'd experienced these past couple of weeks, it felt like months since they'd found a right moment. But it also reinforced that their marriage wasn't part of a real romantic relationship. They were just two people having sex who also happened to be married and having a baby.

'I can't believe you're not having a honeymoon,' Katie said, taking Gigi's mind off how unusual their situation was.

'It's fine,' Gigi said, as they took their seats in the window to admire the harbour views where she sat next to her *husband*.

'And it's criminal that you could only get a half day off work,' Katie went on.

'It was pretty short notice,' Gigi reasoned. 'And we wanted to keep things simple.' She glanced Dante's way and he smiled, ordering zero-alcohol champagne for the table.

'It hardly seems right,' Katie pushed, shooting Gigi a worried look.

'Or maybe it's perfect,' Gigi said. 'A whirlwind wedding for a whirlwind of a trip down under.' She glanced at Dante who nodded, his fingers stroking hers under the table.

'Well, I'd like to raise a toast,' John said holding up his glass. 'To Gigi and Dante. Commitment comes in all shapes and sizes. There's no one size fits all. That you two have so much in common and respect and support each other bodes well for your future. I hope that future is happy for you both and that the amazing journey you're on, your journey as parents, brings you equal joy.'

'To Gigi and Dante,' Katie added with a wide smile.

Gigi touched her glass to the others, her eyes lingering on Dante as she made a silent wish that they'd done the right thing, that this was all going to go to plan. In another few weeks, he'd have completed his final surgical exams and could start looking for a consultant job. Gigi would have completed her locum position in Sydney and they could then tackle the big issues, like where they'd live, how they would raise their baby and when to get divorced.

Everything was going to be fine.

CHAPTER THIRTEEN

LATER THAT EVENING, having returned to work after their wedding lunch, Gigi finished up with her final patient for the day. Throwing herself back into work had helped her manage the surreal feeling that overcame her every time she glanced down at her left hand and saw the shiny gold band encircling her ring finger.

But just because she was married didn't mean anything had to change. This plan she and Dante had created worked because there were no romantic expectations.

Aware that she was staring at her hand again, she ducked it under the desk out of sight. Given Dante's reputation around there and his nickname, she didn't want to flaunt her new marital state or her pregnancy news, which, with the exception of Katie, was still under wraps. But the gossip would spread soon enough, and she'd need to deal with it then, the same way she'd dealt with it back in London when word had got out about Will and Fiona. Of course, it wasn't like she could tell people the truth, that they'd married for immigration reasons.

She ordered a second chest X-ray to check the position of the nasogastric tube the nurse had inserted. She was just about to call the on-call surgeon before heading home, when Dante, the man himself, *her husband*, arrived.

'Hey,' he said, taking the seat next to hers and sliding it close. 'Katie said you have a surgical admission?'

Gigi ignored the thrill of excitement catching her breath—it was just lust and hormones—and nodded. 'A forty-two-year-old woman with a classic history for peptic ulcer disease. She has free air in her abdomen on X-ray and signs of peritonitis, so I suspect the ulcer has perforated.'

Dante glanced at the erect X-ray on the screen over her shoulder and then clicked through to the blood test results. 'Is she haemodynamically stable?' he asked.

'Yes.' Gigi nodded. 'For now.'

'And you've started intravenous antibiotics?'

She nodded again.

'Let's order an urgent CT scan, too,' he said. 'I'll consent her for surgery before I hand her over to the on-call surgeon.'

'Okay, thanks. Do you have a patient to see? I assumed you'd already be home studying.'

'No, I came to see you.' He winked.

'Oh...' She swallowed, still as bewitched by that gorgeous smile of his as she'd been the first time they'd met.

'I wondered if I could give you a lift home?' he asked. 'I have a surprise for you.'

Gigi breathed through the bubble of excitement in her chest, desperately trying to keep her emotions in check, as she'd been doing all day, all week, ever since she'd agreed to enter into this unconventional marriage. 'What kind of surprise?' she whispered, so no one would overhear.

'If I tell you,' Dante whispered back, grinning, 'it won't be a surprise, will it?'

'Sounds very cryptic,' she teased.

He stood and pushed his chair under the desk. 'I'll go see your patient while you order the CT scan. Then we'll head home to change and pack an overnight bag.'

'Okay,' Gigi croaked, too enchanted by the glow in his eyes to remind him of rule number four—no more dates. But it wasn't every day she got married. Surely she could make this one exception for whatever Dante had planned?

Thirty minutes later, having worked together to order tests, reassess the patient and admit her to the surgical ward, they left the emergency department together, Dante's arm around Gigi's shoulders as they headed for the car park.

Gigi emerged from the hotel bedroom dressed in a robe, looking relaxed after her bath. Dante's pulse ricocheted at the sight of her even though this wasn't a real wedding night or even a real date. But no matter how hard he tried to stay immune, their chemistry just wouldn't be silenced.

'Nice bath?' he asked, handing her a glass of zero-alcohol bubbles.

'It was divine.' She smiled and sighed happily as she took in the views of the harbour and city beyond from the suite's windows. 'This is the fanciest hotel I've ever seen.'

'Good,' Dante said. 'I know we said no dates, but I wanted to pamper you a bit. After all, you are carrying our baby and you've been extra tired these past couple of weeks.'

They headed for the terrace, which boasted their own private infinity pool and an outdoor seating area.

Gigi slipped her arm around his waist, resting her head on his shoulder. 'Thank you. It's a lovely gesture. I'm just relieved that the morning sickness hasn't been too bad.'

He breathed in the scent of her shampoo, wanting her so badly he almost couldn't breathe. But then he thought back to their wedding that morning, the moment's panic he experienced when she'd walked in looking breathtaking in her simple sundress and he'd realised he was actually doing this, getting married. Then, like now, he reminded himself of the reasons they'd married and the calm returned along with his control of the situation.

'Do you want to order room service?' he asked as they took a seat on the outdoor sofa. 'Or there's a restaurant downstairs if you prefer.'

She looked up at him, her smile warm and carefree as it had been all day. 'I'm not that hungry at the moment. Maybe room service in a little while.'

'Okay. In that case, a toast.' Dante touched his glass to hers. 'Cheers to us. I know it's not a proper marriage and we're obviously not having a honeymoon, but I want you to know that I have no regrets after today.' As long as they stuck to the rules, nothing could go wrong.

'Me neither,' she said smiling up at him. 'To us, the craziest parents to ever make a baby.'

They held eye contact as they each took a sip. Then she rested her head on his shoulder, sighed and curled her feet up.

'Are you tired?' he asked as they watched the setting sun dip behind the city skyline. 'It was a big day.' Guilt that it had all been a rush and that Gigi had been suffering from morning sickness washed over him.

'I'm okay,' she said. 'I was thinking how lovely your dad is.'

'He's a good man.' Dante nodded. 'I'm sorry your parents weren't there... You really didn't mind?'

She'd decided not to tell the Lanes about the wedding or the baby, which also added to Dante's sense of responsibility. Whenever he finally met them, he'd have some explaining to do.

She shook her head. 'I'd rather tell them face-to-face, when I'm back in the UK,' she said. 'In another couple of weeks I'll be into the second trimester so will feel more comfortable to talking about the baby.'

'They'll be surprised to hear you're married,' he said. 'I hope they don't hate me.' After all, he'd not only got their daughter pregnant, but had also married her in a rushed registry office ceremony without them present. Not the best way to ingratiate himself to the grandparents of his child.

She looked up. 'They won't hate you when I explain. And after everything that happened with my ex and my friend, I think they'll just be happy that I'm happy. They can come to my next wedding,' she said with a smile. 'Plus they can't be angry with me when I'm having their first grandchild, right?'

Dante laughed although his gut twisted with jealousy at her mention of a future wedding. He wasn't ready to think of her with another man. But that was just his need for her and his selfishness talking. Of course there would be other guys after him in Gigi's life. She'd probably fall in love again one day and want to get married for real. Why had he never considered the possibility until now? Their child was likely to have a stepfather someday.

Swallowing down the acid in his throat, he said, 'Well, I'm happy to come with you when you tell them if that will help. I'd rather they were angry with me, if anyone.'

'Thanks,' she said, placing her glass on the table next to his.

When she relaxed back against the cushions, Dante reached for her hand and pulled it into his lap. 'We can make this work, you know—us,' he said, believing the sentiment to the marrow of his bones. 'Just because we're not a couple and won't be living together, doesn't mean that we can't always put our baby first and do what's best for him or her.'

'I agree.' Gigi swallowed, her eyes shining as she held his stare.

'We don't even have to tell our little one the real reason we got married and divorced,' he went on, trying not to think too far ahead into the future because he never wanted to let their child down, or Gigi for that matter. 'The important thing is our relationship doesn't detract from the fact that we both love him or her.'

She nodded again and he cupped her cheek. 'I want you to know that wherever we live,' he said, his voice hoarse with the emotion catching him off guard, 'here, the UK, or somewhere in the middle, I'll always be committed to making us work for our child's sake.'

'I know,' Gigi whispered, herself sounding choked. 'I believe you. And I will too. But don't make me cry. I'm a hormonal mess at the moment as it is.'

'Sorry,' he said, smiling and then brushing his lips over hers, acting on instinct because try as he might to harness it, his addiction to her was unrelenting. They'd put their fling on the back burner since the sonogram. What with Gigi's shifts, his surgical workload and study schedule, and their quickie wedding, which had still required a bit of planning, they hadn't seen much of each other.

But now that the thought of another man had entered the mental picture, he couldn't let it go. He pulled back and cupped her face. 'I know you'll move on one day and fall in love, want a real relationship.'

She frowned, hesitated. 'Maybe one day. But…you might change your mind in the future and fall in love, too.'

There was a hint of a question in the tone of her voice, but Dante shook his head. 'I doubt that will happen,' he replied, adamant because he'd never been in love before and the emotion, the idea of such helplessness still terrified him.

'As the mother of my child,' he said, his stare raking hers so she saw how sincere he was, 'you are likely to be the most meaningful relationship I'll ever have. And our child will always be my first priority. I want you to know that.'

Whereas Gigi would heal from her past betrayals and move on, seek out a loving and committed relationship for real. Marry again. He would be replaced in her life and he'd have to be okay with that. What he'd struggle with even more was being replaced in his child's life.

'Dante...' she whispered, her eyes shining. 'Our child will always be my priority too.' She searched his stare, gripping his hands.

He swallowed, his throat aching. 'Please promise me that you won't push me out of our child's life when you do fall in love again.' He squeezed her fingers. 'Promise me, Gigi. I want to always be there for him or her.'

She shook her head and frowned. 'Of course I won't. I promise. I would never do that to you.'

He nodded, relieved that she believed him and unable to vocalise why he was suddenly desperate for her promises. 'Because I've experienced what it's like to be in the middle of a parental tug of war.' He raised both her hands to his mouth and kissed her knuckles. 'You have to promise me that we'll never play games at our child's expense.'

'I promise.' She swallowed and stared up at him, her breathing speeding up, her lips brushing his like a vow.

As if he'd been deaf to it and could suddenly hear the ticking of the clock counting down the days to when this would be over, he pushed her hair back from her face, holding her stare. 'I won't ever hurt you, Gigi,' he said, his voice breaking because he was splintering apart and only her touch could hold him together.

'I know.' Her eyes shone with emotion as she nodded. 'I won't hurt you either.'

He held his breath, this moment, this conversation seeming more intimate than the vows they'd spoken that morning during their simple ceremony. Marrying Gigi was supposed to have eased his mind, solved their problems and given them some breathing space. But if anything, at the idea that she would one day be married for real, he suddenly felt more unstable, as if all he'd done with his quickie marriage was delay the inevitable. On the one hand, he couldn't imagine not wanting her the way he had every day since they reunited. But on the other, he knew himself well, knew how he'd spent most of his adult life avoiding serious feelings when it came to relationships. And this relationship was the most important one he'd ever had.

'We can't mess this up,' he said, scared that his control of this situation was just an illusion.

As if she saw the panic in his eyes, she whispered, 'It's going to be okay,' leaning close and raising her lips to his enticingly. 'You will always be the most important man in our child's life. I promise. I promise.' She pressed kisses over his face.

For a terrifying second, it seemed as if she could see inside him to his deepest fears. As if with Gigi—this woman who'd become a colleague, a friend, a lover who'd literally turned his life upside down, somehow making it better—he could always be himself, always find himself. That was something he'd never imagined possible.

Caught off guard by the emotions this conversation had raised and still as enslaved by their chemistry as the first day they met, his libido and still constant desire for her undeniable, Dante groaned, burying his face against her neck, and clutched her close, a gnawing sensation in the pit of his stomach. He'd entered new territory with Gigi, their working relationship, their personal connection over the baby, their chemistry which only seemed to be getting stronger and stronger bringing them so close. The kind of closeness he'd always avoided in case it suffocated him or became a weight around his neck.

But now, her promises didn't seem to be enough. He needed more. He needed the all-consuming fire. He needed Gigi. And more than ever, he needed to carefully protect their relationship. Otherwise, he might inadvertently hurt her or mess this up. And given that he would have the most to lose, he couldn't allow that to happen.

CHAPTER FOURTEEN

GIGI'S HEART POUNDED as Dante looked up and peered into her eyes before kissing her softly, slowly as if savouring her lips. Swamped by the emotions of the day, by his heartbreaking vulnerability where he admitted his worst fear, she sat astride his lap and kissed him back. Yes, his insistence that he hadn't changed his opinion on relationships had given her a moment's pause. But of course she hadn't expected him to change his mind about commitment just because they'd married.

'I don't know what's happening to me,' he said, looking up at her, his hands sliding up and down her thighs as they bracketed his. 'I feel…unstable.'

She pushed her fingers through his hair, holding his face. 'It's been a whirlwind, that's all. You rented a room to the cousin of a friend and now you find yourself married to her because she's having your baby.' She smiled, hoping he'd see the funny side, although she too was overcome by the journey they'd travelled together.

Capturing her lips, he kissed her again, as if he needed the connection to settle the way he felt. Dismissing the idea—she couldn't get carried away by what was simply really strong chemistry—she leaned against him, her sensitive breasts brushing his chest and fire spreading through her entire body.

'I've missed you,' she said, leaning back. 'I almost cried when I saw you'd booked a two-bedroomed suite.'

'I wanted you to feel comfortable, not pressured,' he said, his blue eyes serious but almost navy with desire.

'Believe me, I'm comfortable,' she said, pressing kisses down his neck. 'I want you, badly.'

'Gigi...' he groaned, fisting the towelling robe as she shifted closer on his lap and felt the hardness of him between her legs. Then his hands slipped under the robe, along her thighs to her bare backside, shunting her hips forward so his erection was pressed between them.

'Let's go inside,' she pleaded, rocking on his lap, seeking the friction she needed.

He opened the robe and cupped her breast, her nipple pebbling against his palm as he raised it to his mouth.

She sighed with longing, gripped his shoulders and arched her back, pushing her breasts forward. 'Dante...' she moaned as he sucked her nipple, flooding her pelvis with molten heat.

He slid his hand between her legs and looked up at her, watching her moan and melt and burn in the way he made her feel. 'I'm not ready for this to be over yet, Gigi,' he said, his fingers probing her slickness, stroking, teasing, driving her wild.

'Me neither,' she said, sighing as she exposed her neck to his kisses and the delicious scrape of his facial hair.

He tightened his grip around her waist, his fingers slipping inside her so she gasped in delight, rocked her hips faster, saying, 'I need you. Now.'

'I know. I need you too,' he said, kissing her deeply, the urgency building as if he was there with her enslaved by this connection, wanting her as badly as she wanted him.

'Hold tight,' he said, when he dragged his lips from hers.

She wrapped her arms around his neck and, scooping his hands under her hips, he stood, carrying her inside.

In his bedroom, Dante lowered her to the bed and peeled

off the robe, his hands and stare caressing her body as he joined her on the bed, as if making up for the days they hadn't touched.

'You are so beautiful,' he said. 'I've been going out of my mind, seeing you every day, wanting you but holding back because of our…arrangement.' He pulled her close, his kisses turning frantic, Gigi shoving at his clothes until he swiftly removed them, tossing them aside.

'Do you want a condom?' he asked, his gorgeous body braced over hers so she moved her hands over every taut, hard inch of him, desperate to taste his skin, to feel his weight on top of her, to have him inside her, driving them both towards bliss.

She shook her head, reaching for his erection, tugging him slowly so he groaned. 'I want you.'

Dante took her nipple in his mouth once more, trailing his tongue down her abdomen to the spot just below her belly button where their baby grew, where he pressed a kiss.

Gigi speared her fingers through his hair, holding his face, overcome with hormones, her heart leaping that this man who'd always avoided romantic love, already loved their baby.

But she had no time to lament how wonderful a partner Dante could be if only he chose to commit himself to someone, because he moved lower, his tongue once more trailing a path of delicious anticipation, until he'd settled himself between her thighs.

'Dante,' she gasped as their eyes met and his mouth covered her. She arched up off the bed, braced on her elbows, her head spinning as flames streaked across her abdomen to her nipples, weakening her limbs to jelly.

'Tell me when you're close,' he said diving back in, tonguing her until she was sobbing and moaning and crying out his name like a chant to stave off madness.

But this is how he made her feel. Safe. Protected. Precious.

'Dante,' she said her voice full of warning and urgency as he shoved her closer and closer to the point of no return.

He tore his mouth away and lay on top of her, kissing her with wild desperation as he gripped one of her thighs, raised it over his hips and slowly pushed inside her, skin to skin.

She gasped with pleasure as he filled her, her fingernails digging into his shoulders as if she'd never let him go. But she would. She'd have to.

'Gigi...' He groaned, his face buried against her neck. 'I've never wanted anyone this much.'

'Me neither,' she whispered against his ear, inhaling the scent of him, her arms holding him so close they felt like one body, not two.

Slotting the fingers of one hand between hers, he looked down at her and began to move, his thrusts shallow at first, then deeper, deeper, faster. Her lips parted on a sigh as she stared up at him. He swooped in to kiss them, his tongue surging against hers as they rocked together, chasing oblivion, holding onto one another so when they shattered, they'd be there to catch the other's pieces.

She slid her hands down his back to his buttocks and urged him deeper, moaning encouragement, revelling in the possessive way he couldn't seem to get enough of her.

Dante tore his mouth from hers. 'You are the only woman I've cared about this much,' he said, thrusting her higher and higher, his words snatching at her breath because he'd shown her the truth of them, every day.

'Dante,' she gasped, unable to tell him how she felt, because the emotions swelled inside her like a tidal wave, spilling free on a broken cry as she climaxed, her stare locked to his so she witnessed the moment he too surrendered, crushing her close, groaning her name as he came.

Panting hard, he held onto her, his hips still moving with hers, wringing every last spasm of pleasure from their bodies. Even when they were spent, he lay still, as if he wanted them to stay locked together like this forever.

Gigi closed her eyes, breathing him in, scared to move because a part of her felt like something momentous had just happened and she was terrified to break the spell and discover reality.

When he finally rolled to the side, she turned to face him. They stared into each other's eyes, catching their breath, smiling. She reached out and touched his cheek, watched as the emotions he probably had no idea how to manage filtered across his expression: bewilderment, doubt, a hint of panic.

She smiled, guessing he might freak out after such an emotional day. The promises he'd demanded proved his biggest fear was finding himself in the same position as his father—feeling he had no control over his relationship with his child. But just because Dante wanted to be there for his baby, to be an involved father, didn't mean he'd changed his mind about commitment. He cared about her, she truly believed that. But this was still a marriage in name only, even if their physical need for each other showed no signs of weakening.

'I'm going to take a shower,' she said, forcing herself to roll away and leave his bed.

'Okay...' He frowned, sitting up on one elbow to watch her retrieve the robe from the floor.

She hardened her heart, ignoring his look of disappointment, needing some emotional distance to put the events of the day and things they'd just shared into perspective. After all, she didn't want to get hurt any more than he wanted to hurt her.

Determined to stick to the rules and keep her heart safe, she headed for her own room.

* * *

The following Monday morning, sitting at the computer terminal in the emergency department during a quiet moment while she waited for her latest patient's blood results, Gigi couldn't stop her mind from wandering back to her wedding night, no matter how hard she tried to be disciplined. When she'd awoken alone the next morning, every kiss, every touch, every smile and whispered promise they'd made returned, leaving her both dreamily awash with hormones and filled with apprehension.

Dante too had seemed quiet and unsettled as he'd driven them home. She'd convinced herself he'd been distracted by his studies and upcoming professional exams. After all, he'd taken a day off at a crucial time for their wedding. But it was another reminder that no matter how connected they felt when they were in each other's arms, this wasn't a real relationship.

Telling herself that everything would be okay—she trusted Dante not to hurt her and she trusted the two of them to be mature and respectful adults when this was over and to put the baby at the centre of their ongoing relationship as parents—she logged into the computer and checked for her patient's blood results.

'You were miles away then,' Katie said, shooting her a knowing look, taking the seat next to Gigi and logging into the other computer.

Gigi smiled, pretending to look busy. 'It's unusually quiet this morning. I'm not used to it.'

'Enjoy it while it lasts,' Katie said. 'It's never quiet for long around here.'

Just then, Dante appeared from one of the bays, sending Gigi's pulse into overdrive. He looked harassed, but when he spied Gigi, his eyes lit up for a moment, silent communication passing between them. Even in spite of their rules, their caution and reluctance to hurt each other, their physical need to connect was unrelenting. Late last night, after he'd finished studying, he'd tapped at her door, kissed her like the world was ending, then kissed and caressed every inch of her body with a kind of frantic intensity that made her all too aware that their fake marriage, their physical relationship had an expiry date.

She'd put his determined enthusiasm down to stress, but maybe like her, he was counting the days. Soon, his exams would be behind him and then they'd need to extricate themselves from each other as clinically and amicably as they'd formed a legal union. And with their divorce, would come the end of their physical relationship.

'Hi,' she said, her heart pounding as he took the spare seat next to Katie, as if her body was acting irrespective of her cautious mind.

He smiled, his stare lingering on hers as if he too was recalling their desperate coupling of the night before, their simultaneous orgasms where they'd cried out together, their drawn-out goodnight kiss that neither of them had seemed eager to end.

Then he looked away from her and logged into the computer. 'I'm admitting the recurrent pilonidal abscess in bay six,' he told Katie, his voice businesslike. 'He needs an excision and might also need a plastics referral.'

While Gigi clung to the memories of his lust-choked voice, he focussed on typing up his notes, sighing when another of the emergency doctors arrived and handed him another referral.

'Acute appendicitis in bay eight,' the other doctor said.

'Add it to my pile,' Dante muttered, pulling his phone from his pocket and scowling at the screen.

Reluctant to add to his burden but also aware he was due in theatre soon, Gigi slid another A & E summary his way. 'I have a wound infection for you too,' she said, while he waited for his call to connect.

He met her stare as he began speaking to someone in theatres, arranging a slot for his abscess patient. When he hung up the call, he took a brief look at the notes of Gigi's patient. 'Does he need admission?' Dante asked her, quickly and critically scanning her clinical summary.

'I'm…not sure,' she answered, caught off guard by his abrupt manner. 'I'm still waiting for the blood test results to come back. Couldn't you have a quick look at him while you're here? He's elderly and lives alone.' Her face warmed. A week ago he'd have taken the referral, no questions asked.

Was he trying to show her that just because they'd needed to marry, their relationship still had boundaries? Or was he having second thoughts about what they'd done?

'I could,' Dante said. 'But as you can see I'm run off my feet today. If it's just a case of prescribing some antibiotics and making a referral to the district nursing team before sending him home…'

'Okay,' she said in a small voice, ducking her head, uncertain of him and a little embarrassed that he'd publicly put her in her place where a couple of weeks ago he'd have bent over backwards to support her. 'Well,' she said, coolly, 'I'll finish my investigations and come back to you if I think he needs a surgical referral.'

Dante paused, frustration evident in the flattening of his mouth, which only a few hours ago had kissed her with desperation as if he couldn't bear to stop.

'Sorry,' he said with a wince, scrubbing a hand down his face. 'I'm needed in theatre like ten minutes ago. Perhaps you can call my junior to take a look at the wound infection?'

Gigi nodded, wishing they were alone so she could speak her mind and ask if he was okay. Wishing she could touch him and hold him until some of his obvious stress eased. 'I'll do that,' she said. 'You go.'

He paused, looking like he might say something else, something personal. But then he stood. 'See you later,' he said, rushing from the emergency department without a backwards glance.

Gigi watched him go, doubt making her heart heavy. Something was off with him. He was still attentive and passionate when they were alone, and she'd put it down to the big issues they were putting off discussing until he'd sat his exams. Like where to live, finding new jobs, shared custody of their baby. But maybe because she'd experienced initial doubts when he suggested a marriage of convenience, or because she'd felt so connected to him the night of their wedding, she couldn't help but wonder if he was now regretting the rash impulse. Did he feel trapped after all? The last thing she wanted was to be with someone who didn't want her in return, although his physical need for her still seemed strong.

Would he even tell her if he did have regrets? Or would he go behind her back the way he had that first day she'd come to work at SHH?

She swallowed, feeling sick. While she was staring at the glint of her wedding ring full of hormones, daydreaming of his touch, his kisses and the way he reached for her as if he needed her, maybe he was still the same practical, emotionless Dante. Controlling his environment and locking down his feelings, where she experienced a million feelings in a day.

'He's just stressed,' Katie said from beside her, as if she'd picked up on every hidden fear Gigi had.

Gigi plastered on a brave smile and turned to the other woman who'd she'd forgotten was still there. 'Yeah, I know.'

But it was another good reminder for Gigi to guard her emotions. She couldn't get carried away and misinterpret what was going on between her and Dante. He'd never made her any promises when it came to a romantic relationship and after being hurt before, and because she was having his baby, she couldn't afford to make another mistake, feel more than him and get hurt again.

'Your jobs are demanding,' Katie continued, making Gigi's embarrassment worse. 'And his exams are rapidly approaching.'

Gigi nodded, wondering if everyone around them could see that their *marriage* was a one-sided sham because they knew Dante and his reputation well. It shouldn't matter, but after the humiliation she'd experienced after Will and Fiona, she would hate for anyone to feel sorry for her, especially when the entire department discovered she was pregnant with his baby.

'I know…' she said, looking up to see sympathy and concern in Katie's stare. Suddenly, she found herself needing to unburden and set the record straight. 'Can I tell you something?' she said, glancing around to make sure no one else was listening.

'Of course,' Katie said. 'Always.'

Gigi smiled, heartened that she'd found such an amazing friend in Katie. She leaned close and lowered her voice. 'We only really got married because of the baby. It's not like Dante has had a massive change of heart or fallen madly in love with me. And I'm the same. I've made a mistake before and I'm not ready to trust someone else with my heart yet, but I didn't want to be deported.'

Katie's frown deepened, shock and concern in her eyes. 'I see… And you know what you're doing? The two of you?'

Gigi nodded firmly, feeling better already. 'Yes. We both want what's best for the baby, obviously. And neither of us wants to get hurt. But of course because I'm British and he's Australian, it's already kind of complicated.'

'I don't want you to be hurt either.' Katie placed her hand on Gigi's shoulder. 'But I guess the baby is the most important thing.'

'Exactly,' Gigi said, her doubts lingering because in those moments when she and Dante were intimate, she couldn't help but feel that if only he wanted a real relationship, he could be capable of so much more. But he didn't want more. She'd always known that.

'I need to get back to work,' Katie said.

'Me too.' Gigi logged off from the computer.

'But…just be careful, okay?' Katie said, her eyes full of worry.

Gigi pasted on a brave face. 'Don't worry. We've got this, and we're both on the same page.'

But as she headed for her next patient, she wondered if her last statement was still true. His distraction was making her paranoid. The last thing she wanted was to make another mistake or develop feelings for him that weren't reciprocated.

Katie was right. She needed to be extra careful not to get hurt again. To rely on herself and the boundaries they'd put in place. Because the worst thing that could happen was if she stupidly fell for a man who had no experience of and no interest in a real relationship.

After seeing Gigi in the emergency department, Dante's day had gone from bad to worse. He'd spent all day operating. Two of his post-op patients had gone off, one of them needing to be transferred to ICU. And his consultant had gone to his private clinic and left Dante to hold the fort. All he wanted to do when he'd arrived home from work that evening was knock on Gigi's door, kiss her until he felt better and then bury himself inside her until he'd put that dreamy, satiated smile back on her face.

Staring at himself in the fogged-up mirror in the bathroom after his shower, he winced. He'd hurt her with his abrupt dismissal earlier. Trouble was, he didn't know what the hell was going on with him. He ached for her constantly, as if she was the only ray of sunshine in his world at the moment. He'd known his professional exams would bring extra stress to his life. But he couldn't seem to get enough of her smile, her kisses, the way that her laugh settled the panicked churning in his gut. Maybe it was a reaction to all the changes his life was about to go through: consultant job, moving country, a baby...

'Get a grip,' he muttered to himself, pulling on shorts and T-shirt. He just needed to keep reminding himself that this physical addiction to Gigi would pass. That his endless desire for her changed nothing in the grand scheme of things. Neither of them wanted a real romantic relationship right now and he'd never had one of those that lasted beyond two months. That they had the perfect plan in place and simply needed to stick to it.

In the kitchen, he'd just opened the fridge to see what he might be able to throw together for dinner when there was a tap at the door. Gigi stood on the deck carrying a covered container.

'Hi,' he said after opening the sliding door and pulling her inside, his spirits already lighter.

'I made you some pasta. I thought you might need feeding before you start studying,' she said.

'Thank you,' he replied, cupping her face in both hands and pressing his lips to hers because he couldn't stop himself. 'You didn't need to do that, but you're a lifesaver. All I have in my fridge is some suspect cheese and a wilting bag of salad.' He took the bowl from her and placed it on the bench, tugging her into his arms, holding her close, so the reassuring thud of her heart calmed him. 'I don't deserve you.'

Was he taking her for granted? Using her to feel better knowing that aside from their relationship as parents, whatever else was between them would soon end? But he had been honest with her from day one.

'I was making it for myself anyway,' she said, her voice muffled against his chest, 'so it was no trouble to make double.'

He released his grip on her. 'I wanted to apologise for this morning. My consultant had just dumped a whole heap of work on me and there were two patients on the surgical ward going off. It was all happening at once but I shouldn't have taken my stress out on you.' He kissed her again. 'I'm sorry.'

Gigi shook her head. 'Don't worry. I know what it's like. There is a lot going on at the moment. I feel it too. Every time I speak to my parents I feel this pressure to tell them what's happening…with us, about the baby, when I'll be home.'

Dante frowned, frustrated with himself that he was selfishly keeping her in Sydney whereas even though the wedding had bought them some time, of course Gigi was thinking of home and family. 'I know… And I'm sorry. But I can't afford to mess up or retake my exams,' he said, trying to explain the way he still felt…claustrophobic.

'Because of me and the baby?' she asked uncertainly.

'Kind of.' He shrugged. 'I mean, it's not your fault, but it would certainly help us both if I can pass first time around. The clock is ticking. You do need to head back to London sometime, see your family, tell them about the baby. Resits would only delay that further.'

She ducked her head. 'I feel guilty.'

Dante frowned, tilting up her chin. 'Why? You didn't do anything.'

'Apart from getting pregnant.' She offered a hesitant smile.

'We both did that,' he said, brushing his lips over hers. 'And I have no regrets. I can't wait to meet our little nipper.'

She laughed and as predicted, he felt instantly lighter. Just her easy company was enough of a balm.

But as quickly as her laughter came, her expression dimmed. 'I know why we did it, but maybe the wedding was too much.

I was worried that you'd feel trapped and I'm the last person who wants to trap you. The next real relationship I have will be with a man who's so wild about me he won't know that anyone else exists.'

She laughed, but Dante's smile felt fake. Her words should reassure him, but maybe because he was still addicted to her, they left him cold instead. 'He'd be lucky to have you.' Then, because that jealousy was back like a bonfire in his chest, he gripped her upper arms. 'I told you I don't feel trapped. All we need to do is stick to the plan.'

He searched her stare. Was *she* having doubts? Her locum position was coming to an end. She must be homesick, eager to be settled before the baby came along. But the idea of her walking away from what they had made him feel more panicked, not calmer. Maybe that had nothing to do with clinging to his perfect, safe life. Maybe it was simply that they had nothing figured out. If he lost her now, she'd take their baby with her and he'd be back to square one, flailing, scared to lose control of the situation, cut out of the picture.

'It's just a few more days,' he said, pleading. 'Once these exams are behind me I'll have some head space to think about jobs and moving and the divorce. Can you give me until then?' he begged, his heart thumping with fear because he felt balanced on the edge of a knife. As if he could make one wrong move and Gigi, the baby, his future would slip through his fingers and he'd be lost. Trapped. Feeling exactly how he'd tried to avoid all these years.

'Of course,' she said. 'I'm not going anywhere yet. But I should go now. I just came to deliver dinner, not to disturb you.'

'Don't go,' he breathed, wrapping her in his arms. Because he sensed her doubts, because time was passing too quickly, because he was addicted to her touch, her kisses, her moans, he covered her mouth with his and kissed her passionately, erasing his challenging day with one touch of her lips.

But as he kissed her jaw and down the side of her neck, encouraged by her sighs and the way she pressed her body to his, his fears intensified. What if this all-consuming need for her never ended? What if he couldn't bring himself to walk away from their physical relationship when the time came? What if he was losing himself in Gigi and would never be the same after her?

'Dante...' she moaned, dropping her head back so her neck was exposed to his kisses, dragging his mind back to the present, to her, to them, to this connection that only seemed stronger with touch.

'I know I'm asking a lot,' he said, clutching her close, cupping her breast, breathing in the scent of her. 'I'm being selfish. I'm sorry.' He pressed kisses over her face, her closed eyes, her lips. 'But I don't want to mess this up, you and me. It's too important.'

They had trust, respect and honesty, but he still felt on shaky ground, this physical need for Gigi spiralling out of his control. If he could just hold it together a little longer...

She opened her eyes and looked up at him, gripping his wrists when he held her face between his palms. 'We won't mess it up. We agreed. And you never lied to me.'

Because she was perfect, because his need had turned to a full-blown addiction, he kissed her again, parting her lips with his, sliding his tongue into her mouth. He stroked her nipple and she whimpered, writhing against him, and his mind blanked to everything but how good she felt.

'I can't get enough of you,' he said, backing her up against the kitchen island. He lifted her, depositing her on the counter, slotted his hips between her spread thighs, so his erection was bathed in the heat between her legs.

'It's just because we know time is running out,' she said, tugging at the hem of his shirt, rubbing at him through his shorts, pulling him back to her kiss, wanting him even as they each faced the looming inevitability of the end.

His body rebelled at the idea, strung taut with need. He slid his hand along her bare thigh under her dress, his hand delving to where she was wet for him, focussed on making them both feel good so he could forget.

'Yes,' she gasped as he slid his fingers into her tight warmth, her hand around his neck bringing their lips back together in a rush. Then she tore her mouth from his, unbuttoned the fly of his shorts, her hand dipping inside his boxers to grip him, pump him, until he surrendered fully to this burning need that made sense.

'What are you doing to me?' he panted, their kisses turning frantic.

She shoved his shorts and boxers over his hips, tugging him around the neck so he leaned over her. But he needed more. He peeled the strap of her dress from her shoulder and exposed her breast to his mouth, sucking the nipple until she cried out and twisted his hair between her fingers.

Hands around her waist, he slid her backside to the edge of the counter, one arm around her hips to hold her close while he pushed inside her and they both groaned, gasped, their tongues surging together passionately.

She grasped his butt, urging him closer, deeper, riding the wild storm with him, as if she too couldn't bear to stop, couldn't bear for this to come to an end.

He held her tight, secure on the counter while they were locked together, each desperate for release, desperate for this effortless exhilarating connection that surpassed anything he'd ever known. Was it any wonder he was addicted to this rush?

'Dante,' she moaned, crossing her ankles in the small of his back.

Dante dived for her lips, kissing her deeply, groaning when she speared her fingers through his hair and dropped her head back, exposing her neck to his wild kisses as her orgasm struck and she cried out.

He buried his face in her hair as he followed, holding her against his rigid body, dragging in the heady scent of her, basking in her sighs of pleasure, wishing they could stay in this moment, where no doubts existed, forever.

But his first thought as the oxygen returned to his brain, was that their last time to be intimate was coming, any day now. Sickened by his doubts and fears and inability to be the kind of man that Gigi deserved, the kind that was wildly in love with her, forsaking all other women, wanting her for the rest of his life, he withdrew and helped her down from the island.

A moment's awkwardness rushed in. He should say something. Anything to make her see that when she was ready for that man who would love her as she deserved, she'd find him easily. But his throat felt blocked.

'I'll um…let you work,' she said, righting her clothes and smiling up at him, her stare haunted by a hint of sadness that stripped him bare all over again. She knew. Knew that he could never be that man, even if he wanted to.

Wordlessly, because he had no idea what he wanted to say beyond more selfish demands for time, he reached for her hand and gripped her fingers. Even now, breathless, spent, his need for her appeased, he wanted her still. Wanted to lie with her in his arms and laugh with her and make plans and dreams for the future of their family.

Just because he wanted to be a part of their family, didn't mean he could make Gigi any promises. He'd never done that before and if he considered it for too long, he began to feel crushed under the weight of it. But they'd made rules and he had to stick to them. He couldn't risk hurting her the way that other guy had.

'Don't forget to eat,' she said, pulling her hand from his and pointing at the food she'd brought. Bringing him back to the moment. 'I'll see you tomorrow.'

Dante swallowed, his throat raw, as he nodded. 'Thanks.'

He forced himself to watch her leave, determined to try and keep his desire for Gigi contained, to carefully feed it until their time was up, putting care for Gigi's feelings first. Then he would reinforce the defences he'd always relied upon, focus on a future that worked for all three of them, him, Gigi and the baby, and pray that when this was over, he could still find himself in the man left behind.

CHAPTER FIFTEEN

ON GIGI'S LAST day as a locum at SHH, Katie had brought in a cake for them to share in the staff room. A handful of the ED staff had gathered to mark the occasion and bid her farewell, not that she was leaving Sydney just yet.

'To our wonderful Dr Gigi,' Katie said, slicing the cake into portions. 'Good luck with your future career and don't forget us Aussies.'

'How could I?' Gigi said, laughing despite the aching burn in her throat. She knew Katie had invited Dante, but as yet, he'd failed to show and she couldn't help but find that symbolic. Things had changed since the wedding. Subtly, but irrefutably. He was distracted and distant as if preparing her for the end of them. And she'd always known it was coming.

Katie handed out cake on paper plates, passing one to Gigi. 'How are you feeling?' she asked.

'Good. I think my morning sickness is easing,' Gigi said, refusing to cry. If she kept her focus on the pregnancy, maybe she could ignore her wildly veering feelings for the father of her baby. 'How about you?'

Katie nodded. 'That's all behind me now, thank goodness. I wanted to invite you and D to a barbecue Friday. Nothing fancy, just the four of us but you can meet Kev, my husband.'

'I'd love to come,' Gigi said, meaning it. 'Dante has his final exam that day so I can't answer for him.'

She glanced at the door once more, her heart sinking that he hadn't shown up. She'd barely seen him this week, but maybe that was a good thing. Just like he seemed to be doing, she needed to start weaning herself off, physically and emotionally. Except every time she imagined the end, she felt terrified that she was in serious danger of having feelings for him.

She swallowed her nausea, unable to enjoy one bite of her cake. Falling for Dante would make her previous mistake with Will seem like a blip in comparison. Scared to trust her own judgement, she forced herself to avoid even thinking about it. If she could hold off for just a little longer, this would soon be over. She and Dante would talk, figure out a plan for the future and discuss their divorce. She'd even forced herself to print a simple divorce form off the internet in preparation and to remind herself that this relationship was never real or for ever.

Just then, the door opened and Dante strode in. Gigi's foolish heart galloped at the sight of him, her mouth stretching into an automatic smile, every bone in her body eager to go to him as if she was trapped in his magnetic field. He was so handsome and caring and sexy. Was it any wonder that she'd let him get close, especially when she was carrying his baby? When she'd married him, worked with him, was still sleeping with him every chance she had? But just because they were close, didn't mean she could trust her feelings. Trying not to imagine the look of horror on Dante's face if she were to confess she even had them, she pasted on a carefree smile.

'Want some cake?' Katie asked him, cutting a slice.

'Yeah,' he said, looking at Gigi apologetically and adding, 'I can't stay long.'

'Don't worry.' Gigi glanced around. Most people had drifted back to work. But her stomach sank anyway. Why was she so desperate for a few minutes of his company when soon she'd need to walk away from the best relationship she'd ever had?

Only it had never been real.

'There you go,' Katie said, handing him a plate. 'I'll leave you to ask him about Friday,' she added to Gigi. 'I have to get back to it.'

'Want to sit outside for a moment?' Gigi asked Dante, her insides trembling with nerves. 'I'm on a break.'

She shouldn't be alone with him, but she needed to get used to talking to him without wanting to kiss him or touch him or beg him to see that what they shared could be the real deal, if only it wasn't the last thing he wanted.

'Sure,' he said, following her outside. They sat on a nearby bench in the shade of some trees. 'So what's this about Friday?' he asked, distractedly taking a bite of cake.

'Katie and Kev have invited us to a barbeque at their place that evening.'

'Oh, okay. Sounds good, although I'll be pretty wiped out by then.'

'We don't have to go,' she said, her heart sinking because she'd missed him this week and always wanted more of his time. But maybe it was for the best.

'Can I see how I feel?' he asked, and she nodded. 'Although it might be too much like a date.' He looked up and met her stare, his reminder perfectly timed.

Gigi's throat burned as she ducked her head. 'Of course.'

That they'd be breaking a rule they'd put in place to ensure they stayed grounded in reality hadn't even occurred to her. Clearly no matter how hard she was trying to stay immune, her feelings were dangerously close to the surface.

'I'm happy to go alone,' she said, feeling stupid because no matter what she felt for him, it would never be reciprocated. He'd told her that enough times. 'Katie and I have become close, so it might be my last opportunity to spend time with her outside of work.'

'Yeah, of course.'

Oh, how polite this agreement of theirs was. She could no longer bring herself to call it a holiday fling, because for her, somewhere along the way, it had stopped being purely physical.

'I don't suppose you've had a chance to have a look at that London consultant job I emailed through?' she asked, forcing herself to probe her fears that Dante had changed his mind.

'No, not yet.' Dante shrugged, avoiding her stare. 'Although there's no point me applying until I've passed my fellowship exam. That's all I can think about at the moment.'

'Of course,' she said, her doubts building. Maybe he'd had a change of heart about moving to London. Maybe the reality of their situation—a wife, a baby, a divorce—was too close to feeling like a cage for him. Maybe the only feeling he was at risk of having for her was resentment.

'Maybe we should take some of the pressure off,' she said, certain that Dante would always want a role in his child's life. It was just Gigi that was temporary. Gigi he didn't want.

'What do you mean?' he asked, frowning.

Gigi swallowed, her fears that her feelings were real and deep and ridiculously out of sync with his almost choking her. 'I promised I'd give you time, but if I went back to London alone, initially, it would give you more breathing space. After all, it's been a pretty intense time.'

His emotional caution was palpable, and she didn't want to be the source of additional angst for him, not when she was feeling so emotionally conflicted herself. One minute, when she was in his arms or when he kissed her, looked at her as if she was something special, she couldn't help but imagine they could have something more than sex. The next, like now when he seemed evasive and hesitant, it was easy to convince herself that anything she was feeling for him was down to pregnancy hormones or her own stupid lack of good judgement.

His mouth flattened. 'I can't make you stay if you want to leave,' he said carefully, his vagueness only adding to her doubts and as good as shoving her on the plane.

Gigi nodded, her paranoia building because the closer they got to the end of them, the less he seemed to want to put up any sort of fight for her.

But then she'd been wrong about a relationship before. She'd blindly trusted her flawed judgement with her ex and been horribly betrayed and hurt. If she fell for the wrong man again, became the more committed person in the relationship, she'd only have herself to blame, especially when she'd known from the start that for Dante, real commitment meant imprisonment and losing his sense of identity.

'Okay,' she said, standing and dumping her uneaten cake in the nearby bin. 'Well, just let me know about the barbecue.'

Just then a car screeched into the no-park zone outside A and E and a shout rang out as the driver climbed from the car.

'Help. I think my brother is having a heart attack,' the man called, looking wildly around for assistance.

Gigi ran towards the car as a couple of nurses also responded to the commotion. Aware of Dante close behind, she reached the patient just as someone appeared from the emergency department wheeling a stretcher.

Gigi took in the pale and sweating man as she reached for his pulse, noting it was rapid, his breathing laboured. 'Let's get him into resus,' she said, shooting Dante a glance.

The emergency meant they'd need to park their conversation, although it seemed pretty pointless anyway. As this was a medical patient and not a surgical one, she didn't need Dante's help. But as she pushed the patient into resus and began her examination, her mind filtering the tests she wanted to perform, she realised that he was no longer there. He'd gone, drifted off to resume his surgical workload, leaving Gigi alone as if they were no longer a team, something she'd need to get used to.

That Friday, with his final surgical exams behind him, all Dante really wanted to do was sleep for twelve hours straight, preferably with Gigi in his bed, in his arms. But they'd accepted Katie's invitation to a barbecue and he was determined to enjoy the balmy evening after being trapped indoors studying for so long.

And after this weekend when he and Gigi would finally have their talk about the future, tonight might be the last time they'd socialise in Sydney together.

'Want a beer, mate?' Kev, Katie's husband, asked, dragging Dante's attention away from the burning sensation behind his sternum.

Before he could reply, Gigi jumped in. 'Go on,' she urged Dante. 'You've earned it after all your hard work, and I don't mind driving us home.'

Dante smiled and squeezed her hand, the out-of-control feeling that was becoming increasingly insistent as the days went by building as he looked into her beautiful eyes. He could tell something was off with her. Was he hurting her by trying to hold all the balls he was juggling? Asking too much of her? Selfishly needing her physically but holding back anything else, because he felt incapable of more?

'Okay, thanks.' He didn't mind skipping alcohol to keep Gigi and Katie company, but today's final exam had been the culmination of over a decade of hard work and long, demanding hours. 'A beer sounds perfect,' he told Kev, who popped the top off and handed him a bottle.

Just then, Katie appeared from the house with a large bowl of salad, placing it on the table.

'Let me help you carry things out,' Gigi said, and the two

women went inside, chatting together. That Gigi had found a friend in Katie after what had happened to her in the past made him happy. In fact, he was starting to fear that his happiness would for evermore be linked to Gigi. Her smile lit some sort of flame in his chest. Her laughter made him ache for a kiss. Her touch seemed to soothe all the noise in his head. How had he allowed that to happen? Let down his guard? But maybe it was just because of the baby and everything would go back to normal the minute he and Gigi finally called it quits.

While Kev returned to manning the barbecue, where he was grilling four juicy steaks, the two men talked about surfing and Katie and Kev's summer holiday plans. But nothing could fully distract Dante from the thought that now the moment had come to give his and Gigi's roles as parents all his attention, he wasn't ready for what had begun as a holiday fling to be over.

When Katie and Gigi returned, each carrying a plate of food, they too were deep in conversation.

'So it's autumn there at the moment, right?' Katie asked Gigi. 'The weather will be colder than you've grown used to when you get back to London. You'll miss our sunshine, I bet.'

Dante half listened to Kev talk about the new camper van he and Katie had bought, and half tuned in to the women's conversation, the hairs rising on the back of his neck with a sense of dread.

'I will,' Gigi said, keeping her stare averted from Dante. 'But I have to tell my family sometime and the flights get booked up in the lead-up to Christmas.'

Dante froze, his stomach swooping. With the pressure off after their wedding and while he'd knuckled down to study, he'd kept pushing aside any thought of Gigi leaving Sydney but he knew it had been playing on her mind. She promised she'd give him time, but had she already planned the trip back?

Booked flights? Without even telling him, when they were supposed to be doing this together?

Katie looked up guiltily and glanced Dante's way, as if checking what he knew of Gigi's plans. Dante kept his expression carefully neutral, but inside, his worst fears roared awake, the out-of-control feeling he detested so much smothering him. Would she really take their baby back to the UK without discussion? Without him? Was she playing games with him, trying to force her own agenda or test his loyalty while he'd been distracted by his exams?

Just then Gigi looked up and met Dante's stare, a flicker of guilt hovering in her eyes. His stomach fell, his suspicions confirmed. He'd assumed they would make important decisions together, but she'd decided to leave anyway.

'Right,' Katie said, as if sensing the tension. 'Let's eat. I'm starving.'

Kev plated the steaks and everyone sat, loading up plates with salad.

Breathing through the panic that he was about to lose some vital part of himself, whether Gigi stayed or left, Dante swallowed down the clog in his throat and tapped into his reserves of small talk in order to get through the evening until he could speak to Gigi alone.

CHAPTER SIXTEEN

'WHEN WERE YOU going to tell me?' Dante asked as Gigi drove, his voice calm and quiet.

'Tell you what?' she asked, annoyed that his strange mood, which was clearly nothing to do with exam stress, had tainted their evening with Katie and Kev. 'That the need to go back to London and tell my family my news has been playing on my mind? You know that already. It isn't news to you. And I didn't think you'd mind.'

What did he expect? She wasn't a robot. She had feelings, too many feelings, especially after sensing Dante's growing withdrawal since the wedding.

'Have you actually booked a flight?' he asked, looking hurt and confused. 'Are you playing games with me when you promised you wouldn't?'

Gigi gasped, pain hot in the centre of her chest. 'Of course not. How could you even think that? After everything we've been through.'

Dread clogged her throat. They were so ridiculously out of sync. While she'd been battling her foolish feelings for him, trying to give him space while watching him slip further and further away, he'd stayed calmly in control of his emotions, his walls just as high as when they'd met, if not higher. He didn't trust her.

'I don't know...' He scrubbed a hand over his face. 'I asked you to trust me, to give me time, to promise that we wouldn't play tug of war over the baby...'

'I've given you time,' she said, her anger spiking. 'I'm pregnant with your baby. I've stayed in your country. I've waited for you to finish your exams. But the reality is I do have to leave sometime. I need to speak to my family. I feel terrible lying to them, pretending that I'm not pregnant.' Plus she saw now that she had to get away from him, to find some distance and unscramble her own thoughts and put those feelings into perspective.

Dante fell silent and Gigi concentrated on the drive home. When she pulled into the drive, turned off the engine and looked at him, it struck with all the force of a hurricane. She did have feelings for him. Deep, desperate feelings. Why else would his overreaction, his accusations, his continued emotional distance cut so deep and make her want to flee to protect herself?

But where for Gigi, everything had changed since that first night they spent together, Dante was still the same. Still trying to control the uncontrollable. Still scared to feel trapped by a real relationship. Still cynical about love.

'I don't know what more you want from me,' she said, deflated because she'd given him her all and it still wasn't enough to make him change his mind about relationships.

'I don't know what I want, full stop,' he said hollowly. 'I... panicked because I thought you were taking the baby away.'

'Not forever.' She faced him, hurt that he could think such a thing of her. 'I would never do that to you. You said you trusted me.'

When he didn't answer, she went on. 'Don't worry, *I* know what you want,' she said, waiting until he looked up. 'It's what you've always wanted. Your independence. To go back to your casual hookups where you risk nothing because you give nothing.'

When he stayed silent and stared, Gigi left the car and stomped to the apartment, her stomach twisting with nausea that she'd yet again made another terrible mistake.

'Wait,' he said, catching up just inside the door. 'That's not true. I do want you. I wish I could stop wanting you. Maybe then I wouldn't be so…irrational. But I told you from the start that I'm not a "forever" guy. I thought you understood. What do you expect from me?'

Gigi closed her eyes to block out the sight of his bewildered expression. He was so lost, so far out of his emotional comfort zone and she only had herself to blame for thinking he could change.

'I'm not stupid, Dante,' she lied, because she was exactly that. She'd fallen for a man who would never want her back, placing herself in another relationship where she was the more committed person who had the most to lose in terms of being hurt.

'We always knew this arrangement wasn't a committed relationship or long-term thing,' she said, forcing down her feelings while her heart pounded as if bruised. 'You're right, you never lied to me. You told me how you felt from the start.' And no matter how hard she believed he had so much more to give, it was a mistake to think he'd ever change his mind. 'And I told you I don't expect anything from you,' she continued. 'That I was happy to raise our baby alone. It was you that insisted on this marriage to shackle us together, and now you're acting like I deliberately trapped you.'

He reached for her, gripping her arms. 'You didn't trap me. I'm exactly where I want to be.'

Gigi nodded, holding back her tears. 'And I need to go

home. Not forever, not to punish you or keep you away from the baby, but because it's time.'

Dante pressed his lips to hers in a desperate pleading kiss. 'I know. I'm sorry. I don't know what I'm saying or even thinking. You should go home. You're right—I always knew you'd have to go back sometime, I've just been so self-absorbed lately that now the moment has arrived, I selfishly don't want to face it.'

Oh, how easily he'd let her go, where if he gave her just one hint that he wanted something more, she'd fight tooth and nail for him, for them.

'I'm sorry.' He buried his face against the side of her neck and Gigi breathed in the warm scent of him, her eyes closing because she was losing him, losing whatever they'd briefly shared, a connection that was no longer enough for her anyway. She'd changed. He'd helped change her, and she'd outgrown him, leaving him behind.

Then because she loved him and could never have more of him than was growing inside her, she tunnelled her fingers through his hair and brought his mouth up to hers. Trying to block her imaginings of what it might look like if they were together for real, having their baby as a couple, committed to each other as lovers, not just as parents, which was hopeless, she kissed him, knowing it might be the last time.

'Gigi... I'm sorry,' he said when he pulled back, looking desolate.

She shook her head, cutting him off. 'Let's talk tomorrow.'

Desperate to have one last memory of her time in Sydney with Dante, she pulled his shirt overhead and gripped his shoulders, kissing him again as she walked backwards towards the bed. Maybe if she could show him one last time what love could be, he might want it, want her.

Wordlessly, they stripped and kissed with desperate determination. Gigi shoved aside the feeling that she was saying goodbye with her body, wanting him one last time before she had to face facts and walk away. Instead she loved him hard, pressing her lips all over his body, moaning his name as his hands caressed her as if it had been years, not days, his kisses frantic as if he too felt the end approach and wanted to run in the opposite direction. When he finally pushed inside her, she gasped, holding his face so their stares locked.

'I...' he said, his heart racing against hers, his stare tortured and confused and terrified.

Gigi tugged his neck, brought his mouth back to hers, reluctant to hear further evidence of how stupid she'd been, falling in love with a man who didn't even believe in the emotion. This connection had always made sense, had always delivered that heart-pounding rush, searing that love she'd found deep into her heart.

He gripped her thigh, her hip, her waist as he moved inside her. His hand cupped her breast and she moaned, digging her nails into his shoulders as if she could mark him as indelibly as he'd marked her. Their bond was permanent now. They would always be a part of each other's lives for their child. There'd be no escaping him in the future. She would need to face him and know that in this moment, she'd loved him deeper than she'd ever loved anyone.

'Dante,' she moaned as his pace picked up. She wrapped her arms and legs around him and held him tight, imprinting her mind with the feel and scent and memory of him.

Her orgasm snatched a cry from her throat, and she clung harder to his tensing muscles as he went rigid above her and groaned into the side of her neck.

Their hearts banged together, breaths ragged pants. Gigi closed her eyes, wishing the moment could last forever, but shivers erupted over her skin as she faced her reality head-on. 'I love you,' she said, unable to hold the words inside a moment longer.

Dante froze, their bodies still joined, their breath mingling.

'I know.' She winced, wishing she could swallow back the words. 'That's probably the worst thing I could say to you, right?' Her high turned to shame because she'd made another huge mistake. He could never love her in return.

Silently, he reared back, withdrew and sat on the edge of the bed, catching his breath, head bowed, his silence fuelling her nausea.

'It's okay,' she said, embracing her cowardice. 'I know it's ridiculous. I know you don't have feelings for me.' She tugged at the sheet, covering her nakedness because she'd finally given him everything she had to give and he'd yet to respond.

But she knew exactly what his response would be.

He glanced over his shoulder, doubt, confusion and panic shaping his expression. 'Gigi… I… I don't know what to say.'

Gigi shook her head, looked away, sliding to the edge of the bed, turning her back on him while she tried to swallow down the lump in her throat. 'You don't have to say anything.' If only she could take back the words spoken during a moment of weakness, but it was too late now. Too late to stop the feelings that had been building and building over the past month. Too late to un-say those three little words so they could carry on pretending this was nothing serious. Too late to realise her mistake.

'We had a plan,' he said, his voice bewildered, as if she'd betrayed him.

'I know,' she said, with a scoff. 'I've changed the rules,' she said, flatly.

'Why?' he asked, clearly unable to fathom how anyone could feel the way she was feeling. But then he had no idea. No experience of the emotions holding her hostage.

'Because I'm human. I have normal feelings, Dante.' Realising that implied he wasn't and didn't, she rushed on. 'When I came here, when we first met, I didn't know what I wanted. I just knew I needed to run away from the mess I'd left behind back home.'

'But you said you weren't ready to trust again?' he pointed out, clearly still in shock from her admission.

Gigi winced, because he was right. 'I'm not sure I am ready to trust fully. But my feelings are what they are.' She turned to him then, her heart cracking at the look of desolation on his face. 'I'm not like you, Dante. I always knew that avoiding relationships and commitment and love would be temporary for me. That one day I'd heal and want another relationship. I just didn't expect it would happen so soon, or with you.'

'But you promised,' he said petulantly, clearly deaf to the momentousness of what she was saying.

Wasn't that fitting? They were so clearly out of sync that Dante, the man she'd stupidly fallen in love with while carrying his child, couldn't even comprehend the depth of her feelings.

Embracing them rather than minimising them to appease his feelings, she continued. 'I know I've changed the rules, but I've also changed since I met you, even since I married you. You helped me to change by helping me to heal from my past. I can't simply change back and be that former version of myself just to keep pretending that our arrangement works for me. I know what I want, now. I want a real relationship, commitment, love. I want more. More than you're willing to give. I want you to be as in love with me as I am with you.'

'Hang on a second...' He tugged on his boxers and stood, facing her with such an expression of being lost that her heart clenched with empathy. He was so out of his depth.

'You don't have to say anything.' Gigi shook her head. 'I

know you don't feel the same way. Your fear and pity is written all over your face.' Her heart sank like a stone but then hardened.

She stood too, faced him. 'Which is why I need to go back to London,' she said, her own fear a metallic taste in her mouth. 'Knowing that I've made another mistake, that I stupidly love someone incapable of loving me back will hopefully kill my feelings sooner rather than later, but only if I'm away from you.' She held the sheet to her body, chills breaking out over her skin. 'I have to leave, now. Back in London, I'll get over it.'

Dante's frown deepened, his hand scrubbing at his hair. 'I thought we'd agreed to figure this out together. I thought we were on the same wavelength, but now you've changed the rules. Where does that leave me?'

'I know, and I'm sorry,' she said. 'Believe me, I wish I felt differently. I wish I'd been able to be intimate with you and carry our baby but still stay detached the way you have, but I couldn't do it.'

She raised her chin, resolved. 'It won't be forever. Give me a few weeks to pull myself together, the way I've given you time. It's the least you can do.'

Frustration clouded his stare and tugged down his mouth. 'Okay, but I can't help but feel you're running away like before and taking the baby with you. You said it's not, but from where I'm standing it feels like a punishment.'

Her throat burned hot with unshed tears. Of course he would think that she was playing some sort of manipulative game. Punishing him for not loving her back.

'We're not children playing tit for tat in the playground,' she snapped. But his assumption told her exactly how he felt about her. Despite what they'd shared, despite the fact that they'd created a life and were going to be parents, he obviously thought so little of her.

'I would never hurt you that way,' she said. 'But I am leaving, as soon as I can. It's self-preservation. I'll go home, tell my parents about the baby and pull myself together.' She pulled on her robe and dropped the sheet. 'In fact, I think the feelings I have for you are fading already,' she muttered. 'I wish I'd never said anything.'

She faced him once more, her mind made up. 'We can discuss the logistics via email or on the phone. Or I can come back to Sydney for another visit. Unless you decide to look for a job in London when we can discuss things in person. But now, I'd like you to leave, please.' She glanced at the door.

Looking lost, he reached for his clothes and pulled them on. Gigi held her body still and unrelenting. She needed him to go before she broke down in front of him and she'd already been vulnerable enough, she'd given him her whole heart and it wasn't enough.

'Okay, I'll go,' he said, pulling his T-shirt down so his accusing stare landed on her before he moved towards the door.

Before he could leave, Gigi threw out one last home truth. 'You asked where this leaves you and the answer is exactly where you want to be. You think you're making a choice to be alone, to stay in control of your feelings and keep hold of your precious independence, but what if it's not a choice, Dante? What if it's just your fear making the decisions?'

He stalled but said nothing, his rigid back to her.

'And if you are ruled by your fear,' she added, 'then you've actually trapped yourself, condemned yourself to being alone forever. I hope that's truly what you want.'

As she headed for the bathroom, her heart breaking all over again, Gigi heard the door slide quietly closed.

CHAPTER SEVENTEEN

THE NEXT MORNING there was a tap at Katie's guest room door where Gigi had spent the night. Gigi snapped out of her self-indulgent trance, looking up from where she'd spent the past five minutes staring blindly at the carpet. 'Come in,' she called.

Katie poked her head through the open door and smiled, obviously trying her best to hide her worry. 'I made breakfast. Want to join me?'

'Thanks, Katie.' Gigi rose and left the room although she wasn't remotely hungry. 'And thanks for putting me up for the night. I really appreciate it.'

The minute she'd emerged from the shower the night before and taken in the unmade bed, she'd known she couldn't stay a minute longer in Dante's apartment. She'd called Katie to beg for a bed for the night, tossed the sheets in the washer-dryer and packed her suitcase at the speed of light.

'Let's eat on the deck,' Katie said, watching Gigi carefully in a way that made her feel fragile.

But quite the opposite in fact. She was strong. Strong enough to heal her battered heart after Will had discarded it and strong enough to walk away from Dante and another big mistake when it was obvious that he could never return her feelings.

Woodenly, Gigi followed Katie outside where the sun was shining on a perfect Sydney morning. Gigi shivered, despite the fact she was wearing a hoodie. It was just the shock, an adjustment to her expectations, although she'd known that confessing her feelings to Dante would freak him out.

'Want to talk about it?' Katie asked as soon as they sat, handing Gigi a mug of tea.

'What is there to say?' Gigi sighed, wishing she would hurry up and get over him. 'You warned me about him on my first day. I only have myself to blame for expecting that I was different from all his other women. I just feel stupid because I convinced myself that he had more to give.' She should have seen it coming, just like with Will. Only she'd convinced herself that Dante was different. Because he was nothing like her selfish ex.

'I'm sorry,' Katie said, taking a sip of tea. 'It's hard to watch him pass up on something so good simply because he's scared.'

Gigi shrugged, her mind consumed by Dante's lost expression. 'Relationships never come with a cast iron guarantee. We're all just out here hoping that we've found the person we can trust with our heart, a person that wants us as much as we want them. But he doesn't want me.'

Just like Will hadn't wanted her...

'Do you trust Dante?' Katie asked, quietly, thoughtfully, giving Gigi pause, because she'd assumed she did.

'I'm having our baby,' she said automatically, aware that it didn't answer the question. 'I told him I've fallen in love with him. How much more can I give without hurting myself?'

She broke off, confused. Because she'd told Dante she loved him, but also that she wasn't ready to trust fully. And then she'd kicked him out, as if she'd expected the worst from him even before she'd opened her mouth to tell him the one thing that should always come free of conditions or limitations: I love you.

'And he didn't say it back,' Katie said flatly.

Gigi shook her head. 'No, but I wasn't expecting him to say that. He's never been in love. He never wants to be. Doesn't believe in the emotion. I guess I just hoped for something he's incapable of, because I wanted it so badly.'

'Unless he does want more but doesn't realise it,' Katie offered.

Gigi looked up, shocked. 'I can't wait around forever on the off-chance,' she said with a firm shake of her head. 'Which is why I'm flying home. Tonight.' She'd spent most of a sleepless night going over their last conversation, until finally she'd booked a flight to London. 'I've been in a relationship where I'm the more committed person before and I got really badly hurt.'

But was Katie right? Could Dante have feelings for her but he was terrified to admit them or believe in them, because he'd spent so long avoiding this chaos called love?

Katie nodded thoughtfully. 'So you're scared too.'

Gigi cast her another sharp look. 'Of course I'm scared, because of my past. Because I'm having Dante's baby. Because me loving him isn't enough of a reason for him to want me in return, so I'm just going to get hurt again.'

Katie's stare was full of understanding. 'I've known Dante a long time and I've never seen him so content as he is with you. Maybe he just needs a bit more time to process your feelings *and* his own. Because he's spent so long convincing himself that love is something he doesn't need. Maybe he simply has to realise that it's something he now wants.'

Gigi's heart galloped painfully, icy fear in her veins. 'You think I should give him another chance?' Was Katie right? Had Gigi also clung to her fear? Shielded that last bruised and battered part of her heart, fully expecting Dante to let her down because of her history?

What if Katie *was* right? What if out of her own fear to be rejected again, she'd expected the worst from Dante, set him a test by telling him she loved him and then watched him fail, as she'd known he would? As if all along, she'd been waiting for his betrayal so she could be proved right to protect her heart? Because she might have blurted out her feelings in a moment of intimacy, said the words *I love you*, but could she really love him and not trust him wholeheartedly?

'I'm not telling you what to do,' Katie said when Gigi stayed quiet, her mind reeling, 'but you have all day before your flight to London tonight. I'd hate for you to leave Sydney and then feel as if you've made a mistake once you're on the other side of the world.'

Gigi swallowed, her heart thudding with fear and the kind of longing that told her it wouldn't be easy to run away or move on from this. 'I'd hate that too,' she whispered, realising Katie was indeed right. 'I'm done making mistakes. Letting fear guide me.'

It seemed so obvious now that last night she'd still been protecting her heart from rejection, still acting out of those deep-seated fears by yet again running away. Even if Dante couldn't love her back, she owed it to herself and to him to be honest, to let him know that she trusted him with all of her heart, even the damaged part.

Abandoning her untouched tea, she headed for the shower.

Dante awoke the next morning after a rough night with little sleep, his first thought to go to Gigi and sort things out. He couldn't let her leave on last night's sour note. He had no idea how to fix this, but he had to try. Having taken a brief shower, he hurriedly dressed and then knocked on the apartment door.

The wait seemed endless, the silence rolling his stomach with nerves. When his patience snapped, he peered through the window, his stomach plunging to the ground as he took in the empty apartment, the stripped bare bed, all trace of Gigi gone.

With a trembling hand, he unlocked the door and stepped inside, finding the bathroom door ajar and the room empty, confirmation that Gigi had left, without even saying a proper goodbye.

And he only had himself to blame. She'd opened her heart to him and he'd rejected her, hurting her just like her ex.

Feeling dead inside, he glanced at the bed, spying the only thing that she'd left behind—an envelope with his name written in her handwriting.

With a sick sense of dread and deep regret hollowing out his stomach, Dante sat on the edge of the mattress and opened the envelope. He expected a goodbye letter, more home truths from Gigi that he wasn't sure he'd ever be ready to hear. But when he unfolded the paper his heart took another tumble. It was divorce papers and she'd signed them, a blank space at the bottom for his signature. He turned the document over, checked the empty envelope, willing some personal message to materialise only to be disappointed. But his disappointment was self-inflicted. For a while he'd had everything: an exhilarating and passionate love affair, a mutually respectful relationship, a future he was excited about. Now, thanks to his own actions and by his own stupid choice, he was alone.

And he'd never felt more suffocated.

Hearing a car pull into the drive, he sprang excitedly to his feet. Perhaps she'd come back. Changed her mind. Decided to give him another chance to figure out the complex mess of his feelings and say the right thing.

When he rounded the side of the house, he saw his father's car in the drive and a new wave of emptiness engulfed him.

'Hi, Dad, what brings you over?' he said when his father had climbed from the driver's seat.

'I brought you and Gigi a gift. Sorry, I know it's early, but I picked this up from the framer's this morning and I was excited to give it to you.'

Dante swallowed, guessing what the gift might be. 'Come in,' he said, leading the way to the main house where he tossed the divorce papers onto the kitchen island and flicked on the espresso machine. 'Want a coffee?' Maybe caffeine would shock his system into something other than numbness.

John hesitated, looking around before taking a seat on one of the bar-stools. 'Sure, if you're having one.'

For a few minutes, Dante drowned out any possibility of conversation with the grinding of coffee beans and the frothing of milk. But when he slid the coffee in front of his dad, his gaze finally fell to the rectangular-shaped wrapped gift, his heart sore as if impaled by shards of broken glass.

'Is that what I think it is?' he asked, taking a sip of his coffee to calm the storm inside him. It was so hot he almost scalded his top lip.

'Is Gigi here?' John asked looking around once more. 'I wanted to give it to you together.'

'No,' Dante said, looking away from his father's hopeful expression. 'I'm afraid she's gone.'

'To work?' John asked, sliding the gift towards Dante across the counter.

'No, she's on her way to London, I think,' he said, his nausea building. How could he have been so stupid as to let her leave? To ignore her words and wallow in his own head? To throw away the only meaningful relationship of his life? She'd been right. He'd chosen this cage in which he now found himself locked.

'Gone for good?' John asked, frowning with disappointment.

All Dante could do was nod as the weight of his shame and devastation dragged at his shoulders.

'What happened?' John's frown deepened and Dante experienced an irrational surge of guilt, as if he'd been a naughty little boy and now had to confess to his crimes.

'We had a...disagreement,' he stuttered, feeling inadequate and out of his depth because in letting her leave, he should feel freer, but felt the opposite.

'So? Make it right,' John said with a scowl. 'Don't just let her leave.'

'It's not that simple, Dad.' Dante sighed and pushed away his coffee. 'I warned you that our relationship was practical, not romantic. You should know me by know. When have I ever introduced you to a woman I'm dating before?'

He'd only introduced John to Gigi because of the baby. But as that thought left his mind, another thought muscled in. Even if there was no baby, he would still feel the same about Gigi leaving. He still selfishly wanted her to the very depth of his soul.

'But Gigi is special,' John said, stating what Dante knew but hadn't been able to rationalise. 'I thought you'd finally found the one for you.'

Dante shook his head, confused and sickened. 'I don't believe in all that. Gigi understood that at the beginning, but then... I don't know, she changed her mind. And I started to feel trapped as I feared I would.'

Only that didn't make sense. He felt trapped now, with her gone. But what he'd been feeling before then was some other thing.

'Trapped? Why? Because of the baby?' his father asked.

Dante swallowed hard, a fresh wave of fear closing his throat. 'No, I'm excited about the baby.'

He'd hurt Gigi, let her down, just like her ex. But deep down, despite what he might have stupidly said in the heat of their argument, he knew her, knew that she would never put their child at the centre of a manipulative game.

'I just... I can't explain it short of saying that I saw what love and a real marriage did to you and I never wanted to be caged that way.' Or so he'd thought.

But now, with Gigi gone and with him a signature away from the quickie divorce he'd wanted, he'd never felt more lost.

'I see,' said John, his gaze dropping.

'I'm not saying it's your fault,' Dante rushed on. 'You're a great dad. I just... I guess after being at the mercy of Mum's manipulations growing up, I never wanted to feel that out of control again.'

'But Gigi isn't like that,' John reasoned. 'And there's no greater chaos than love,' he said sadly, as if Dante had missed out on something wonderful.

Dante looked up sharply. 'I'm not in love,' he said. 'I wish I was. It would be so much easier.' If he could love Gigi, he could make her happy.

Shivers of dread snaked up his spine. What was stopping him from loving Gigi? He certainly had strong and demanding feelings for her, stronger than any he'd ever experienced. She'd been a constant in his head every day since they first met. He was addicted to her company, her smile, her laughter. She made his awesome life brighter and richer and more joyous.

'Aren't you?' John asked as if blind to the confusion in his son.

Dante shook his head, adamant. Love couldn't feel like this—turbulent, urgent, all-consuming. Otherwise no one would ever seek it out.

'I can't think straight,' he muttered. 'I feel out of control all the time.' He rubbed the back of his neck and paced, scared he might actually pass out. 'I want her to be happy but I don't want her to leave.'

'That sounds like love.' With an indulgent expression that made Dante feel even more confused, John tore the wrapping from the gift he'd brought, which as Dante had predicated was a framed wedding photo of him and Gigi, and slid it across the counter.

Dante peered at the image, his flailing heart fighting its way into his throat. He and Gigi stood on the sunny waterfront outside the registry office, backdropped by the boats and skyscrapers of Sydney. Staring up at him with a serene smile, Gigi looked so beautiful he caught his breath as a sharp pain stabbed between his ribs. The photographer had captured the exact moment when Dante had whispered to her that he had no regrets.

But unlike the man in the photo, Dante's current regrets were suffocating, stealing his breath and fogging his thoughts. Had the whirlwind of the baby and the rushed marriage blinded him to what was happening inside him? Had he shoved down his feelings out of habit, but they'd been there growing stronger and stronger all along? Was his father right, was he in love with Gigi and he'd let her walk away? Could that explain the way he was feeling now, as if the world might actually end if he didn't find her before she stepped onto that plane?

'What about the baby?' John asked, looking worried for his son.

Dante scrubbed a hand over his tired face as he paced the kitchen once more, his racing mind making it impossible for him to stay still. 'We agreed we'd put the baby first, no matter what happened between us. She'd never keep me from being a father,' he said, knowing instantly that that sanitised version of his and Gigi's relationship was no longer enough for him. He wanted more than a divorce and a shared custody arrangement. He wanted Gigi in his life, every day. He wanted to feel these terrifying feelings knowing that she would be there for him, the way he wanted to always be there for her, not just at work, but in life.

'So what's the plan? Where will you live?' John asked, his understandably concerned questions like arrows, piercing Dante's battered psyche because he had no answers.

'I don't know,' he said, his breathing becoming shallow as he panicked.

'Are you just going to let her walk away with nothing resolved?' John pushed.

'I don't know.' He turned a desperate stare John's way, silently pleading for help.

'Are you going to deny your feelings for this woman? Because I can see them all over your face.'

Dante dropped his face into his hands, his mind screaming for him to act. Now. To find Gigi and make this right.

John rose and rested his hand on Dante's shoulder. 'I'm sorry that you're so scared of this. I feel responsible.'

Dante shook his head. 'You're not, Dad. I just convinced myself I was happy with so little. Gigi was right.'

John gave a dismissive shake of his head and went on. 'I assumed that because you had the rest of your life so sorted—good job, a nice house, an active social life—that you were exactly where you wanted to be.'

'I was,' he said feebly, thinking back to the time before Gigi, when everything had made sense. 'Until I met her.'

'But now nothing makes sense, right?' John asked as if he could read his son's mind. 'Not without her.'

Too stunned to argue, Dante nodded, the panic building to un-survivable level so he feared he might actually drop dead.

'You love her,' John said, simply. 'It's no wonder. You have so much in common and she brings out a side to you that's lovely to witness. Don't let my choices, mine and your mother's, rule *your* happiness. We had our time. In the beginning, we were as desperately in love with each other as you are now. And even after the divorce, I wouldn't change a thing, because I'm still happy. I have an amazing son. I've lived the life I wanted to. Now it's your turn to do the same.'

Dante gripped his father's arm. 'It's too late, Dad. She told me she's fallen in love with me and I let her leave anyway and now she's gone and I don't know where. All I can think is that the flights to London usually leave at night, so I might have time to find her.' Maybe Katie would know where she was.

'It's never too late to be honest,' John said.

'Honest…?' Dante winced, recalling how arrogantly he'd banged on about his honesty when all this time he'd been lying to himself. He wasn't content alone, he'd just been scared to feel this helpless.

But now, thanks to Gigi and their baby, he had everything to lose, and everything to fight for.

CHAPTER EIGHTEEN

DANTE KNOCKED ON Katie's front door, his heart in his throat. After what seemed like an endless wait, the door opened and Katie appeared, looking stunned to see him.

'She's not here,' she said, inviting him inside. 'She borrowed my car and has gone to find you.'

Dante rubbed his hand down his face. 'How long ago did she leave? She'd not answering her phone.'

'I know,' Katie said with a wince. 'She left it outside where we had breakfast.'

'Has she gone to the apartment?' Dante asked, trying to think straight, willing Katie to have the answers. 'Will she wait for me?'

'I don't know. Might she look for you at the hospital?' Katie suggested.

'I'm not on call today, but I did plan to go in this afternoon to check on my ICU patient.' Realising that might be a possibility, Dante gripped Katie's shoulders and pressed a kiss to her cheek, his pulse flying with renewed excitement. 'Good thinking.'

'Wait,' Katie said, as he turned tail and headed outside. 'What are you planning to say? Don't hurt her again. She's already pretty devastated.'

'I won't, I promise,' he said, waving as he raced to the car, unable to spare a second longer.

He broke some speed limits on his drive to the hospital. But faced with the idea that they might miss each other, that Gigi would leave for London before he had a chance to tell her how he felt about her, he struggled to care.

He started his search in the emergency department, frantically checking with every staff member that might have seen Gigi. With every 'no, sorry,' his chest burned hotter with rising panic.

Hoping she might look for him in the department of surgery, he rushed there, checking with the receptionist only to be disappointed. Then he recalled how Gigi would have needed to hand in her security pass after her final locum shift. She would only be able to access the public parts of the hospital anyway.

Frantically retracing his steps, he passed through the emergency department waiting area, scanning the rows of patients waiting to be seen for the sight of her. Dejected and desperate, he trailed back outside into the sun, planning to return to Katie's and wait it out. She had to go back and collect her suitcase.

As he crossed the road, he looked up and his heart rate soared. She was there, sitting on the bench where they'd shared cake on her final day.

'Gigi,' he called out, jogging over.

At the sound of his voice she looked up from the ground, her eyes lighting for a second before she obviously recalled the way he'd behaved last night.

'Thank god I found you,' he said, collapsing beside her on the bench and taking her hands. 'I'm so sorry about last night. I was a total idiot. I can't believe I walked away from you.'

She swallowed nervously, her beautiful stare wary. 'It's okay. I did kick you out.'

'I deserved that,' he said, squeezing her hands. 'I let you down when I promised I'd never hurt you.'

She shrugged. 'It was my own fault.'

'No.' Dante shook his head, suddenly scared that she no longer loved him. 'It was all me. You were right. I was terrified. I did trap myself. I had no right to call you on broken promises when I let you believe that I had no feelings for you, which was such a lie.'

'You don't have to say that if it's not true,' she whispered, her teary stare searching his.

'But it is true,' he said so urgently she flinched. 'I've been going out of my mind these past few weeks, thinking I was going insane or stressed because all I wanted to do was be with you and I couldn't seem to get enough of you. I'd never experienced anything like that before, so I didn't know what was happening to me.'

She smiled up at him sadly. He cupped her face, holding her stare captive, urging her to see that he meant what he was saying. 'I didn't realise that how I feel is what love feels like,' he said. 'I've never felt it before. I never wanted to, but it happened anyway because you're amazing and wonderful and exactly what I need and want.'

'Dante,' she pleaded, blinking away the sheen in her beautiful eyes. 'It's okay. You don't have to love me back. You don't have to say it. We'll figure everything with the baby out just like we said.'

'No, Gigi. I'm not just saying it to make my life easier. I love you. I woke up this morning with a raw ache in here.' He rubbed at his sternum with his fist. 'I want you. I want to build a real relationship with you, not just because of the baby, but because I can't live without you. I thought if I could control my feelings, that my life would return to normal after you. But there is no normal that doesn't include you. I know I might have realised it too late, that you might not have feelings for me any longer after the way I behaved, but I want you to know that I love you. That I'm still terrified, but mainly of losing you. That I don't want to mess this up so if you can forgive me and help me to make this right, I'll stop being scared of commitment and commit myself to you.'

Tears spilled over her lashes and Dante wiped them from her cheeks with his thumbs. 'Don't look so scared,' he said. 'I promise that if you give me another chance, I won't let you down or hurt you again.'

'I'm not scared,' she whispered, smiling through her tears. 'I know you're capable of love. You've shown me how big and open your heart is these past few weeks, even if I was too hung up on the past to properly interpret it.'

'Then what?' he asked, his gut rolling because maybe he had killed her love and it was too late for them.

'I just love you more than I did last night,' she admitted, fresh tears falling. 'I was still scared then, without realising. I was looking for betrayal and expecting to be hurt because that's what happened before. I'm sorry I didn't fully trust you. But today, I'm ready to give you all of my heart, even the damaged part I've been protecting.'

Dante pressed his lips to hers, his feelings bubbling over. She still loved him. It wasn't too late. He could make this right.

She pulled away again, her hands on his shoulders. 'But I need to know. Will that make you feel trapped?'

Dante shook his head, drawing her into his arms. 'I'm the first to admit that I have no idea how to be in a long-term relationship. But for the first time in my life, I want to be in one, with you. Will you help me? I don't want to mess up again.'

'Of course I will. We'll figure it out together.' Leaning in, Gigi kissed him, her tears wetting his cheeks. He held her tight, a sense of euphoria bursting in his chest. He could do this, love this woman. He had no choice in the matter.

She pulled back and rested her forehead against his. 'But what will we do about the divorce?'

Dante brushed her hair back from her face and pressed his lips back to hers, unable to stop kissing the woman he loved. 'We can tear up the application or I'll sign it if you prefer. Either way, it makes no difference. I'll want you, be committed to you and only you as long as you want me.'

'And if I want you forever?' she asked, happiness glowing in her eyes.

'Then that will make two of us.'

She kissed him once more, then fell serious. 'I booked a flight to London. I leave tonight.'

Dante nodded, smiling bravely. 'And you should go. Tell your family about our baby and the Aussie guy who's crazy about you the way you deserve. I'll stay and work my notice and apply for a job in London and join you two—' He placed his hand over her still flat belly, over their baby. 'As soon as I can.'

She nodded, more tears falling. 'I'll miss you.'

He nodded too. 'I'll ache, every day until I see you again.' His voice broke because being without her was going to be tough, but nowhere near as tough as the fear he'd experienced when he'd thought he'd lost her for ever. 'I love you, Gigi.'

Then he took her home and made love to her one last time, before driving her to the airport.

EPILOGUE

A month later...

THE INTERNATIONAL ARRIVALS area at Heathrow Airport was busy with people who were, like Gigi, waiting for the sliding doors to open and for their loved ones to emerge. Gigi glanced up at the digital display board for what felt like the millionth time, finding Dante's flight number and seeing that it had landed thirty minutes ago.

For the past month since she'd left Sydney, they'd talked every day, sometimes twice or three times a day. In that time, Dante had passed his final surgical exams, registered with the UK's General Medical Council and secured a consultant surgeon position at King's Surgical Hospital, where Gigi was also working as a locum emergency doctor.

The sliding doors parted and Gigi's grip on the metal rail of the barrier tightened with anticipation. Her stomach soared only to swoop with disappointment when a small group of cabin crew emerged, wheeling their identical black carry-on cases after them.

Reasoning that Dante would need to wait for his checked case, she dragged in a calming breath and prepared to wait. But she couldn't resist staring at the doors, willing them to open to reveal the man she'd fallen deeper and deeper in love with every day that they'd been apart.

Then, as if she'd wished hard enough to command the universe, the doors opened and a tired-looking Dante appeared. She gasped as his stare scanned the waiting crowds, seeking her out. A flash of disappointment registered in his expression but then their eyes locked, and the love she felt every time they talked beamed from his stare.

Gigi waved, while weaving her way through the crowd towards him. Dante picked up his pace, his stride lengthening to get to her in return. She broke through the crowd just as he passed the barrier and threw herself into his arms.

'I missed you so much,' she cried, clinging to his shoulders, her legs wrapped around his waist as she laughed and cried and peppered his face with kisses.

'I missed you too,' he said, holding her close in both arms, having dropped his suitcase. 'I thought I might die, that flight was so long. Someone needs to invent teleportation so I can get to you quicker.'

Laughing, her heart feather-light that he was finally there, she slid down his body and reluctantly released him so they could clear the pathway for those people arriving behind Dante.

'I can't believe you're actually here. My husband,' she said, grinning and taking his hand and leading him towards the exit because he'd never signed those divorce papers. 'That was the longest month of my life.'

'Mine too,' he said, stopping to scoop one arm around her waist and kiss her properly. 'You look fantastic, way more beautiful than I remembered. How are you, my wife? How's our baby?'

His questions rushed her but she didn't mind, she was equally delighted to see him. 'He or she is fine,' she said, finally registering that he only had one small carry-on case. 'But where's the rest of your luggage?'

'I didn't bring any,' he said, slinging his arm around her

shoulders as they headed for the car park. 'I knew a checked bag would only slow me down at this end so I just brought carry-on so I could get to you quicker.'

Gigi laughed in delight, her heart almost bursting with love, her arm around his waist tight as if she'd never again let him go. 'Well, I guess you can buy anything you might need here,' she said, as they stepped outside the terminal into a crisp and sunny autumnal day. 'Welcome back to London.' She paused to kiss him once more, lingering, losing herself in their passion, their connection, the excitement and euphoria of their love.

'Thanks,' he said when she let him up for air, his lips brushing hers as if he just couldn't stop kissing her. 'But I have everything I could possibly ever need or want, right here.'

He held her in his arms as people walked around them, their three heartbeats—his, hers, the baby's—fast, as if now, finally together again, they were home.

'Me too,' she whispered, blinking up at him and holding him just as tightly.

* * * * *

*If you enjoyed this story,
check out these other great reads
from JC Harroway*

Manhattan Marriage Reunion
The Midwife's Secret Fling
Forbidden Fiji Nights with Her Rival
Secretly Dating the Baby Doc

All available now!

MILLS & BOON®

Coming next month

HAWAIIAN KISS WITH THE BROODING DOC
Scarlet Wilson

'You can sometimes be a little grumpy at work.'

For a moment, Jamie looked tense, but then Piper noticed his shoulders relax as he sank back further into the chair. 'And you think you'll win me around by telling me this?'

There was a hint of amusement in his voice. She kept things light. 'Well, I figured you already knew anyway.'

He let that hang for a few moments. 'Maybe. I just don't like to get too friendly with people at work.'

Wow. How to sting. She tilted her head and contemplated him for a few minutes. 'You spend more than eight hours a day at work. Sometimes you can be there for more than twenty-four hours. Why would you want to have no friends?'

'It's complicated.'

He didn't expand. But she wasn't going to let it go.

'You're not grumpy all the time. At least not around me.'

She met his blue gaze straight on. It was a challenge. They were out of work now. And she had to know if the flirtations, glances, and that touch the other day, was all just a figment of her imagination. This—whatever it was between them—seemed like a two-way thing to her. If she was wrong, she wanted to know. Before she became the talk of the hospital again. And before she started to get her hopes up.

Continue reading

HAWAIIAN KISS WITH THE BROODING DOC
Scarlet Wilson

Available next month
millsandboon.co.uk

Copyright © 2025 Scarlet Wilson

COMING SOON!

We really hope you enjoyed reading this book.
If you're looking for more romance
be sure to head to the shops when
new books are available on

Thursday 17th July

To see which titles are coming soon, please visit
millsandboon.co.uk/nextmonth

MILLS & BOON

FOUR BRAND NEW BOOKS FROM
MILLS & BOON MODERN

The same great stories you love, a stylish new look!

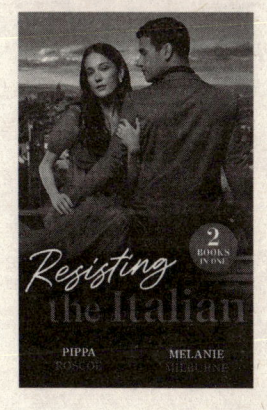

OUT NOW

Eight Modern stories published every month, find them all at:

millsandboon.co.uk

afterglow BOOKS

Afterglow Books is a trend-led, trope-filled list of books with diverse, authentic and relatable characters, a wide array of voices and representations, plus real world trials and tribulations. Featuring all the tropes you could possibly want (think small-town settings, fake relationships, grumpy vs sunshine, enemies to lovers) and all with a generous dose of spice in every story.

@millsandboonuk
@millsandboonuk
afterglowbooks.co.uk

#AfterglowBooks

For all the latest book news, exclusive content and giveaways scan the QR code below to sign up to the Afterglow newsletter:

SCAN ME

afterglow BOOKS

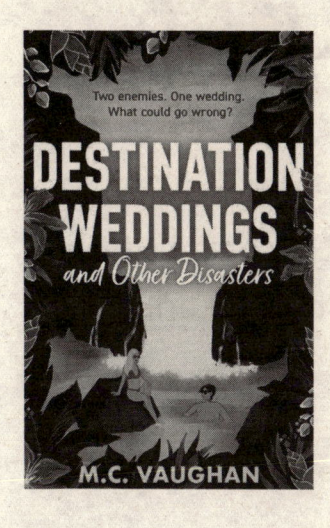

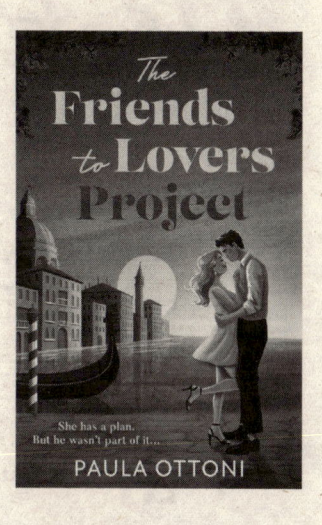

DESTINATION WEDDINGS and Other Disasters
Two enemies. One wedding. What could go wrong?
M.C. VAUGHAN

The Friends to Lovers Project
She has a plan. But he wasn't part of it...
PAULA OTTONI

- ✈ International
- ♥ Enemies to lovers
- 💗 Forced proximity

- 👫 Friends to lovers
- ✈ International
- △ Love triangle

OUT NOW

Two stories published every month. Discover more at:
Afterglowbooks.co.uk

LET'S TALK
Romance

For exclusive extracts, competition and special offers, find us online:

- **f** MillsandBoon
- **X** @MillsandBoon
- **◉** @MillsandBoonUK
- **♪** @MillsandBoonUK

Get in touch on 01413 063 232

For all the latest titles coming soon, visit
millsandboon.co.uk/nextmonth

OUT NOW!

Opposites Attract
Workplace Temptation

3 BOOKS IN ONE

CHRISTY McKELLEN · BARBARA WALLACE · STEFANIE LONDON

Available at
millsandboon.co.uk

MILLS & BOON

OUT NOW!

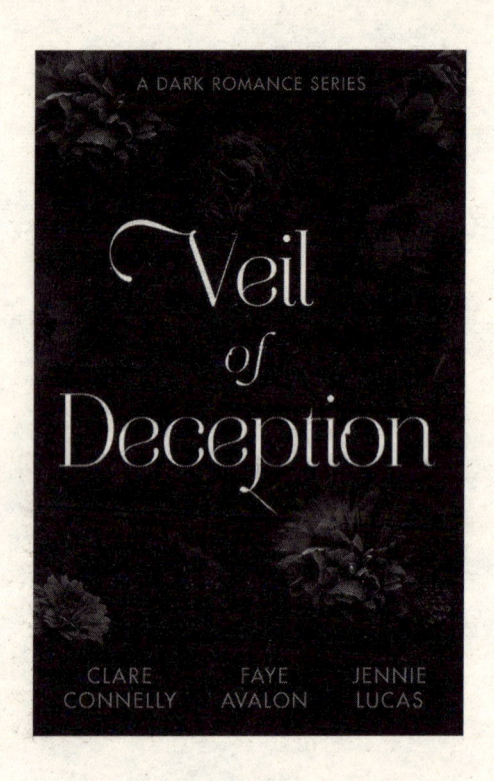

A DARK ROMANCE SERIES

Veil of Deception

CLARE CONNELLY FAYE AVALON JENNIE LUCAS

Available at
millsandboon.co.uk

MILLS & BOON

OUT NOW!

SECOND Chance
— HIS UNEXPECTED HEIR —

3 BOOKS IN ONE

LOUISE FULLER   AMANDA CINELLI   HEIDI RICE

Available at
millsandboon.co.uk

MILLS & BOON

OUT NOW!

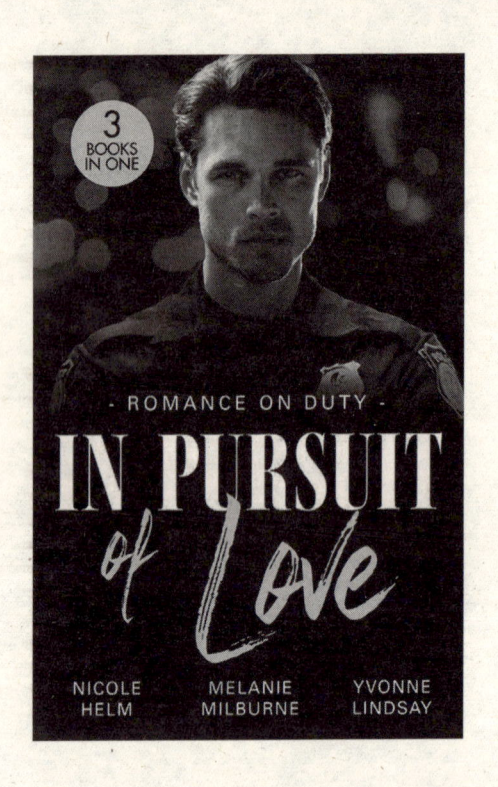

3 BOOKS IN ONE

— ROMANCE ON DUTY —

IN PURSUIT of Love

NICOLE HELM   MELANIE MILBURNE   YVONNE LINDSAY

Available at
millsandboon.co.uk

MILLS & BOON